FINDERS

The second book in the Retribution

gangland c

The race is on… An early prison rel … marriage.

Family betrayal.

When Saul Powell is released early from prison, it causes mayhem for the family firm. His brother, Jonah, has enough problems trying to keep semblance amidst the chaos, not to mention his fast approaching unwanted marriage.

But even Jonah's problems pale into insignificance compared to what Robert Adams is discovering about his mother, Dulcie – the woman he's always put on a pedestal.

In the meantime, Teagan Fraser is also facing a dilemma – one which could ruin her life completely.

Can anyone come out of this nightmare unscathed?

"Edie Baylis has delivered another truly gripping read. Full of action and twists and turns, I couldn't stop turning the pages! 5 well deserved stars!" - *Caz Finlay, Author of Bad Blood Series*

What readers are saying about *Finders Keepers*:

- "...This is one of those books that on finishing a chapter I realise I've held my breath through most if it.....just brilliant!!"
- "...Great story, with strong characters and I would give it more than five stars if I could..."
- "...Another fantastic book from this author...
- "...Highly recommend to gangland fans and can't wait for another instalment..."
- "...Had me on the edge of my seat..."

Also by Edie Baylis

Retribution Series

An Old Score (Retribution #1)
The Final Take (Retribution #3)
The Retribution Box Set

Allegiance Series

Takeover (Allegiance #1)
Fallout (Allegiance #2)
Vendetta (Allegiance #3)
Payback (Allegiance #4)

Hunted Series

The Status Debt (Hunted #1)
The Family Legacy (Hunted #2)
The Target of Lies (Hunted #3)
The Hunted Series Box Set

Downfall Series

Until the End of Time (Downfall #1)
Escaping the Past (Downfall #2)
Vengeful Payback (Downfall #3)
The Downfall Series Box Set

Scarred Series

Mirrors Never Lie (Scarred #1)

FINDERS KEEPERS

RETRIBUTION #2

EDIE BAYLIS

First published in Great Britain in 2021 by Athame Press.
This paperback edition published in 2022 by Athame Press.

Front cover photography: Kiraliffe/envato.com Erik Lattwein/Dreamstime
Back cover photography: Greg Jeanneau

ISBN 978-1-9161627-6-1
e-ISBN 978-1-9161627-5-4

Athame Press
Unit 13230 - PO Box 6945 – London – W1A 6US

PROLOGUE

2005

SAUL POWELL TIPPED his third pint down his neck and looked around the Kings Arms finding it fitting this place should be his first port of call, considering what he'd done here was what landed him a long stretch. 'You've no idea how fucking good this tastes, mate,' he said, a wide grin across his face. 'It's the little things in life you miss the most.'

Keith Grogan returned the smile, his one gold tooth amongst the other slowly decaying ones glinting in the yellow glow of the overhead lights, their stained glass shades doing nothing to help the dimly lit interior of the room.

Despite it being a sunny afternoon, the Kings Arms always appeared to be in a perpetual state of winter – its worn and gloomy interior not encompassing any hint of the outside seasons, courtesy of the frosted glass windows blocking out all natural light and the shabby green curtains no good for anything, short of cutting down the draught from the ill-fitting, rotten frames.

Personally, Keith wanted to go somewhere a little more salubrious to celebrate Saul's early release after seventeen long years at Her Majesty's Pleasure, but Saul was insistent they came here, preferring this back street pub rather than one of the many pubs that had transformed into wine bars in his absence. He had little penchant for wine, preferring a good old pint rather than some poncy overpriced grape juice, but at least wine bars offered a more pleasing vista than this place.

His eyes strayed to a pair of elderly women sitting opposite, fags in trap and legs akimbo, complete with wrinkled stockings, one avidly scratching herself, whilst the other picked through a packet of bacon crisps she'd tipped onto the sticky tabletop.

'Appreciate you collecting me, Keith,' Saul continued, pulling a new packet of cigarettes from his jacket, his cold blue eyes scrutinising his friend. 'No issue getting the time out, I take it?'

Keith opened a bag of pork scratchings, offering them to Saul and seeing the quick refusal, happily began cramming them into his mouth. 'The question wasn't even asked.' His face slid into a sneer. 'He's tied up organising the show's rota since the woman who usually does it has done a runner.'

Saul put his pint down none too gently. 'Gwen? She's done a runner? Why?'

Keith shrugged. 'Yeah, Gwen. Not sure why exactly. She hasn't exactly done a runner, she just hasn't been seen for a few days.'

Saul rolled his eyes. 'That says it all really. Instead of sorting out where the fuck our haul has gone, my dearest brother is only concerned with which bird is dancing with who on the stage, the fucking prick. That's been Jonah's fundamental problem all along. His priorities are all to pot.'

Keith glanced around uncomfortably. Several people had been eyeing them since they'd arrived and he didn't want to attract any undue attention, however much he agreed with Saul's opinion. Plus it was awkward hearing Jonah get slated. The man was still his boss. *For now*. Truth was, thanks to his penchant for insisting on treading lightly around civilians, Jonah had allowed this situation to drag on for longer than it should have.

Saul chugged down the rest of his pint. 'Everything will be changing shortly, my man. Unfortunately for Jonah, he'll be stepping down now I'm back.' He grinned widely. 'You're sure he's no clue I've been released?'

Keith shook his head. 'None whatsoever. I haven't said a word. That's what you wanted, wasn't it?'

'Absolutely.' Saul's bared teeth resembled a snarl rather than a smile. 'It will be a surprise for him and everyone. One that's very much overdue.' Standing up, he slapped Keith on the back. 'And you, my friend, will help me put the firm back on the right footing and get some semblance back into the fucking place.'

Keith was just about to remark about how pleased he was to return to working the way he excelled at, when the distinct change in Saul's expression made him hesitate and instead follow where his old bosses eyes had moved their intense focus to.

'Did you hear that?' Saul hissed. 'Did that wanker over there say what I think he fucking said?'

'Eh? I didn't hear anythi…'

'I'm sure that cock said something about me. That lot over at that table have been fucking staring since we came in.'

Keith had no time to respond before Saul jumped up, knocking his chair over and barged rapidly towards the group of men.

'What did you just say?' Saul roared, fronting up to the man sitting at the back of the round table. 'You talking about me?'

The man wearing a grubby donkey jacket smirked, his piggy eyes glinting. 'All I said was you're a dead ringer for that bloke in nick. That geezer from the Powell firm. No offence, mate, it's just you look a bit like him, that's all.'

'And what's that supposed to fucking mean? What do you mean, no offence?' Saul yelled, the whole pub now deadly silent.

Keith glanced warily at the barman who looked like he

might be thinking about placing a call into the Old Bill. That was the last thing Saul needed an hour after being released from nick. Causing problems would mean his licence being revoked and he wanted Saul returning to prison probably less that the man himself did.

'I'm waiting...' Saul raged. 'What did you mean by no offence? Come on?'

'Fucking hell, mate. I didn't mean anything! Some people might not take kindly to being likened to that nutter, that's all.' The man grinned. 'Word has it the Powells are losing their clout around these parts nowadays.'

Hearing this, Keith got to his feet to intervene, but he was too late. He watched with growing apprehension as, in one swift movement, Saul smashed the man's pint glass on the table and then deep into his face.

'Nutter, am I?' Saul screeched, watching with satisfaction as the man's face split, large ribbons of flesh hanging from his cheekbones. With minimal effort, he dragged the howling man over the table, snorting in derision as his companions scrambled out of harm's way.

'No, please...' The man raised his hands in a futile effort to protect what was left of his face.

With women screaming, Saul rained debilitating punches into the man's face, his nose collapsing on impact. 'My firm's losing its clout? That's the general consensus is it?'

Keith's eyes darted back to the barman, his hand hovering by the phone. *Shit*. This wasn't how he'd foreseen the afternoon going, but he couldn't let this tosser call the cops. Pulling his pistol from his waistband, he aimed at the barman who lurched backwards into a shelf of neatly stacked glasses, sending them crashing to the floor.

With his hand still around the neck of the man he'd beaten to a pulp, Saul looked at Keith – his trusted right hand man and smiled.

Turning, he faced the room. 'Listen here, you bunch of cunts. I don't know what shite has been flying around about my firm, but if I ever hear *anything* untoward coming out of any fucker's mouth, I'll cut their bastard tongues out, do you hear me?'

Planting a kick to the side of the now silent man's head, Saul's mouth formed a menacing smile. 'Do I need to make my point any clearer with this one here?' He nodded to the unconscious man, his ruined face seeping thick blood onto the garish carpet. 'Or will everyone remember that it's rude and *very* silly to bandy around hearsay?'

Keith took his eyes off the barman and glanced at Saul, the mania clear in his face and a mixture of both elation and fear grew. *Things were definitely back on.*

'I am Saul Powell,' Saul roared, 'and let none of you forget it!' He smiled at the sea of silent acknowledgments from the room. 'Now, let's not spoil my homecoming by causing problems, shall we?'

Seeing everyone nod, Saul gave Keith the sign to put the gun away, confident none of these fuckers would involve the Old Bill. He glanced at one of the men. 'You want to get your mate cleaned up? No hard feelings, but he's spoiling the look of the gaff, don't you think?'

Grinning, Saul slapped the man on the back and stalked over to the bar, grinning widely at the terrified barman. 'Another two Carlings, please mate.' He nodded to the shelf of smashed glasses. 'Make sure there's no bits of glass in the drinks, yeah?'

Nodding furiously, the barman flicked on the lager tap, eyeing Keith moving back to the table in the still silent room.

Saul turned and smiled. 'Carry on as you were, folks. Nowt worse that a quiet pub.'

Keith leaned back in his chair and happily sparked up a fag. Saul was back alright. He'd get everything back on track and things would now be sorted.

One

June 2005

GWEN VELLA WATCHED THE POSTMAN making his way up the road and aimlessly wondered whether there was anything for her.

She placed her hands around her mug of coffee, not knowing why, considering it was the tail end of June. It looked like it would be a decent summer this year, but what did it matter? Everything would be ruined if Lena had anything to do with it. To be frank, everything was ruined *whichever* way she looked at it.

Seeing the postman walk past the path leading up to her small block of maisonettes, Gwen got up from her chair by the window and padded despondently through to her little kitchen. She usually enjoyed watching the world go by in her spare time, but for six days now she'd stared miserably out of the window – and today, just like the others, felt that despite the bright blue sky and the abundant sound of birds, it should be grey, wet and dismal to mirror how she felt.

Even though there was hardly a patch of greenery around, unless the odd window box and postage-sized squares of grass in front of the maisonettes counted, Gwen liked her little place. It may not be much on the grand scale of things, but to her, it was her sanctuary. Now, thanks to Lena Taylor, she'd been ripped from that sanctuary and chucked headlong into a seething mass of writhing venomous snakes.

How she wished she'd not bothered seeing if Lena was alright during the engagement party. If she hadn't made the effort, she wouldn't know what she now did. But then, being ignorant of Lena's knowledge wouldn't stop the conniving little cow from using it.

It was six days since Gwen's world had been rocked upside-down and the longer it went on, the worse it became. She knew her out of character disappearance would have been noticed. She also knew the time to act was limited – becoming tighter with every minute that passed. Furthermore, the passing of time was not revealing any solutions – if anything it was making everything more complicated. It certainly wasn't getting her any closer to solving what had been unexpectedly dumped on her.

Gwen pulled a loaf from her bread bin, then replaced it, unable to face eating. It was already 2pm and she hadn't even bothered getting dressed. Sitting down on one of the two chairs at the small kitchen table, she put her head in her hands. *What was she going to do?*

What had happened between her and Jacky Powell all those years ago had been relegated to the annals of time. Aside from her, the only other person who knew was Jacky – and he had taken their secret to his grave. At least that was what she'd thought until the night of the engagement party. It hadn't crossed her mind this subject would come back from the dead to haunt her.

Being around Jonah and Saul as young lads after they lost their mother helped put her guilt aside, but now it had reared its ugly head again. And the pain it would cause now would be a thousand times worse than if the truth had come out at the time.

Gwen choked back a sob. She'd lose everything. Worse

than that, Jonah would despise her and that would break her heart. Losing his trust, love and respect would be a lot worse than losing her job and reputation. A lot, *lot* worse.

A lone tear escaped from her eye and rolled slowly down her cheek.

Although a lot older than her, Jacky Powell had been a handsome man. She'd thought that ever since the day she'd started work at the Feathers back in 1973. His very presence exuded power and strength and although she had a good idea from the off what he did – much not being above board, he was always charming and respectful to everyone.

Although a lot of the girls' pure aim was to seduce Jacky Powell, he'd never taken any of them up on their offers. He was far too loyal to his wife to ever entertain such a thought. *That was until it happened...*

Gwen smiled sadly. She hadn't meant for it to happen and couldn't remember exactly when it *did* happen, but it had happened all the same.

A few years after being promoted to managing the show at the Feathers, Gwen had also become Jacky's personal confidante. She'd offered him an ear and given him a different take from those belonging to people who only dealt with things one way. She was good at thinking of viable options - ones with less risk to the firm and she and Jacky had become close. That was all there was to it; no ulterior motive from either side. It was purely business.

But one night it *did* happen. As they'd pored over the books and bounced ideas off each other, a switch had flicked. To this day she couldn't say how or why, but before she'd known it, their lips had met, fast turning into a mass of intertwined limbs.

After this first encounter, despite the guilt, neither of them could stop themselves. It was more than sex. *A lot more*. Gwen had fallen head over heels with the man.

Jacky, as always, was honest in as much that he would never leave his wife. He loved Carole but he'd loved Gwen too and she'd accepted this without question. She'd loved Jacky too much not to.

There were times when they'd tried to knock things on the head, the guilt of betraying Carole eating away at both of them, but not enough to stop. They couldn't. They were in far too deep, yet no one knew about their affair. Not *one* person and it was imperative that no one found out. Gwen certainly didn't want to be the cause of breaking up Jacky's family – leaving two young sons with only occasional access to the father who doted on them.

She admitted she used to dream that one day she'd marry Jacky and have a baby of her own. A son – like Jonah. She wanted to give Jonah another brother – a *normal* one - not like Saul. That boy had always been cold; unhinged. *Odd.*

She'd even been genuinely pleased when Jacky announced he was going to be a father again. That was ok – her love for him was unconditional and their affair continued. Until it went wrong…

She'd been holed up with Jacky the night Carole collapsed in excruciating pain, bleeding heavily. At fourteen weeks' pregnant, she'd been feeling unwell for a while, but no one had expected that and along with everyone else at the club she'd waited on tenterhooks whilst Jacky had dashed to the hospital.

He hadn't returned that night, nor the next and at that point Gwen realised it was bad. When Jacky finally returned three days later, he'd turned grey overnight and the spark in his eyes had gone. Even after all this time she could still picture the raw pain on his face as he'd announced to his concerned staff that Carole and the baby had died from an undetected ectopic pregnancy.

Gwen turned her mug around on the table sadly. Scans weren't commonplace in those days, but the surgeons tried; they really had. They couldn't save the baby – no one could, but neither could they stop the haemorrhaging inside Carole and her heart failed on the operating table.

Within the space of a few hours, Jacky had lost his unborn daughter and his wife.

The guilt that followed plagued *both* of them. After this, their relationship - affair, ended. It wasn't finished by either of them – it was just never instigated. *Ever.*

Gwen had continued closely working with Jacky – that didn't change - just the other side of their relationship was deleted – like it never happened in the first place.

Throwing herself back into her work and helping out with the boys was the only saving grace she had to assuage her torment.

Gwen found herself making her way back to the window, realising that for the first time in over thirty years she didn't want to return to work. Someone had been aware of the well-kept secret all along and had sat on it all of this time. And because *they* knew, Lena knew. And now Lena knew…

Two

'YOU'VE GOT TO BE SHITTING ME?' Mike barked, his steadily greying hair falling in strands over his forehead. Scraping his fingers through it, he glanced up at Heath busy uploading a new advert on to their account on the AutoTrader website.

Pushing his leather chair away from his desk, he stalked over to his son in the office at the back of the large, newly refurbished showroom and threw the opened letter on the top of Heath's keyboard. 'Look, like I said. We're fucked!'

Glancing up warily, Heath unfolded the letter and scanned the contents. His face fell. 'Twenty-eight days? Jesus Christ! How can they expect you to find this sort of amount in that time?' He looked at the letter once again. 'This has to be illegal. They've got to give you several warnings before it goes this far!'

Mike flopped back into his chair and sighed. 'They did…'

'What do you mean? This is the first time I've ever seen one.'

'That's because I haven't mentioned it.' Mike pulled open the bottom drawer of his desk to retrieve a half-empty bottle of Scotch. 'I wasn't entirely honest with you before…'

Heath swivelled around in his chair and folded his arms, getting the distinct feeling he wasn't going to like what he was about to hear.

'I should have told you everything from the start, but I thought perhaps we stood a chance with this stuff... this stuff that should have been ours...'

Heath's irritation mounted. 'You told me you owed 40k for June's bills and an invoice!' He remembered the conversation well, because he'd been gobsmacked to think that *anyone* would have bills amounting to forty grand a bloody month. 'What else is there?'

Mike shook his head. 'Nothing. There's nothing else – that's the extent of it and that much is true, but what I didn't tell you was I was on my last warning before repossession and bankruptcy.' His fingers knotted together. 'I didn't tell you that I've been unable to make the payments for a while either and, well, it's all snowballed. My last chance was last month and I... I thought what with this Helen Shepherd stuff that we could pull it off.'

Heath jumped up and paced around. 'This is my business too – or rather, it should be! You should have said!'

Mike put his head in his hands. 'I know, I know. I didn't want you to have to worry about it as much as I was, but there's no choice now because our chance of getting our hands on that stuff has gone.'

Heath spun around and glared at his father. 'Of course there's still a chance. We don't know anything for sure yet.'

'I'm having to hide the letters that I'm getting delivered to the house from your mother. The bank is starting to put the repossession order for the house into place. Unless the full outstanding amounts are paid it will go ahead and I don't know what I'm going to tell her.'

Heath scowled. All these years he'd looked up to his father, but these last few weeks had uncovered what a defeatist he really was.

Well, *he* wasn't defeatist. 'I'll sort it,' he muttered.

Mike threw his hands in the air. 'How? You can't. Not now. It's too late. I knew that the moment you told me about those men you saw at Dulcie Adams' house. They were members of the Powell Firm. Who else would it have been? They've got their stash back and that Helen Shepherd woman's dead now too – you saw the news yourself. We're just bloody lucky they didn't see you.'

Heath stared at his father pointedly. 'Christ, Dad. I doubt they even know we exist!' 'And you're right – Helen Shepherd is dead - they killed her. It also looks like they've got the goods, but that doesn't mean it's over.'

'Don't be so ridiculous!' Mike barked. 'What are you going to do? Take on people like that? Just accept it, Heath. It's over and I… *we* are finished here.'

Heath slammed his fist on his father's desk, watching a framed certificate of excellence fall from the wall with the reverberation. 'That's your answer to everything, is it? Throw the fucking towel in? Well, I'm not like you!'

He grabbed his suit jacket from the back of his chair and shrugged it on. 'I'm not accepting this - at least not until I've done everything in my power to change it.'

Stalking from the office, Heath strode across the showroom, ignoring a customer beckoning for assistance. His father could deal with that for once.

He would do his utmost to get back what was rightfully theirs and would do whatever was needed to achieve that. *Nothing* was over until the fat lady sang and she hadn't opened her fucking mouth yet, so there was still a chance.

• • • •

TEAGAN SMILED sympathetically as Robert tapped away at his computer, desperately trying to override the distraction of Dulcie as she pottered around the flat's small living room.

She caught him eyeing Dulcie with irritation as she picked up a selection of his items, inspected them and put them back down again. She knew he was trying his very hardest to bite his tongue and that working was being made increasingly difficult by both his mother's and her presence. The flat was small – especially after the space available at Footlights, but if they hadn't come here, she didn't know what would have happened. No doubt Dulcie would have been placed in some kind of home – as was Helen's intentions.

Teagan's brows knitted together. She didn't want to think about Helen, but hadn't done much *but* think of her in the six days since it had happened. Since Helen's horrific actions had been uncovered, Teagan had had very little sleep. This wasn't because of the usual reason because since Helen's despicable ploy of feeding Dulcie those prescription drugs had ended, Dulcie was no longer plagued by night terrors. In all respects, Teagan's sleep should now be uninterrupted and peaceful, but it was far from that. Her sleep was now filled with looping dreams.

Although Robert had refrained from going into detail about James' body in the garage of Helen's house, Teagan had overheard the statement he'd given to the detectives and she'd been unable to get the image of the man's caved-in skull, its contents splashed across the concrete floor of the garage, out of her mind.

It had also broken her heart to hear Dulcie speak about what had happened that night Helen had been shot. Dulcie must have been so frightened and despite Helen's actions, she still hadn't uttered a bad word about her only daughter.

The other thing bothering Teagan was the knowledge she had on Robert. Despite his outwardly aloof and cold manner, he did care very much about his mother and he'd also recently shown Teagan a huge amount of kindness too.

That was why Teagan felt bad that she hadn't told him what she knew of his father. Keeping something so big from him upset her and she wasn't comfortable with it, but she'd promised Dulcie and she had to honour that promise. It was only right Dulcie should be the one to tell her son who his real father was.

As Dulcie wandered off towards her bedroom, Teagan glanced back at Robert, his thick brows knitted as he perused his screen. 'I'm sorry to encroach on your space so much,' she said. 'I wonder when the police will tell us Dulcie can return to Footlights?'

Robert looked up, his face stern. 'I've already said you can stay as long as you like - although it's different having people around.'

'Do you think Dulcie will want to go back to Footlights? You know, after…'

'I don't know whether everything has hit her yet.' Robert glanced in the direction of the hall to make sure his mother wasn't in hearing distance. 'It's only been, what? Six days? Perhaps it will hit her after the funeral.' His lips pursed. 'She's expecting me to go, but I've already told her, I have no wish to pay my respects to that woman.'

Teagan swallowed hard. Dulcie would need Robert there – he'd always been her rock, but she couldn't say she blamed him. How could he pay his respects to someone who had let him down so horribly? Talking of funerals, it was Alan's funeral tomorrow and she supposed she should go, but she wasn't looking forward to that either.

Teagan smiled softly. 'You've been so good making sure your mother and me are ok, but what about you? Are you alright?'

Robert sat back, surprised. He rubbed his hand over his cleanly shaven chin. 'I haven't really thought about how I feel.'

Teagan nodded. 'You must get some time for yourself. If… if I can help in any way, then please say.'

Robert stared at Teagan, his cold blue eyes penetrating into hers a little too long. 'Thanks, but I'm not much one for talking.'

As he turned back to his screen signifying the conversation was over, Teagan rose from her chair. She must remember that however close she felt to Dulcie, she mustn't overstep the boundaries. The Adams' were still clients, even if Dulcie and now, Robert, felt more like family.

• • • •

'WHEN ARE WE GOING TO DISCUSS the wedding?' Lena crossed her long shapely legs, giving Jonah an eyeful up her small tight skirt.

Jonah huffed irritably at Lena's blatant attempt to distract him. He knew exactly what was underneath Lena's skirt – he'd been there enough times and didn't need reminding that was what had got him into this mess in the first place. 'I'm busy,' he muttered, looking back down at his paperwork.

'Why have you brought all that rubbish home?' she whined, secretly miffed that her ability to manipulate him appeared to be waning.

Since the engagement party Jonah had been as cold as a fish. Although she'd smoothed over the fiasco of the diamonds theme and was still very much entrenched in his life and home, she wanted more than that. His reluctance to discuss their upcoming wedding, coupled by the fact that nothing had come of the atom bomb she'd lobbed in Gwen's direction was unnerving. She'd have thought at the very least *something* would have been mentioned by now. It was six days since Gwen had disappeared without as much of a word, short of saying she was sick and Lena thought Jonah would have come running to her long before now for help in organising the show in Gwen's absence, but he hadn't said a thing.

In fact, it was worse than that – he'd said nothing about anything. It was all very well getting her feet under the table at the club, but she couldn't have him backing off about the wedding. That would wreck everything and then all of this bullshit would be for nothing.

Getting up from the large round armchair, she wandered over to Jonah and draped her arms around his neck. 'Is there anything I can help with?' she purred, surreptitiously eyeing the paperwork. 'Are those the dance rotas? Why don't you let me have a look? I could p…'

'I'm fine,' Jonah snapped, quickly putting the paperwork into a pile.

Lena pouted. 'Just trying to help,' she said, sulkily walking away. 'So, when can we discuss the wedding?'

'For Christ's sake!' Jonah barked, slamming his pen down. 'Don't you think I've got enough on my plate?' Lena knew nothing about what had gone on with Dulcie Adams, or that all of his attempts to discover who had lifted the haul was getting nowhere. And now he had to fudge the rotas at the Feathers too, whilst all she wanted to do was discuss the wedding? A wedding he didn't even goddamn want?

'What exactly do you want? I've signed the registry office forms and given you the go ahead to arrange whatever you wish for the wedding and the reception.' He raised an eyebrow. 'I'm presuming you won't be as stupid to do something along the lines of the engagement party this time?'

'But that's just it, Jonah. I want you to be involved. After how you behaved at the party about my choice of decorations, I'm frightened to do what I think would be nice.' Lena made her eyes fill up with tears on cue and ran her hand over her still perfectly flat stomach. 'It's not good for the baby.'

Jonah waved his hand dismissively. 'Get a wedding planner. That will take the pressure off.' *If Lena could call anything she dealt with as pressured?* But the one thing he didn't want was anything happening to that baby inside her. That and that alone was the only reason Lena was still breathing. 'And you're sure you didn't see Gwen at the party after I left?'

'Oh, you mean after you disappeared for hours without telling me? How embarrassing was that?' Lena sniped.

'Like I said when I got back, I didn't have the time to unwrap you from your host of admirers. We had an emergency at one of the warehouses,' Jonah countered. At least Nero had sorted out an alibi because they sure as hell needed one after those wankers had got to Dulcie Adams first, leaving him in the frame for the dead body.

'And for the record, like I told *you* before, I didn't see Gwen,' Lena lied, hiding her scorn. 'It's clear she's upped and left.'

Jonah shook his head. 'She wouldn't just do that.' He got to his feet. 'That's why I'm going around there now to see what's happened. Something's not right. I just hope it not too serious.'

Lena stiffened. *He was going to Gwen's?* The old cow had best remember what the deal was here because there was no way she wouldn't use her newfound knowledge courtesy of Uncle Ron to her advantage, like she'd promised. But if Gwen had done a runner, then she wouldn't get what she wanted *that* way either. The second bloody plan that had been scuppered. She needed to have her feet well and truly under the table long before the wedding. And time was running out.

She needed certain things to be nicely in place before the cat came out of the bag because when it got to the part when her *real* name was read out, Jonah would know, as would everybody else, that she wasn't Lena Taylor at all.

It was a gamble, but with his belief there was a baby on the way, it was pretty much guaranteed he'd swallow the 'discrepancy' for the sake of his reputation.

Yeah, he'd take the hit that he'd married an O'Hara on the chin, because otherwise he'd look a prize cunt for ditching his pregnant fiancée at the altar and she knew all about Jonah's principles where family was concerned. When the baby unfortunately never materialised due to 'natural causes', well… it was just one of those things…

THREE

JONAH PULLED UP OUTSIDE GWEN'S ADDRESS. Getting out of the car, he nodded politely to the people congregating outside their houses to acknowledge him.

He knew the Feathers and the Powell firm's notoriety was renowned in the area, along with many other parts of the city and he hoped his presence at Gwen's house wouldn't cause any hostility. Although with any luck it would bring her some well-deserved kudos rather than anything detrimental.

Knowing Gwen, she wasn't the sort to broadcast their association. She always kept herself to herself, but it shouldn't do her any harm to have a personal visit from him. She'd been a faithful member of the business for so very long – both to him and his father before him and the rather sad observation that he had given her little credit for that nagged painfully.

That's why he was here now. He was worried. *Very worried.* For Gwen to be off sick for six days in a row was unheard of. He couldn't remember a time when she hadn't been in work. Even when she'd been really unwell in the past, she'd always struggled in. There had even been one occasion when she'd had an operation and insisted on taking the rotas to work on from her hospital bed, so for her to not put in an appearance, nor to call was a red flag.

The thought of Gwen suffering alone was not something he would allow. She had no family; no husband or kids – the business had always been her family and, if he admitted it, she had been more like a mum to him since his own mother had died, so making sure she was alright was the very least he could do.

Glancing back at his top spec Range Rover, Jonah loped up the steps to Gwen's maisonette, balancing the bags of supplies in one hand as he pressed the doorbell. He'd grabbed a selection of staples; bread, cheese, some ready meals and tea and coffee from the shops on the way over, but he'd happily pop back out for anything else she might need.

He was just about to ring the bell again when the door opened. 'Morning!' he said, smiling to hide his shock at the state of Gwen. She looked like she hadn't washed in days, was deathly pale and her skin was tinged with grey.

'J-Jonah?' Gwen cried. 'What are you doing here?'

'Thought I should make sure you're alright!' Jonah frowned. 'But you don't look like you are…'

Gwen hovered unsteadily on the doorstep and said nothing, her mouth frozen. *Did he know? Had Lena told him?*

Jonah held up the bags of shopping. 'I've brought you some supplies. You going to invite me in?'

Finding her voice, Gwen stepped aside. 'Yes, yes, of course. Sorry. Please come in.'

Walking into Gwen's tiny hallway, Jonah turned and smiled. 'Right, I'll put the kettle on and then you can tell me how you are and what I can do to help.'

Gwen smiled weakly as she shut the door. *If only someone could do something to make this better, but they couldn't.*

• • • •

GWEN KNEW SHE HAD TO DO IT. What choice did she have? She'd wracked her brains, yet hadn't been able to come up with anyone who would know of her secret or furthermore, speak of it to Lena. The sad truth was it might not even be someone who worked at The Feathers at all. It could be anyone and was like looking for a needle in a haystack. Either way, she was finished and she knew it.

There was no way she could return to work. She couldn't go *anywhere* around here either now someone knew her history. Even if they didn't say anything, Lena would.

Lena would definitely open her trap to get what she wanted. Having nothing to throw back to counter it, Gwen had reached the realisation with a sinking heart, that she had little choice but to do what the horrible woman wanted. Even if it meant losing her job and Jonah's respect, she'd much rather level with him than submit to that money-grabbing little tart's blackmail.

It was no use. She had to bite the bullet and it may as well be now.

'So.' Jonah stretched his long legs out, almost filling the entire width of Gwen's kitchen and sipped at the tea he had insisted on making. 'Have you seen a doctor? Is there anything I can do?'

Gwen's eyes filled with tears. Jonah's Savile Row suit looked out of place in her home, but she loved him for making the effort to come and see how she was. That in itself made things even worse.

Jonah sat forward, worry etched across his rugged face. 'Gwen? What's wrong? It's not something serious, is it? Please tell me you haven't got something serious?'

Gwen shook her head and brushed away the tears. 'No, nothing like that.' She took a deep breath. 'I'm just exhausted.'

Jonah grinned. 'Well, that's easily rectified. Have yourself a couple of weeks off – all expenses paid. God knows you're long overdue for a holiday – like about thirty years if I remember rightly!'

Gwen smiled sadly. 'There's no need. It won't help. I've been doing a lot of thinking; it's been in my head for a while now, if I'm honest.' *This was anything but honest, but she'd got to do it rather than him finding out and it destroying him.*

She stared at her mug as she turned it around in her hands, but knew she had to look at Jonah if she wanted him to believe her. He wouldn't buy any of it if she didn't meet his eyes. *Come on Gwen, you can do this.*

'Ok, I'm listening,' Jonah pressed, his face still lined with worry.

Gwen took a deep breath and placed her hands in her lap so their trembling wasn't visible. 'It's been a really hard call to make, but I've come to the conclusion that it's time for me to retire.' She kept her eyes on Jonah without giving way to the tears pressing to escape.

Jonah's expression could not be classed as anything other than abject shock. 'Retire?'

Gwen could already feel her resolve crumbling. 'I know it's probably a shock, but I've been doing this for over thirty years and, like I said, I've never had a break. I…'

'Gwen, you can have all the breaks you need. All you have to do is say,' Jonah said, his concern accelerating. *Gwen Vella retire? She couldn't. He needed her too much.*

'I didn't mean that you've made it difficult for me to have any time off because you haven't,' Gwen said quickly. 'It's me. You know what I'm like. I live and breathe my work, but it's getting too much now. I'm not at the age where I can keep up with it anymore and I don't want it to get to the point where I let you down.'

'You can't possibly be serious?' Jonah's face cracked into a smile. 'You'd miss me too much for a start!'

Gwen couldn't return his smile. She would miss him. She'd miss him, the club, the work – the combination of all of that made her tick, but she couldn't do it anymore. Not now Lena knew. 'Of course I'll miss you, but it's the right time, love. I'm too old for this lark. I…'

'You're not even sixty!' Jonah cried.

Gwen bit the inside of her cheek to keep herself in check. 'I've made my mind up. It's time to replace me… replace me with some fresh blood. Give someone else a chance to put their ideas into practice.'

Jonah raked his fingers through his hair. *And to think he'd been in a half-decent mood today.* 'How the hell am I supposed to replace someone like you, Gwen? I don't *want* to replace you! What about reduced hours? Would that sort it?'

'It won't work, I'm sorry,' Gwen said. This was harder than she'd thought. It was torture. And this bit would be even worse... 'I've been thinking that Lena might be a good proposition to take over my role? *God, how those words stuck in her throat.*

'Lena?' Jonah choked, his hand spilling tea onto the little table. Angrily mopping it up with a piece of kitchen roll, he stared at Gwen suspiciously.

Gwen nodded. 'You two are getting married and she could do with being more involved. I may have been a bit hasty in my opinion of her as she does have good ideas. I think that perhaps th...'

'What's she said?' Jonah barked, his eyes narrowing.

Gwen paled. 'N-Nothing. She's said nothing, I...'

'You're a shit liar! This is Lena all over. What the hell has she done to make you come out with this?'

Gwen looked at Jonah and nausea rose. She had to think of something and *quickly*. 'I-I just feel I'm coming between you both and I don't want to cause problems.'

Jonah closed his eyes and inhaled deeply, but despite this his ragged breathing escalated as his anger grew. He thought Lena had been disturbingly quiet the last few days. He'd even stupidly succumbed to her advances last night, feeling that her pregnancy must have finally kicked in and mellowed her. But this... If Lena had any hand in forcing Gwen to leave...

Gwen interrupted Jonah's train of thought by grabbing his hand over the table. 'Lena hasn't said anything. I haven't seen her,' she lied. 'It's no secret that we don't get on, but by staying I feel I'd be doing you a great disservice. This is your chance to be happy an...'

'Happy?' Jonah raged. 'Why would Lena replacing you

make me happy? You know as well as I do that she causes ructions. I don't want her in there and I won't lose you either.'

Gwen sighed. 'Don't be too hard on her. I think she genuinely wants to be involved, but this business with the engagement party hasn't helped.' She couldn't quite meet Jonah's eyes, still questioning how she was uttering this rubbish in Lena's defence.

Jonah sat back against the hard kitchen chair and folded his arms. 'I do not want to replace you with Lena. I can't stand the fucking whore.'

Gwen blinked, shocked. 'But you're marrying her! Why, if you feel like that? Love, if you don't want her, then tell her to sling her hook.'

Jonah raked his fingers through his hair so hard that Gwen was surprised he didn't rip some of it out. 'I've got to marry her. It's the right thing to do.'

'Not if you feel like that, it isn't,' Gwen said.

Jonah sighed. 'Lena's pregnant so what choice do I have?'

Gwen gasped. 'Pregnant? Are you sure? How far along is she?'

Jonah shrugged miserably. 'Got to be nearly two months.' He met Gwen's eyes. 'What the fuck am I going to do? Please don't leave, Gwen.'

Seeing the utter distress on Jonah's face, Gwen grasped his hands. It was times like this that this man wasn't the head of a dangerous London firm, but the little boy that had been so bewildered after losing his mother. This put a different slant on things.

She couldn't leave now. Not when Jonah needed her. And right now he needed her more than ever. She had no idea how this would work with what Lena's threats, but she had an idea… 'Ok, love, I won't leave. We'll work something out that works well for everybody, I promise.'

FOUR

SAUL SAUNTERED INTO THE FEATHERS, his smile wider than one belonging to a Cheshire cat. It had been amusing seeing the doorman's double take as he'd reached the entrance. He'd clearly been recognised and it wouldn't be long before his unexpected arrival circulated faster than the Black Death. *Yeah, everyone would know of his return soon enough.*

He glanced appraisingly around the lobby. It had definitely had an overhaul and it looked good. Real good. *Classy.*

Not bothering to wait for Keith to park the car, Saul slammed through the double doors into the staff corridor. He was just glad Keith was driving today. After their relatively enjoyable afternoon at the Kings Arms he'd had a few more than he should have to get away with going behind the wheel, but at least the coke Keith had the foresight to bring livened them both up.

The last thing he wanted was not to be on the ball when the moment came to take his throne. His smile cracked wider. He'd been waiting a long time for this. A long, *long* time.

Moving down the corridor to the main office – the office which had been his father's, Saul spotted two girls leaving one of the many dressing rooms. 'Hey up! Who are you two little beauties?'

Turning, the women stared at the tall, well-built and devilishly handsome man striding towards them and blushed, smiling coquettishly.

Approaching the perfectly-dressed women donned in skin tight high-cut leotards, complete with plunging necklines and adorned with glittering sequins and jewels, Saul's eyes made no excuse from running over their lithe bodies and down their long legs encased in fishnet tights, complemented by high black stilettoes. Seeing beautiful women after such a long enforced drought was a very welcoming homecoming.

Reaching out, he placed his hand against the wall, using his body to corner them. 'I presume you two ladies are starring in tonight's show?' he said confidently, flashing the smile that, if he remembered rightly, went down a treat.

The women glanced at each other, silently sharing their uncomfortableness of this stranger's close proximity. Remaining professional, the taller of the two women smiled. 'Yes Sir, we are, however the show will be starting soon, so if you'll excuse us. It may well be time to go and grab your seat out front.'

Saul grinned. *They didn't know who he was.* Well, why would they? They were too young to remember him from when he'd been here virtually every waking second of the day and night.

He traced a thick meaty finger down the woman's face, its trail continuing along her throat and down towards her ample cleavage. Squaring his body, he grabbed her hand and pressed it against the hardness in his trousers. 'Think we've enough time before your stage call to get better acquainted, don't you…?'

The woman snatched her hand away, her eyes darting towards her colleague. 'Sir! Please do not do that! This area is staff only and…'

'I know the area is staff only, you silly bitch!' Saul hissed, grabbing the woman by the shoulders and slamming her against the wall. If people thought they could treat him like a muppet, then that idea needed to be quashed immediately.

Leaning his weight against the woman's body, her eyes wide with fright, Saul smiled, all pleasantries gone. 'If you want to remain staff, I'd advise you to change your fucking attitude.'

'I'm getting security!' the second woman cried, hastening towards the doors, only to run straight into Keith. 'Mr Grogan!' she squeaked. 'This man… he…'

Keith watched Saul release the dancer he'd pinned against the wall, his eyes dancing with both mischief and lust. *Yep, Saul was definitely still Saul.* 'It's fine ladies. This is Mr Powell.'

Rubbing her bruised shoulder, the taller woman glanced worriedly at the man who had just treated her like cattle. 'Mr *Powell*?'

Saul turned towards her and smiled coldly. 'Yes, *Saul* Powell. You may well have heard of me? Most people have.' His grin widened. 'I'll put your rudeness tonight down to a misunderstanding and I trust you'll be more friendly next time we meet? Now fuck off and do what you're paid for.'

Not needed to be told twice, the two women hurried down the corridor to the backstage area.

Chuckling, Keith looked at Saul. 'I should have warned you that Jonah insists perks are to be taken only when they're offered.'

Saul's eyes narrowed. 'Does he buy them fucking flowers first too! Well, fuck that! This isn't a convent. I've got some catching up to do in that department. Where is he, anyway?'

Keith shrugged, tapping on Jonah's office door. 'In here, I guess. Either that or with his fiancée.'

'His what? And you're knocking the door too? What is this? Fucking school?' Saul yelped. He'd only been here five minutes and there were already several of his brother's rules that would need revising. And what was all this about a fiancée?

Pushing the door open, Saul barged in, all set to give his brother the surprise of his life, but the only person there was Nero Banks, who promptly dropped a tumbler of whisky to shatter on the wooden floor.

'Not expecting me?' Saul drawled. 'It seems no one is. Where's my brother?'

Quickly composing himself, Nero stepped forward to shake Saul's hand. 'Saul! It's been a long time. I'm expecting Jonah back any minute.'

Jonah would not be expecting this and he doubted whether he would be over the moon about it either.

• • • •

LENA HAD BEEN CHUFFED TO BITS when Jonah called to say she should come to the club. That was until she'd got there to find Gwen sitting in the office. This what not what she'd had in mind. Not even slightly.

She eyed Gwen malevolently. Thought she could play games, did she? Well, she hadn't got time for this. 'I didn't expect to see you here.' Lena's eyes narrowed pointedly, before turning to Jonah. 'There's something I think you should know ab…'

'Sorry, Lena. I haven't got time to run through how everything will work right now. I'm needed in the office.' Jonah hadn't missed Nero frantically beckoning when he'd arrived not five minutes ago. He didn't know what had happened, but judging by the man's expression, it didn't look like it was good.

Besides, he hadn't got any inclination to babysit Lena. He glanced at her sulky face. He couldn't say he was happy about Gwen's suggestion or that he understood it, but if it was the only way to keep her at the club, then he'd take it.

He had to say he was unsure how they would cope working alongside each other, but Gwen was confident it would work. She knew what she was doing and if she thought it would be fine, then it would. He hoped so anyway, because he needed things ticking over nicely and with no distractions so he could get back on the Dulcie Adams case. Enough time had passed as it was, giving whoever had lifted his haul a head start with disappearing off the radar, so the quicker he could get back on it, the better.

Perhaps now Lena had something to occupy her time, she wouldn't be such a snotty ungrateful bitch, but one peep out of her – one step out of line and the deal was off. There was only so far he'd bend – even for Gwen. On the upside, it would only be a matter of months before Lena's pregnancy would force her back to the confines of the house. She was far too vain to be around lithe dancers once her belly got big.

Seeing Lena's scowl deepen as he moved towards the door, Jonah smiled. 'Gwen and I have discussed everything and she'll fill you in. Now, I really must get on.'

Lena waited until the door had closed before approaching Gwen's desk, ignoring the second smaller one – presumably for *her* use. Pushing a stack of paperwork out of the way, she placed her handbag down and retrieved her packet of cigarettes.

Taking her time to light one, Lena inhaled deeply before helping herself to a large measure of vodka. She perched on the top of the desk. 'I'm not sure what you think you're doing,' she said, scrutinising Gwen pointedly. 'The deal was that I would *replace* you, not join you.' A ghost of a sarcastic smile appeared across her heavily made-up face. 'I can sit here this evening with you if you like, but grasping one last night in your job is a little pointless, considering I can have the conversation with Jonah tonight when I get home, or tomorrow morning. Anytime I like, really.'

Lena inspected her bright pink fingernails and she daintily tapped her cigarette ash into the thick crystal ashtray. 'I can't decide whether I pity you for your desperation or whether I'm angry that you're trying to call my bluff.'

Gwen remained silent. She'd let Lena dig her hole. Let her believe just for a little bit longer that she was in control. She may have *some* control over the situation otherwise she wouldn't be forced to be sharing her bloody office with the gold-digging little cow, but Lena was nowhere near as much in control as she thought and she'd soon be realising that.

Lena's false-lashed eyes turned to Gwen as she reached for

the bottle of vodka for a top up. 'You're very quiet. Realising you'd have been better off not coming back? It will be difficult leaving again under such embarrassing circumstances when you've only just returned.' Her smile widened. 'And to think people were concerned over you! I wonder how they'll feel when they discover why you were hiding in the first place? I can't imagine how they'll feel when they discover you were the dirty bit on the side of Jonah's father? The bit on the side who made him miss his wife's death?'

Gwen flinched, but she wouldn't rise to it. She would never let this malicious bitch know exactly how deep her words cut. 'I'd probably feel as uncomfortable as you will when Jonah finds out you're knocking vodka back, chain-smoking and doing coke by the gram. As you quite rightly know, we all know how he feels about family, so I doubt he'll take kindly to you poisoning his baby. And, let's face it, the baby is the only reason he's marrying your sorry arse in the first place!'

Gwen experienced a small ping of victory seeing Lena's face pale significantly. 'Yes, he told me that apparently you're pregnant.'

Lena's mind whirred. Jonah had *promised* he wouldn't tell anyone and out of all the fucking people to tell, he'd told Gwen? *Shit.*

'I'm surprised any pregnant woman would be so stupid to put away the amount I've seen you down lately...'

Lena's eyes flashed. 'Are you saying I'm not pregnant?'

Gwen shrugged, her eyes lingering on Lena's washboard stomach. 'How would I know? But it would be sensible to suggest to Jonah that it's unlikely. It's either that or you're knowingly poisoning his baby... Or do we try and work alongside each other? Of course, the choice is yours...'

Standing up, Lena slugged down the remains of her drink then placed the glass heavily on the silver cabinet tray. *Fuck.* She was between a rock and a hard place here. Damn Jonah for opening his gob.

Her overplucked eyebrows knitted. Gwen couldn't *prove*

she wasn't pregnant could she? No, she couldn't, but Jonah could. Jonah could demand to see her doctor's notes. Or worse, book a private scan and accompany her. He'd be the sort to do just that. What Gwen said was true – Jonah was only marrying her because of the baby – she knew that, but if he knew there was no baby…

Her pulse cranked up a notch. *For fuck's sake.*

It had all been so perfect. So ideal. So perfectly executed, yet now Gwen could cost her everything…

Gwen swallowed her smile. 'So what's it to be, Lena? You look after my secret and I'll look after yours? Or shall we put our cards on the table to Jonah instead and see what he thinks?'

Lena clenched her jaw. As much as she resented this, she had no choice. At least not for the next few weeks. After they were married it would be a different fucking story. 'We'll work together,' she mumbled.

'Sorry?' Gwen said, her eyes glinting. 'Didn't quite hear that.'

'I said, we'll work together,' Lena spat through gritted teeth. Now, not only did she still have to put up with Gwen, but she also had to find somewhere new to drink and to do coke too. *This was just shit.*

'Good. I think that's the best choice all round. Right then. I'll continue dealing with the girls, being as we all know none of them like you. And you… oh, let's see… how about you deal with the admin for the VIP list? That doesn't involve dealing with anyone face to face, so you should be ok.'

Lena's eyebrows shot up. 'Are you taking the piss?'

Gwen plastered on a mock-hurt expression. 'Of course not! I want to show Jonah that we can work together. Why don't you take a seat at that desk over there and I'll show you how everything works.'

Scowling, Lena snatched her handbag and angrily stalked to the other side of the room.

Gwen watched with smug satisfaction, however, she was under no illusions that Lena would take this lying down. The woman would bide her time as to when she would tell Jonah, but if Lena thought Gwen was happy to keep *her* secret, she was very much mistaken. She was not selling Jonah out to this woman just to save her own skin.

Regardless of the fallout it would personally cause, that was not something she would consider. She would let Lena believe that for as long as it took to make sure the wedding did not happen. As long as that didn't go ahead, she'd take whatever that meant on the chin, however painful it was.

FIVE

JONAH GENUINELY DIDN'T THINK there was much left in his life that could make him want to bin everything off and retreat to an unknown corner of the globe, but finding Saul in his office proved there were still things left to cause that strong reaction.

His head was spinning. Nero looked equally as perturbed, but Keith didn't. Keith looked excited, but it was hardly surprising. Keith had been Saul's right hand man on the enforcement side of the firm and being very similar in personality, they'd worked well together. It was expected he should be elated at Saul's unexpected release, but Jonah was not.

The exact opposite.

It wasn't just Saul's release that was the problem, it was what would happen now he was back.

Jonah watched Saul help himself to a full tumbler of his best whisky. By the looks of it, he'd had several already. And that wasn't all either. Judging by the state of his pupils, his brother's long-standing habit of masking the effects of alcohol with cocaine hadn't waned either.

'Great surprise, eh, bruv?' Saul grinned as he leant back in the chair, his feet firmly planted on Jonah's desk.

Jonah tried to smile, yet his face was reluctant. He had to get everything ironed out quick smart. That he could only do between him and Saul, hence why he'd told Nero and Keith to leave them to it.

Behind Saul's façade of jollity and saying he was glad to be back, there could only be one thing on his agenda – and that was to take control of the firm – to take the seat he believed should have been his from the off. The one that he was pointedly sitting in right now.

'How come you've been released?' Jonah asked. 'I thought you'd got another two years left to serve?'

'Yeah, funny how things work out, isn't it?' Saul winked. 'Let's just say the new prison Governor had a favour done by the Powells back in our dad's day, so I called in the debt.'

Jonah saw the glint in his brother's eyes. 'You mean you blackmailed him?'

Saul raised his hands in submission. 'Blackmailed? You insult me!' He grinned. 'Just *suggested*, Jonah, that's all.'

Jonah shook his head and smiled despite the position he found himself in. Saul had a brass neck that was for sure. Getting up, he walked over to his cabinet and poured himself a shot of whisky whilst there was still some left. He held the bottle towards Saul – pointless really because it was obvious his brother didn't need asking if he wanted a refill. Seeing the slight nod, Jonah topped up his glass.

Sitting back down, he decided not to rock the boat by telling Saul to get the fuck out of his chair and took a swig of whisky instead. 'Let's cut to the chase. What do you want?'

A nerve twitched in Saul's eye. 'What do I want? What do you mean, what do I fucking want?'

'From the firm? From the club? What are your plans? I'd rather you laid your cards on the table,' Jonah said.

Saul placed his glass on the desk. 'Ok, I want my place at the head of this firm. Had it not been for prison, I'd have taken the reins when Dad died, not you.'

Jonah nodded. It was what he'd expected. As much as he liked to think he could pre-empty how his brother's mind worked at least on *some* respects, he hoped he was right on this one. If he wasn't, then everything would go to shit. 'As much as that may be true, situations dictated that you couldn't take the reins. *I* did and I've done a bloody good job. Changing that now isn't sensible.'

Saul slammed his fist down. 'Sensible? To who? It's my right to be head of this firm. *Mine.* It's what Dad would have wanted.'

Jonah doubted that. He strongly believed their father was secretly relieved that Saul couldn't take over. The man was too unpredictable and unstable to carry on the family values, but he wouldn't voice that. He'd let Saul believe he was making the decisions.

He folded his arms across his chest. 'Regardless of what you think, I've got good relationships with our suppliers – the coke side of things is ticking over nicely, the club is pulling in the most accolades ever and the VIP waiting list is the longest it's ever been. We've got several business openings in the pipeline and the money lending is doing ok too.' Jonah ran his tongue along his teeth. 'Whether you like it or not, you steaming back in will affect all of that. As you well know, people like to know who they're dealing with, and let's face it – no one has dealt with you on anything but money lending, which is only a percentage of the firm. Rebuilding trust with you at the helm will set the business back months.'

Saul frowned, accentuating the latest scar above his eye. 'From what Keith told me you're getting slack on the extortion.'

Jonah scowled. *Thanks, Keith.*

'I also didn't appreciate the first thing I heard the minute I got out was some twat thinking it's clever to mention our firm's losing its clout.'

Jonah bristled. 'We haven't lost any clout? Who the fuck said that?'

Saul shrugged. 'Irrelevant. He won't be saying it again, put it that way.' He leant forward, his massive forearms bunching up the paperwork on the desk. 'Have you allowed the firm to get a pussy-whipped reputation, Jonah? This isn't the Women's fucking Guild.'

Jonah's anger surged. 'No I have not. I'm running a business – a *proper* fucking business! There's more to all of this than caving people's heads in. I don't know whether you've noticed, but I've also been trying to recoup the haul that Pointer pulled. It is *that* which has taken precedence lately.'

Saul's eyes flashed. 'And a fat lot of good that's done. You've got precisely no fucking where.'

Jonah jumped to his feet and Saul followed, both big men squaring each other off, staring at each other with pent-up frustration.

Jonah wanted to pummel his brother to the floor. He'd got enough stuff to deal with without Saul sticking a spanner in the works, but at the end of the day, Saul was his brother. Like his father had drilled into both of them, family comes first – even if that family contained a loose cannon; an unexploded bomb – someone with the capacity to destroy everything.

Jonah sat back down reluctantly. 'I didn't expect you to get out so soon and in all truth, I didn't *want* you to. I knew you'd charge in and fuck everything up.' His eyes focused on the equally blue ones of his brother, now staring at him with even more discontent. 'Whatever your beef is with what you think I should or shouldn't do or have done with Dulcie Adams, screwing things up here I will *not* sanction. If you're sensible about this we could work it to our advantage.'

Begrudgingly, Saul sat down himself, his unbridled anger still bubbling dangerously. 'I'm listening.'

Jonah kept his voice moderate, yet confident. It was the only way he could do this. It wasn't his first choice, but it was the lesser of two evils. Anything else would start a war within the family and cause even more grief. At least this way he could remain in control of his brother. 'I suggest we take *joint* control. Nothing happens over anything without joint agreement. You have your strengths and I have mine. We pool them and work together. Come out on top on every side.'

Saul remained silent. *Joint control? That was supposed to be ok, was it?* He could see Jonah had dug his heels in on this. He could force the man out, but in reality where would that leave him? He'd been out of the loop too long to blindly pick up from scratch. Whether he liked it or not, he needed Jonah's knowledge, but that didn't mean he couldn't achieve what he wanted if he was careful. And very clever…

He sucked in his bottom lip, his mind scooting over different scenarios. 'Ok, but I want full shout of the extortion – that's my forte,' Saul said, his voice clear there was no room for manoeuvre. 'You take care of the club side. The rest is joint.'

Jonah sat silently. That was exactly what he'd wanted. Turning his whisky tumbler around on the desk, he pretended to mull it over. 'Ok, but that includes Dulcie Adams. Any decisions on that are joint. I'll bring you up to speed where we are with that next.'

Saul got to his feet to refill his glass. Turning his back, he grabbed the Scotch and slowly unscrewed the lid. Thanks to Keith, he knew exactly where they were with Dulcie Adams, but he'd let Jonah think what he liked. He'd play the game, but knew how he would deal with at least part of that already and Jonah would have no choice but to put up with it.

Turning back around, Saul lifted his drink. 'Well, here's to us and the family firm,' he said, smiling as Jonah clinked his glass. 'Now, what's this I hear about you getting married?'

• • • •

HEATH TURNED THE CORNER into Frogmore Road and gritted his teeth. Teagan hadn't replied to one single text and he'd been texting her for days. Neither had she returned any of his calls.

He hadn't particularly wanted to drive all the way back up to Maidenhead to call on Teagan out of the blue, but what choice did he have? He had to get the lowdown on what was going on and this was the only way.

Pulling up outside Footlights, he glanced around. Although he doubted whether those men – the ones who must have knocked off Helen Shepherd, would be lurking around the scene of their crime, he didn't want to walk straight into trouble.

Getting out of the car, glad to see there were no police cordons surrounding the house, he looked up at the imposing old property, its general lack of repair not having improved. Walking up the crumbly stone steps to the front door, he tentatively rang the bell.

Getting no response, Heath pressed the doorbell again – this time for longer. He glanced up at the tightly shut curtains surrounding the bay window of the front sitting room. There didn't look to be any activity in there, but maybe Teagan was watching him right now from one of the upstairs windows?

What should he do? Impatiently moving from foot to foot and becoming rather annoyed, Heath pressed the bell again.

'There's no one there.'

Swinging around, Heath spotted a middle-aged woman at the bottom of the steps near the pavement. 'Sorry? Are you talking to me?'

The woman pointed to one of the houses on the opposite side of the road behind her. 'I live over there. Are you the press?'

'Press? No. I'm a friend.' Heath said. 'I'm looking for Teagan - she's the carer of the lady who lives here.'

'Oh, they've gone,' the woman said smugly, proud to be privy to the information. 'They went after that dreadful incident last week.'

'Yes, I heard about that,' Heath muttered. *Gone? Where had they gone?* 'I just wanted to see how she was. Do you know where they are?'

The woman smoothed down her hair. 'I don't, but the police have been here all week. They only packed up and left last thing yesterday.'

Heath nodded impatiently, but stopped himself from asking if watching her neighbours was her only source of entertainment. 'Do you happen to know when they're coming back?' *Being as you seem to know everything else...*

'I don't know the woman, even though she's lived here for years, we never saw much of her. Very eccentric by all accounts.' The woman's lips pursed. 'I wonder if she murdered her daughter? Maybe she's locked up? Do you th...'

'Thanks for your help,' Heath interrupted and turned his back, cutting the woman off mid-flow. Classic busy-body - no use whatsoever.

'Although...' the woman continued, 'I don't suppose she'd have left with the girl and that man if the police suspected she'd done it.'

Heath froze. *Man?* He turned back around. 'A man, you say?'

The woman nodded. 'Oh yes. The night it happened both the old lady and the girl left with a man. I think it was her son. I've seen him before.'

Heath walked down the steps. 'Do you happen to know where this son lives?' he asked, trying not to fixate on the large hairy mole on the woman's cheek.

'No I don't, but he's a bit of an odd ball too,' she said, frowning. 'Who did you say you were again?'

'I didn't,' Heath muttered, walking past the woman back to his car.

If the police had finished at the house then didn't that mean Teagan and Dulcie could return? Although perhaps Teagan's services were no longer required? Perhaps the son was looking after the old woman himself, or he'd moved her into an old folks' home?

Pulling open the door of the Lexus, Heath fished out his mobile and dialled Teagan's number again.

• • • •

SAUL GRUNTED, grabbing the hips of the woman straddling

him on the dressing room chair, his strong arms effortlessly forcing her to up the pace.

Slamming her onto him harder and harder, he closed his eyes in irritation as the petite blonde began making obligatory noises. 'Shut it,' he hissed.

He didn't need her acting like she was enjoying herself to make him get off. She sounded like someone was half killing her and if anyone burst in and interrupted him from unloading into this silly cow, he'd go tits.

Finally feeling his climax building, Saul dug his fingers into the woman's hips thrust with savage force, the back of the chair banging loudly against the mirrored counter. Gritting his teeth, he growled loudly from the back of his throat, before finally relaxing.

Catching his breath, he looked at the woman's sweaty bleached hair stuck to her face and flinched as she placed her hand on his cheek. 'You don't need to paw me,' he snarled, knocking her hand away.

'Sorry, I…'

'You said you wanted to see me?' Keith said, walking into the dressing room. 'Oh, sorry!'

'It's fine. We're done.' Without even looking at the woman on his lap, Saul roughly pushed her off, sending her sprawling to the floor.

Tucking himself back into his trousers, he stood up and glanced at the woman with disdain. 'Cheers love, but can you fuck off and get your kit back on elsewhere? We've got business to discuss.'

Scrabbling around to gather her knickers and clothes, the woman pointlessly covered her modesty with the bunched up fabric and scuttled past Keith and Saul, red-faced.

As the door closed, Keith perched his big frame on the dressing table. 'What's up?'

Saul sparked up a cigarette and blew the smoke out towards the brightly illuminated mirror. 'This guy – the one you were telling me about. The guy with the burner phone?'

'Stoner Joe?' Keith frowned. 'What about him?'

Saul rolled down the sleeves of his white shirt, slotting the gold cufflinks into place. 'I want you to touch base with him. Pay him a visit or call. I want the latest on the old witch. I want to know what the old girl's plans are and see if the tart looking after her has said anything. She's the stoner's missus, isn't she?'

'That or an ex, who knows?' Keith said. 'Don't think he does!'

Saul looked at Keith, his eyes cold. 'Do it low key of course. You know the score.' He raised an eyebrow. 'And I don't need to say that this is between me and you?'

Keith nodded. He understood completely. The meeting Jonah had called for the inner circle had come as a bit of a surprise in as much that Saul was willing to accept joint control of the firm. He'd been fully expecting a nightmarish showdown of power between the Powell brothers, but it all made sense now. *Saul had his own agenda.* 'What about Nero? Is he in this too?'

Saul shook his head. 'Fuck Nero! Let's keep this just between us for now. Less hassle.'

'I'm on it.' Keith hurried out of the dressing room.

• • • •

GWEN LOOKED AT THE EMPTY CHAIR at Lena's desk and frowned. She'd hazard a guess where the girl had been for the last half an hour. The woman must be thicker than the average plank if she didn't realise it was obvious that she'd sidled off to the toilets to shove powder up her nose, but let her carry on – the quicker the hole was dug, the better.

There wasn't long to find something to catch Lena out on though. And it needed to be something set in stone, rather than speculation - enough to make Jonah cancel the wedding.

Gwen frowned. She was 99% certain that Lena wasn't pregnant, but what if she was wrong? If the sneaky cow was truthfully carrying Jonah's child, then *she* was turning a blind eye to the conniving tramp's cocaine and vodka habit. If something happened to that baby because of Lena's vices, Gwen knew her disbelief would not be an acceptable excuse for keeping her mouth shut.

Gwen glanced up at the door – no sign of Lena yet. Was there time to get another look through her phone to see if she'd had any further texts from that mysterious 'UR' person?

Deciding now was as a good a time as any, she pushed back her chair and hurried over to Lena's desk, reaching for the over-sized Gucci bag on the floor. Opening the zipper, she peered inside. *Damn, she'd taken her phone with her.*

When the office door suddenly swung open, Gwen span around, stomach somersaulting, relieved to see it wasn't Lena, but less relieved to see Saul instead.

Saul cocked an eyebrow, his gaze moving from Gwen to the large handbag. 'Am I interrupting something?'

'I thought I'd split coffee,' Gwen blustered, hoping her cheeks weren't as scarlet as they felt. She forced herself to smile. 'Settling back in ok?'

Saul leant against Gwen's desk, his blue eyes scrutinising her. 'Yes, it's good to be back on home turf again after so long.' He smiled – a smile that didn't extend to his eyes. 'I know I saw you at the meeting earlier, but I thought I should come and say hello properly. You've been at this firm longer than I have and it's been a long time since I saw you.'

Opening his arms wide, Gwen reluctantly stepped into Saul's embrace, her skin bristling as he enveloped her into a hug. Pressed against his hard chest, her nostrils were invaded by the overpowering scent of his expensive aftershave, horribly aware his heavily muscled arms could squeeze the life out of her any time he wished.

She'd forgotten just how much this man unnerved her. His mere presence set off alarm bells and his close proximity made the silent danger even more intimidating. Although she wanted to push him as far away from her as possible, Gwen couldn't let his invisible ability to make her skin crawl get to her.

Physically, he was appealing; he had the same qualities that both Jonah and their father shared. There was no doubt that all of them were extremely handsome, well-built and powerfully charismatic, but Saul – Saul possessed a strange, detached coldness – an indescribable something that set the nerves on edge.

Glad when he released his hold, Gwen quickly sat down at her desk. 'I'm pleased to see that you and Jonah made the decision to run this as a joint venture.' Although the man engendered dread at the very base of her being, she had known him too long not to speak candidly. She wouldn't tread on eggshells around either of the Powell boys.

Leaning casually against the opposite wall, Saul smirked. 'Yes, it's the most sensible thing to do. I want this firm to work.'

Gwen nodded, not believing a word. Saul was not a rational person. 'Jonah's done a good job keeping the business at the top of the game and I wouldn't want anything to spoil that.'

A flash of anger crossed Saul's face before hiding it behind a dazzling smile. 'You're looking great, Gwen. You haven't changed in the seventeen years since I last saw you.'

Gwen pursed her lips. 'That I very much doubt, but nice of you to say.'

Saul nodded at the empty desk. 'And her?'

'Have you not met Lena yet?'

Saul winked. 'Nope. But I've heard about her. Fancy my brother getting himself hitched. I never expected that.'

'Nor did I,' Gwen muttered, wondering if Jonah had also mentioned to Saul the reason he was marrying the horrible woman.

'What's she like?'

'See for yourself,' Gwen said, spotting Lena peering through the glass of the office door.

Six

JOE WOKE UP with a mouth like an Arab's sandal. He stuck his arm out from under the duvet and fumbled for his alarm clock.

Reluctantly opening his eyes, he focused his swimming vision on the clock's face, his stomach dropping. He tried to unscramble his brain to work out what day it was – the last few days were a bit of a blank, but as his memory kicked in he sat bolt upright, dread weighing heavily. *Shit. It was today – Alan's funeral.* Christ, what time was he supposed to be there or was the hearse coming here first? He couldn't remember.

Wiping the sleep from his eyes, he pushed his unwashed hair off his face and tried to make sense of what was going on.

Joe glanced to the right, a mixture of relief and disappointment to see the other side of his bed empty, like it had been more often than not recently. Yes, disappointing that his dick had seen little action these past few weeks, but then he'd hardly been in any state where he would have been up to the job anyway. At least by not having any contact with the opposite sex, he avoided getting involved with someone who might add to his problems.

Pulling himself out of bed, he swayed unsteadily, the

leftovers of what he'd consumed last night making themselves known. *God, he felt rough.*

He glanced at the pile of empty cans on the floor and the overflowing ashtray full of dog-ends, along with a half-smoked spliff and his stomach lurched.

And then he spotted it.

It was still there. Unfortunately, he hadn't dreamt it.

Staggering across the room, Joe picked up the newspaper from the floor and plonked back down on his sagging mattress. The page he'd been reading last night – the one which had been the precursor to his latest drinking session, was still open. He forced himself to look at it again, just to double check that he really hadn't been hallucinating:

Probe Into Murder Investigation Grinds to a Halt

Police investigating the brutal murder of Helen Shepherd, 44, partner of local estate agent Shepherd, Percival and Proctor, have finished their work at the scene of the crime.
Helen Shepherd died from a single gunshot wound to the chest last week at the home of her elderly mother, Dulcie Adams. Mrs Shepherd's death came after her husband, James was found also brutally murdered at the couples' home earlier that evening (22nd June). Police believe the killer was known to Mrs Shepherd as there were no signs of forced entry at either property and it was thought nothing had been taken.

Unfortunately, no unexplained fingerprints or other evidence has been unearthed at either property and police are left trying to piece together the motive from a description of the attacker by the victim's mother, who witnessed her

> *daughter's murder from her hiding place.*
> *There has been a worrying spate of brutal murders/attacks and disappearances in Maidenhead recently, and although nothing has been confirmed, it is widely questioned as to whether the Shepherds' deaths, the disappearance of Ken Manning – another Maidenhead estate agent and another recent local attack could be linked?*
>
> *Mrs Adams, who has been staying with relatives since this ordeal, is hoping to shortly return to her home and asks that she is left to grieve the death of her beloved daughter in peace.*

Joe reached for a carton of orange juice at the side of his bed, grateful to find there was still some left. It tasted a bit rank and he had no idea how long it had been there, but he had to get this foul taste out of his mouth. If only it would also remove the knowledge that it looked very much like the keys he'd delivered to that psycho has been used…

That was the first thing he'd thought when the murder was first reported a few days ago, but this latest update proved it. *No forced entry…*

He shivered. Now those nutters had finally got what they wanted would they leave him alone?

Joe stared at the burner phone. He remembered he'd been all set to destroy that last night. Surely there was no need for it now? But there was just something… something that was telling him this wasn't over yet. And he was dreading what that meant.

He moved to the mirror and stared at his reflection. *Christ, he looked bad.* He'd have a shower, hope his hand remained sturdy enough for him to shave without slitting his own throat and then iron his new shirt. Whatever happened, he'd make an effort for Alan today. It was the least he owed him.

Burying Alan would signify the end of this shitty chapter in his life and perhaps then he could move forward?

Despite not wanting to, the urge to look at the phone again was overwhelming. Gingerly picking it up, Joe switched it on. *Fuck. A message.*

With shaking fingers he opened the text:

`Call me. Now.`

Feeling a fresh cold sweat break out on his brow, Joe obediently pressed the call button.

• • • •

JOE'S NAUSEA INCREASED as he made his way to the Plough and Harrow. Why he'd suggested meeting here he had no clue. He was sure he must be having some kind of mental breakdown. Had he lost all sense?

He shouldn't have looked at that burner phone again. He should have kept his eyes as far away from it as possible; or thrown it away, eaten it, *anything*. Looking at it must have put out a prompt to the ether for the psycho to get back in contact.

Stupid, stupid.

As he turned into the road, Joe spotted the nasty outline of the man and his pace slowed. How long could he drag out reaching there?

Sighing, he continued at a normal pace, realising the longer it took, the more time it gave his mind to dream up worst case scenarios and he'd already imagined far too many of those.

'Alright?' Keith said as Joe approached.

'Not bad,' Joe muttered, thinking he was *far* from alright because he was here. With *him*.

Keith nodded towards the door of the Plough and Harrow. 'Fancy a drink?'

Joe stared at the man with half an ear. What were they? Mates or something? The fucker had tried to drown him in his own fucking toilet! 'I'd rather make this quick if you don't mind.'

Keith cut Joe a look. 'In that case, walk.' He moved off up the road, leaving Joe to scuttle behind trying to keep up with his long strides. 'What's the news?'

Joe glanced sideways. 'What news? I don't have any news.'

'Don't play thick, dumbass,' Keith spat. 'Are they back in the house?'

Joe's brain worked overtime. 'Who?'

Keith stopped dead and Joe walked straight into him – the man's back as hard as a brick wall. 'I haven't got time for this,' he snarled, turning around. 'Your missus. Is she and the old bitch back at the house yet?'

Joe shook his head. 'I don't know.' *Why did it matter? These guys had got what they wanted, hadn't they?*

'I'll make it a bit simpler. I forgot how fucking stupid you are. Has your girl told you anything? Anything at all about the police – that sort of stuff?'

Joe frowned. 'No.'

'Where are they?'

Joe shrugged. 'I haven't seen her. She texted me the other day to say she was coming to the funeral and that was it.' He looked down at his suit. 'That's where I'm going now.' *You know, the funeral of my mate that you killed…*

Keith's eyes narrowed. 'She must have said something. You need to fucking think.'

Joe swallowed, remembering all too clearly the last time he'd been slow in giving his answers to this man. 'I haven't seen her.'

Keith's mouth formed a snarl. 'Then find out everything you can today. I want to know where they are and if they're back at the house. I want to know what the police have said. I want to know every fucking detail. *Everything.* Do you understand? I'll call you later, so make sure to answer.'

Without waiting for a reply, Keith sauntered off down the street, leaving Joe feeling like the groundhog nightmares had begun all over again.

SEVEN

TEAGAN IGNORED THE muffled buzzing of her phone from the bottom of her handbag, glad she'd remembered to turn the ringer off. There wasn't much worse than someone's phone ringing loudly at a funeral, apart from perhaps it being your own funeral.

She suspected it was Darren Harding. He'd sent her many texts and left several voicemails over the last few days, but she'd been loath to return them. Admittedly, she was being a bit of a coward by putting off getting back to him, but his general attitude the last time she'd seen him was not the best and well, they didn't have what she'd thought in common after all.

After Joe, Teagan decided she was done with spending time on detrimental relationships and besides, she'd had other things to deal with. But she would have to at least return his calls and explain what had happened. Despite her decision about not wanting to pursue a relationship, it wasn't fair to blank him. But she'd deal with that later. Right now it was more important to be here for Joe.

Aside from how things had worked out between them and what he'd put her through, she still cared for him and felt it only decent that she should make the effort to come to Alan's funeral.

She eyed Joe dressed in a suit and less unkempt than the last time she'd seen him, glad he'd made the effort to spruce himself up. But he still looked worried. *Stressed.*

As Alan's coffin was lowered into the earth, Teagan bowed her head and bit back the urge to cry. She watched Joe also fighting against the tears and reached out to squeeze his hand.

The last couple of weeks had been so confusing and difficult, Teagan felt drawn to Joe. Not in the way she used to be, but by his familiarity. Right now she needed someone around her that she didn't need to second guess. Although Robert had been less abrasive since Helen's murder, she couldn't talk to him – not about most of the things that were bothering her.

'Thanks for coming. I really appreciate it. Are you joining us at the pub?' Joe asked as the small group walked away from the graveside. 'I mean, I know you said you didn't want to see me again, but being as it's the wake, I…'

'I'll join you, yes,' Teagan said. 'It will do me good to be out of the house for a while.'

'The house? Are you back there already?' Joe asked. 'I wasn't even sure whether you'd still be needed.'

Teagan walked beside Joe, glad that the handful of others were some distance ahead. 'I'm not sure what's going on. We're both still at Robert's, but I don't know whether Dulcie will want to return to Footlights, or whether she'll want me there if she does.' She turned to Joe. 'I really should apologize, Joe. When I first saw that man running out of the house, my first instinct was that it was something to do with you.'

Joe burnt inside. 'Me? I told you all of that other business was sorted,' he lied. 'I said I was sorry and…'

'Hey,' Teagan raised a hand. 'I know that. It just went through my mind. I realise you'd never have done that.'

'No, I wouldn't,' Joe said, only wishing that was true. Sickness ate away at his insides. 'Do the police know who it was yet?' he asked, dreading the answer.

Teagan shrugged. 'They've all but admitted they haven't got a clue. Dulcie put together a photofit of the man she saw, but I don't know how much help it's been. I couldn't add much because I only got a glimpse as he left the house. As far as I know they haven't arrested anyone.' She lowered her voice. 'Robert thinks it's all to do with Helen and that she was involved with lots of things no one knew about.'

Joe hoped his frown looked convincing. 'She certainly was a dark horse.' Stopping, he placed his hands on Teagan's shoulders. 'I know we're no longer together, but I was still terrified for you when I heard what had happened.' *Did that sound sincere enough?* He hoped so because his main fear was of something happening to *him* rather than her. He needed info. 'Did… did these people take anything?'

Teagan shivered involuntarily. 'Not as far as I know, but they were definitely looking for something.'

Joe frowned. He'd love to know what had been lifted from that house, courtesy of the keys he'd supplied and what all this nightmare had been about in the first place.

'I mean, the place had been turned over by those… those scum, whoever they were, but Dulcie didn't seem to think anything was missing. Although saying that, the place was such a mess, she didn't have much chance to look before we went to Robert's.' Teagan pursed her lips. 'Do you know, it's funny because out of all of Dulcie's beautiful things that got ruined, the only thing she was bothered about was a little box that she didn't want the police finding. She's given it to me to look after until everything's sorted.'

Joe's skin bristled. 'Oh? What is it then?'

Teagan hesitated. 'Just personal stuff.'

'Haven't you looked?'

Teagan stared at Joe incredulously. 'Looked? Of course not. I've broken enough of that woman's trust already thinking I was doing the right thing with what I told Helen, without snooping through her stuff as well!'

She glanced around furtively. 'I shouldn't be telling you

this, but I've got to tell someone. I feel dreadful because I can't say anything to Robert.' She watched Joe nod in sympathy. 'Robert has a different father to Helen - a man from where Dulcie used to work. She was planning on running away with him, but he never came back. Dulcie thinks he must have been killed. It's so sad.' She shook her head. 'Anyway, this box contains stuff from Robert's father – love letters or something. The thing is, Robert doesn't know. Not yet, anyway.'

Teagan glanced at Joe. 'That's why she's given it to me. If the police or Robert found the box then everything would come out and as I'm sure you appreciate, she didn't want Robert to find out that way.' She suddenly looked weary. 'Oh God, Joe. I feel so bad for Dulcie. Fancy all of this happening. It doesn't bear thinking about. I don't know how I'll feel if I'm not needed anymore. It might sound daft, but I'm so attached to the old lady. She feels so much more to me than a client.'

'I'm sure it will all work out,' Joe muttered, his heart racing as they continued walking towards the pub.

• • • •

HEARING THE FRONT DOOR SHUT, Dulcie looked up. 'Is that you, dear?' she called.

'Yes, it's only me.' Taking her jacket off, Teagan placed it on the coat stand and walked into the lounge where Dulcie sat on the sofa, a book perched on her lap. 'Where's Robert?' she asked, immediately spotting Robert wasn't in his customary position at the computer desk wedged in the corner of the room. Alarm rang through her. Surely he hadn't gone out and left Dulcie on her own?

Dulcie patted the seat next to her. 'What are you flapping for?' she laughed. 'Robert's in the shower. I think he wanted to get away from me.' She raised her eyebrows. 'But don't mind him. Tell me how it went. Did it go ok?'

Teagan nodded. 'As funerals go, it went ok I suppose.'

'And from the smell of you, you had a few drinks in this young man's memory?' Dulcie smiled.

Teagan blushed. 'Oh dear. Is it that obvious?'

'Well, why not? Talking of which, would you mind pouring me a gin? Robert will moan, but he's in the other room, so he can't.' Dulcie winked mischievously.

Teagan moved to Robert's cabinet, the beautiful antique furniture placed in this 1970s flat never ceasing to surprise her.

'Make sure you have one too,' Dulcie called.

'I probably shouldn't…' Teagan said, pouring a large gin and tonic. Normally, she didn't drink in the day, or very much at all, but today it wouldn't hurt. She could certainly do with something to help her to relax. 'I already feel a bit light-headed after the ones I had this afternoon with Joe.'

Dulcie's painted eyebrows arched. 'Oh, don't tell me you're back with that imbecile?'

Teagan walked back to the sofa armed with the glasses. 'No! Just talking at the wake, that's all.'

Dulcie glanced in the direction of the doorway, then lowered her voice. 'You haven't said anything to him about… you know…? About that box?'

'Erm no…' Teagan said uncomfortably. She might have told Joe about the box, but she hadn't gone into detail had she? She couldn't remember what she'd said now. She'd got a bit carried away, relieved to talk to someone who knew her so well, even thought it was Joe.

'You've still got the box haven't you?' Dulcie asked, gripping Teagan's arm.

Teagan moved her arm out of the grasp that was fast becoming painful. 'Of course. I told you I'd look after it. I keep it in my handbag.'

'You've been walking around with it in your handbag?' Dulcie cried.

Teagan frowned. 'Don't worry, I won't lose it.' It was only letters – hardly the crown jewels, although they were probably the same thing as far as Dulcie was concerned. Maybe she had been thoughtless taking them out with her? 'I didn't want to leave them lying around here in case Robert found them. You said you didn't want him to kn…'

'No, I don't want him to know,' Dulcie cried, looking at Teagan, her bright blue eyes searching. 'I still haven't told him.'

Teagan patted Dulcie's hand. 'There's enough going on at the moment, so leaving it a bit longer won't make much difference.'

'When are you seeing that Darren again?' Dulcie quickly changed the subject. 'Now *he* is a nice man.'

'Erm…' Teagan fidgeted. *Damn. She still hadn't called him back.*

The phone ringing saved her from answering. 'I'll get that.' Putting her glass of gin down, Teagan picked up the telephone. 'Hello? Yes, but I'm afraid he's busy at the moment. Can I take a messa… Oh… Ok… No, I understand, bear with me a moment.'

Placing the receiver down, Teagan mouthed, 'It's the police.'

Hurrying up the corridor, Tegan saw the door to the bathroom still closed. She was just about to knock, when the door flew open, along with it a cloud of steam. 'Oh!' she yelped, jumping back.

Robert stood in the doorway, a towel around his hips. 'What is it?' he snapped.

Teagan coloured furiously. 'The phone… It's for you. It's the police…' she squeaked. 'They said it's important.'

Huffing, Robert strode along the hall and Teagan leant back against the wall. She hoped she hadn't given him the impression that she was staring at him. Robert was… *Robert* and the last thing she wanted to do was give him the wrong impression.

EIGHT

'I'M NOT ENTIRELY CONVINCED I'm happy for you to go back to Footlights, mother,' Robert said.

'We can't stay under your feet forever, Robert and the police have now said I can return home,' Dulcie said miserably.

Robert looked at his mother, trying to read her. 'Like I said, you're welcome to stay here for as long as you need or want to.'

'Are you sure?' Dulcie sniffed. 'It's just... it's just I feel uncomfortable... and I...'

'It's fine. I've already told you.' Standing up, Robert walked over and patted his mother's hand, then looked in Teagan's direction. 'That goes for you as well, of course.'

'Thank you,' Teagan muttered, before turning back to the sideboard that she was aimlessly dusting for the fifth time.

'I'm going to have a lie down,' Dulcie said quietly. 'I need a bit of space.'

Robert watched his mother leave the room. 'I'm worried about her,' he said, as Teagan moved objects around the sideboard. Striding over, he stared at her. 'Do you not think you've moved those around enough?'

Teagan blindly continued dusting the overly polished surface. She didn't want to go back to Footlights. The prospect of it being just her and Dulcie in that massive house now terrified her. After what had happened she didn't know whether it would ever not terrify her, but how could she let Dulcie down now when she needed her more than ever? When Dulcie was ready to return to Footlights, then she would accompany her, regardless of her fear.

Her heart raced, her hand polishing the surface quicker and quicker and more frantically. Everything span around and around in her head.

'Will you stop it?' Robert roared, grabbing Teagan's arm, holding it still. 'What the hell is the matter with you?'

Teagan froze and blinked, her eyes wide; the stress of the last couple of weeks hitting her like a sledgehammer. She felt her eyes fill with tears and her heart pounded mercilessly in her chest. 'I… I don't know… I…'

She stared at Robert's big hand clamped around her arm holding it motionless and she felt faint. Totally overwhelmed, the tears spilt from her eyes and she began to shake.

Although it was not a manoeuvre he'd normally make, Robert pulled Teagan against his chest. 'You need to calm down,' he said slowly, holding her close. 'Now breathe.'

Teagan buried her face in Robert's shirt. She couldn't. She was panicking. Panicking about everything.

• • • •

LENA PULLED ON the high-legged lycra swimsuit and admired herself in the mirror. This one was the least clumsy and cumbersome she'd been able to find.

She couldn't remember the last time she'd worn a full swimming costume. School, probably. With a figure like hers, she was definitely a bikini girl, but it wasn't like she was lying on the beach. This whole ridiculous ensemble was the only thing she'd come up with to aid her plans. Her nose wrinkled, not quite believing she was reduced to this in the pursuit of her dreams.

But she had to be careful. Not personally having any

knowledge of the subject, she'd done some digging and the trick was not changing too much too soon. Bringing the screen of her mobile back to life, Lena crossed her long legs and sat on the bed. Jonah wouldn't be back for a while, so she'd got plenty of time.

Flicking through the open tabs of her internet app, she found the site she'd been studying earlier. Her mouth twisted in distaste as she glanced through the photos, centring on the people who were naturally slim like her.

What possessed people to want to publicly document how fat they became week by week until they morphed from a slender size eight into a gargantuan beachball by the end of forty weeks was beyond her, but by the looks of it, it was a fairly popular practice.

Now, what was she supposed to be? 8, 9, 10 weeks? How far along had she told Jonah she was? *Come on, Lena – think.*

She gritted her teeth. Grabbing a quart bottle of vodka from the zipped compartment of her handbag, she unscrewed the top and took a good few gulps. Now she'd have to use that repulsive mouthwash again before Jonah returned. How many more weeks did she have to do this shit for? And *this*…

She glanced at the kitchen roll on the bed. This was one step beyond the bloody pale.

Men didn't notice stuff, but now Gwen had made it clear she doubted the authenticity of this baby thing, she had no choice but to ensure no one became suspicious.

Studying the photos on her phone, she flicked from one to the next, then another and back again. *Right. Ok.*

Pulling a whole host of sheets of the ultra-quilted kitchen roll off she carefully folded the layers into a long rectangular pad, then did the same with another bunch of sheets and smoothed them down to ensure no lumpy bits.

With a deep sigh of resignation, she carefully fed the padding through the right leg of her swimsuit and adjusted it into place. Turning sideways, Lena looked at herself in the mirror. That looked exactly what it was. *Fake.*

Readjusting the padding again, she looked forlornly at her reflection. *Too big.*

Lena carefully extracted some of the layers and went through the same process. *That was better. A very slight bump.* And it looked pretty damn realistic, even if she did say her herself.

Pulling a dress from the wardrobe, she slipped it on and smoothed the lycra down over her "bump". Her face screwed up. It looked too obvious, plus the lines of the swimming costume were clear.

Irritated, she reached for the vodka and took another swig whilst she rummaged around for a less clingy dress. *For fuck's sake.*

Putting on a different dress, she stared in the mirror. That was better. *Much* better. A very slight hint of a bump; noticeable, but not blatant. *Fuck you, Gwen.*

Lena scowled at her reflection again. She felt disgusting. A fat, flabby bastard. She pushed her pink glossy lips together. *Swallow it, Lena. It will be worth it in the end.*

Grabbing the kitchen roll, she shoved it into the bottom of her wardrobe. She'd need to add more sheets every fortnight until she no longer had to keep this charade up. Plus she'd have to make sure Jonah didn't see her naked, which also meant she'd be very frustrated for the next few weeks too. For God's sake.

Lena finished the last of the vodka, glad for the warming sensation it brought. She stared at the paper bump and gingerly touched it. *Did it feel real?* She didn't know. What did it matter?

Feeling stupidly self-conscious, she grabbed a thin jacket and slipped it on. The bump would only need to be glimpsed occasionally. But how would she deal with no sex for the next 7 or 8 very long weeks… *Damn Gwen and her suspicions.*

Lena glanced at the clock. Time for a couple of lines of coke and then she'd better dig out that mouthwash.

NINE

SAUL SHIFTED UNCOMFORTABLY in the cramped confines of the passenger seat of Keith's car. 'You sent Team B out on the collections?'

Keith moved out to the outside lane of the M40. 'That's what you said in the meeting, wasn't it?'

'Yep,' Saul agreed. It had been good informing the enforcement teams they would be taking orders directly from him from now on. There were several men remaining who had been present in his team originally and it was good to see them still involved, but many of the faces in this room this afternoon were new. Keith had hand-picked them and said they could be left to their own devices with minimum guidance, so Saul was quietly confident they were decent. That didn't mean he wouldn't keep a very close eye. He also intended to be present himself on a lot of the collections.

Saul grinned. The gaffer being there always had the effect of instilling an extra amount of fear – from the punters to the staff alike. He'd never been one to sit behind a desk and not get his hands dirty like Jonah had taken to doing. Oh no, *he'd* be getting involved. Well, he would be once all this other business was sorted and that wouldn't take much longer. *Not now he was on the case.*

'Tell me again what this prick reported.'

Keith grinned. He'd been pleased with what the stoner had come back with and he knew Saul was too. It was more information than either of them expected and put a whole new slant on things.

'The girl said they're still at the son's gaff and didn't know whether they would return to the Amityville House of Horrors at all.' He chuckled to himself with his apt naming for Dulcie Adams' place. A perfect name for the creepy dump of a place.

'And you think the girl is in possession of the diamonds?' Saul said, barely able to believe they'd landed such a bonus.

'I don't know for certain, but that's the impression. Adams gave her something personal that she didn't want the police to find,' Keith said.

'The dippy bitch didn't have the nous to look?' Saul scoffed. 'I mean, what sort of fuckwit wouldn't look?'

Keith laughed. 'Her, obviously. She thinks the world of this old crone, so the stoner says.'

'Hmmph, that won't do her any favours.' Saul lit himself a cigarette and wound down the window. 'With this is mind, we haven't got much to lose but to lift the bird.'

Keith gripped onto the steering wheel to stop himself swerving into the central reservation. '*Lifting* her? The young girl? What the fuck?'

Throwing his head back, Saul laughed loudly. 'Oh, Keith, you've been working with Jonah too long.' He could see Keith's anger bubbling from his remark which only made him want to laugh harder. 'I told you I'm sorting this and not fannying around. We'll lift the bird and see exactly what she's holding for the thieving witch. I reckon she knows a lot more than what she's let on to her stoner boyfriend.'

Keith nodded, trying not to let Saul's barbs rile him. 'Perhaps. We'll just have to hope that she don't talk.'

Saul snorted in derision. 'Talk? She won't be talking.'

Keith nodded again, adrenaline flowing once again with the

prospect of what he suspected that meant. 'Don't rush though because from what I remember, she's a nice looker.'

'Even better,' Saul grinned. Grabbing his own crotch, he laughed. 'Always up for use, this one! Now, how much further is it to the son's place?'

'Not long. I know where it is, but I never got as far as going there. I wanted to go and see the man because I had a good idea for doubling up on the job. According to the dweeb estate agent I dispatched he's got a huge gambling problem,' Keith said. 'The Shepherd bitch told the dweeb that this Robert prick had all but sold his mother up the river for money.'

'Sounds like a prize cunt if you ask me. I suppose Jonah stopped that,' Saul said, flicking his fag end out of the window.

'Yes he did. He wanted us to concentrate on the stoner,' Keith continued. 'But yes, this bloke must be a prize wanker. It must run in the family.' He paused, remembering the part that he hadn't yet mentioned. He knew he had to, but it was a question of *when* the right time was. And there probably wasn't a right time because whenever he spoke about it he was fairly sure what kind of reaction it would get. 'Talking of which, I learnt today that Robert Adams' real father isn't who he thought it was.'

'What are you going on about?' Saul snapped. 'Auditioning for a research job on *'This is Your Life'*?'

'No, Robert Adams is the son of Michael Pointer…'

Saul shot forward hard. 'You fucking what?'

Keith nodded. 'Yep, he's Pointer's son.'

His body rigid, Saul sat back in the car seat and Keith felt the manic rage coming off him in waves as they took the slip road off the motorway to Maidenhead. 'What are you going to do?'

Saul cracked his knuckles, his icy stare fixed out of the window. 'I haven't decided yet,' he spat through gritted teeth.

• • • •

DRIVING BACK DOWN THE ROAD, the enticing aroma

from the bag of fish and chips on the passenger seat made Robert's stomach rumble in appreciation.

He chewed his bottom lip impatiently. Even though he'd only been gone fifteen minutes, it was uncomfortable leaving his mother and Teagan alone in the flat. It was the not knowing that was the worst thing. The not knowing exactly what had happened with Helen and why.

Robert brushed his hair from his face and placed his hand back on the steering wheel, noticing he was gripping it tightly. If he only knew, however bad, what Helen had been involved in to cause all of this, then at least he would know what he was dealing with. *Who* he was dealing with. But he didn't and neither did the police and he didn't like not knowing. He liked things to be neat. *Ordered.*

He'd seen the photofit his mother had put together with help from the police artist and the result wasn't a face he could say he'd ever seen before or even marginally recognised, but if his theory was correct and all of this business was linked to Helen, then the truth was it could have been anyone. No matter which way he looked at it, she had to be involved, but what had she been so desperate to cover up to make her kill her own husband and poison her mother to the point of madness?

Cold anger seeped up Robert's spine like it did every time he thought about the situation. None of it made sense.

And then there was that estate agent – the one who had disappeared. His forehead crumpled in concentration. The police had been interested in questioning Helen several times over that. Was it possible she was behind that too?

As it was, it stood he'd lose a shed load of money after pulling out of the purchase of that apartment Helen convinced him their mother needed, but he didn't care about the cash. He didn't want anything connected to his sister.

Robert blasted his horn at the car in front taking its sweet time. He needed to get home.

The question was, how would he feel when his mother returned to Footlights? Would whoever killed Helen return?

Had they got what they were looking for? What they believed Helen had secreted in a property she was connected with?

A creeping dread trickled down Robert's back. What if they came to his flat?

Teagan was a worry too. From what he'd seen tonight; the way she'd all but shattered in front of him, she wasn't coping as well with this situation as he'd believed.

Robert pulled up outside his block of flats and sat motionless, the engine idling. Over the next couple of days he'd go to Footlights himself and get it sorted. He'd get everything cleaned up and tidied away regardless of whether his mother ever moved back there.

Turning the motor off, Robert grabbed the fish and chips and got out of the car, scowling at a car further down the road, its headlights on full beam right in his face.

TEN

TEAGAN PLACED DULCIE'S BREAKFAST on the table and poured her a fresh cup of tea. She felt a lot better today. The release of her pent up emotions yesterday had been cathartic, although she was mortified to have broken down in front of Robert. She didn't want him to think her incapable.

Dulcie's nose wrinkled. 'I don't think I'll ever get used to this instant tea you insist on, Robert,' she moaned. 'Tea should be left to steep in a pot, not these tasteless bag things. They're not the same.'

Teagan bit back a smile watching Robert raise his eyebrows from his desk in the corner of the room. *Dulcie really was a case.*

'Can you not buy a tea pot?' Dulcie continued staring at her son, only the top of his head visible behind his screen. 'Robert? Can you even hear me?' She looked at Teagan. 'Can he hear me?'

'Robert's working, Dulcie,' Teagan said quietly.

Dulcie rolled her eyes. 'Is that what you call it? I have no idea what that boy does, tapping away at that plastic box all day and night. Where has the life gone in this world?'

Teagan glanced at Robert once again. From her position she

could see the irritation forming on his face, his jaw clenched.

'I wonder if I've even got a tea pot left? There was so much smashed... The place will still be in such a mess...' Dulcie's voice tailed off, her voice sad.

'How do you fancy getting out for a while?' Teagan suggested brightly. 'You've been cooped up here for a week now. You haven't even seen the light of day! Perhaps we could go for a walk or even a bite to eat at lunchtime somewhere?'

Robert glanced up. 'I'm not sure that's a good idea. Mother's still very nervous of going anywhere an...'

'No, I'm not!' Dulcie interrupted. 'I'm feeling a lot better actually. Just because I'm not quite ready to face the mess at Footlights doesn't mean I don't want to go anywhere at all.' She pursed her lips like a sulky child. 'It's hardly likely anything's going to happen to me, is it? It wasn't *me* those people were after.'

Robert frowned. 'Even so, I...'

'Do you know, I think I'll go to bowls. It's on this afternoon and I haven't been for weeks!' Dulcie looked at Teagan wide-eyed. 'Like you said, it will be good for me to get out of the flat.'

Teagan looked at Robert apologetically and gave him a small shrug. She wished she hadn't suggested anything – she hadn't meant to cause additional worry. 'Ok, I'll call a taxi and drop you off there later.'

'There's no need. I've got some things to do this afternoon, so I'll take you on the way,' Robert added, thinking he might as well make a start with cleaning Footlights up this afternoon, being as now he didn't have to worry about leaving his mother alone.

• • • •

'WHERE'S EVERYONE ELSE?' Nero asked as Jonah impatiently drummed his fingers on the desk.

Jonah frowned, wondering the same thing. He knew Saul had an enforcement team meeting this morning, but he'd specifically made sure Saul was aware this meeting about Dulcie Adams had been arranged and he was keen to voice his suggestions as to how to move things forward. They'd agreed to work together on that side of things, so Saul had best be sticking to that.

Surprisingly, there had been no ructions from Lena, so it looked like Gwen was keeping all of that under control, which was good. It also meant he'd been able to give some long awaited concentration to the next plan of action. 'Saul and Keith should be here. I presume their meeting has run over,' he said, irritation evident.

Jonah straightened his cuffs and folded his fingers together. 'We'll start without them.' He wasn't impressed how Keith had drifted away since Saul's return either. It also hadn't gone unnoticed that Keith had been privy to Saul's release, yet chose not to mention it. He'd even had the audacity to collect Saul from nick during company time. He shouldn't be too surprised as Keith was one of Saul's men, but he had thought that over the years of Saul's absence, Keith would have developed some loyalty by now, but what he had displayed seemed to have evaporated since Saul came back on the scene.

'What's the plan then?' Nero asked. 'Touch base with the stoner again?'

Jonah chewed his lip. 'Nah, I think we've got everything we're going to get out of that one, so I suggest we go after the son – Robert Adams.'

He glanced up as the door opened, watching unimpressed as Saul and Keith sauntered in. 'You may well remember he was mentioned some time ago and we decided not to go down that road, but maybe now it's time.'

'Started without us, I see?' Saul said caustically, cutting Jonah a withering look.

Jonah returned the cool stare. 'You weren't here, so yes. Time is of the essence.'

'Oh, so you've noticed that?' Saul muttered, making a big point of clattering his chair as he made his way to his desk. It wasn't fitting for him to share an office with his brother. A childhood full of sharing a bedroom had been enough, but he wasn't accepting the office next door. *This* office – the main office, should be his and if Jonah was still laying claim to it, then so would he.

'Jonah was just saying we should concentrate on the son – Robert Adams.' He glanced at Saul. 'We had information some time ago that the man has a gambling problem and a lot of debt, therefore the chances of him being open to exchanging info for money is high.'

Saul glanced at Keith. Jonah going after Adams right now was not what he wanted to hear. He was keeping the knowledge about Adams' link to Pointer to himself and didn't want his brother involved.

After taking up position outside that crummy flat last night, they'd been saved a lengthy stake-out when the man put in an appearance early doors. He and Keith had been there less than an hour before Robert Adams had left his poky flat and driven off. Tailing him, he hadn't gone anywhere exciting – just to the fucking chippy, but it had given them ample opportunity to eyeball the man.

Saul had very nearly passed out when he'd set eyes on the guy. The stoner hadn't been lying and Keith's info was bang on. Based on the handful of photographs he'd seen of the two-faced prick who had shafted his father, the bastard was a dead ringer for Pointer – there was no question who had fathered him, so no – Jonah digging on Adams was not something he'd agree to because he was having the wanker to himself.

Saul folded his arms across his wide chest and made a big show of looking pensive. 'Yeah, Keith mentioned you'd previously got intel on the bloke. Off that estate agent, Manning, wasn't it?'

Jonah nodded. 'That's correct and now we've got as much as we can from the stoner, Adams should be our next target.'

Saul shook his head and inspected his fingernails. They had *no way* finished with the stoner. Besides, he'd been *very* useful so far – not that Jonah would know that. 'I don't agree. Going after Adams now isn't the best thing to do.'

Jonah bristled. 'Why's that?'

Saul looked between everyone in turn. 'The police are still digging and they're bound to be in close contact with the family - probably on a daily basis.' He paused thoughtfully. 'Putting a tail on Adams now could mean walking straight into a frying pan.'

He held out his hands theatrically. 'I'm just taking a leaf out of your book, Jonah, and avoiding the heat whilst it's still on full flame.' Saul could see disagreeing had rattled his brother no end, but he couldn't have Jonah and that eyjit Nero digging around now he and Keith were onto something. *They just needed a bit more time.*

'What are you suggesting instead then? We can't leave things much longer. Enough time has passed already to give the wankers who took our haul and shot Shepherd a head start. The police could be digging around for months yet.'

Saul nodded 'I agree, but we don't want to give the cops a hot trail back to us, do we? I suggest we leave it at least another few days – just until we get clarity on where the cops are at with the investigation.' He glanced around the room again, seeing Keith nodding enthusiastically. Even Nero looked like he could see sense in the theory. 'In the meantime, I'll get feelers out to see if there's been any word as to who was behind this and I don't mean on the street or places we've tried before. I have a few contacts who aren't linked who might prove useful.' He raised his eyebrows. 'I'll also use some of my other contacts to get confirmation on the investigation.'

Saul rubbed his hands together. He was doing well here. 'It's no secret that I want to get to the bottom of this and neither is it news I didn't agree with how the 'original' approach panned out… The way that was done achieved very little, short of being detrimental.' He looked at Jonah pointedly. *Yeah, brother – that was a dig – a BIG one and aimed right at you. Did you like it?*

'But what's done is done and we must concentrate on where we're at now. I for one am all for avoiding going back inside and the *last* thing I want is us all ending up in nick for the sake of rushing things?' He smiled widely. 'Trust me, we'll catch up with who's lifted our goods and we'll also put the record straight with Pointer's tart and the fucking O'Hara's while we're at it, but we need to be careful and do one thing at a time.'

Gritting his teeth, Jonah felt like punching Saul in the face. Saul made him sound like a prize twat; purposefully rushing things because he'd fucked up? *He* hadn't fucked up. Saul was up to something and he didn't like it. He didn't trust his brother one iota.

'I guess it makes sense…' Nero reluctantly agreed. Despite everything, Saul's take on things did seem the most sensible and logical way to go about this. Not that Jonah liked it, judging by his face. His neck tightened, hoping this wouldn't become a tug of war between the Powell brothers. After all, it was all of their necks on the line.

Saul looked at Jonah. 'Well? Do we have an agreement?'

'The O'Hara's are long done, but as for the rest of it - Ok,' Jonah said resentfully. 'We'll wait another week and then weigh up where we are again from there. In the interim we'll use this time to get as much info as possible, plus catch up with the other parts of the business which have taken a back seat the last couple of weeks.'

'Yeah, we have started running a bit behind pace…' Saul jibed. 'Good job I'm back, isn't it?' He grinned. *He* was in control whether Jonah realised it yet or not. The O'Hara's weren't done – far from it. There was still that tosser who'd ended up in the loony bin to deal with. Just because he hadn't physically been part of any of it meant jack shit. The man was related to that turd, Sean O'Hara and he'd done fucking years because of that joker – so anyone left related to him was fair game.

Biting back his rising rage, Jonah closed the hardbacked notebook on his desk. 'If that's everything, then I've got some calls to make.' He had to abruptly close this meeting before he got up and knocked Saul's teeth down the back of his throat.

ELEVEN

TEAGAN HESITATED ON THE TOP STEP, her heart racing. She watched Robert jam the key into the lock of the big old red door and shoved her hands deep into her pockets to stop them shaking.

Robert pushed the heavy door open. 'I didn't ask to you accompany me.'

'It's fine,' Teagan said, smiling bravely. 'We'll get more done with the two of us. At least we know Dulcie will be safe at bowls.'

Robert was right. She didn't *have* to offer to help. Teagan had gone along for the ride when he'd dropped Dulcie at bowls and it was only after Dulcie had got out of the car had he admitted he was going to Footlights, so it was only right she should help. But nerves were getting the better of her. Being back in the shadow of the big house brought the horror of the night Helen was murdered rushing back like a freight train.

Taking a deep breath, Teagan stepped over the threshold and her nose wrinkled up. The house smelt musty – unused. It was funny what a week of leaving an old house empty did. She followed Robert into the gloomy hallway, pushing aside the ridiculous notion that Helen's body might still be lying exactly where she'd last seen it.

When Robert disappeared into the front sitting room, Teagan forced her reluctant legs to follow suit. 'Oh my God! I'd forgotten how bad it was!' she gasped.

Her eyes darted around the piles of smashed ornaments, the tipped-out drawers and scattered paperwork. She'd seen it before, but in her rush to locate Dulcie and the following shock of that night, she hadn't taken on board just how trashed everything was.

She stared at several framed photographs of Dulcie's dancing days at the Feathers, some she remembered having been hung on the wall, others on sideboards, now smashed on the floor. 'It will break Dulcie's heart to see this,' Teagan sighed, feeling slightly tearful.

'Yes, it's a bit of a state, isn't it?' Robert muttered, tentatively treading over pieces of porcelain and glass. 'I know I wanted her to get rid of all this stuff, but it I didn't mean for it to be like this…'

Teagan scanned the devastation once again. 'Where do we start?'

Robert grimaced. 'In here. The police have warned me there's still a lot of bloodstains upstairs, so I'll deal with that.'

Teagan nodded gratefully. 'I'll get that stuff you brought with you from the car. If you could put some of those boxes together, I'll stack the saveable things in those whilst I'm tidying up. Can I have the keys?'

Fishing the car keys from his pocket, Robert threw them to Teagan and started rolling his sleeves up.

Teagan ran down the steps to the car, breathing in lungfuls of fresh air. Being in the house was making her dizzy, but she knew it was all in her mind. She pulled a bottle of bleach and a roll of heavy-duty bin bags from Robert's boot. Pursing her lips determinedly, she made her way back into the house. *Everything would be a lot better once the house was back to normal.*

Not relishing the momentous job in hand, Teagan wandered

back into the sitting room. 'I've got some bin bags, so I'll start wi…'

She froze seeing Robert crouching on the floor staring at something intently. Blind to her presence, his eyebrows knitting closely together, his forehead crumpled in concentration. She edged closer, spotting a crumpled up piece of newspaper in his hand. *Oh no… That wasn't what she thought it was, was it?*

'What the fuck is this?' Robert muttered, his voice hollow. 'It was scrunched up on the floor.'

Standing behind Robert's crouched figure, Teagan could now see what he had was exactly what she hoped it wasn't. *Shit.* How had that newspaper cutting – the one Dulcie kept in the little table, ended up discarded on the floor? That was the cutting Dulcie showed her before – the one she treasured. *The only photo she had of Michael.*

Robert got to his feet, his face waxen. 'Your face tells me you've seen this before…' he growled. 'Well? Have you?'

Teagan instinctively stepped backwards from his piercing stare, her feet slipping on smashed pottery. 'I…'

Robert thrust the creased clipping towards her, the fragile paper all but ruined. 'This man…' He pointed to the centre of the photograph. 'Who is he?'

Teagan stared at the image of Michael Pointer - the very same image which had made her realise immediately the man was undoubtedly Robert's father. She blinked rapidly. *What should she say? How should she handle this?*

Robert's face contorted with rage. 'Answer me!' he roared, 'Have you seen this before?' He stabbed his finger on the old newspaper. 'It's like looking in the fucking mirror!'

Teagan looked at Robert's pained face and felt sick. She would have to tell him. She couldn't lie – it was pointless and by the looks of it, he'd already worked things out. 'I-I only saw it myself recently,' she faltered. 'Dulcie… she…'

'Who. Is. He…?' Richard barked, sweat beading on his brow. He paced over to the fireplace, leaning on the mantle with his big forearms and put his head in his hands, before swinging around, his eyes wild. 'I look just like him.'

Not knowing what else to do given the situation, Teagan spoke softly. 'He's your father... I'm sorry... I...'

'*This* person is my father? Jesus fucking Christ!' Lurching forward, Robert grabbed the nearest intact bottle from Dulcie's drinks cabinet. Tipping port liberally into his mouth, he gulped at it greedily, then wiped his mouth with the back of his hand. Slamming the bottle down, he grabbed Teagan by the shoulders. 'She told *you* this? You? My mother told *you* that this person is my father, yet never told *me*?'

Teagan trembled, the rage in Robert's face frightening her. 'S-She wanted to tell you. She was *going* to tell you, but...'

'But what? She decided just to tell YOU instead?'

'Please Robert, it wasn't like that. She only told me because she needed to tell *someone*. Someone who wasn't involved. She'd never told anyone an...'

'So Peter Adams wasn't my father...?' Robert dropped his hold of Teagan and his big shoulders sagged. 'What is this person's name?'

Teagan swallowed hard. 'M-Michael. That's all I know. I-I don't think she mentioned his surname. I've felt awful not being able to tell you, but it wasn't my place and...'

'Save your excuses!' Robert spat. He stormed back to the cabinet and took more gulps of the port. 'Who is this *Michael*?'

Nausea crashed over Teagan. Robert wasn't supposed to find out like this. 'I-I don't know. He... he worked for someone at the Feathers. Dulcie said they were getting married. She'd been with him for a while and after your father... after Peter died, they were going to be together.' She watched all manner of emotions passing over Robert's face one after the other. 'He was supposed to come back for her, but never did. She thinks he was killed.'

Robert's eyes narrowed. 'So what is she? The fucking Black Widow? First my father – or should I say *Peter* dies and then this guy too?'

Teagan moved tentatively towards Robert and reached to

touch his arm. 'Don't say things like that. Dulcie loves you dearly an...'

'Why didn't she tell me then? Robert screeched, shrugging off Teagan's hand.

Teagan shook her head in despair. 'I-I guess it was hard. She said once Michael didn't return there was no point... She didn't want you to be known as a... as a...'

'As a *bastard*, you mean?' Robert raged, his breathing ragged. 'Did Helen know?'

Teagan shrugged. 'I don't know. Dulcie didn't seem to think so.'

'I bet she did! Helen always had a problem with me. Always had a fucking issue – saying I was the favourite! It's probably half the reason behind what she did.'

Teagan held her hands out in despair. 'I really don't know, but Dulcie gave me a box. The night it happened... She didn't want you or the police to find it. It's got things from Michael in it. She kept it under the floorboards in her bedroom.'

Robert raked his fingers through his hair. 'She'd got it all worked out hadn't she? Christ! I can't believe this, I just can't believe it! Is there anything else?'

He picked up the bottle of port, finding he'd finished it and launched it against the wall sending fragments of blue glass scattering across the room.

Teagan shrieked and grabbed Robert's arm as he rummaged around for another bottle. 'Robert! Stop this. Don't drink any more! We've got to pick Dulcie up later.'

Swinging around, Robert threw Teagan's arm away before grabbing her again and shaking her. 'Don't tell me what to do! Why the hell should I stop? She's lied to me. Fucking lied!'

Teagan stared up at Robert; saw the hurt combined with rage. 'She must have thought she was doing it for the best.'

'And you were part of this too? You lied as well – the hired fucking help? The hired help who knows more about my own bloody heritage than me? What the fuck?' Robert shook Teagan again, his eyes wild.

Biting back the hurt, Teagan grasped Robert's forearms. 'Stop it, you're hurting me. I'm sorry, Robert, I really am. If I could change any of it, I would. I didn't want to upset you.'

Feeling tears brim, Teagan blinked them away, despair rushing over her like an avalanche. Everything was now so much worse. So, *so* much worse. She looked back up at Robert, his cold blue eyes met hers – focused and intense, yet filled with confusion and just wanted to hide until all of this went away.

Suddenly turning his back, Robert began clearing up the sitting room. In silence, he boxed up bits and pieces whilst Teagan swept up the broken ornaments into the dustpan.

• • • •

LENA BATTED HER FALSE EYELASHES as Saul Powell slouched against the empty bar in the VIP suite. 'Oh! I didn't expect you to be in here.' She consciously ensured her cleavage was nicely on show under the jacket she'd carefully buttoned up over her 'bump'.

The bloody kitchen roll was itching her skin like buggery and the whole palaver was getting right on her tits. Gwen hadn't commented or said a bean, even though Lena had made the express effort of making sure her jacket was undone when she was on her own in the office with the old cow.

Even though it wasn't a chore coming across Jonah's brother, it had ruined her plan of getting a sneaky snort in while no one was looking. A function was booked for tonight and Gwen was flapping whether their champagne supply was adequate. Of course it was fucking adequate, they had crates of the damn stuff. Lena smiled. She should know because she'd been half inching bottles on a regular basis for yonks and that was the only reason she'd jumped at the chance to check over the VIP bar stock whilst the place was empty.

'I'm not disturbing you, am I?' Saul drawled, his eyes moving over Lena's enhanced bust.

Loving the attention, Lena couldn't help running the tip of her tongue along her glossy bottom lip. *Old habits die hard...*

'Not at all. I'm just checking the champagne quota for tonight.'

'Well, that's simple enough,' Saul winked, springing up and effortlessly vaulting the shiny silver bar top.

Lena giggled with both admiration and a heady helping of lust as she eyed his taut buttocks inside his well-tailored trousers. 'You're very supple for a big man.'

'That I am.' Saul fished a bottle of Moët out of the chiller. 'If you didn't belong to my brother, I'd happily show you just how supple.'

Lena heated, her pulse quickening as Saul popped the cork with his thumbs. Tipping the frothing champagne into his mouth, he grabbed two glasses. 'Best I help you test this. Just to double check it's up to the Feather's usual standards of course…'

Lena laughed. *Hallelujah! She was gagging for a drink.* 'Don't mind if I do!'

Pouring the champagne into the crystal flutes, Saul walked around the bar and handed one to Lena, then clinked his glass against hers. 'I suppose I should formally welcome you into the family,' he winked.

Lena leant towards Saul, the heady smell of his aftershave more intoxicating than the champagne she was desperate to neck and smiled as seductively as possible. 'Thank you.'

'So,' Saul continued, perching on a high leather-topped bar stool. 'How did you manage to bag my brother? I mean, apart from the obvious.' His eyes pointedly ran over Lena's large breasts. 'But *married*? I didn't think I'd ever see the day!'

'I guess once he'd had me, he didn't want to risk losing me…' Lena purred, purposefully jutting out her bottom lip. In her experience men liked that kind of thing. She leant forward just that little bit more, giving Saul a perfect view deep down her top. Sitting on a stool, she crossed her long legs slowly and ran her nail down the exposed flesh of her thigh.

Saul watched Lena carefully. He'd seen a thousand birds like this and shagged plenty of them. There was nothing particularly special about this one. A corker of a figure and decent-looking to boot, but remove the hair extensions, the two kilos of slap, plus the implants and she was just your average munter, like they all were.

Nah, there was sod all special about this one, apart from her *thinking* she was special. He'd bet his last few quid she was the sort who'd quite happily jump on him if given the chance.

He placed a big meaty hand on Lena's thigh, leaving it lingering and noticing she made no attempt to move it. *Yeah, just as he thought.*

Lena sipped her champagne, glowing at Saul's hand on her leg. *So he was testing her? Bad luck Saul. I'm one step ahead of you.*

She'd happily take the opportunity for a tumble with this one in the sack, but she wasn't stupid and wasn't ballsing this up now. She smiled slowly. 'Of course being pregnant, it's only right to get married.' Her hand moved to her stomach, lovingly stroking the stash of kitchen roll. 'Neither of us can wait until this one arrives.'

'Then it's double congratulations,' Saul smiled, removing his hand. *The silly fucker*. Jonah had got this tart up the duff? Well, more fool him. Another example of why he shouldn't be in charge of the firm if he was going to fuck up so royally.

Hopping off his stool, Saul necked his champagne. 'Right, I'll leave you to it. I've got places to go and people to see.'

TWELVE

TEAGAN DIDN'T THINK anything could be much more cringeworthy. She glanced at Robert, his eyes fixed ahead, his hands gripping the steering wheel.

She squirmed uncomfortably. And she'd thought things couldn't get any worse? Well, she'd been wrong. Things were now a *lot* worse.

She stole another glance at Robert, his face set like stone, his expression thunderous. Unspoken words burnt the end of her tongue, but that was as far as they got. How could she look Dulcie in the eye now knowing she'd told Robert about his father?

She wanted to talk to him about it, but every time she opened her mouth her vocal cords were rendered useless. She'd only just started having civilised conversations with the man and now he felt like she'd betrayed him.

Pulling up outside the indoor bowls centre, Robert pulled on the handbrake and turned to Teagan. 'I assume we both acknowledge that today wasn't what I was expecting.'

Knowing her cheeks must be pillar box red, Teagan nodded, not wanting to meet Robert's eyes. 'I'll make myself scarce when we get back so you can talk to Dulcie,' she whispered, her throat dry. Finally looking at Robert, she watched a nerve twitching in his jaw, anger burning behind his eyes and hoped this wouldn't change anything.

Spotting Dulcie rushing towards the car, waving frantically pulled Teagan from her worrying thoughts.

'That was great!' Dulcie exclaimed as she clambered into the back of the car. 'It was lovely to see everyone again. Of course, they were all devastated about Helen.'

Teagan shuffled in the passenger seat, painfully aware that Robert was struggling to contain his anger. 'Oh, erm, glad you had a good time.'

'And what have you two been up to?' Dulcie chirped.

Teagan risked a glance at Robert. *No reaction whatsoever.* 'We, erm, we made a start clearing Footlights up.'

'Oh!' Dulcie gasped, her face falling. 'How… how is it?'

'A mess, but we made some headway, didn't we, Robert?' Teagan said, the words jamming in her throat.

'Yep,' he said tersely.

'What's the matter with him?' Dulcie cried. 'I hope you put him to good use?'

Teagan tried to laugh, but the sound that came out of her mouth sounded more like she was being strangled. She needed to get out of here *now*. 'If you wouldn't mind dropping me off here,' she said quickly. 'I'll pick something up for tea.'

'We'll wait for you, dear,' Dulcie said.

'No, it's fine. I could do with some fresh air - the dust has got to me. I'll walk back – it's not far.'

As Robert drew to a halt outside the line of shops, Teagan clambered out of the car, daring to glance at him as she closed the door, but he didn't move his eyes from staring straight ahead.

As Robert and Dulcie drove off, Teagan leant against the wall of a shop and inhaled deeply, glad to be out of the claustrophobic space. She didn't want to be about when Robert had the conversation with Dulcie about his father either.

• • • •

AND THAT'S IT, IS IT? Saul snarled, malevolently eyeing the copper from the back seat. Was it not bad enough to hear that his brother had got that dippy tart in the family way, let alone *this*?

He glanced at the pile of empty sandwich packets in the footwell, his nose screwing up in distaste. These bent coppers were all the same – treating their motors like a fucking caravan. 'That's all you've managed to get? I expected a bit more for five hundred quid!'

DC Blackburn shrugged. 'There's nowt else to say, mate, that's why. That's all there is to know.'

Saul snarled inwardly. *He wasn't his mate*. 'I know it's a different station to you, but being as you're CID, surely you can do better than that? Isn't that what I pay you for?'

DC Blackburn's squinty eyes peered at Saul in the rear view mirror, his irritation clear. 'As I said, if there was anything else to say, then I'd have fucking told you. I know the score and, like you, I know how this works.' He rubbed his stubbly chin. 'I've seen the photofit the old bird put together and I'm telling you now if that is likened back to any of you lot, then I'm Mahatma fucking Gandhi!'

Saul grated his teeth. He might be paying a bastard copper for info and out of principal he hated that from the off, but like it or loathe it, it was an unfortunate necessity in his line of work. The trouble was, he didn't trust any of them and never would.

'Why are you so bothered anyhow?' DC Blackburn asked. 'Is there something I should be aware of that you need to give me the heads up on?'

Saul scowled. *Hardly!* 'Don't get rocks in your head! I just heard something in the boozer and want to make sure no one's being fitted up for getting your solved crime numbers up, that's all.' He crossed his arms menacingly. 'You out of all people know how this works when a face gets released. Some people would love the opportunity to get me and mine slung back in jail for something – *anything*, just so it means I won't tread on any plans they might have cobbled together in my absence.'

Total bollocks. At least where *he* was concerned. No one would *dare* cross him, but this numbskull could believe what he wanted. Saul smiled coldly. 'I'm just looking out for potential trouble. No more, no less.'

The detective shrugged his large shoulders. 'Then I'd safely say you've got nothing to worry about - and I heard that from the horse's mouth. I went out for a beer with one of the DCs pulled over to work on that case and although I didn't ask the question directly, the Powell name wasn't mentioned.'

Saul nodded. That was good, but what about the rest? *He'd have to play this casual.* 'What was it all about anyhow?'

DC Blackburn chuckled. 'Fuck knows. Some sexually frustrated estate agent with a mother-hating complex got herself tied up with some undesirables, by the sounds of it. The woman was clearly a loon. Drugging her own mother and killing the husband and all.' He tapped his temple. 'Fucking barking!'

'Who was this bloke the old dear saw then? The one in the photofit?' Saul asked. Regardless of what this fool said, if the cops were still digging around, then he needed to know.

'Christ knows. The old dear was that doped up and scatty, I'm surprised she could remember what she looked like herself, let alone anyone else! They're taking her description with a pinch of salt and the general consensus is that it was some kind of money lender that she owed or even a lover.' He shrugged. 'Between you and me, although they're not closing the case, they're not expecting results either. It's not being treated as priority.'

'Hmm,' Saul muttered nonchalantly, as it if didn't matter, but it did matter. *A lot.*

'They've wound up at the scene too. Found nothing of any use, so not a lot to go on. The old bird is free to return if she wants and they've also released the crazy daughter's body. From what I've heard, she's being stuck in the ground sometime soon.'

'Oh, well,' Saul shrugged. 'Not a lot going on then?' Handing the man a roll of notes he slapped the DC on the back and opened the car door. 'Cheers for the update. Keep me posted if anything should crop up.'

'Will do,' DC Blackburn nodded, shoving the wad of cash in his breast pocket and started his car before slowly driving away.

Saul sauntered down the road back to his own car. He'd thought that had been a waste of money, but the investment had paid off by the end.

The Shepherd bird's funeral was coming up then? The perfect time to grab the girl who could have her hands on his haul when everyone else was otherwise preoccupied. All he needed to do was find when and where it was happening.

• • • •

TEARS FELL FROM DULCIE'S EYES as she sobbed in earnest. *What had that silly girl told Robert for?* She could have thought up an excuse if she'd wanted.

She'd never thought this was on the cards. For Teagan to have broken her trust like this was unthinkable. *Unbelievable*, in fact and something she hadn't factored into being an option.

Dulcie dabbed at her face with her handkerchief, her hands shaking. Not only had the girl got in first with the most important piece of information that she had to give Robert, but she was plotting to steal him off her too and probably had been all along. Oh yes, this afternoon she'd sensed the atmosphere the second she'd got in the car.

Had something happened between that little hussy and Robert? All this butter wouldn't melt act? Well, if it had, it wouldn't happen again – she'd make sure of it. Robert was *her* son. He was a piece of Michael and she would not allow anyone to take that from her. She'd kept Robert close all these years; made sure he never got too involved with any women, which hadn't been too difficult. Oh, there had been plenty of brief encounters, but Robert's natural inability and inherent dislike of forming relationships with anyone made anything more lasting impossible.

But was that about to change? Was it possible that somehow after all this time the wiring in Robert's brain had shifted?

Dulcie shook her head in annoyance. Before she could spend time thinking about that and its implications, she had to deal with *this*.

'Darling, I didn't want you to find out this way, genuinely I didn't,' Dulcie sobbed. 'There was never a right time to tell you… I knew it would upset you.'

A nerve twitched in Robert's temple. 'I'm more upset because you didn't tell me. You should have.'

Dulcie dabbed at her eyes again. 'I know, I know.' She had to keep Robert on side. Short of his father, he was the only thing that mattered, but she must play this carefully. 'Your father was a wonderful man. I loved him deeply.'

Robert's jaw clenched. 'But you let me believe Dad, or rather, *Peter*, was my father? Why?'

Dulcie looked at her son pitifully. 'It seemed the best thing to do after… after Michael disappeared…'

'Who was he?'

'Michael worked for the people who owned the Feathers. He was loyal and worked hard – not that that helped him in the end,' she spat, her eyes narrowing. 'Bastards, the lot of them. They killed him - they *must* have. He wouldn't have just left me.'

Robert sighed. He'd listened to his mother for half an hour; listened to her sobbing about how she'd lost the love of her life, but there was still one question he needed the answer to. 'This Michael Pointer – was he Helen's father too?'

'God no!' Dulcie exclaimed. 'She was definitely Peter Adams' daughter. You though…' She placed her hand on Robert's, 'are your father's son and the last thing I wanted was to hurt you. I-I was only trying to protect you.'

'Did Helen know?'

Dulcie put on her most hurt look and nodded sadly. 'I didn't realise, but yes she did. I don't know how she found out, but she did. She told me the night… the night she was killed.' She sniffed loudly. 'I-I think she must have known for a while. Maybe that's why she hated me so much. Maybe that was part of the reason she wanted to kill me? She believed I favoured you…'

Dulcie made a show of wringing her hands together. 'I've always loved both of my children equally,' she lied. Robert was and always had been her favourite. Helen was an unfortunate accident which ruined her life, but at least she was gone now. 'Do you forgive me?' she whispered. 'I was going to tell you. I need you to believe that because it's the truth.' She looked at her most prized possession, her big blue eyes doleful and her bottom lip trembling.

Robert nodded brusquely. 'I understand that you had my best interests at heart.'

'Oh, I'm so relieved!' Dulcie cried. 'I've been carrying this burden around all your life, dreading the day I told you.' She snivelled. 'Terrified that you'd hate me…'

Robert smiled, although he felt less than happy. 'I could never hate you, you're my mother.'

Dulcie leaned against Robert's chest, waiting as he wrapped his big arms around her. 'You do remind me so much of your father,' she said. 'I wish Teagan hadn't interfered. It was not her right. No wonder the girl scuttled off.'

'I didn't give her a lot of choice,' Robert said. *The less he thought about Teagan, what had happened and what he'd wanted to happen, the better.*

'Hmph!' Dulcie muttered. 'I'll still be having words with her.' If it were up to her, she'd tell the girl to get on her way, but right now her hands were tied. That little tart had the box and the contents of that were Robert's. Furthermore, she hadn't forgotten about Darren Harding and she needed Teagan for that side of things too.

Lifting her head from Robert's chest, Dulcie looked up.

'You will accompany me to Helen's funeral, won't you? Please say you will. You're all I've got and things have been so difficult…'

Robert scowled. 'If I must.'

'Thank you, son,' Dulcie smiled, patting his hand. He was a good boy, Robert and no one else was having him.

Robert sighed inwardly. He wanted to ask his mother about that box Teagan had mentioned, but didn't think he could take anything else on board today. Tomorrow he'd continue cleaning up at Footlights. *Alone*. He couldn't risk another lapse like today.

As much as it pained him to admit it, he'd become suddenly overcome with the unexpected urge to kiss Teagan. It had come from nowhere. He'd kissed plenty of women in the past, but he'd never felt such a *need* to. And today he'd felt that need.

Getting up, he stared at himself in the mirror, visualising the carbon copy of himself he'd seen in that newspaper cutting. *Michael Pointer?*

The urge to discover more about the man who fathered him was strong, but nowhere near as strong as the urge to have Teagan underneath him and neither of those things were viable.

He scraped the back of his hand across his forehead. Why was he beginning to feel things? He'd always wanted to experience what other people took for granted, but it unnerved him. He didn't do feelings, everyone knew that, so why now?

THIRTEEN

'BUT WHY FUCKING MARRY IT?' Saul snapped. 'I've got a few kids knocking around and they're just the ones I know of! There's probably a fair few more that I've yet to be made aware of, but I'm sure they'll become known to me once their slag mothers realise I'm out of nick and think they can hit me for backpay of child support.' He grinned. 'They'll have a long fucking wait!'

The smirk fell from Saul's face as he glared at his brother. 'Seriously though, what the fuck were you thinking?'

Jonah knocked back his whisky. His third so far since Saul had broached this subject. His brows furrowed. Lena had been blunt in her wish not to breathe a word about her pregnancy until she was past the twelve week mark, yet *she'd* opened her trap? And to Saul of all people? Now, because of her, he was getting earache.

The stupid bloody woman. Was there no end to her talents? Or rather, lack of them.

Saul waved his hand in front of Jonah's face. 'Hello? Calling Planet Zog! Are you receiving me? Or are you too busy dreaming of fluffy babygros, musical mobiles and happy ever fucking afters?'

'Shut your mouth!' Jonah roared.

'Answer me then!' Storming over, Saul refilled his own glass. 'Can't you see what she's doing? She's trapping you. What the hell do you want to marry something like *that* for? Yeah, great for a shag, but *this*? Even let her pop the kid out if she insists on keeping the fucking thing, like they invariably do if there's a few quid in it for them, but *marrying* it? Have a day off! Christ, you can't marry her, I won't let you!'

Jonah laughed loudly, then slammed his glass down on the desk. 'You won't *let* me? What the hell has who I marry got to do with you? What makes you think you can dictate my personal life?'

Saul tipped the whisky into his mouth, then smacked his lips together loudly. 'What you do affects me where the business is concerned. If you think I'll stand back and allow you to think with your dick and be blindsided by big tits whilst the company wallet is being emptied by that gold-digging tart, then you've got another think coming!'

He pointed his finger level with his brother's eyes. 'Because that's what Lena is - a fucking gold-digger and you know it, yet you're all loved up with a constant hard-on for the bitch!'

Jonah smacked Saul's hand away. 'Get the fuck out of my face! How dare you stand there and say th…'

'Ah, look! Immediately jumping to your darling's defence! Wise up, brother, for Christ's sake. She's laughing all the way to the bank.' Saul's mouth twisted into an ugly sneer. 'I never thought you'd be so saft as to do the love thing.'

Jonah almost choked on his tongue. 'Love? Love's got fuck all to do with it!'

Saul threw his hands in the air. 'Then chuck her some money every so often and leave it at that! She's taking you for a sucker and everyone knows it! You're such a fool! I'm only telling you what Dad would have said. He wouldn't have stood for this shit. He'd have told you t…'

'Our father would have insisted I did exactly what I'm

doing,' Jonah raged, white anger pumping through his veins, his nails digging into the palms of his hands. 'I take it you conveniently forget when you go around impregnating hosts of women, adding them on to your fucking tally sheet, that Dad didn't appreciate that sort of thing. He was more against shirking responsibility than anyone else I know.'

'That was different!' Saul muttered, puffing his chest out. 'Mum was special. Besides, I expect he had a few on the go regardless.'

Jonah's eyes flashed with malice. 'No he did not. Our father never looked at any woman besides our mother, so fuck off. I'm doing what is expected of me whether you like it or not.'

Saul shook his head. 'Then get yourself a pre-nup sorted sharpish, you prick. And if you don't, then I promise you there will be no wedding. Lena will not get her grasping hands on any of the firm's money.'

• • • •

WHITE-FACED, GWEN SCUTTLED AWAY from the door of Jonah's office just in time, retreating into her own office just as Saul stormed out.

She'd been about to tap the door to speak about the phone call she'd received from the press regarding tonight's function. There were some additional details she'd wanted to check about the extra security needed for a high profile football team on the premises when she'd frozen, unable to ignore the raised voices from inside the office.

She'd also been unable to ignore the subject being discussed, which starkly reminded her that there was no way she could risk either of the Powell boys, but especially Jonah, finding out about what had happed in the past between her and Jacky.

A deep wave of nausea entombed her. For once she wholeheartedly agreed with Saul. Jonah shouldn't and *couldn't* marry Lena. But her reasons for that were entirely different. It was imperative Jonah was made to realise that of his own accord without too much interference. If she pissed him off it would leave her wide open for Lena to spill her guts as a means of payback.

• • • •

HEATH SCROLLED MINDLESSLY through the newsfeed on Facebook and checked his Messenger inbox once again in the hope that he had inadvertently missed a message from Teagan, but there was nothing.

The last one was thanking him for a nice afternoon – and that was way back when they'd first met up. All other messages since then had been via text and he knew he hadn't got any new ones there, because he'd just double checked them too.

He ran his hand over his chin. This was silly. He had to do something. Since discovering Teagan was staying at Dulcie's son's place he'd been unable to locate where the man lived, despite his best effort. This was surprising because being a dab hand with computers he didn't normally have issues locating people, but this time he'd drawn a blank where Robert Adams was concerned. It was so frustrating.

Heath glanced at the desk opposite, his father's chin resting in one hand as he aimlessly leafed through a pile of paperwork. The man was becoming more morose by the minute. He'd lost all fight and completely given up by the looks of it, accepting he'd be bankrupt before the summer was out.

He grimaced. That was not the attitude needed in a situation such as this and was not helpful by anyone's standards. It was certainly not the attitude *he* took, but it looked like he was on his own where sorting this out was concerned.

He stared out into the deserted showroom. They didn't even have any customers, for fuck's sake!

Opening a new Google tab, Heath clicked on the Maidenhead news website he'd been following closely since Helen's death. From what he'd read the other day, he got the distinct impression the police investigation had been scaled down. Being as they'd wrapped up at the house too, it didn't look like any further news would be forthcoming on that story for the time being, which didn't leave him much more to go on.

With nothing further in the papers, no Helen, Teagan blatantly ignoring him and Robert nowhere to be found, there were no means to source more information. He frowned. The only real direction to head and the one his father was adamant he didn't take, was to go to the Feathers himself and deal with it from there.

Heath was convinced the men he'd seen at Footlights the night of Helen's death were something to do with that firm who ran the Feathers - the ones who it was believed were the cause of his grandfather's death, as well as Helen Shepherd's. If it *was* them, then surely that was the only avenue left to explore?

Wait! What was this? His eyes focused on the small section of obituaries:

> ***Helen Shepherd** – Funeral to be held on 3rd July at 11.45am at St Peter's Church, Maidenhead, followed by a wake at The Temple Hotel. All flowers to be sent to Greaves Funeral Directors, Stone Road...*

Heath smiled. Well, that was it. He'd go to Helen Shepherd's funeral. Teagan would be bound to be there.

FOURTEEN

ROLLING HIS SLEEVES UP, Robert silently scanned the sitting room at Footlights. Although he and Teagan had broken the back of cleaning up this particular area yesterday, a lot more could have been achieved had it not been for getting side-tracked.

As it was, he'd been up half the night, unable to sleep, haunted by the combination of disappointment and confusion about his unexpected parentage, along with the simmering resentment that no matter how much he attempted to dilute his anger for his mother's hiding the truth from him all these years, he couldn't stop it from bubbling under the surface.

Both of those unpleasant situations were contradicted by the unfamiliar aching for Teagan; the woman who had been lying mere feet away the other side of the wall in the next bedroom all night.

These things clamouring for attention in his mind did not belong together and made relaxing enough to sleep properly impossible. To make matters worse, the small amount of sleep he had snatched was filled with vivid dreams; the lucid and graphic images of Teagan causing him to frequently wake, mortified to find the proof of his hunger on his sheets in sodden patches. *How old was he? 12?*

Robert snatched up a pile of stacked paperwork from the floor. He prided himself on his ability to remain above base desires and raw emotion. This strength had always served him in good stead; giving him a modicum of control that most people were unable to maintain, but now he was becoming just like them and hence in unfamiliar waters.

Shaking his head with irritation, he opened his mother's bureau to place the paperwork back where he presumed it had been pulled from.

His eyes kept wandering to the newspaper clipping, now folded on the top of the sideboard, but he resisted the urge to look at again. He didn't need to study the image of Michael Pointer further because it was indelibly ingrained on his brain as clearly as the reflection he saw each time he looked in the mirror.

No, he was better off not using any more energy speculating over things he was unlikely to get the answers to. But he'd keep that clipping. Maybe once the shock subsided he would search for answers elsewhere?

Stuffing the paperwork back in one of the bureau's compartments, Robert frowned, again wondering if Helen had been aware of this, whether it explained any of her behaviour?

Unable to fit all of the paperwork into the bureau, Robert tugged at a small drawer. He'd shove some of it in there. It could all be sorted properly later. Right now, the most important thing was to get the house back into a habitable state. He still had the whole of the upstairs to do and that he *really* wasn't looking forward to.

Absentmindedly cramming in as much paperwork into the small drawer as possible, huffing when it wouldn't fully close, he yanked it open again, pushing his fingers to the back, feeling something trapped.

Robert pulled a small leather-bound notebook out. Staring at it he hesitated, but despite his reluctance, felt unable to stop the pages falling open and stared at the handwritten notes. *His mother's handwritten notes.*

....

'ARE YOU DRUNK?' Lena whined, watching Jonah throw his suit jacket scruffily over the back of the sofa. For God's sake – he smelt like a brewery. If she'd known he would bathe in whisky she wouldn't have bothered torturing herself with that mouthwash to mask the smell of the vodka she'd chugged.

'I'm not drunk,' Jonah snapped, making his way to the drinks cabinet. That wasn't entirely true - he was more than half-cut and if he had it his way, he would get very drunk tonight. At least that way he might get a bit of peace.

How dare Saul dictate his personal life. It wasn't up to his brother who he goddamn married. It wasn't up to *anyone* – apart from himself and if he wanted to marry Lena, then he would do just that. The problem was, he *didn't* want to marry Lena, but that wasn't the point.

Jonah's hand rested on the whisky bottle. Saul was correct on one thing and stupidly, it was something he hadn't considered. He should have a pre-nuptial agreement in place. Regardless of his promise to uphold his deeply instilled family values, he also had to protect the business from all eventualities and that was something Lena would have to accept.

Deciding she should try and ease the atmosphere and make the best of the situation, Lena slid her toned arms around Jonah's neck. 'Have you had a bad day, babe?'

'It hasn't been the best…' And having the person whose big gob had caused the latest bit of aggro hanging around his neck wasn't helping. Shrugging Lena off, Jonah concentrated on pouring himself a doubly large scotch.

'Ooh!' Lena jibed. 'Who's in a snotty mood? And there was me about to discuss the wedding. I want to invite some of my friends.'

'Weddings aren't the best subject tonight,' Jonah snapped. 'Besides, have you even got any friends? I've never seen any, neither have I heard of any. I haven't seen any of your family either, come to think of it. Are you a friendless foundling or something?'

He gulped at the whisky, knowing he was being needlessly unkind, but he couldn't help it. Lena was getting on his nerves. Wedding this, wedding that. All of this shit was her fault and Saul kicking off about it was the last thing he needed. It was bad enough keeping an eye on him to make sure he was playing ball without Lena handing the man more fuel for the fire.

Lena's eyes momentarily narrowed, quickly swapping her expression to a hurt one. 'Why would you say something like that to me?' she sniffed. 'That's horrible.'

Jonah topped up his whisky. 'Like I said, I'm not in the mood to talk weddings.'

'You never are!' Lena cried. 'But it's only a few weeks away. Everyone invited are *your* people. I haven't got anyone from *my* side and…'

'Invite who you want. I've already told you that,' Jonah roared. 'Just do what you like - you usually do!'

Lena watched Jonah gulp at his fresh drink and her nerves jangled. Something had rattled his cage. 'There's no need to be aggressive. Why are you in such a bad mood?'

Jonah swung around, swaying slightly as he did so. 'If you must know, it's because of you!'

'Me? Why me?' Lena's stomach plummeted. *Oh no.* Gwen hadn't said anything, had she? They had an agreement and if Gwen had broken that, she'd make sure the old hag was finished in this town quicker than she could shake a stick. She scowled. She should have stuck to her original plan. She could have told Jonah all about Gwen. After that he'd have been far too irate to even listen to anything the old witch might say.

Jonah moved closer, backing Lena up against the wall. 'All this shit about not mentioning the baby to anyone, then you tell my fucking brother? Thanks to you I've had nothing but abuse off him this afternoon.'

Lena blinked rapidly. Jonah scared her when he was like this - especially when he was drunk. And regardless of him denying it, he *was* drunk. She didn't see it often. She eyed the whisky bottle on the side. He'd be even drunker soon, having already polished off half of that in the ten minutes since getting home.

She'd screwed up again. She'd been stupid by not thinking carefully enough about what repercussions telling Saul would bring. *Stupid, stupid.*

'Saul thinks I'm ridiculous for marrying you,' Jonah slurred. 'He wants me to stop the wedding.' Smirking at the shock on Lena's face, he stumbled back to the drinks cabinet. 'Yeah, or at the very least get a pre-nup sorted.' He shrugged clumsily. 'Everyone thinks you're a gold-digger, so it's probably a good idea.'

Cold flooded from Lena's feet up to her hair. *Fuck. A pre-nup? Oh, bollocks. Quick, think... THINK!*

About to turn the tears on, she refrained just in time. She was due at that function shortly and there was no way she was redoing her makeup. It had taken a bloody age to get it perfect and she looked the business. *Apart from the kitchen roll baby.*

It had crossed her mind to give the 'bump' a miss tonight, but then thought better of it. It would be just her luck that tonight was the night Gwen got suspicious. But a pre-nup? She might as well not have bothered with any of this if Jonah went down that line.

As panic set in, a glimmer of an idea formed. It was risky, but she'd take the chance. At least it would give her breathing space to think of a way around this pre-nup crap before it actually happened. Besides, Jonah was far too volatile right now for her not to smooth things over.

Casually undoing the button of her jacket, she sniffed loudly. 'It hurts that you and everyone else thinks so little of me. I know we've had our ups and downs, but I want to marry you, Jonah. I love you and I don't want our baby to be born a bastard.' She looked at him sadly. 'I'll sign your pre-nup if that's what you want, you know I will. It's *you* I want, nothing else.'

It wasn't an issue. She'd think of something to get out of that when the time came, but tonight she'd say what was needed. Plus, she had a few more ideas up her sleeve.

Finishing his newest drink, Jonah sloppily topped his glass up, surprised Lena had so readily agreed. 'You still haven't explained why you told Saul? I thought you wanted to keep the baby quiet?'

He watched Lena perch on the armrest of the chair and it was then that he noticed it. *Maybe he just hadn't looked properly before, but it was there.*

His eyes remained glued to the small, but definite bump where Lena's perfectly flat stomach had previously been and his heart hammered, a thoroughly unexpected jolt of pride slithering up his spine.

Lena clocked where Jonah's drunken eyes were focused and seeing his expression, smiled inwardly. *Bingo.*

Taking the opportunity to wring as much out of the situation as possible, she placed her hand lightly on the kitchen roll baby, not wanting to squash it out of shape. 'It's this dress, isn't it?' she gasped. 'It makes it obvious and I've got that function tonight too. How stupid of me. I'm sorry, babe. I'm running out of things to wear that fit properly, but I'll go and change. I'm sure I've still got something…'

She moved to get up but Jonah stopped her. 'Leave the dress on.' A strange mixture of pride rolled around his head as he reached towards Lena's belly. 'You look… amazing. Beautiful…'

'Don't,' she whispered, twisting away. 'I'm really self-conscious about it at the moment.'

Jonah cupped Lena's face in his hands. 'I'm sorry I shouted at you,' he said, placing his lips on hers.

Lena enjoyed the kiss – far too much, but as it became deeper and more urgent, Jonah's hands wandering dangerously close to the stack of kitchen roll, she had no choice but to pull away. She looked hungrily at the unmistakeable bulge in his trousers and cursed the day she'd had this stupid idea. She was gagging for a good seeing to. 'We'll have to wait until later, babe. I've got to go to that function.'

Jonah backed off sulkily, his eyes still focused on Lena's belly. *That was his baby in there. His.*

Lena looked suitably downcast. *The final piece of the plan ready to go...* 'And you really want to know why I told Saul…?'

Jonah's drunken grin slid slowly from his face. 'Yeah, as it happens, I do.'

Lena sighed dramatically. 'I don't… don't want to cause any grief between the two of you… I…'

'Just spit it out,' Jonah said. There was little even Saul could do to spoil the fuzzy sense of pride he felt at this precise moment.

Looking up at the ceiling, Lena blinked rapidly as if she were stopping tears from falling. *Come on, Jonah. Suck it up.*

Moving forward, Jonah held Lena gently by the shoulders, unease prickling. 'Lena? Tell me what the problem is.'

Lena sniffed loudly. 'I-I had to tell Saul about the baby because I knew it would make him stop…' Her voice was small, quiet. 'He kept trying to paw me… Touch me… I…'

Jonah's eyes narrowed, like someone had flicked a switch. 'He did fucking *what*?'

FIFTEEN

FLICKING THROUGH THE PAGES of the notebook, Robert realised it was a diary. Not the type you'd get nowadays with the date printed on every page, but a plain book with the dates written in his mother's hand, the tiny writing making it difficult to read.

He scanned some of the entries; 1962, 1963, notes about a show opening, having a row with a girl in the dressing room... The standard witterings of a young woman.

Robert was about to close the book and put it back when he stopped:

> **6th Jan 1964**
>
> *Pegasus show a hit, but boa makes me sneeze! Ha ha! Getting more frustrated and hate sneaking around, but things are far too deep with M.*

Robert frowned. 'M'? Michael? His eyes scanned the next entry, squinting at the tiny writing:

> **29th Jan**
>
> *I've asked P for a divorce and he laughed! How I hate*

him. He has to go.

P? That must be Peter? Peter Adams?

3rd March
Nearly got caught with M tonight in Nobby's bar. SO came in, but M says he's ok and won't say anything. We have to be careful.

Irritation prickled. By the sounds of it his mother had been seeing Michael Pointer behind Peter's back for some time and the concept he'd cultivated about her began to quickly deteriorate. And who was 'SO'? Someone that Michael was involved with by the sounds of it.

His nose wrinkled with distaste, not wanting to read further, but found himself unable to stop his eyes moving over the small words:

14th Aug
I told M it's me or S. To my relief he chose me! I knew he would! All I need now is to get rid of P and S and then everything will be perfect.

Was 'S' the same person as 'SO'? Robert chewed his lip, hating abbreviations. But it said 'choosing S'? Was 'S' a woman? Shrugging, he continued:

9th Sept
Love love LOVE M

12th Sept
M promised to sort P. I have to believe him. It has to happen. It's the only way.

Robert frowned. 'Sort P'? What was that supposed to mean? A growing glimmer of unease formed.

19th Sept

I can't breathe! He's done it! M has done it!!! I'm so SO happy!

20th Sept

P's "accident" made the papers. I was named as the distraught wife. How funny! Pretending to be upset when I'm celebrating is more difficult than I thought.

Robert blinked and re-read the entries. Was this what he thought it was? Was she saying that Michael Pointer had killed Peter? *'Pretending to be upset'?* No, it couldn't be, could it?

25th Sept

I'm worried they'll find out. M says no one will and that everything is covered. AND M's divorcing S! He's seeing a solicitor and then we're getting married!

Robert swallowed the rising bile. He wasn't wrong. Michael Pointer had killed Peter Adams. But how? He frowned. However he'd done it, he'd made it look like an accident. He froze, vividly remembering his mother had always said that his father – or rather, *Peter*, was killed by a car outside the Feathers. Hit by a car which hadn't stopped when he'd left work one night... *Oh, shit! It was no accident.*

Pointer had killed Peter Adams or arranged for someone else to do it. Either way, the man was responsible and Robert also realised it was apparent that his mother had known all about it, and worse, *welcomed* it. *Maybe she'd even helped plan it?*

Feeling sicker by the second, he turned the page, detecting the noticeable tremor of his fingers:

27th Sept

I'm in shock! M wants me to leave Feathers and move

away! JP may cause problems but M has plans. I'll move anywhere M wants to go as long as we're together.

He growled audibly, the sound vibrating in the back of his throat. Had his mother been brainwashed by this Michael, or was she as manipulative as he was?

7th Oct

I'm having M's baby!!! I'm pregnant! So happy! It's all I have ever wanted in the 2 years we've been together. I could scream it from the rooftops! Wheeeee!!!

Robert shivered. Pregnant? Pregnant with *him*?

He did a quick calculation. Yes, it must have been him.

Bending over the bureau looking at this little book, his legs felt decidedly shaky. He reached across to the cabinet and grabbed a bottle of spirits, not much caring what it was. Unscrewing the cap, he took a gulp and grimaced, all his senses screaming at the gin. He hated gin, still it would do.

Moving to the sofa, he plonked himself down and looked back at the notebook:

20th Dec

My last show at Feathers. I'm sad to leave, but now I'm starting to show there's no choice. I love this baby, but not as much as I love M. Wish we could be together this Xmas. Maybe if S was dead too we could?

He shook his head with disbelief. This was unbelievable. He didn't recognise the woman who had written these things - the woman who he'd put on a pedestal all of his life. This woman wasn't his mother - she wasn't this person. His mother was nice. Or rather, he'd *thought* she was nice…

Robert had always held his mother with the greatest respect and admiration for raising two young children as a widower.

But her husband dying and leaving her pregnant wasn't exactly what had happened. Peter Adams wasn't the one who'd got her pregnant the second time and neither had he died. He'd been *murdered.* Murdered by her lover – Michael Pointer – his *father*.

The name echoed loudly around his head and he took another long swig directly from the gin bottle, hating the bitter taste. But no amount of bitter-tasting gin was as foul as the taste the contents of this notebook was leaving in his mouth.

And she was wishing 'S' dead? Pointer's wife? Did Pointer kill her too?

Robert feverishly turned the page:

> **25th Dec**
> *This will be the last Xmas I will spend without M. We'll be a proper family by next year.*
>
> **28th Jan**
> *Maidenhead is so different to Soho and I don't like it. I want to return as soon as it's safe to do so. M is still there. Wish he was here with me. I can't wait much longer. The way is clear so why hasn't he come?*

Robert frowned. So she'd moved? Moved to Footlights or somewhere else in Maidenhead? Why Maidenhead? He backtracked a few pages, but there were no additional explanations.

> **30th Mar**
> *One last job (again) and then M's coming. I'm lonely and the house is too big.*
> *Helen is growing to look more like P every day. Makes me sick. Wish she was in the same place as her father!*

He sighed, his breath ragged. *His mother had wanted Helen dead?* Feeling light-headed he read the entry again. What job was she referring to? Pointer worked at the Feathers - she'd told him that the other night, but who did he work for and as what? What on earth was he, or both of them involved in?

28th Apr
Counting the days!

10th May
M doing another job tonight and promises faithfully this is the last, one EVER. And it's a BIG one! The one to make everything possible. I have to believe him.
Baby restless. It's definitely a boy! I'm getting as big as this house and will pop before the month's out, I'm sure! Ha ha!

Another reference to a job? Robert's heart picked up pace. What was this Michael Pointer doing? Killing people? Stealing? What?

17th May
Had an argument because I want M here, but found out tonight that it's finally happening. Also discovered M bought Footlights for ME! For us. He's so clever – making it look like it came from P's insurance.
But it's even better than that. M's just left to return to Soho for the FINAL time. He's telling JP he's retiring. He's leaving the firm. Yes, LEAVING! Thanks to M we've got more than enough now. Plus more. And I've been trusted with it all! Can't explain how excited I am.

Robert put the notebook down and stared at the wall, shaking his head in confusion. This was crazy! Peter's death, this house; Pointer – his job. A firm? And they'd *'got more than enough'*? What? Money?

And Michael was retiring from JP's firm? Whoever JP was?

Oh, Christ, this was way too messed up.

Robert wiped the sheen of perspiration off his forehead with the back of his hand.

> **18th May**
>
> *Waiting to hear from M. He was supposed to call to tell me how it went with JP.*
>
> **3rd June**
>
> *Haven't seen M. I'm worried. He'd better not miss this baby being born. It will be any day now.*

Robert frowned and turned the page impatiently. *That was it? Nothing else? That was the last entry?* He flicked through the remaining pages just to make sure he hadn't missed anything. *No, there was definitely nothing else.*

He slumped back against the sofa in bewilderment. His mother had been sleeping with a man who had arranged to remove her husband from the planet, making it look like a tragic accident to boot. And as for the rest?

What sort of woman was she? Not the woman he'd spent his life believing she was, that was for sure because she'd been stupid enough to spell the real truth out in black and white.

SIXTEEN

DESPITE THE ALTERNATING cold then hot shower he'd had this morning, Jonah knew he looked rough because he felt nastier than a badger's arsehole.

Lena slamming the door around 2am when she returned from the function at the Feathers had jolted him from his drunken sleep on the sofa, but even then he'd been able to do little more than grunt in appreciation when she'd knelt down and unzipped his trousers.

It was surprising his body had even worked, the state he'd been in, but whatever she'd done with her mouth had the desired effect of coaxing things into life. He'd still been far too drunk and half-asleep to do much more than lazily lie back whilst she'd brought him some much needed relief and then afterwards, he'd shamefully fallen straight back to sleep again.

Waking back up at 6 this morning on the sofa, he'd found himself covered in a woollen throw and could have quite happily turned over and stayed there, but as the memory of the night before filtered into his mind, he knew he had to get up and deal with it.

Jonah grimaced, unsure how Lena had talked him down last night. He'd been all set to go and give Saul the kicking of his life, but when she'd got upset, saying how stress would hurt the baby, he'd agreed to leave it until he'd calmed down and was sober. He wasn't having *anything* hurt his baby. It was probably a good job he'd left it because the state he'd been in he'd have undoubtedly wrapped his Range Rover around the tree at the bottom of the road. But he would be dealing with Saul sooner rather than later. There were some things that were off limits and Lena was definitely one of them.

Jonah had now been at the club for half an hour, but was yet to set eyes on his snake of a brother and when he did, it wouldn't be pretty.

Adrenalin pumping through his veins, he eyed the new bottle of whisky on the side in his office longingly. Although the very thought of the taste made him want to heave, he knew a few of those were the one thing guaranteed to cure or at least tone down this bloody hangover.

Instead, he eyed Gwen tentatively. This was supposed to be a catch-up meeting, yet she'd said nothing. He gulped at his coffee, irritated at the alcohol-induced shaking of his hands.

'You'll be glad to hear it went well last night,' Gwen said suddenly. 'I expect Lena filled you in with that already?'

Jonah wiped the back of his hand across his mouth and lit a cigarette, the first drag almost making him blow chunks over his desk. 'She was still asleep when I left.'

Gwen frowned. Last night she'd been hoping to catch the tart red-handed. Catch her with another man or with coke up her nose – *anything*, just so she had something solid to make Jonah cancel the wedding, but Lena hadn't done anything amiss. She looked at him with concern. He definitely wasn't on form this morning. 'Is everything alright, love?'

Jonah looked at Gwen, his eyes hooded. 'Why do you ask?'

Gwen fidgeted. 'I half-expected you to pop into the function last night and was surprised you didn't. I thou…'

'I wasn't in the best frame of mind,' he said. 'I figured it was better to stay away.' He wouldn't mention that he'd got so drunk he'd eventually passed out.

Gwen nodded sympathetically. 'Try not to let any beef you have with your brother get to you. You knew as well as I did his return would rock the boat, but…'

'What's he been saying?' Jonah snapped.

'Nothing!' Gwen gasped. 'He's said nothing. I've barely seen him! I-I heard you two arguing yesterday. I couldn't help but overhear.'

'Oh that,' Jonah picked up his cup and realising he'd already finished it, rattled it back into its saucer. Yeah, the row about Lena and the wedding. Of course. Now it all made sense. His fucking brother wanted Lena for himself. Well, he could have had her before she got a child of *his* inside her. It would have been a lot better all round if Saul was stuck with her, but he wasn't and now she was out of bounds.

'I need words with him,' Jonah said, his temper spiking again.

Seeing Gwen's concern, he knew he had to tell her. She'd only worry or get the wrong end of the stick. 'This has nothing to do with the firm.' He tapped his pen on the desk, even that muted sound causing the pounding in his head to worsen. 'Saul thinks I should get a pre-nup.'

Gwen raised her eyebrows. Another sensible thing the son from hell had suggested? Maybe he had learnt something in almost two decades of being incarcerated? 'Perhaps that isn't a bad thing?'

Jonah slammed his pen down. 'Do you know what? I'm getting a bit tired of everyone having an opinion on my private life!'

Gwen sat back, a little startled. It had been *him* who told her he was unhappy with Lena. *Something had shifted.* Was Lena finally getting her claws under Jonah's skin? She hoped not because it would make the already daunting task of stopping this wedding impossible.

'Lena's already agreed to a pre-nup. Saul won't be expecting that, not that it's any of his business.'

Gwen smiled. 'I know you and Saul have your problems,

love.' She squeezed Jonah's hand, adding, 'We all do.'

Jonah stood up and paced the length of his office. 'I'm going to be a father, Gwen.' A sloppy smile formed on his face. 'And I'm over the moon about that.'

Gwen tried to smile, she really did, but it wasn't easy. Was now the time to mention her suspicions? That there probably was no baby at all?

'But Saul,' Jonah continued, 'he's got his own agenda and I'm not having it. He knows Lena's pregnant.'

'How? I thought you said no one knew?'

'No one was supposed to know, but Lena told him.'

Gwen's mouth pursed into a knowing pout. So Lena was looking for extra clout with Saul? Bandying around her new-found position to give herself more bargaining power? God, she was a sneaky mare, that one.

'I can't see by your face what you're thinking, Gwen,' Jonah barked. 'But you're wrong. My cunt of a brother only knows because he was all over her – pawing her like a tart. She told him about the baby so that he would stop!'

Gwen stared at Jonah in shock, his expression frightening her.

'I'm going to fucking kill him,' Jonah added, his voice dripping with venom. 'No one and I mean, *no one* puts their hands on my child.'

Gwen swallowed sharply. This was bad. If this was true, Saul was in deep shit. Jonah's inbuilt want of Lena's pregnancy had unleashed a protective side. But he was protecting the very person whom Gwen believed to be lying about everything.

• • • •

DULCIE'S GAZE RESTED INTENTLY ON TEAGAN. How she wanted to tell her to pack her bags and get out, but she couldn't. Not yet. Not whilst the girl still had the box. She needed it back, but dare not risk having it in her own possession – not whilst everything was still up in the air.

Even though inside her anger pulsed like a strobe light, she had to keep things on an even keel until she knew where she stood. Until it was safe. But she would say something. *She had to.* She had to pull on her best acting skills and make the girl feel bad. Like, *really* bad. Putting a mammoth guilt trip on the silly little cow would be more useful in the long run.

Dulcie's mouth formed into a small smirk. If she played it correctly, then it would also help with any designs Teagan may have on Robert too. Her anger pulsed once more. Just thinking of something developing between the two of them made her blood boil.

She hadn't seen the prospect of this coming at all. Robert had only previously displayed contempt for the girl, but since Helen, something had changed. Dulcie's eyes narrowed. Trust Helen to have the capacity to cause issues in her otherwise perfect plan from beyond the grave. The conceited, spiteful bitch of a daughter that she was and always had been. Always thinking of herself – just like her bloody father, that girl.

But she hadn't mistaken the atmosphere between Teagan and Robert. It looked like something had happened between them, but she wasn't sure what.

A kiss? Sex? She didn't know. Either was bad enough, but Dulcie couldn't risk the small chance of it becoming more than that.

Dulcie watched Teagan potter around, clearly stuck for something to do. It wasn't like she had much left to clean in Robert's poky flat. She'd already cleaned it a thousand times. The girl felt awkward - that was plain as day. Oh, Teagan knew full well that Robert must have spoken about his father whilst she'd made herself scarce at the shops, yet she hadn't said a word and the silence sat like an elephant in the room.

Robert had disappeared today too. For the first time in *years* he'd gone into the office and Dulcie couldn't quite work out whether his motive was to put space between *her* or Teagan. Robert had always stuck to his rigid cast-iron routines; nothing ever changed how and when he did things – it never had, but now it was…

The thought of her beloved son drifting away grated painfully. It was thanks to Teagan that he'd discovered the truth about his father in the worst way. She'd had it all planned how she would tell him, but now it was spoilt and if that girl had ruined the relationship she had with Robert, then she'd be making her pay.

'Is there anything you want to watch on the television? I can see if that antique program you like is on or maybe find you a film?' Teagan said brightly, jolting Dulcie from her thoughts.

'No thank you,' Dulcie said frostily.

Teagan caught Dulcie's eyes, then looked away. 'Oh, ok... erm... well, how about a game of cards? I know Helen's funeral tomorrow must be playing on your mind, so I...'

'Yes, the funeral is playing on my mind, but so is why you felt the need to tell my son about Michael,' Dulcie snapped, her voice icy.

Teagan froze. She'd been waiting for this. Actually, she'd wanted to broach it and explain, but she didn't know how to. Dulcie was so fragile lately and the guilt she felt about inadvertently making things worse hung around her neck like a dumbbell. 'I'm sorry... I...'

'You *knew* how important it was for me to tell Robert myself.' Dulcie's eyes shot daggers at Teagan and she willed herself to rein in her wrath. *For now at least.*

Teagan sat next to Dulcie and hesitatingly reached for her hand. 'I know and I'm really sorry,' she spluttered. 'The last thing I wanted was to make things worse.'

'Hmph!' Dulcie snorted. 'Well, you have. It's really upset him. And it's really upset *me*!' Her face crumpled. 'I can't lose another child.'

Teagan watched in horror as tears poured down Dulcie's face and felt her own eyes brim. She clutched harder at the old lady's hand. 'Oh Dulcie, I'm so sorry. I...'

'I trusted you!' Dulcie wailed. 'Is it not bad enough that Helen betrayed me so badly without you doing it too?'

Teagan's heart shattered into a thousand pieces and her

tears fell freely. 'That newspaper clipping... It was on the floor... I'd gone to get some bin bags and when I came back, Robert... Robert was looking at it,' she sobbed.

'On the floor? No, you showed him. You knew where it was kept,' Dulcie cried. 'You showed him, didn't you?'

Teagan looked aghast. 'I didn't, I swear. I care for you so much, I'd never do anything to hurt you. He found it screwed up into a ball. I *swear* I didn't show him.'

Dulcie continued sobbing but her mind was whirring. *You do want to hurt me though, because you want to steal my son from me.* The memory of Helen screwing up the clipping and chucking it onto the floor seeped into Dulcie's mind, but she wasn't going to admit that. 'How else could he have known the details if it wasn't for you? I'll lose him now.'

Teagan grasped at Dulcie's hands. 'Oh Dulcie, you won't. Robert loves you. And he didn't need me to tell him. He... he said looking at that picture of Michael was like looking in the mirror... I could hardly deny that.'

Dulcie ramped up her sobbing. 'Robert doesn't love people!'

'He loves you, I'm sure,' Teagan cried. She'd never forgive herself if Robert turned his back on Dulcie because of this.

'What if he never forgives me? He said he won't come to Helen's funeral and I need him there,' Dulcie wailed, the lies tripping off her tongue.

'Don't worry, I'll talk to him,' Teagan soothed, devastated for her part of the problem and equally aghast at having volunteered to get Robert to change his mind. She knew exactly how he felt about Helen, but resigned herself to the task. It was the least she could do to make Dulcie's life less painful.

'I suppose you've given Robert that box too?' Dulcie whimpered.

'No, of course I haven't. I've still got it, just like you asked. Regardless of what it may look like. I didn't mean to betray you.'

Dulcie dabbed at her face with a handkerchief. *Good.* So

Teagan still had the box and she was still playing ball.

SEVENTEEN

GWEN STARED BLINDLY at the paperwork in front of her, her mind centred on what would happen between Jonah, his brother and that woman. She was so wrapped up in her thoughts she barely noticed Saul enter the office until he was almost on top of her. 'Christ!' she spluttered. 'You nearly gave me a heart attack!'

'Don't do that! We could do without you going AWOL again,' Saul grinned. 'Got a cuppa for me?' Sitting heavily on the edge of Gwen's desk, he glanced around. 'Take it the tart hasn't put in an appearance? Still, at least she got more people to sign up to the VIP list, so she's good at something, short of flashing her tits and honey trapping my brother.'

Gwen gave Saul a wary glance. His presence always made her uncomfortable.

Saul lowered his voice. 'She's no good that one. She'd have quite happily fucked me the other day. I gave her a bit of the old charm to see if she'd flirt and did she ever! You should have seen the way she was looking at me!'

Gwen stared at Saul accusingly. 'What did you do to her?'

Saul raised his eyebrows. 'Do to her? Christ, Gwen! I wouldn't touch that slut with Keith's! I did sod all, apart from prove a point, yet she couldn't have pushed her tits in my face any more without fucking suffocating me!' He wiped his hand across his brow and laughed. 'I thought I was going to fucking die!'

His face suddenly turned into a scowl. 'Joking aside, she's got my brother over a barrel. I told him what a stupid cunt he it, but he can't see it. I won't let him marry her, Gwen – baby or not.' He bared his teeth into a snarl. 'Half of this firm is mine and she's not getting her hands on it.'

Gwen was speechless. *So Saul hadn't been all over Lena?* She studied his roguish face, pretty sure he wasn't lying. Should she risk telling him her suspicions and getting him on side? It could backfire horribly, but she had to do something.

Saul folded his arms. 'You're looking at me funny. Whatever that bitch has said, it's bollocks, believe me. I want her gone from here. She's a cunt. And cunts are only good for one thing, but I'll leave that specific pleasure to my blindsided fuck of a brother who wants to play happy families with the dog.'

Gwen took a deep breath and lowered her voice to a whisper. 'I shouldn't be saying this, but I don't know what else to do.' She swivelled round in her chair to face Saul. 'She told Jonah you tried it on with her and furthermore, I don't believe she's really pregnant.'

Saul's eyes narrowed. 'Is that so? The lying bitch! I guess I'll have to find that out after I've put this shit right with my brother.' Lena had made an even bigger mistake now. Whether she was pregnant or not made little difference. If she was, she wouldn't be for much longer. Either way, she would be out of here.

• • • •

TEAGAN DID HER BEST to stack the plates on the small work surface in Robert's kitchen. Her hands were still shaking and her eyes still red from the soul-destroying conversation she'd had with Dulcie this afternoon.

During dinner, with Robert still not back, Dulcie was back to her usual bright chirpy self – as if that dreadful conversation between them earlier hadn't taken place at all. When Robert appeared just as she and Dulcie were finishing up, Dulcie had cheerily informed him that his tea was keeping warm in the oven. Teagan had barely been able to look at him as he'd hovered in the doorway, brusquely saying he'd grabbed something on the way back.

When he'd headed to the bathroom and the shower began running, Teagan had breathed a sigh of relief. Now Dulcie had gone for a lie down, leaving her to clear up and worry about when she would have the conversation with Robert about going to Helen's funeral tomorrow, like she'd promised.

What a bloody mess. The whole equilibrium had shifted. Dulcie was heartbroken and although it was true Teagan hadn't purposefully told Robert about his father, she should have still checked something hadn't been left lying about for him to find.

Now she wasn't even sure whether Dulcie believed what she'd said and with a heavy heart, felt the old lady's trust in her might indeed be broken beyond repair.

• • • •

HEARING ROBERT COME OF THE BATHROOM, Dulcie lay immobile on the top of the bed listening as his footsteps passed her bedroom.

She was planning how to act at tomorrow's funeral. The trick was to behave suitably distraught but not so much to detract from the belief that she was handling the death of her daughter well and with dignity. It was more than imperative everyone maintained the perception that she was brave as well as coherent.

However, it would undeniably be difficult not to scream for joy when Helen was officially out of her life. Plus, the funeral marked that the police did not suspect her having any hand in it. Another reason why she'd been so keen that Helen's final journey after the church service should be a fast track to the crematorium.

Dulcie smiled. She was leaving nothing open to chance. *Not a thing.*

Her brow suddenly furrowed, as she realised in hindsight that Robert was going towards the kitchen. *And Teagan was in there.*

Silently swinging her legs off the bed, she moved to the door, her hand slowly turning the handle. Hearing voices, Dulcie stiffened. He was in there. *With her.*

Holding her breath as she slipped out of the bedroom, Dulcie padded up the hallway.

• • • •

'OH, YOU'RE IN HERE!' Robert's gruff voice startled Teagan so much she almost dropped the plate she was drying. 'I'll leave you to it.'

Turning around, Teagan looked at Robert. His face was fierce. *Angry.* 'Wait!' she cried. She'd promised to speak to him, so she might as well do it now.

'What is it, Teagan? I'm tired.'

'I... I...' She glanced at the impatience on Robert's face, the thick lines across his brow. She wanted to reach out, tell him not to be angry and that she cared how he felt. She didn't want any awkwardness between them. She wanted it to get back to like it had been before when she'd felt like they were becoming friends. 'Your mother... she...'

'I don't want to discuss my mother,' Robert growled. The only way he'd got through the day was by breaking his cardinal rule and going into the office. Even spending the day and half the evening with those half-wits was preferable to sitting in the same room as his mother, knowing what she'd done. *Knowing what she was really like.*

'Dulcie wants you at Helen's funeral,' Teagan blurted. 'It would mean the world to her if you changed your mind and agreed to go.'

'I already told her I'd go.' Robert snapped, pointedly not

looking at Teagan because he didn't want anything to deflect him from his inner rage. 'I don't *want* to go, but I said I would. She knows that. What's the matter with her?'

Teagan frowned. 'Oh! She said...'

Robert finally glanced at Teagan and frowned. 'Have you been crying?'

'No...' Teagan flapped her hand and turned towards the sink, already feeling the burn of new tears.

Robert strode across and placing his hand on Teagan's left arm, turned her none too gently towards him. 'What has she done? What has she said to upset you?'

Teagan shook her head. 'Nothing really. She believes I told you about your father, but I think we've sorted it out now.' She stared at Robert's hand, his fingers wrapped around her arm.

Robert scrutinised Teagan. What he wanted to say was not to listen to anything that his mother said because none of it was true, but he couldn't. If he said that then he'd have to explain why. He'd have to recount what he'd found in that notebook and he wasn't ready to physically put that into words. Speaking of it would make it real.

The closeness of Teagan and the strange surge in emotions weren't helping either. If he didn't walk out of here soon, he ran the risk of kissing this woman and he didn't want to. Thinking like that upset his concentration and he didn't like it. It ruined the routine.

'You look strange. What's happened?' The worry in Teagan's voice was audible. 'Please tell me what's bothering you.'

'You're bothering me,' Robert growled, stepping towards Teagan, until hearing a loud crash from the hallway made him stop in his tracks.

'Robert! ROBERT!' Dulcie screamed, her voice filled with panic.

Jumping back, Robert stared at Teagan in confusion. Shaking his head in utter frustration, he went to see what had happened to the mother he no longer knew, angrier than ever with his inability to stop himself from succumbing to what was making his life even more confusing.

EIGHTEEN

LUCKILY, TEAGAN HAD A BLACK DRESS and smart jacket in the clothes she had brought with her for the contract at Footlights, so she didn't feel out of place, but despite it now having just turned July, it was surprisingly chilly in the small church.

Walking behind Dulcie and Robert, Teagan looked anywhere but at the tall frame of Robert, his hand on his mother's elbow. He'd completely blanked her so far today. Things were awkward. She'd been sure he'd been about to try to kiss her last night and she didn't know what to do about that.

She'd begun to really like Robert – as a *friend*, but if he was beginning to think something else could be on the cards, then things would become impossible. His behaviour, apart from a couple of strange looks recently, had always been the opposite of attraction, but last night she'd got the distinct impression something had shifted and that was the last thing she wanted.

How selfish was she? Dulcie's fall last night was a stark reminder to Teagan that she wasn't here to worry about her client's son. She was here to look after Dulcie. Shame engulfed her. *Stop it, Teagan*, she admonished. Her thoughts and concentration should be on Dulcie. *Nothing* else. *Especially today*.

Nearing the top of the aisle, Teagan faltered seeing a framed photograph sitting atop Helen's oak casket on the stand. Helen's eyes burrowed into her as she paused, unsure where to sit. She wasn't family, so shouldn't sit on the first row of pews. Considering the circumstances, there was a surprisingly good turnout at the funeral. She cautiously eyed the faces of the other mourners, presuming the majority were Helen's work colleagues and associates.

Moving towards a pew several rows back, Teagan was stopped by an usher. 'Please sit up at the front, Miss,' the man said quietly, placing a hand gently on Teagan's arm. 'Mrs Adams has requested you take your place with the family.'

Flustered, Teagan hurried back to the front, conscious the softly piped music had stopped and was eager to be seated before the service started.

Sitting down, refusing to dwell that she was ushered to sit next to Robert, Teagan swallowed nervously and fixed her gaze on the statue of Jesus on the altar. The organ cranked up, blasting the intro the first hymn and along with everyone else she stood, leaning to pick up her order of service, her hand accidentally brushing against Robert's leg.

'Sorry,' she whispered, glancing at him. Catching Dulcie looking, Teagan smiled sympathetically, but was shocked by the glimpse she caught behind her eyes. It was almost... almost *venomous*.

Feeling increasingly uncomfortable, Teagan fumbled with the order of service searching for the words for the hymn and cleared her throat ready to sing.

• • • •

HEATH ARRIVED LATE AT THE CHURCH. The traffic out of London hadn't been kind this morning and the service had been well underway by the time he'd slipped into the church.

He'd wanted to arrive early so that Teagan would see him when she arrived. He'd planned on sitting with her, using the opportunity of offering well-timed sympathy to glean much needed brownie points. He understood she must be hacked off with him for not hanging around the last time she'd seen him, but getting her back on side was the only way to discover what was going on. If he hadn't spotted the obituary notice then he'd have missed a prime opportunity.

At least he was here now and that was the main thing.

Miming the words to the hymn, Heath glanced around the church. Where was Teagan? He couldn't see her anywhere, but he had spotted Ms Botox.

The woman with the surgically frozen face he'd first met in Shepherd, Percival and Proctor last month sat on the adjacent row of pews. Being as she was staring right at him, she'd spotted him too, probably wondering why the random person who had wandered into the estate agents about a house he'd never moved forward with, was doing here. She could surmise what she liked. Her opinion was of no interest. He was here for one thing and one thing alone.

When the hymn finished, Heath sat back down and patiently listened to the vicar closing the service. It was only when Helen's coffin was carried out, followed by the immediate family, did he finally spot Teagan. His eyes immediately tracked to the big man walking next to her – the one who had rushed up to her on the pavement *that* night.

Heath shuddered. Getting a much better look than he'd managed to do the night of all the trouble, Heath was unnerved just how similar the man was to his father – a menacing, bigger version.

Heath nodded respectfully seeing Dulcie falter ever so slightly when her piercing blue eyes spotted him and ignored the glare he received from the son, but when Teagan clocked his presence, her mouth formed a perfect 'O' of surprise. She slowed down almost to a stop, only continuing to move forward when the son put his hand on the small of her back, propelling her forward.

Heath smiled. Now Teagan had seen him all he had to do

was allow the graveside formalities to take place and then he'd talk to her. He had every intention of inviting himself to the wake and since he was here she could hardly ignore him.

Getting much needed information from Teagan was worth putting up with Ms Botox and Dulcie Adams' creepy staring tactics.

• • • •

JONAH WAS STILL STEAMING that he was yet to catch up with Saul. The man, clearly guilty as sin over Lena had been keeping his distance from the Feathers. Jonah had even tried calling him at home only to get no answer.

Oh, Saul knew what he'd done alright and knew the shit would invariably hit the fan, but evading the confrontation only made it worse.

Jonah frowned. He would have driven round Saul's house himself if it hadn't been for Lena. When he'd mentioned he was going, she'd become tearful, begging him not to go. Usually, that would have irritated him no end and he'd have gone regardless, but now things were different.

His usually hard expression softened, picturing Lena in the chair looking ever so slightly vulnerable, her eyes dewy with unshed tears; one hand cradling the little bump. *His baby.*

Lena's developing pregnancy was changing her – not just physically, but mentally too. Her usual brash, demanding nature had been replaced by a different, more vulnerable and quite frankly, *nicer* side of her – one that made him want to protect her. It was a strange turning point. Apart from lust, Jonah never thought he'd feel anything other than irritation for the woman, but now he was starting to feel something. Something different… *Protective.*

The downside was that she'd gone off sex, which was frustrating, especially when all he wanted to do was run his hands over her changing body and feel what he'd created inside her. But she wouldn't let him anywhere near her.

Remembering Gwen was sitting in his office with the

figures from the night of the function for him to look over, Jonah snapped himself from his daydream. 'I must say, I'm pleased with this. Lena's done a very good job,' he said, his eyes running over the list of numbers.

'I too was pleasantly surprised,' Gwen admitted. 'You'll also be pleased with the amount deposited by *OK* magazine for the exclusive use of photographs from the event. That was also something Lena negotiated.'

Jonah raised his eyebrows as he took the print-out of the company bank statement. Truth be told, Lena was doing a lot better in her new role that he'd expected. She'd embraced the work, was improving the takings, had organised her first event both effectively and profitably and, from what he could tell, wasn't causing problems with Gwen or anyone else.

Apart from this business with Saul, things on the home front had unexpectedly improved dramatically. 'Is Lena working well with you?' Jonah asked. 'What I mean is, there's no animosity?'

Gwen shrugged. 'No, she's been fine.' Jonah was happier today and she didn't want to ruin his good mood by pissing on his bonfire with her suspicions. Not until she'd got cast-iron proof.

Jonah smiled. 'You were right to push me about involving her. It's done her the world of good.'

I bet it has, Gwen thought caustically, making sure her face outwardly appeared benign.

'Now Saul's the only fly in the ointment,' Jonah spat, his cold expression returning. 'I still haven't got hold of him, which makes it even more obvious he knows he's in the shit.'

'About that,' Gwen said. 'I saw him yesterday. After you had gone, I should add.'

Jonah's eyes narrowed. 'How unsurprising for him to show up after I'd left for the day. Did you tell him what Lena said?'

'No!' Gwen spluttered. 'That's for you to do.' She could hardly say she had told Saul. Neither could she admit she'd confided her suspicions over Lena's pregnancy either.

Guilt raged; the concept of betraying Jonah sitting heavily, but she'd done it purposefully to avoid hurting him. 'We were talking about something else, but from the things he said, I don't think what Lena told you can be right.'

Jonah folded his arms. 'Don't tell me you've fallen for his bullshit? I thought you were more intelligent than that! Are you saying Lena's lying? You never had any trust in her, but y…'

'I'm not saying that at all,' Gwen exclaimed. 'I think perhaps she may have misconstrued the situation. The fact that Jonah was protective of Lena at the moment was all too painfully obvious and she didn't want to rub Jonah up the wrong way.

'That I doubt,' Jonah growled. 'Saul's a bastard. Lena was extremely upset. She didn't even want to tell me what had happened, so I find it unlikely she'd have misread anything.'

Gwen held her hands up. 'Ok, ok. Just saying it might be possible, but you'll do what's needed, I know that.' *And Lena would be relying on that too, the sneaky cow.*

There had to be something she could find on the woman to nip all of this in the bud before it really was too late and the little bitch succeeded in milking the business and ruining what was left of the Powell family.

NINETEEN

DULCIE KEPT HER FACE NEUTRAL, kindly even, when really she wanted to scratch the eyes out of Teagan's pretty little head. It was a good job she'd possessed the foresight to conveniently stage that fall to break up their tryst in the kitchen last night, otherwise something could have occurred between her son and that woman.

Her jaw tightened. She'd seen the way Robert had looked at the girl and that was the most worrying thing.

Although it was many years ago, Dulcie well remembered the comments from Robert's teachers. How they'd gone on about his lack of empathy, his insistence for routines, not mixing with the other children. They'd almost insinuated there was something not quite right about him.

Dulcie tutted indignantly. *Something not quite right about him indeed!* Robert was fine – perfect. Extremely bright and extraordinarily talented, he just wasn't a social butterfly. What was wrong with that? Besides, he had a good relationship with *her* and that was all that mattered. These so-called 'foibles' of his meant she didn't have to worry he'd squander his life on pointless relationships, or get involved with the wrong crowd.

But now, if her suspicions proved to be correct, something

was beginning to change in Robert's way of thinking and that had to be quashed without fail. She must be on her guard, but she couldn't watch them *all* the time, so it was a blessing in disguise that Darren Harding had appeared today. It was perfect timing and something to diffuse this horrible situation.

'It's obvious Darren's made a big effort to be here today, which I think is very nice,' Dulcie said. 'And you don't need to apologise for his presence. I've told you before, he's a lovely young man.'

Teagan glanced in Darren's direction and watched him stare out over the Temple Hotel's manicured lawns. She knew she'd have to make the effort to go and speak to him, but in all honesty she didn't want to. It felt wrong.

Dulcie placed her hand on Teagan's arm. 'Please don't let what I said before put you off.' She smiled. 'I know I said he had a resemblance to my Michael, but surely you realise I was talking utter rubbish?' Her watery blue eyes saddened. 'It was the pills - they made me chatter nonsense half the time.'

That first time she'd seen Darren Harding was the only time in years that she'd let her guard down. Seeing the Pointer features had knocked her off kilter and thrown her from her usual controlled and strategic behaviour. It had been remiss of her. Very remiss indeed.

Dulcie chewed the inside of her cheek. It was possible her theory about Darren Harding was wrong After all, the resemblance was not obvious, but there *was* a resemblance. Her instinct was telling her the same and she needed to find out, but the only way to confirm that was to coax Teagan into getting close to the boy.

The Powells being on to her was bad enough, but she had to rule out this other possibility too. Maybe this would kill two birds with one stone? Once that was done she could move on to step two of her plan.

Teagan smiled weakly. 'Don't think about those pills, Dulcie. All that's over now.'

'But it won't be if you allow what I said to cloud your

judgement,' Dulcie implored, tapping Teagan reassuringly on the arm. 'You deserve a good man in your life.' *Just not my son.*

Teagan glanced at Darren again, then her eyes flicked to Robert talking to two women, who she presumed were Helen's work colleagues. Maybe she was worrying too much about this whole thing?

Dulcie waved at Darren and beckoned him over. 'Let's see how he is.'

Teagan cringed. 'Oh no, Dulcie, please. I don't th…'

'Rubbish! What I said has put you off. You're thinking of me, but you shouldn't! I saw with my own eyes how happy you were when you went out with that boy and how pleased you were when he sent those flowers, so don't give me that. Ah, here he is…'

'Hello Mrs Adams.' Heath held out his hand to shake Dulcie's. 'My deepest condolences. I'm so very sorry about Helen.'

'Yes, indeed.' Dulcie nodded, pretending to agree appreciatively. 'It is decent of you to pay your respects like this.'

Heath kept his smile in place, despite the presence of Dulcie's bony hand in his making him itch. She was still studying him. He could feel it. Despite her pleasantries and actual words, her eyes spoke a different story. 'I know I only met Helen a handful of times, but I wanted to be here.' He glanced at Teagan. 'How are you, Teagan?'

Teagan coaxed her mouth into a slight smile. 'I…'

'Teagan's been a saviour and I wouldn't have coped had it not been for her wonderful support,' Dulcie cut in, placing her hand on Teagan's arm. 'But I'm afraid all of this business with Helen has interfered with you two love birds.'

Blushing furiously, Teagan couldn't bring herself to look at Darren. 'Dulcie, I…'

Heath made himself stare at Teagan longingly like he was supposed to. 'Teagan's a very special woman and I'm hoping we can pick back up where we left off at some point soon.'

Teagan fought to keep her feet rooted in position, rather than running in the opposite direction. *God, this was embarrassing.*

'There dear, you see?' Dulcie said, inwardly smiling at Teagan's awkwardness. 'I told you there was no need to worry. He's still interested.'

'I…'

'Ah, Robert!' Dulcie exclaimed. 'Have you met Darren Harding? Darren, this is my son, Robert.'

Extending his hand as Robert approached, Heath tried not to take it personally that this man dwarfed his own six foot height. 'Nice to meet you, Mr Adams, although I wish it was under happier circumstances. My condolences.'

'Thank you, Mr Harding.' Robert shook Heath's hand just that little bit too hard. 'Do you work at Shepherd, Percival and Proctor?'

'No, I met Helen when I was interested in a property she was advertising an…'

'Darren also knew Teagan from school. Isn't it a small world?' Dulcie gushed. 'They've been dating.'

'Dating?' Robert said, his eyes on Teagan. *So this was a boyfriend?* 'How very… nice…'

Teagan burnt with humiliation. *This was dreadful.* She wished Dulcie would be quiet and then felt immediately guilty. Poor Dulcie, she was such a sweetheart thinking of others even on a day like today. She wasn't to know how desperately awkward this was.

'I was just saying to Darren how amazing Teagan has been,' Dulcie continued animatedly, looking for any slight reaction from Robert. 'Oh Robert, you should have seen the beautiful flowers this lovely young man sent Teagan only the other week! Absolutely gorgeous! Oh, love's young dream, eh?' She clutched Heath's arm and winked conspiringly. 'My son's only ever been interested in working and computers! I think I'll be about 95 before he gives me grandchildren!' *Did you hear that, Teagan? Robert's off limits.*

'I'm sure Mr Harding isn't interested in my bachelor status, mother,' Robert growled. There was something odd about this Darren Harding character. Had he seen this guy somewhere before? 'What school did you say you went to, Mr Harding?' he asked, studying the man suspiciously.

Heath blinked. *Shit. Which school did Teagan go to again? Oh God, he couldn't remember. Fuck.* 'I… erm…'

'What a strange thing to ask,' Dulcie snapped. 'You do talk drivel sometimes, Robert!' She turned to Teagan. 'So, when are you two going out again?'

'Erm, I don't know,' Teagan said a little too sharply. 'Would you excuse me?' Grabbing her handbag from the table, she hurried off in the hope of finding the Ladies cloakroom, unable to remain in that awkward, crucifying situation for one moment longer.

While everyone else's attention was centred on Teagan's abrupt departure, Heath's eyes tracked back to where he'd seen that invite on the table. He'd seen it while Dulcie was talking, but now, being as everyone else was otherwise preoccupied, he had the opportunity to take it.

Moving carefully to one side, Heath reached behind him, using his own body as a screen and stealthily snatched up the invite that someone had carelessly left lying about. Careless because he'd seen the print at the bottom of the card in black and white. An RSVP to Robert Adams with an address underneath, clear as day. *Robert's address…*

Shoving the invite into his trouser pocket, Heath turned to Dulcie and smiled cordially.

• • • •

LENA GRINNED. The function for that West Ham footballer last night had been a resounding success. The press were out in their droves and the place was bursting from the rafters. Consequently, she'd spent as much time mingling in the VIP suite as protocol allowed.

It had been annoying because there were several footballers

present that she wouldn't mind a bit of a tumble with. One especially had been giving her the eye. He'd even offered her a few lines of powder of which she'd had to regretfully decline. She'd have gone for it had she not spotted Gwen. With her cat-like vision, Gwen would have clocked her taking a snort even if she were on the bloody moon! But Lena knew how she had to play things at the moment and it wasn't worth rocking the boat. She had, however, found her way into several of the official photographs, making sure the reporters got her name down in their notepads too.

She flicked through the latest issue of *OK* magazine and her eyes lit up. *Fabulous*! They'd got the story out already. Flattening the double spread out on the desk in front of her, she beamed seeing herself featuring in the article's main photograph along with the rest of the football team, their manager and wives/girlfriends.

Suddenly a small frown appeared on her otherwise crease-free brow. *Damn*. Stunning as usual, but that purple bandage dress had showcased the padding. She couldn't remember taking her jacket off during the evening. *How had she been so careless?*

A photograph more than worthy of inclusion in the ever-growing album of her posed with celebrities, pop stars and household names – she'd spoilt by being slack with her camera angles. If it hadn't been for that it would have been her most favourite picture yet, but all she could now see was that she looked a right fat fuck.

Lena peered closer and inwardly shrugged. She couldn't have it both ways. Ok, so the kitchen roll bump may have spoilt her photo collection, but the fast approaching end result would be more than worth it. From now on she'd have to be strict with keeping her jacket on during photo opportunities because the only lasting reminder of this whole charade she wanted was her wedding certificate and the following bank balance.

Smacking her glossy lips together in satisfaction, Lena pulled her phone from her bag and scrolled down to Uncle

Ron's number, quickly tapping out a text:

> Get a copy of this weeks' OK Mag. I'm on p9. Spot anything different about me? 😊 Will call you later this week to make arrangements. xx

Gwen watched Lena quickly shove her phone back in her bag as she entered the office, then scornfully eyed the magazine open in front of her. 'Busy?'

Lena's pink lips pursed. 'Actually, I was reading the coverage of the West Ham party.'

Raising her eyebrows, Gwen wandered across to Lena's desk. 'They've printed a story already?'

Lena sat back proudly. 'Not just *they* – it's *OK* magazine. Good publicity for the Feathers, don't you think? Nothing but glowing compliments and great photographs. See for yourself.'

Gwen peered over Lena's shoulder, inhaling a steady waft of spirits and wrinkled her nose in contempt. Admittedly, she had to give Lena credit for the function. She'd organised it well and the takings were very healthy. Saul was correct in as much that the requests for VIP club membership had skyrocketed and even Jonah was impressed with the cheque for the photographs.

Lena stiffened from Gwen's close proximity but remained upbeat, even though she wanted to smash the manipulative old cow in the temple with the heavy glass ashtray. 'What do you think?'

Gwen scanned the article. It certainly did give the Feathers glowing references and there were plenty of colour photographs showing the interior of the club in a good light as well as showcasing a range of footballers and celebs enjoying themselves. But it didn't go unnoticed that Lena had strategically sneaked into three of those pictures.

She read the small print of the caption underneath the main photograph:

The West Ham team and their manager celebrate

in style, along with Lena Taylor – Events Organiser and fiancée of Jonah Powell, owner of the esteemed Feathers Club in Soho.

Gwen sneered silently. 'What's this 'events organiser' thing?'

Lena huffed. 'What was I supposed to say? They asked me what my involvement in the club was and being as I'm dealing with the VIP list and also arranged the event, I thought the statement was fair enough? What's wrong with it?'

Gwen shrugged. 'Nothing, I suppose. You did well.' Although it pained to give the girl a compliment, regardless of everything else, credit where credit due.

Lena glowed smugly. 'I've also taken the initiative and set up a new incentive scheme.' She fished a print-out from her in-tray. 'Being as the waiting list for standard VIP membership is so long, I've sent the option live on the website for Platinum membership for a limited time only.'

Gwen frowned. 'But we're almost at capacity as it is! We can't take on too many more elite members.'

'The chances of every single VIP member wanting to be on site at the same time is virtually impossible. For that reason, everyone in business knows you can double book pretty much anything without causing problems,' Lena said pompously.

She didn't actually know that, but had read something along those lines on an American website and it made sense, but of course nothing would be good enough for Gwen Vella.

Lena folded her arms defensively. 'The opportunity to purchase Platinum membership is only available for 24 hours and has been sent to everyone on the VIP waiting list.' She grinned excitedly. 'They get a few extra perks for this on top – all easily viable and nothing that will cost much, but Platinum members pay an extra grand for the privilege.'

Gwen's eyes widened. 'A *grand*? On top of the VIP price? They'll never go for that!'

Lena's smile was so wide it looked like her face may crack

in two. *God, she loved being right.* 'That's where you're wrong. The scheme went live at 9 this morning and 90% of the places have already been snapped up.' She waved the list the printer had churned out. 'The whole sign-up process and responses are automated too, so it's not even any extra work.'

She pulled the desk calculator towards her, her long talons clacking on the buttons. 'So... by my calculations, that's 180k extra in the bank this morning.'

Gwen forced a smile. Ok, so Lena had done good on this too, but that didn't change what she thought of the girl and still didn't trust her.

Lena looked back at the double page spread in front of her. 'And for the record, I didn't ask to be included in those photographs. I look alright though, don't I?'

Gwen swallowed her sarcastic retort. Of course there wasn't the slightest thought Lena would have gone out of her way to pose with anyone even slightly well-known... And now the girl was fishing for compliments?

'You don't think my dress looked stupid?' Lena pushed.

'I'm sure if you thought it looked stupid, you wouldn't have worn it.' Gwen looked at the photograph again, hiding her reaction when, on closer inspection, she saw the bump under Lena's tight dress.

She felt queasy. *Lena wasn't lying? She really was pregnant? Oh shit.... What about what she'd said to Saul?*

Lena smirked. She knew if Gwen hadn't noticed before, she had now. She may have thought she'd hidden her reaction, but she hadn't. *Far from it.* She watched Gwen pretending to be interested in the picture, when really she was gutted. *Back at you, bitch.*

Clearing her throat, Gwen moved across to her own desk. 'You looked great,' she muttered through gritted teeth. Sitting down, she pulled the rota towards her, her mind whirring. 'I'd better run though this and make sure everyone's here who should be for tonight.'

Lena stretched theatrically, raising her arms to the ceiling.

'Oh, I'm so stiff!' She stood up, knowing Gwen was looking. Lowering her arms, she placed her hand on her 'bump'. *This was working just perfectly.* 'Do you mind if I go for a walk? I've been cramped up at my desk for hours. I'll grab us a couple of teas from the kitchen on my way back?'

Quickly moving her eyes from Lena's stomach, Gwen hoping her smile looked genuine. 'Yes, thanks. That would be great!'

Slipping her jacket on, Lena left the office and closed the door behind her.

Gwen sighed heavily and stared at the desk in front of her. There was no mistaking it - Lena's stomach was no longer perfectly flat. It may be small, but the bump was definitely there. *So now what?*

Although Lena had done a decent job with the function, the incentive for the VIP waiting list and was being over the top falsely nice, there was no mistaking the girl was still drinking. Despite the smell of the Polo mints, the undeniable scent of alcohol was noticeable and it was equally likely that she was shoving powder up her nose too. She had to tell Jonah – it was *his* child after all. At least she *presumed* it was…? But she also had to tell Saul she'd been mistaken and the girl *was* pregnant.

Picking up the phone, she dialled Saul's number, getting more frustrated than ever when it rang out. Hanging up, she paced around the office, until hearing the 'ding' of a notification, she rushed back to her phone.

Seeing nothing on her screen, her eyes tracked to Lena's phone visible in her handbag under the desk. Taking the chance, she grabbed the phone before Lena returned. Seeing a new text message, she opened it:

> Nice work sweetheart. It suits you! Ha ha! Me and Noeleen aim to be over by the end of the month. Call me to arrange arrival plans.

Gwen frowned. It was from that same person. And

Noeleen? Where did she know the name from? Her brow furrowing, she quickly changed the message status to unread then shoved Lena's mobile back in her bag.

TWENTY

ROBERT WATCHED HIS MOTHER still busy talking to that Darren Harding person. Shoving his hands in his suit jacket pockets, he clenched his fists, irritation mounting.

Why was his mother pushing Teagan to make another date with the man? He'd seen her face and she hadn't looked too pleased about being put on the spot. And why had the bloke come to the funeral anyway? The man hardly knew Helen and furthermore, there was something about him that didn't add up. He didn't even seem to know where he went to school? Something wasn't quite right about him. Robert admitted that *none* of this should bother him, so why did it? He was tying himself up in knots and that achieved nothing.

He glanced around the room, openly scowling at the ghouls from Helen's firm. He presumed he'd be lumbered with dealing with that too now she was gone, but he didn't want involvement in that partnership. Not even *slightly*. He didn't want to be *here*, let alone involved in anything his sister had been part of.

Were any of the people who had instigated this nightmare here right now? The person who had shot Helen and terrified his mother could be in this very room, yet he had no way of knowing. No one looked anywhere near what his mother had described and none of them looked the 'type', but then sometimes it was the least expected ones…

Robert kept his hands buried in his pockets to stop himself from dragging his fingers through his hair. His brain was still reeling from what he'd read in that notebook. He'd barely had time to process any of it.

He stared at his mother, now having moved on to talk to a funny-looking woman. *Someone else he didn't know.* His mother was putting on a very brave face considering she was allegedly so upset about Helen, yet here she was, nattering away, plus playing cupid for the home-help. But then again, it was now apparent he didn't know anything about his mother or who she really was.

Since they'd had words she hadn't divulged anything further about Michael Pointer either and he had lots of questions he wanted answers to. There was little point asking whilst she was acting as blasé as if she'd merely omitted something akin to going to Eastbourne for the weekend, rather than not mentioning that the man he'd believed to be his father for forty years, wasn't.

And now Teagan was bulldozing his thoughts as well?

Robert sighed. He still didn't know what had come over him. The girl had irritated him from the moment he'd set eyes on her, yet she'd now become relevant? It was stupid.

His eyes narrowed. He'd noticed how embarrassed Teagan had been when her boyfriend rocked up. At least it underlined the sort of woman she was. His jaw clenched harder. So why was it bothering him so bloody much? Aside from the whole thing being utterly illogical, allowing the girl to affect him to this extent was even more absurd.

Feeling heat rise under his collar, Robert looked back towards his mother, now once again chatting happily to that Darren Harding man and decided he had to get out of here for a while.

Slamming his wine glass down onto the nearest table, Robert ignored the curious glances his actions brought and stormed from the hotel's function room. To his horror as he rounded the corner of the corridor, he came face to face with Teagan as she stepped out of the Ladies cloakroom. Glowering, he made to walk straight past.

'Robert? Are you alright?'

Swinging around, Robert noticed Teagan's eyes were pink, like she'd been crying again. His hand moved, drawn to pull her against him, but instead hastily diverted it.

Teagan lightly touched Robert's arm. 'What's the matter? Is Dulcie alright?'

Stiffening, Robert shrugged her arm away, his eyes narrowing. 'Why wouldn't she be? It's her daughter's funeral, so I expect she's having a wonderful time!' Despite his sarcasm, considering what he'd read in that notebook he wondered if that were actually true.

Teagan blinked in surprise. 'I-I didn't mean it to sound like th...'

'If you'll excuse me.' Robert shoved his hands back in his pockets and turning on his heels, continued walking down the corridor.

'I think we need to talk...' Teagan rushed after Robert, placing her hand on his arm.

Swinging around, Robert cornered Teagan. 'What about?' he growled.

Teagan stared up at Robert. He wasn't even close, but his big frame dwarfed her. 'Since the other day, you know... well, I feel things have become difficult between us and I don't want them to be.' She swallowed nervously. 'I felt we were getting on well before and I don't want anything to spoil that. Also, you never said whether you spoke to Dulcie about your father. Is it that what's upset you?'

Robert stared at Dulcie incredulously. 'What gives you the right to question my personal business?' Unable to stop himself, he raked his fingers through his hair, messing up his neatly slicked-back look. 'Listen, I think the lines have become blurred. I made it clear the other day about that, so please don't feel you can question me like this. You shouldn't have been party to any of this knowledge in the first place, so don't act like you have the right.'

Teagan dug her teeth into her lip – anything to soften the ice-cold stare Robert was giving her. 'What? I...'

'Teagan,' Robert snapped, his voice hard. 'I do not need your concern, nor your attention. I suggest you divert your time to your boyfriend, rather than me.'

'Darren isn't my boyfriend. He's...'

'It is of no consequence to me who he is, so you don't need to justify or explain yourself.' Robert's irritation with himself and everyone else – especially Teagan, grew exponentially. His jaw clenched, a nerve twitching. 'Let me explain something simple. I'm not a twenty year old lad, I am forty, Teagan. That's point one. Point two is if you cannot remember that some lines should not be crossed, then the most sensible thing for you to do is move on.'

Teagan felt as if she'd been punched in the stomach. 'You want me to leave? But you... W-What about Dulcie?'

Robert scowled. 'What about her? I'll make sure she is well looked after. I think it's the best thing to do under the circumstances.'

Indignation flooded Teagan and she grabbed Robert's arm. 'What? So you can shout and scream at me? Blame me for not running to you about who your father is and something your mother told me in confidence? You know, your mother - who I happen to care about very much? And then after I offer to come and help you clear up a *murder* scene, which, I might add, is *not* part of my job description, you accuse me of blurring the lines?'

Robert stared at Teagan in horror. 'Shut the fuck up!' he hissed, glancing around. 'You can't shout that out!'

Teagan folded her arms, her eyes angry. *This man was the bloody limit!* 'I can't shout what?' She ignored the woman walking past the bottom of the corridor who did a double take. She also ignored the rage in Robert's face. He wasn't the only one who could get angry.

Robert gripped Teagan's wrist. 'I'm warning you, keep your voice down. This is a funeral, you disrespectful bitch!'

'*I'm* disrespectful? You've spoken to me like a piece of shit since I first met you. I'm sorry about what happened with your father, I really am, but that doesn't mean we have to allow it to change anything. Now you're saying you want me to leave because you aren't big enough to live with that?'

Pulling her wrist away from Robert's grip, Teagan turned on her heels leaving Robert to stalk off in the opposite direction.

• • • •

SAUL FLICKED YET ANOTHER CIGARETTE butt out of the car window. The way he was going there would be a whole twenty pack's worth of nub ends on the floor.

He glanced at his mobile, seeing a missed call from Gwen. What did she want now? He'd told her yesterday that he'd put things straight with Jonah as soon as possible and he'd also said he'd deal with Lena, but she had to give him fucking chance! As much as he had more respect for Gwen than he did for most people, he didn't need her harping on.

His eyes fixed on the large back room visible from the side car park that, from his enquiries, he knew to be The Temple Hotel's function room. 'Palladian. Nice…'

'What?' Keith spluttered, a lump of half-chewed Twix shooting from his mouth to stick on the dashboard.

Saul nodded towards the long arched windows of the hotel. 'Those windows. They're 'palladian'. It's a style from the Georgian period.'

Keith raised an eyebrow and smirked. 'Oh, right…'

Saul grinned. Keith could think what he liked, but he didn't care. He liked buildings and this one had splendid features. Not that he was big into architecture or anything, but thanks to a book from the prison library which had helped while away the time, he had learnt a little and also appreciated nice-looking buildings.

'That room is where everyone we want is,' he said, nodding

towards the windows backing onto the grounds.

'We've been here a while and haven't seen anyone leave, so what's the plan?' Keith moaned. He'd had enough of car stake-outs.

Saul was well aware of how long they'd been here and he could have instead done with sorting out whatever shit that tarty slut had said to cause aggro with Jonah. Oh, he knew what she was doing, but she was playing with fire, which was a very stupid and reckless thing to do. *One which she would deeply regret.*

And as for this bullshit about babies… He would quite enjoy telling Jonah there was no need to marry the slapper and wouldn't be breaking his oh, so pious morals because there was no fucking baby. But time waited for no man and he couldn't hang around to speak to Jonah or plan how to wreck Lena's two-faced wretched life just yet. Neither did he have time to return Gwen's call because *this* was more important.

Saul sparked up yet another cigarette, hoping the choking smoke within his newly purchased BMW was enough to put Keith off his constant eating. The man's slobbering was making him feel fucking sick, but nowhere near as fucking sick as knowing the people he wanted to get his hands on were only a few hundred yards away. *So close, yet still so far.*

'Can we gate-crash a wake?' Keith asked.

'Well, we *could*, but that wouldn't be the greatest idea,' Saul said sarcastically. 'What we do is we sit here. We watch and we wait. Someone will come out sooner or later.'

'And if they don't…?'

Saul scowled. *Was Keith trying to wind him up?* 'Then we wait some fucking more.' He turned to face his right hand man. 'I told you we were lifting the girl and if it takes us all day, all night, plus tomorrow and the day after that until she comes out and gives us an opportunity, then that's how it is, ok? At the end of the day, you're either in this or you're not and I want to know which it is because you're getting on my tits.'

Keith nodded hastily. He should have known better than to

question anything. Sometimes he forgot he was working with Saul rather than Nero and it would do him good to pay more attention to remembering that.

'Although…' Saul added, leaning forward in the car seat. 'I think we may have just got lucky. Pass us the fucking binoculars, would you?'

Twenty One

HEATH SCOWLED AT his bank balance. He really could have done without dipping into his savings, especially for something so bloody expensive. And something that he didn't really even want either. But there was no other choice. He needed this whether he wanted it or not.

He'd been fortunate to land the option in the first place. The last time he'd enquired there was a minimum six month wait for this sought after membership, but whoever had opened a special offer to purchase membership with additional benefits had done him a massive favour.

Of course, it had also come with an additional price tag, but it was the only way.

Flicking over to his email app, Heath pulled up the confirmation:

Platinum VIP Access

Dear Mr Pointer,

Congratulations on securing the opportunity to become part of the Feathers Elite. As well as the exceptional benefits the standard VIP membership offers (listed in the terms and conditions), you are also granted the following in addition:

- 2 free bottles of house champagne per month
- Guaranteed booking of the sumptuous VIP Function Lounge
- Choice of canapes on entry during each visit
- Early bird access to cabaret premiere sittings

To take advantage of these additional benefits, please read the **Platinum** section of our website, or enquire at the VIP reception.
Please collect your Platinum VIP Membership Card from the club reception. Your card will be ready for you within 48 hours of receipt of this email, along with an entry pass for one guest as part of your access.
Please note: Formal dress/black tie to be worn at all times in the VIP Suite.

Your membership details are as follows:

Name: Mr Heath Pointer
Membership: Platinum VIP
Valid from: 03/07/05
Expires end: 02/07/06
Membership No: 57862

We look forward to welcoming you to the VIP Suite at the Feathers Club.

Enjoy your membership with us.

Warmest regards

Lena Taylor
Events Organiser and VIP Manager

Heath grinned. *That was it then.* He was now a fully-fledged member of the Feathers club in Soho.

Opening his phone's browser, he typed in the address for the Feathers website and navigated to the *'What's On'* section. He'd better hope his father still had that tux that he could borrow because he was going to need it.

• • • •

IT HAD TAKEN TEAGAN a good twenty minutes to calm down from her fury at Robert's arrogance. And now he wanted her to leave?

How could she abandon Dulcie? She couldn't and furthermore, *wouldn't.* It wasn't up to Robert. The only person who could tell her to leave was Dulcie herself and as far as she knew, Dulcie wanted her there.

Teagan gathered up her hair that the summer breeze pushed across her face and twisted it into a loose ponytail. For her, the prospect of leaving wasn't about the money or being out of a job. She'd expected to be out of a job when Helen said Dulcie was being moved to a residential apartment, so it wasn't about that. The truth was she loved Dulcie dearly and admitted she now saw her like a substitute grandmother rather than a client.

Maybe Robert had a point? Perhaps she *had* blurred the lines and overstepped being an employee to thinking more like she was part of the family?

Teagan forced the forming lump in her throat away. Whether how she felt about Dulcie was morally right or not, her whole attitude towards the Adams' was unprofessional. Perhaps she *should* leave?

Her mouth set determinedly. No. *She'd* manufactured this issue by allowing an attachment to Dulcie to form and mistakenly getting involved with family business.

Teagan walked determinedly back along the path through the manicured grounds to the hotel. She'd return to the wake, act like the heated exchange between her and Robert half an hour ago hadn't happened and behave completely normally. *Like an adult.*

Tomorrow she would push to move back into Footlights with Dulcie as soon as possible. She'd fight her nervousness about being alone in that big place and just get on with it. They would have to do it sooner rather than later because it wasn't feasible to remain in Robert's small flat indefinitely – especially now with such an uncomfortable atmosphere.

Teagan glanced at the hotel in the distance, surprised she'd wandered so far through the extensive grounds. Maybe she should take Dulcie's suggestion about Darren on board? Perhaps the stress and frustration surrounding Helen had unfairly coloured her view? After all, she'd been keen initially.

Teagan set her chin as she continued up the path. She wouldn't waste any more time analysing things with Robert. She was more than capable of dealing with the awkward situation as a rational person should. It wasn't the end of the world and she was damned if she would allow this to disadvantage Dulcie. It was as simple as that.

• • • •

KEITH HURRIED ALONG THE PATH. The girl was moving quicker than he'd factored into his timing. He eyed the black shoes on the end of her shapely legs. How women walked in those spiky contraptions always bemused him. If he wore those, within five minutes not only would his feet resemble something from *Swamp Thing*, but he wouldn't cover ten yards, let alone anything else. Thankfully, that didn't apply.

Upping his pace, his face screwed up with exertion, hoping it didn't look obvious he was trying to catch up with the woman. Ok, so there was no one else around – not a soul. It was the perfect opportunity and not one they'd expected.

He'd resigned himself to waiting around for hours, possibly *days*, but once this opening unexpectedly presented itself and although it was a hell of a risk, he did agree with Saul that they couldn't afford to pass up it up. Especially as so much time had already been wasted over this whole caboodle. The sooner this was wrapped up, the better.

Keith was the first to admit that spending the last few weeks trailing women around for reasons other than what he'd normally associate with giving the fairer sex his attention, hadn't been his favourite. Wild goose chases in the pursuit of the Powells' nest egg were tiresome and more now than ever he wanted to return to his normal line of work. He envied the team they'd left back at the firm. How he'd love to be punching some bastard in the face and collecting overdue payments right now, rather than poncing through some bloody dressed-up hotel garden after a slip of girl that some stoner reckoned had access to a shed load of rare jewels! *Bloody stupid, the whole thing.*

As a light sheen of sweat broke over Keith's brow, he was glad to finally close enough distance between him and the girl. He glanced behind him, just able to spot the bonnet of Saul's black BMW behind the hedge in the distance.

'Excuse me?' Keith called. Frowning at the lack of response, he tried again, this time louder. 'Excuse me? Miss?'

Slowing, Teagan looked over her shoulder at the man behind her and felt a glimmer of unease.

Realising he'd got the girl's attention, Keith smiled. 'Sorry to shout, love. Don't suppose you've got the time?' Continuing towards Teagan, he shrugged apologetically. 'Stupidly I've left my phone at home. I'm meeting someone and can't remember whether we'd arranged to meet inside or out here.'

Relaxing, despite the man's unnerving appearance, Teagan smiled. 'Yes, of course.' Opening her bag, she reached for her phone.

'You here for a business meeting?' Keith said pleasantly, waiting as Teagan rummaged around in her bag. *When should he do it? Now or wait?*

'A wake, unfortunately.' Teagan frowned. 'That's funny, my phone's not here.' Sighing, she remembered placing it on a table before rushing to the Ladies. 'Oh, I'm ever so sorry. I've left it inside. I think the time is abou…'

Moving forward, Keith grabbed Teagan's arm. 'Don't do anything silly.'

'W-What are y…'

'I *said*, don't do anything silly. Link your arm through mine and turn the fuck around,' Keith growled.

Heart racing, Teagan did as the big man said, too terrified to even look at him.

'That's better.' Keith patted Teagan's hand and held her arm in place. 'Now, put a smile on your face. Or at the very least, don't look so fucking scared. Let's go.'

Teagan forced her jelly-like legs one in front of the other. Making her mouth turn up slightly, to anyone who might see them, they looked like a couple going for a stroll as they ambled slowly back down the path in the direction she'd just come from. *The opposite way from the hotel.*

Her mind picked up speed and panic intensified. 'W-Where are we going? What do you want?' she squeaked, her mouth dry.

Keith grinned menacingly. 'Don't worry your pretty little head about that.'

Nausea engulfed Teagan, realising she hadn't seen anyone else around. If she screamed, no one would hear. *What would this man do if she did scream?* 'I haven't got any money, I…'

'Listen, bitch,' Keith hissed, digging his meaty fingers into the flesh of Teagan's arm. 'I don't want your money. There's someone waiting to have a word with you, that's all. There's no need to panic. Be cool, calm and collected and don't do anything rash. If you do as I say, everything will be fine.'

Teagan nodded frantically and plastered back on a smile of sorts. It probably didn't look too convincing, but it was the best she could manage. *Who could possibly want to talk to her?* She had to think – think of how she could get out of this situation.

Dizziness suddenly overwhelmed her. *Oh, shit. No!* This was them, wasn't it? This beast of a man was something to do with those people who had broken into Dulcie's house and killed Helen. Her eyes darted towards the massive bull-headed man with an iron grip of her arm. He wasn't the one she'd fleetingly seen that night – she'd have recognised him, but this one was *part* of it. He *had* to be.

Teagan glanced to her right. Could she make a run for it? She hadn't even got her phone, but she had to get away from this man and these people, whoever they were.

Continuing along the path, Teagan's head span with unfeasible ways of changing the dreadful unfolding situation, but all hope of getting away evaporated when she realised they were heading towards a black car.

Twenty Two

LENA INSPECTED HER FRESHLY PAINTED NAILS and sipped from the bottle of vodka kept in the back compartment of her bag, wishing her nails would hurry up and dry. Gwen was on a late lunch and planned on popping to the stationers afterwards, so there was plenty of time to relax, as well as make a couple of phone calls.

Lena scowled. The swimming costume underneath her clothes had shifted right up her backside, making it more uncomfortable by the second, but she could hardly readjust it whilst her nails were still tacky. *Bloody thing.* She wasn't smudging the varnish for that, despite the irritation. This whole swimming costume thing was driving her up the wall. Wearing lycra all day made her sweat like a pig, not to mention the straps chafing into her bloody shoulders all the time.

She glanced down at the 'bump' under the knitted jersey of her light pink dress and prodded it irritably. That was driving her nuts too *and* she'd have to add another layer of kitchen roll next week to keep things on track. Soon *everyone* would notice, not just the people she *wanted* to notice.

Taking another big mouthful of vodka, Lena scowled. She was gasping for a smoke, but she'd never get away with it in here – unless she said one of the dancers had been in to discuss the rotas? *Yeah, sod it. That's what she'd do.*

Pulling the cigarettes and lighter from her handbag, Lena lit up and exhaled the smoke gratefully. Doing a quick mental calculation, her face fell. The wedding was still six weeks away. Christ, by that time she would supposedly be around 15 or 16 weeks' pregnant. She'd never get away with it for that long, let alone having to abstain from having a shag.

Jonah would bound to be frustrated by that point, despite her going out of her way to ensure he was pleasured at least once a day, but he was a very hands-on man and would expect to get those hands of his on her sooner rather than later. But how could she allow that to happen whilst *this* was in situ?

She glared at the kitchen roll padding once again.

No, she'd most definitely have to do something about it.

Pulling her purse from her handbag, Lena extracted a small key and unlocked the bottom drawer of her desk. At least working here she had somewhere that certain things could be safely stored. Not like at home, in case Jonah came across them.

Pulling at the envelope containing the paperwork for the registry office, Lena scanned the documents for the telephone number and quickly stabbed the digits into her mobile, taking care not to catch her nails.

As the call connected, Lena glanced up at the door as a double precaution, perpetually on edge in case someone came in.

'Hello? Hi, I'm hoping you can help me. My wedding's booked with you for the 20th August… Yes, that's right, this year… I was wondering if you had any cancellations? I was hoping for a sooner one… Yes, I'll hold…' *Come on, come on. Please have a cancellation…*

Lena drummed her fingers on the desk as she waited, hoping her nail varnish would withstand it. 'Hello? Yes, I'm still here… I'd really appreciate it if you could swing something… A-A family member is unwell and we really want him to be able to see us get married and… Oh, you have?'

Lena's heart beat frantically as she scribbled down the date, now not caring if her varnish got smudged. 'That's fantastic! Thank you so much!' Her face split into a wide smile. 'Yes, yes of course. It's Jonah Anthony Powell and Lena Margaret O'Hara. Yes, O'Hara… that's correct… Brilliant! Is there anything else I need to do? We don't need to sign any more forms? Ok… No, that's fine. Thanks again. Bye.'

Ending the call, Lena sat back in the chair. What a bit of luck. That made everything *so* much more palatable. It might make juggling around the venue and caterers a bit of hassle, but it shouldn't be impossible being as money wasn't an object.

Gleefully, she took a long celebratory swig of vodka and scrolled through her contact list. She might as well tell Uncle Ron the good news while she had the chance.

'Hello?' Lena cried excitedly. 'Yes, I know! Looks the part, doesn't it? But I'm not ringing about that. There's been a change of plans… No, no – in a good way! The wedding's been brought forward…'

She happily swirled around in her chair. 'Guess when it is now… Go on, guess… No, the 20th July! Two and a half weeks' time…! I know, it couldn't be better… No, he doesn't yet, but I'll tell him tonight… You'll still be able to come won't you? I'll let you know when and where as soon as everything's confirmed … Yes, you too… Can't wait! Bye.'

Before Lena could spin her chair back to face the right way, Gwen made sure she quickly stepped away from the glass-panelled office door before she was spotted.

• • • •

EVERY FIBRE IN TEAGAN'S BODY screamed against getting into the back of the black BMW. As Keith steered her closer, her whole being primed to run; run as fast as she could to anywhere that might offer a chance of getting out of this situation.

Her eyes darted around the rows of cars within the fenced off car park. Although she could make a dash for it, she might run into a dead end. Looking at the high wire perimeter fence surrounding the open air car park, she couldn't see any cut-through points. She'd also seen no one. *Not one person.*

With one hand still tightly around Teagan's arm, Keith opened the back door of the car with his free hand. Sensing the girl's reluctance, he tightened his grip, 'You're not going to do anything stupid are you? Remember what I said, if I were you.'

Despite the threat and the futility of escape, primal instincts took over and Teagan pulled against Keith. 'Let me go!' Her voice was high-pitched and terrifyingly loud.

Snarling, Saul opened his driver's door. 'Get the fuck in, bitch!' he spat, his eyes narrow slits. He glared at Keith. He'd made it clear there should be no fuss and the girl was fussing. Couldn't Keith even lob some chick into the back of a motor?

Seeing the man in the car, the blood drained from Teagan's face. Wasn't that the man she'd seen running from Footlights? No, but the meaning was the same. These *were* the people Joe had been involved with - the ones he'd ripped off for drugs and the ones who had killed Helen.

Teagan shook violently, Robert was wrong. These people weren't to do with Helen. They'd killed Helen *because* of Joe. They'd killed Helen because of *her* own involvement with Joe. *And now they would kill her*.

Joe had lied. He hadn't sorted things out with them at all. They must believe she was still holding the drugs that Joe stole. *God, no!*

Suddenly pushed forward, Teagan thrashed around, blind panic overtaking coherent thought. 'No, I won't let you! You can't!' she shrieked, her eyes wild.

'Fucking sort it!' Saul hissed, glancing around. 'And *quickly*!'

Slapping his meaty hand over Teagan's mouth, Keith manhandled her into the car with minimal effort, such was his brute strength. Following her into the back seat, he'd barely closed the back door before Saul wheelspinned off.

Struggling to breathe, her mouth and nose covered with

Keith's massive hand, Teagan's panic increased, her heart thumping wildly. Head twisted to one side, she stared up at Keith whose free hand held both of hers twisted behind her back, keeping her pressed into the leather upholstery, his elbow firmly against the small of her back.

Teagan forced her brain to function; to remember anything to give the police clues as to her whereabouts or the identity of these people, but found it would not stop swarming with pointless thoughts. Hyperventilating through her terror, she couldn't concentrate on anything enough for more than a split second. Not that she could see much from her position. The only thing that was obvious was an overpowering smell of freshly valeted car.

'You fucking dipshit,' Saul snarled, swiftly turning out from the hotel's staff car park onto the main road. 'I thought I said subtle. That was *not* subtle.'

'She just went batshit!' Keith grumbled. 'What else was I supposed to do?'

Huffing, Saul turned the music up as the car accelerated. He'd have words with Keith about this, but for now the main thing was getting the fuck out of here. Luckily, no one was about and he'd already made sure there was no CCTV in the car park.

Teagan felt bile make its way up from her stomach and repeated to herself over and over to calm down. Panic would get her nowhere, apart from thrown out at the side of the road and that was if she was lucky. If she was calm there was a chance of reasoning with these people and explain she knew nothing about Joe's drugs or where he'd put them. Although reasoning with them was a long shot, she had little other options. Apart from that, her best bet was to work out where they were taking her.

It was only after a relatively short space of time by gauging the speed of the car, with rising horror she knew they were now on a dual carriageway – the one which, if she was correct, led to the motorway.

Her heart crashed in her chest. If they were heading towards the motorway and judging by the strong accents of the two men, they were going to one place and one place only. *London.*

TWENTY THREE

DULCIE SAT ON THE SOFA wringing her hands together nervously. 'I can't believe she's done this.' She looked up at Robert imploringly. 'What will I do?'

Robert concealed his irritation behind an unfazed expression, refusing to show that Teagan's lack of presence bothered him.

Yesterday, when after an hour, Teagan failed to return to the wake, he'd found himself getting more and more annoyed, reaching the conclusion that she was doing it as a childish attempt to gain his attention. Despite the growing urge to look for her, he'd remained where he was, swallowing his internal irritation. Honing his concentration, he'd continued politely chatting to the other mourners, all of whom were adept at skirting around the glaring issue that Helen had been shot dead shortly after her husband had been discovered with his brains splattered all over the garage floor.

He wondered whether any of them believed it to have been a random attack by a psychopath, or whether Helen had been involved in something which had cost both her and James their lives. Or even whether it had been *Helen* who had killed James and then someone had decided to off her?

Whatever anyone else thought remained unsaid, but Robert knew what *he* thought. Having to stand there pretending that he didn't was akin to having the soles of his feet burnt off with acid.

Based on what his mother had written in her own hand, watching her playing the devasted parent was another ill-fitting piece. Teagan throwing her teddy out of the pram was the final insult.

Finding Teagan's phone lying on one of the tables, Robert had truly believed she'd have skulked back eventually. Even if her game was to make him worry for a few hours before returning, he'd thought the moment she'd realised she'd left her phone, she'd have come back like a shot, but she hadn't.

Once the final stragglers had left the wake, he'd picked up the mobile and placed it into his pocket, all set to give her a mouthful the minute he'd got back. Because that's where he genuinely believed she'd be - back at the flat, sulking like a child. But there was no sign of her. And there still *wasn't.*

Now, Teagan's heartfelt proclamations of saying how much she cared for Dulcie were hollow and fake in the light of walking out on the woman she deemed to think so much of.

Robert's eyebrows furrowed lower. But then that was Teagan all over, wasn't it? A lot of things had come to the fore about people's true nature of late. And it was damn well infuriating.

'Robert?' Dulcie whined. 'Are you even listening? What am I going to do?'

Robert glared at his mother before dropping the stern look. 'It's quite obvious what's happened,' he said, desperately keeping a handle on his growing anger. 'Short of nailing them together, you all but arranged it!'

Dulcie frowned. 'Arranged it? What are you talking about?'

Robert sighed. 'Darren! Teagan has gone off with that Darren Harding, just like you wanted.'

Dulcie bit back the urge to slap some sense into her son. Was the stupid boy jealous? *How could that be?* 'If that were the case, then surely she'd have told me she was spending the night with her boyfriend?' She watched a slight flinch cross Robert's face with warm satisfaction. 'Last night may have been Teagan's night off, but to not say anything, well, it's very disappointing.'

'Hmm,' Robert nodded. 'Or perhaps she's had enough. You upset her by blaming her about my father, so maybe it's to do with that?' Let his mother shoulder some of the responsibility for once. Besides, that reason was preferable to thinking it was what *he'd* said was what had caused Teagan to leave. He needed her – needed her to prove to himself he was normal after all.

Dulcie scowled. 'You're blaming me for being upset Teagan told you something so important, when it should have been *me*?' Remembering the game she needed to play, her face softened. 'Anyway, I didn't shout. I just said I was upset, which I was. But we sorted it out. Or at least I thought we had.' A glimmer of worry ignited. 'Wait a minute! Are you insinuating that she's left? As in, for good?'

Robert shrugged nonchalantly. 'How should I know? Perhaps?'

Dulcie's breath caught. 'S-She can't!' Her mind whirred. *Had the girl gone with the box? Oh God - if she'd taken the box...*

Trying not to show her rising panic, Dulcie opted for the more sensible approach of emotional manipulation. She threw her hands in the air, sobbing loudly. 'Oh, I can't bear it! She can't leave! She mustn't. I need her here, Robert. Teagan's been the one to keep me going throughout all of this.'

She put her hand on Robert's, not noticing him stiffen at her touch. 'That's not to say you haven't been fantastic because you have. But Teagan, well, it's different. I-I had the kind of relationship with her that I'd always wanted with Helen... Helen was too cold... She hated me...'

Yes, she did and now I know why, Robert thought bitterly.

'You must get Teagan back!' Dulcie wailed, throwing herself against his chest. '*Please* get her back.'

'Mother, I think you're being over dramatic. She's probably with that Darren and will be back soon.'

'But I need to know,' Dulcie cried. *She was worried sick, but not as sick as she would be if the little hussy had done a runner with her jewels.* The thought made her feel quite ill. And if she'd done a runner with her jewels, had she also done a runner with Darren Harding? Was this part of a convoluted master plan? One to put her own well-thought out scheme to shame?

She clutched at Robert's shirt. 'Please, Robert. I need Teagan. I rely on her. I need to know if she's coming back.'

Angrily brushing his mother's arm away, Robert stood up. 'I won't chase after Teagan because she's decided to act with such rudeness. Walking out of Helen's wake with not so much as a word and then not even having the good grace to let us know that she wanted to spend the night sleeping with that *man*, making us – making *you* worry about her whereabouts is unacceptable.'

He grabbed his jacket from the back of a chair. 'I'm going into the office.' Snatching up his car keys, he stormed out of the flat.

Dulcie flinched as the front door slammed, the shockwaves reverberating up her spine. She took a deep breath and exhaled slowly.

This was bad. As much as her son had tried to hide it, Dulcie knew him too well. Making out he was angry over Teagan's bad manners and perceived disrespect, when in reality it seemed he was seething with jealousy over that little tramp being in the arms of another man. If Robert really was starting to have deep feelings, that certainly didn't bode well for her plans. She needed Teagan here and she needed her to be with Darren Harding, but how was she supposed to engineer that whilst her son was steaming around like a green-eyed monster? It would never do.

But what if the girl *really* had a hidden agenda with Darren all along? What if she'd taken the box and done a runner with that man?

Dulcie's heart beat at an alarming rate. She'd guarded those jewels for forty years. They were hers and Robert's now, not for the benefit of anyone else!

But Teagan thought the box contained love letters, didn't she? Unless she'd opened it? Unless Darren had told her to open it? Or was it possible that she was working for the Powells?

Dulcie sucked at her lips. *Stop it. Stop it!* She was being ludicrous. Teagan didn't have the capacity to pull off either of those things. That limitation was the exact reason why she'd been chosen.

She closed her eyes to get a handle on her escalating panic. *Wait!* Didn't Teagan say that she'd stopped taking the box around in her handbag?

Dulcie's mouth twitched into a smile. If she had, then it meant the box was in this flat. Most probably in the girl's room.

She'd be generous and give Teagan the benefit of the doubt until this afternoon, but if she didn't show in a few hours, then she'd turn the little tramp's bedroom over until the box was found.

• • • •

GWEN GRABBED HER MORNING COFFEE and sat in her usual chair looking out of the window of her maisonette, but despite the sun shining brightly, she felt anything but.

She picked at the start of a snag in her tights, hoping it didn't turn into a ladder, then glanced at the clock on the mantlepiece. Still ten minutes before she needed to leave. Enough time to finish her drink. Raising the cup to her lips, she blew on the coffee. She'd left it a bit late to have a hot drink, not that it would matter if she spent another hour sitting here before going into work. She always arrived early, but sitting around wracking her brains for an answer she didn't have was getting her nowhere, short of frustrated.

Gwen's lips pursed. She'd seen Lena sipping at the vodka yesterday without a care in the world as she rattled away on the phone, absentmindedly patting that bump of hers. But who had she been on the phone to? That's what she wanted to know. Unfortunately, she'd only heard the tail-end of the conversation, but had heard enough to know that the wedding had been brought forward. And whoever Lena was telling, it was clearly someone who was attending.

She also wanted to know what was in Lena's desk. Last night she'd hung around even later than usual in the hope that once Lena had left for the night, she'd get a chance to look in that drawer of hers. Nosy, she knew, but she'd watched her stuff some paperwork back in there before carefully securing the key back in her purse and felt sure that something in that drawer the girl went to great pains to lock was worth seeing.

Standing up, Gwen finished her now drinkable coffee and straightened down her skirt.

Slipping on her court shoes, she grabbed her handbag and walked towards the front door. Hopefully she'd get the chance to either look though Lena's phone again today or even better, get in that drawer.

TWENTY FOUR

KEITH LOOKED AT SAUL, experiencing an uncharacteristic flutter of nerves at the expression on the man's face. 'He said she had it. I know that's what he said,' he repeated. He'd already said that about ten times so far, yet he was still being stared at like a compulsive liar.

'You also said he wasn't blagging you,' Saul growled, not happy with this latest turn of events.

Since the minute they'd picked up that girl last night he'd been looking forward to this moment. True to form, he'd chosen to drag out revealing the pièce de résistance until today to ensure the magnum of Bollinger chilling in the fridge was cold enough for the long-awaited reveal.

This situation – the one where he held in his hands the haul of exquisite pink diamonds lifted from the firm's grasp was one of the daily images that had replayed on loop in his mind every single day of his long seventeen year stretch.

He could have done this last night, but he'd wanted to savour it and draw out the anticipation a bit longer. Now he had, it was all for nothing. *Nada.*

Keith stared at the contents of Teagan's handbag. There was the usual collection from a woman's bag on the table: a purse, lipstick, mirror, a couple of tampons and some stuff he didn't know the words for – that gunk birds put on their faces.

Gingerly reaching out, he peered inside the now empty black leather bag, staring into the compartments and tugged at one of the side zips. 'You've checked all of these?'

'What do you take me for? Some sort of cunt?' Saul slammed his fist on the table. 'Of course I've fucking checked them!'

Snatching the bag from Keith, Saul shook it violently before throwing it across the small kitchen where it rebounded off the wall and landed with a soft 'whump' on the lino. 'That stoner twat must have been winding you up and you being the thick bastard that you are, swallowed everything he told you.'

Keith stiffened. He would kill that fucktard stoner. He was not a thick bastard and didn't appreciate being called one, even by Saul Powell. 'The guy had no reason to make it up! That's what he said *she* said,' he seethed. 'I told you at the time I wasn't sure if it was definitely the diamonds, you know that.'

'Well, whatever it was, it isn't in the bloody bag. You said it was something of Michael Pointer's and there's fuck all in here relating to Michael-fucking-Pointer, unless he had a penchant for lipstick and bastard tampons!'

Keith swallowed his irritation and shrugged. 'Then it must be still at Footlights or at Robert Adams' place.'

'That is of course, presuming someone else didn't lift it like Jonah thinks,' Saul added, scraping his hand across his face in sheer frustration. 'Christ, I'm fucking sick of this! I just want my shit back and now we're lumbered with that silly bitch in there.' He jerked his head in the direction of the bedroom.

Keith cringed. He hadn't liked how that had gone last night either. Saul had made a right mess of the girl's face and shooting her up with smack was a bit unnecessary, but then she had been making a racket. 'I guess now we can dump her somewhere? We could do without a bird adding to the problem. If she hasn't got what we're looking for, then it's pointless holding onto her.'

Saul stared at Keith incredulously. 'Sometimes I wonder whether you've ever had a brain cell or whether you come out with crap just to wind me up.'

He watched Keith's face crinkle in confusion and felt more than he had in a long time like slicing the man's other ear off so he didn't look so ridiculously unsymmetrical. 'The girl's going nowhere. Grow half a brain! You really think we can let her walk now? Just because she hasn't got them on her doesn't mean she doesn't know where they are or who's got them. She must know and so we'll keep her until she tells us.'

'And if she doesn't?' Keith asked, unsure whether he wanted to hear the answer.

Saul smiled. 'She will.' Grinding the remains of his cigarette out on the kitchen table, he stood up. 'In the meantime, clean this shit up.'

• • • •

TEAGAN AWOKE, her head pounding and nausea like she'd never experienced before pulsing through her body. Her eyelids felt glued together, her whole face stuffed with cotton wool.

She tried to open her eyes, each one weighed down with concrete blocks, her mouth as dry as a bone. She found one eye wouldn't open; the pain pulsing behind it breathtaking. Reaching up to touch it, she couldn't, her arms... *What had happened to her arms?*

Panic rising, she pulled against whatever was trapping her, confusion spiralling. Fuzzy memories filtered into her head. *Those men... The car... She couldn't remember anything else. What the...?*

Eyes adjusting to the room shrouded in darkness, Teagan blinked, each movement excruciatingly painful. She could see very little: the outline of a window; a chink of light behind curtains. Various shades of black and white with a small helping of faded colour swam in her mind.

With her senses gradually coming to life, she realised she was lying on a bed. *Whose bed? Where was she?*

Tears sprang into her eyes and her breathing became laboured as, with growing horror, Teagan realised she couldn't move her arms because she was manacled by her wrists. *She'd been handcuffed to a bed.*

Yanking frantically against the restraints, all she achieved was to make an unholy racket as the cuffs banged against the metal bed frame. That and the pain where they had chafed against her wrists.

The speeding in her brain intensified and her stomach clenched. Heaving, she scrambled to sit up; the restraints stopping her from adopting a full sitting position. As her stomach heaved violently once more, the best she could manage was to twist her head and vomit stinging bile partly over herself, the rest across the bed.

Sobbing, Teagan felt she might pass out when she heard the key turn in the door.

'Feeling unwell?' Saul flicked on the light, his eyes dancing with mischief. The girl on the bed was a pretty thing. Or she had been until he'd clumped her.

He would have preferred not to have to had to smash her in the face and by the time they'd arrived at one of the flats he'd presumed she'd calmed down enough for it to be safe, but the minute Keith got her out of the car, she'd kicked off again. Still, the one eye, blackened and swollen almost shut, would heal and it didn't mean he had to look at her.

She'd was lucky that was all she'd got. At least the swift clump had knocked her silly enough to drag her into the flats unhindered. To anyone who'd happened to spot them, she looked like the classic pissed-up tart being helped home - a common sight around these parts. No fucker would say anything even if they had noticed because he owned all of these flats, plus most of the tenants were toms anyway, so they didn't give a shit. It was water off a duck's back where they came from.

Once they'd got her into the flat, the stupid bitch had kicked off again. Screaming, screaming and fucking *screaming.*

Blathering how she'd had nothing to do with the stolen drugs. Saul shrugged. He hadn't a clue what she was going on about. No one had half-inched any drugs - they wouldn't be that stupid, but he worked out fairly quickly that they wouldn't get anywhere questioning her whilst she was in such an angsty state, so the best thing was to reset her head. She'd soon become more pliable. They always did with a shot inside them.

The silly tart hadn't even seen it coming, but there had been a split second of sheer terror when she realised she'd been spiked. She'd been just about to scream, yet hadn't quite managed it before the heroin hit her square between the eyes. And she'd be getting as much of that as necessary to keep her quiet and create a bargaining chip to make her talk. Because she *would* talk once she became reliant, he would make sure of it.

Saul stepped forward, watching Teagan attempt to back away up the bed. *Pointless really - she couldn't go anywhere.* 'I've brought you some water,' he smiled. 'Looks like you could do with it.'

In reality, he felt like drowning her for wasting his time. He may well yet do just that, but not now. Unscrewing the top of the plastic bottle, Saul pulled Teagan upright and held the bottle to her dry lips. She gulped at it gratefully, some going in her mouth, most spilling down her black dress.

Saul grinned, aroused by the thought of her nipples straining against wet clothes and pulled the bottle from Teagan's lips. 'Are you going to behave yourself today and tell me what I want to know?'

'I-I don't know what you want,' she croaked. 'I don't know anything about the drugs. Please, you have to believe me. Please just let me go. I really don't know ab…'

'Still playing games?' Saul's eyes narrowed. 'That's not an advisable route to take, little girl. There's only so much I will put up with before I get really cross. I'm not interested in these drugs you keep going on about. I just want what's mine. I've been through your bag and I'm very disappointed to find my goods are not in there.'

Teagan blinked in confusion, along with the sinking realisation that she really needed to use the toilet. 'Please, I don't know what you mean. I…'

'Look,' Saul hissed, grabbing one of Teagan's breasts and twisting it. 'It's easier if you do things my way. Your boyfriend was adamant that *you* are in possession of what's mine.'

Yelping in pain, tears sprang from Teagan's eyes. 'Can you unlock me. I-I need to use the toilet.'

Grinning, Saul perched on the end of the bed, his fingers running slowly up Teagan's thigh. 'And you think I'd be so stupid as to do that? You'd try and run away or whack me with something!' He laughed heartily. 'You think I don't know what you lot are like?'

Teagan moved her leg from Saul's touch as if his fingers were branding irons.

Saul shifted quickly. 'I rest my case. You tried to kick me then. Don't know when to stop, do you?' he growled. 'All I want to know is where my stuff is. The stuff *she* gave you.'

Teagan looked bewildered. 'I don't know about any stuff and I don't have a boyfriend!' She clenched her teeth, the pressure on her bladder increasingly painful, her mind too fuzzy to think straight. 'Look, I… *Please* untie me.'

Saul laughed again. 'Your lies are starting to bug me, but I tell you what, despite your behaviour, I'm in quite a good mood. How about I make you come? Orgasms stop the urge to piss.' His hand moved back to Teagan's thigh, his fingers inching under the hem. 'It will relax you too. You look like you could do with a release of tension. Maybe then you'll be more inclined to tell me the truth?' He palmed his rapidly swelling crotch. 'After that, I'll let you return the favour…'

Teagan bucked away from Saul's hand. 'GET OFF!' she screamed, freezing as hot urine flowed over her legs, soaking her dress and the bed.

'Urgh! You dirty bitch!' Saul spat.

Openly sobbing in humiliation and terror, Teagan began screaming in earnest, banging her cuffed wrists against the bed frame and making a racket loud enough to split her own head. 'Let me out of here!' she shrieked. 'LET ME OUT!'

'For fuck's sake!' Saul growled. 'You're not making this easy!' Fishing out the syringe, he held it up, smiling as Teagan's eyes widened in renewed terror.

'No! NO!' she sobbed. 'What's that? What is it?'

'The same as you enjoyed last night,' Saul snapped, forcing her elbow prone against the bed frame. 'I'm trying to be reasonable with you, yet you're determined to piss me around. Well, listen up, girl – it won't fucking work!' Grabbing an elastic strap, he threw it around her arm, tightening it with his teeth.

'NOOOOO!' Teagan screamed, eyeing the point of the needle as it slotted into her vein. *They'd injected her last night? With what? What was it?* 'Please! Please don't! I…'

It was too late. She felt it rush up from her feet to the back of her eyes and her body went limp as she fell into the void. The world turned grey and she could only lie back, blissed out, unable to even react or feel any emotion when Saul unzipped his trousers.

TWENTY FIVE

ROBERT SAT IN HIS CAR in the work's car park and drummed his fingers on the steering wheel. If he'd thought going into the office would offer him any means of concentration, he'd been wrong because he hadn't achieved more than a ten-second burst of thinking about something other than Teagan's whereabouts.

Teagan, Teagan, Teagan - forever squirrelling into his thoughts and driving him crazy.

Ripping the cellophane from the packet of cigarettes, Robert fumbled with the lighter he'd just purchased. Lighting up, he leant back against the head rest. He'd knocked fags on the head ten years ago and here he was – the rush of the first drag on a long-awaited cigarette just as satisfying as it always had been. Taking a couple more deep drags in quick succession, his head swam from the nicotine rush.

He frowned deeply. After a few hours had passed this afternoon, he'd called home, making out he was calling to check his mother was alright, rather than to ask the only question banging around his head: *Had Teagan returned?*

Thankfully, the question had been answered without him having to ask. *And the answer was no. Still no sign of Teagan.*

No message. No phone call. Nothing.

Promising he'd be home within a couple of hours, Robert had returned to staring at his computer, pretending to study the rows of code, but there was a niggling worry that wouldn't go away. Would Teagan really have just upped and left without a word? Even if she'd been angry enough to react like that last night, surely she would have been in contact by now? If not with him, then with Dulcie? He knew how much Teagan cared for his mother, so her lack of contact made no sense.

Robert impotently toyed with what to do. Finally resigned to making the call, he slapped the button for the glove box and retrieved Teagan's phone.

Two texts.

Heart picking up the beat, he unlocked the phone, grateful Teagan was so trusting she'd felt no need to password it:

> `How are you doing? Give me a call sometime. Joe xx`

Robert frowned. *Who was Joe? Another boyfriend?* Irritated, he moved onto the next text, his skin bristling seeing it was from Darren Harding:

> `Great to see you. Call me xxx`

He glanced at the time the message had been sent. 9.18am. If Teagan had spent the night with the man, had he sent that after she'd left?

Robert frowned. Hang on. If she'd been at Darren's and left before 9.18 this morning, then surely she'd have been back *hours* ago?

He glanced at his dashboard clock. *Almost 6pm.*

Unease glimmering, Robert pressed the call button, waiting impatiently as it rang out. He would have to play this carefully.

'Teag!' Heath said. 'Great to hear from you!'

'It's Robert Adams.' Robert said, his voice clipped, already aggravated by the sound of the man's voice.

There was a pause. 'Oh, erm... Mr Adams. Is everything ok?'

Robert clenched his jaw, immediately wanting to punch the man in the face. Of course everything wasn't ok. Would he really be phoning up otherwise? 'I'm... erm... I'm just wondering if you've seen Teagan today? She's left her phone and it's late wi...'

'Today?' Heath interrupted. 'No, I haven't seen her since the funeral when she left with you. Did she say she was coming to see me?'

'No, she didn't,' Robert said hastily. 'I think my mother must be confused with what was said. Sorry to have bothered you.'

Hanging up, Robert stared at the mobile. How he resented apologising to that smarmy bastard. There was something really not right with that man and he wished he could put his finger on it. Throwing the phone on the passenger seat, he lit another cigarette, slowly blowing the smoke out so it plumed across his windscreen.

So Teagan hadn't spent the night with Darren Harding? The man had been genuinely surprised. But if she hadn't spent the night with Darren Harding, then where had she gone?

Wait a minute...

Robert's face screwed up in concentration as he recalled Darren Harding's exact words. Hadn't he just said, *'I haven't seen her since the funeral when she left with you'*?

Teagan hadn't left with him. She'd stormed off *from* him.

Robert bit the inside of his cheek. Who the bloody hell had she left with then?

• • • •

JOE SHOVED HIS PHONE BACK in his jeans and picked his pint back up. He took a long swig, disappointed to see that he'd almost finished. He glanced at his housemate. Down to his last quid, he hoped Dave would shout him a few more beers.

'Everything alright?' Dave asked.

Joe nodded. 'Yeah, everything's fine.' *But was it?* He turned his cigarette packet around on the sticky pub table.

When Teagan's name flashed up on his phone half an hour ago, his heart had sunk. He hadn't spoken to her since Alan's funeral last week and had to admit he'd been quite glad about that - it was less hassle. Plus, since he'd called that nutter to give him the info, he hadn't heard anything more, meaning he'd dared to believe things might finally be over where that lot was concerned, but now he wasn't so sure.

That bloke – Robert Adams, the one who had just called, sounded less than happy. And why had he been using Teagan's phone? He'd asked of course, but the man was gruff, almost rude - extremely reticent to give anything away.

Nodding in appreciation when Dave signalled to his empty pint glass, Joe watched Dave make his way to the bar for refills.

But why would Robert Adams call to ask if he'd seen Teagan? Joe frowned. Like he'd said to Robert, as far as he knew she was staying at his flat? When he'd asked if that wasn't the case, the man had blatantly ignored his question. *Rude fucker*.

Teagan hadn't been exaggerating when she'd said the man was a miserable bastard. But if she wasn't with that old bat, Dulcie and wasn't at the flat, combined with that miserable fucker phoning round contacts from her phone, then it looked like something had happened.

Needles of wariness prickled up Joe's spine. This wasn't anything to do with him, was it? Had that Robert bloke discovered he'd pinched Teagan's keys for Footlights or had the police discovered he was the link to letting those psychos in?

The reasoning behind Teagan's disappearance only really bothered him when Robert Adams asked for the second time if he was at the wake yesterday. For a start, Joe hadn't even known there was a wake yesterday, but when the man said it was his sister's wake and asked if he'd met Teagan at the hotel, had alarm bells began clanging.

With a pounding heart, Joe glanced at the bar in the search for his top-up, seeing Dave three deep in the queue and huffed impatiently. For fuck's sake. It wasn't even 6.30 and the place was rammed. It would be yonks before he got served and he was gagging for another drink.

Stubbing his fag out in the chipped ashtray, Joe wracked his brains for everything he'd said to the nutter. From what he could remember, which wasn't too clear being as he'd had a skinful the night in question, there hadn't been a lot to say.

All Teagan had said and all he'd repeated was that her and the old bat were staying at the son's place and they didn't know when or if they'd be returning to Footlights. That was it, so what was the big deal? Fuck all, that's what. And no, he hadn't been hanging around some strange hotel. What sort of tosspot did this Robert Adams take him for?

Wait! He'd also said something else on. What was it? Joe frowned, his brain hurting. That was it. Teagan had mentioned something about the old boot giving her a box. He'd thought it strange because she hadn't wanted the cops to find it. Something about Robert having a different father to the other kid.

Joe sparked up another cigarette. Yeah, that was it. The box contained something of Robert's real father and he'd been amazed Teagan hadn't looked in the stupid thing to see what it contained, he knew he would have.

He rolled his eyes. And all she'd banged on about was not wanting to break the old witch's trust. Well, fuck that! He'd have looked. Teagan was far too soppy for her own good.

Joe glanced towards the bar again, pleased to see Dave getting served. *At last.* His mouth salivated with the prospect of a fresh beer and sat back happily. That was until cold dread swamped him.

Had he told the nutter about the box? He closed his eyes to recall the conversation word for word. *Shit, he had - he knew he had.* He hadn't thought much of it at the time, but now…

The clear memory of what those blokes had said when they'd bashed their way into the house terrifying the lives of him, Dave and Alan, leapt into his mind. They'd said the old woman was in the possession of something of theirs that they wanted back. Had what he said given those blokes the impression that *Teagan* had what they been after? *Fuck.*

Sweat broke out on Joe's back. He could already feel his T-shirt sticking clammily to his skin.

'Here you go.' Dave deposited two fresh pints on the rickety table. 'What's the matter with you? You've gone a funny colour.'

'Just gagging for another drink,' Joe muttered, reaching for his pint.

Dave laughed. 'Jeez, if you're at the point where you're withdrawing after five bloody minutes without a beer, then you've got some serious problems, mate!'

Joe slurped at his new pint. *Serious problems?* That could be likely, but how the hell did he find out without dropping himself in the shit?

TWENTY SIX

DULCIE HAD WAITED all morning, plus the afternoon and Teagan *still* hadn't shown her two-faced self and she wasn't waiting any longer.

She tugged viciously at yet another drawer in Teagan's cupboard, impatiently shovelling her way through the contents. Picking up handfuls of clothes, she dumped the items on the bed, shaking each one out just in case the box was cunningly concealed within one of the neatly folded tops.

Her anger increased, adrenaline pounding as she fruitlessly tossed each item to one side. It was plain to see how, make no mistake about it, the double-crossing little mare had done a runner.

Dulcie bit back the tears of frustration. She might have known the only person she could ever trust was herself.

Hadn't she learnt that enough over the course of her life? Look what had happened to her Michael. He'd only ever worked his backside off for those Powell bastards. They *owed* him those jewels and yet they'd killed him for taking what was rightfully his. Disgusting, greedy bastards the whole lot of them. *And as for Teagan…*

Dulcie's eyes darted around the room. Where else would

the conniving little cow think to stash the box? It had to be in here somewhere?

She should have shot Teagan the same night she'd shot Helen. And she would have, had she thought something like this was on the cards.

Dulcie scowled, her face becoming ugly and twisted as she snarled in pure rage. She'd genuinely believed the girl to be pliable and deemed her perfect for coaxing Helen into the trap she'd waited so very long to spring. And Teagan had helped immensely.

Dulcie sighed heavily, her breath ragged. By being so involved with how things unfurled with her darling daughter, Dulcie knew she'd taken her eyes off the ball with Teagan and missed what was under her nose all along. The girl had her own bloody agenda. *Everyone always did.*

As she rummaged under the bed, such was her annoyance with both herself and her rage, she didn't notice the front door shutting.

Dulcie pulled at Teagan's suitcase, fumbling to unzip it, her hands shaking. Yanking open the main compartment, she stared at an old receipt – the only thing there. She opened the compartment in the vinyl lid and shoved her arm deep inside to feel around. *Nothing.*

She was just about to sling the whole thing back under the bed, when a small pouch-like section in the wall of the case caught her eye. Putting her hand in for good measure, she felt around. *There was something there. It was hard. Was this it?*

Heart pounding, Dulcie pulled out the object, relief flooding over her like a waterfall. *Thank God for that.*

She shook the box gently. What if Teagan had opened it and taken the contents? Had she thought about *that*?

She shook it again, pointless really, being as it was impossible to tell whether it was empty or not. The small box was fashioned from thick wood and the diamonds were carefully wrapped in strips of material, so it wasn't like they'd be jangling about. They must still be in there. *They had to be.*

She was the only one with a key and the box nor the lock was damaged.

Dulcie smiled. Grabbing the bed frame, she pulled herself from her aching knees to her feet and shoved the box into her cardigan pocket. She wasn't leaving anything to chance now and would keep hold of this, regardless of whether the Powells or Pointers were on her tail. She'd find somewhere else to place it. Somewhere where no one except *her* could get their hands on it.

'What are you doing?'

Dulcie swung around in shock to find Robert standing in the doorway of Teagan's bedroom.

'I said, what are you doing, mother?' Robert repeated, his eyes full of suspicion.

• • • •

'I HAVEN'T SEEN EITHER OF THEM,' Nero insisted. 'What's the issue?'

Jonah scowled. Saul and Keith disappearing was becoming a frequent occurrence. Aside from his disrespectful play for Lena, he didn't trust what his brother was planning with the business either.

Both enforcement teams were busy and things *seemed* to be running to plan, but in real terms that meant little. Saul and Keith were rarely on site and that only caused Jonah to wonder exactly what they were up to. Saul hadn't even mentioned Dulcie Adams for a few days either and that alone set off alarm bells. Saul setting up new arrangements behind his back wasn't part of the deal. Everything apart from the enforcement and the show side of things should be agreed by both of them and even then, out of courtesy, expecting updates wasn't unreasonable, but he'd had no updates from anyone – including Keith.

Lena dropping it on him last night that she'd got the wedding brought forward was a shock too. He knew she'd wanted it sooner, but what was the issue? As far as he was concerned, she was already visibly pregnant, so what difference did a few more weeks make?

It had made all the difference to Lena as she'd been overjoyed by the date change. From his side, now he'd resigned himself to marrying the woman and being able to physically see *why*, the prospect wasn't quite as offensive as it had been, so realistically, the date change didn't matter. If it made Lena happy, then fine, but he could do without this extra distrust between him and Saul.

Jonah looked back at Nero. 'When was the last time you saw them?'

'I saw Keith this morning, but I haven't seen Saul since, oh it must have been the day we had the West Ham function.' Nero glanced up at the ceiling to kick start his memory. 'Yes, it was because I remember thinking I hoped they didn't drink all the champagne before the thing started!'

'Keith and Saul were drinking champagne?' Jonah frowned. Keith hated champagne and he knew for a fact his brother wasn't a fan either.

'Nah.' Nero shook his head animatedly. 'Lena and Saul.'

Jonah stiffened. Wasn't that when Lena said Saul had tried it on? He'd broach this carefully, reluctant to let Nero know how much of a mess things were with his family. 'What was Saul doing in the VIP suite?'

Nero shrugged. 'Lena was checking the stock and Saul wandered in and poured them both champagne.'

Jonah forced himself to laugh. 'Drinking the club champagne, eh?'

Nero laughed too. 'Lena looked like all her Christmases had come at once! She loves her champagne, that one.' Seeing Jonah's face cloud, he realised in hindsight that he probably shouldn't have said that. He kept forgetting Lena's new standing as Jonah's fiancée. 'Sorry, I…'

'It's not a problem,' Jonah lied. So Lena had been chugging the champagne? 'I hope they didn't leave stocks short for the function?' *Come on Nero, what happened. Did you see anything?*

'I was checking the security barrier at the top of the stairs, so I doubt they even noticed me. Saul didn't hang around long anyhow,' he grinned. 'I think your Lena scared him off!'

A nerve twitched in Jonah's neck. 'Scared him off?'

Nero laughed heartily. 'Oh, you know what she's like – ever the showgirl. Saul couldn't get out of there fast enough when she all but shoved her cleavage in his face!'

'She did *what*?'

'That didn't come out quite right,' Nero countered. 'I didn't mean she got her tits out or anything like that, but… that top she had on… well, she kept leaning over and your brother was directly in line!'

Anger travelled up Jonah's arms to pound relentlessly in his chest. 'Did he touch her?'

Nero raised his eyebrows. 'Touch her? No? Why would he have done that? They were just chatting.' Creeping dread that he'd inadvertently started something became apparent. 'What's happened?'

Jonah shook his head, his jaw tightly clenched. 'Nothing.' *And that was the crux of it. Nothing had happened, so why the fuck had Lena made out otherwise?* His jaw tightened further. Was this another one of her games?

'Shit, I can tell by your face that I've said something out of turn. I didn't mean to insinuate that Lena was…'

'You haven't,' Jonah held his hand up and looked at Nero. 'I'm just on edge. First time fatherhood and all that.' He had to explain his questions before the whole firm got wind there was bad blood between him and Saul. And it wouldn't be long before everyone knew about the baby just by looking at Lena.

Nero's eyes widened. Standing up, he masked his shock by extending his hand and shaking Jonah's heartily. 'Congratulations. I didn't realise.' He eyed Jonah cautiously, the strain behind the man's eyes clear. Now he really was roped to that woman for all eternity.

Jonah forced his face into a smile. 'Thanks. It's a new thing for me, but it's not common knowledge, so I'd appreciate it if...'

'I won't say a word,' Nero said, watching Jonah pour two shots of whisky.

Facing away, Jonah closed his eyes in utter frustration. Why was Lena trying to drive a wedge between him and Saul? Wasn't there a big enough one there already? Turning around, he handed a whisky to Nero. 'There's something I want you to do.'

Taking the glass, Nero leaned forwards. 'Whatever you need.'

'I want you to find out where Keith and Saul are going. They're absent a lot and I need to know why.'

Nero nodded slowly. 'You think there's a problem?'

'I don't know, but I need to find out,' Jonah sighed, sitting down heavily. 'You remember last time it was discussed and Saul was supposed to be getting info as to whether anything's still being dug into with Dulcie Adams before we move forward? Well I've heard nothing.'

Nero frowned. 'You think he's acting alone?'

'I fucking hope not, but I guess that's what I'm thinking.'

Twenty Seven

ROBERT STARED AT THE CONTENTS of the wooden box, barely able to believe what he was seeing and even less able to get his head around what his mother was saying. 'But you haven't explained how you happen to be in possession of *these*.' His eyes tracked back to the collection of jewels that his mother had unwrapped. Now, he was no jeweller, but he had a fair idea these were worth a substantial amount of money.

'I've already told you these belonged to your father. He gave them to me to keep for when he returned but…' Dulcie looked down sadly. 'As you already know, he didn't return...'

Robert's eyes remained locked on the sparkling jewels. 'Yes, but where did *he* get them from? What are they anyway?' He knew exactly what they were, but wanted to see how much of a fool his mother took him for and exactly how far she was prepared to go to evade the truth.

'I don't know where Michael got them. That wasn't the kind of thing you asked a man back in those days. As for what they are, looking at the colour, rubies perhaps?' she lied.

Robert's eyes narrowed. *Rubies, my arse. They are pink diamonds and worth a fucking fortune.* 'Are they stolen?'

Dulcie adopted a horrified expression. 'Stolen? No!

Michael wasn't like that!' Robert wouldn't understand Michael's work. He was a shielded and sensible boy - he always had been, she'd made sure of that. He didn't need to know the ins and outs of what had gone on back in the day. Besides, she didn't know all of the details surrounding the diamonds and had never asked. There was more to be gained by acting dumb and she didn't want Robert going holier than thou on her. *Time to change the subject into something a lot more beneficial.*

Dulcie sniffed loudly, furiously dabbing at her eyes with her handkerchief. 'Your father entrusted these to me for our and, of course, *your*, future. The night he gave these to me was the last time I ever saw him and are the only things I have left.' She squeezed Robert's knee. 'Apart from you of course. You're the most priceless thing he could have *ever* left me, but now I hope you can understand why these mean so much and why I was looking through Teagan's room. I... I guess I wanted to prove myself wrong and that she hadn't taken them.'

Inwardly, Dulcie was disappointed she'd had to show Robert the diamonds. It wasn't supposed to be like this – she'd got it all planned when to reveal their nest egg and it wasn't now, but now he'd caught her red-handed it was the only available option. What she hadn't expected was to have to use Teagan as a scapegoat. That *really* messed up her plans. It also contradicted everything she'd said so far about the girl. *Damn and blast it.* Still, she'd just have to make it convincing. At least it solved the problem of Robert wanting anything to do with the woman and she could keep him for herself – the way it was always supposed to be.

Dulcie frowned. Losing Teagan also meant she'd lost the inroad to Darren Harding. She'd just have to think of something else. A pain the in the neck, but the lesser of two evils.

Realising Robert still hadn't spoken, Dulcie upped the angst. 'I'd hoped my imagination was running away with me. I-I'd ignored the things I'd seen before because I didn't want to accept they were true.'

Robert pushed his frozen voice box into life. 'What things?'

Dulcie conjured a loud sob from the back of her throat. 'Being here on my own all day gave me a lot of time to think. I-I was thinking of possible reasons for Teagan abandoning me and the more I thought about it, the more I remembered things which have been fuzzy because of those awful pills Helen gave me.' *Yes, get a dig in about Helen and one to Robert for leaving her alone. That would play on his mind and keep him closer.*

Robert stared at the box in his mother's hand, wishing she'd get to the point. 'Go on...'

Dulcie blew her nose and snuffled miserably. 'Several times I caught Teagan going into the pink bedroom at Footlights – you know, the one I didn't like anyone in? She knew the room was out of bounds but went in when she thought I was asleep.' She clutched Robert's arm. 'One time I even caught her pocketing a silver trinket box!'

Dulcie flapped her hand, glad to see by Robert's face that her words were hitting home. 'She denied it, of course – and acted most upset to be accused of stealing. She claimed she was picking it up off the floor, blaming me for knocking it off during one of my night terrors. A likely story, I realise that now, but at the time I was so confused because of those drugs...'

Robert didn't pull away from his mother as she latched onto him. He wanted to, but also wanted to hear everything she'd got to say.

'There was a few more times – something and nothing then, but now... now it all makes sense...' Dulcie paused for effect. 'Things in the sitting room went missing. Only small things, but I knew she'd taken them. I guess I didn't want to believe it even though it was obvious. I dearly loved that girl.' She began crying again. 'I'm broken hearted and feel so, *so* betrayed. What a stupid old fool I am.'

'No you're not,' Robert said. 'She fooled us all.' He knew that was what his mother wanted him to say, so he'd said it, but he didn't believe it. He didn't believe a word of it. 'The thing I don't understand is if you believed Teagan was stealing from you, then why you didn't say anything?'

'I did!' Dulcie exclaimed. 'I told Helen, but she accused me of imagining it. I know now that was part of her plan to make me believe I was going insane – or maybe she genuinely didn't believe it was true?'

Robert sighed. Teagan had told him about a box she'd been given for safe-keeping. Why would she tell him if she'd been planning to steal it? His brow furrowed. It was possible, but unlikely. Still, he'd play the game.

'Oh God, I was so stupid to tell Teagan about the box!' Dulcie sobbed. 'She could have stolen *everything*!'

'But she didn't, so it doesn't make sense.'

Dulcie bit her lip. *No it didn't, did it? Quick, think of something.* 'She must have been planning on taking it, otherwise it wouldn't have been stashed in her suitcase, don't you see? Oh Robert, when things started going round my mind earlier, I went to check the box was still in my bedroom where I put it. I felt guilty for even *thinking* about suspecting her. I thought the world of Teagan and now…'

'Right, then and…?' Robert's impatience bubbled. This was not right. This was not how it was. His mother had given the box to Teagan to look after. She was lying again…

'My worst fears were realised when it wasn't in my room.' Dulcie waved her hands in the air. 'I knew then that she'd taken it and planned to steal it. Even then I sat for another hour before I could face proving myself right. And that's when *you* came back, just as I found it. I still can't believe it!'

'It still doesn't explain why she hasn't taken it with her,' Robert mumbled.

Dulcie's eyes narrowed. 'She must be planning on returning for it. She must still be with her boyfriend.'

Robert nodded. 'Yes, I guess you must be right.' Except Teagan wasn't with her *boyfriend*, as his mother succinctly put it. Neither had she taken any of her clothes. Teagan hadn't planned on doing a bunk at all and according to the 'boyfriend', she'd left the wake with a man…

Despite his dislike of the man, Robert believed that Darren

hadn't seen her since the funeral. But what he *didn't* believe was that Darren knew Teagan beforehand. Since the man's uncertainty at the funeral as to where he's been to school – the school Teagan had attended, Robert had done his own digging. He wasn't a computer expert for nothing and quickly discovered that no one with the name 'Darren Harding' had *ever* been to Teagan's school.

Why the man had lied was a mystery. Was Darren Harding some kind of con-man? 'We should call the police.'

'Oh no, Robert! *Please* don't do that! I can't bear those people all over the place again. Is it not bad enough that I've had weeks of that already because of Helen? I just want to get back to normal.'

'But if Teagan has done what you say, then you should press charges,' Robert snarled. His mother was lying. Like it seemed she always did.

Dulcie clutched the box tightly to her chest. 'She hasn't stolen this, thank God and that's the main thing, but I don't want her back in our lives.' She looked up at her son, mistaking his grave expression as wrath for Teagan. 'Please tell me you won't allow her back into our lives. I've been let down enough and I can't take any more.'

'Don't worry. I'll deal with it,' Robert muttered, his mind whirring, unsure where even to start.

Teagan was in trouble and he had the creeping suspicion that his mother was something to do with it. He was worried. *Very* worried. He would need to find out where Teagan was and quickly because he had to know if she was the one to make him feel for real or whether what he'd experienced was a one-off fluke. If it was still present, then it was his to have.

TWENTY EIGHT

JOE STARED AT THE PLATE IN FRONT OF HIM. He couldn't recall making a fried egg sandwich, but he must have.

Lifting the top slice of bread, he poked the egg with his finger. His face screwed up. *Was he losing the plot?* Had he got to the point where he was so derelict to have no idea what he was doing? He couldn't cope with going la-la on top of everything else. Or was his mind so taken up with other things that he was wandering around on auto-pilot? He suspected it to be the latter, but even so, didn't like it.

Joe continued staring at the sandwich. It wasn't like he was going to eat it. He felt too sick to even think about putting that in his mouth. The image of the greasy egg going round; bits sticking to the roof of his mouth caused his stomach to roll disturbingly.

Walking into the small kitchen, Dave eyed Joe as he pushed the plate across the table as far away as possible. 'Not eating that?' When Joe shook his head, Dave grinned. 'I'll have it then!' Picking up the sandwich, he hurriedly stuffed it into his mouth.

Joe watched a gloop of brown sauce slide out of Dave's mouth and quicky looked away, his guts churning. He couldn't remember putting brown sauce on it either…

Dave sat down, the contents of his mouth visible as he spoke. 'What's the matter?' Getting no response, he wiped the sauce off his chin with the back of his hand. 'Oih! I'm talking to you! Why are you sitting there like a space cadet? You haven't been on the weed already, have you?'

Joe shook his head. 'No.' At least he didn't think so, but then again, he couldn't remember getting up either. Either way, it wasn't a bad idea. He could do with something to shut his head off.

'Then what the bloody hell is wrong with you?'

Joe shrugged. 'I didn't get much sleep.' That was rather an understatement. In reality, he didn't think he'd had *any*.

'I'd have thought you'd have slept like a log. We put a fair few away last night.' Picking up the second half of the sandwich, Dave added a liberal helping of salt over the remaining part of the frazzled egg. He studied Joe suspiciously. 'You were acting strangely yesterday as well.'

Joe sighed. The last thing he needed was Dave interrogating him. It wasn't like he could say what was on his mind considering he hadn't been honest about anything for some time. 'I'm fine.'

Dave's eyes narrowed. 'You haven't had any more grief off those psychos, have you? You said all of that was sorted out.'

'Of course I haven't,' Joe snapped. Well, it was true. He hadn't heard anything since he'd reported back to the nutter after the funeral. Such was his paranoia he'd even checked the burner phone first thing - that he *did* remember and there were no missed calls, texts or voicemails, so why did he have the growing suspicion that Teagan's disappearance was linked to them?

He'd been up all night talking himself into the disappearance being coincidence - just happening to occur after he'd given out the info about her having a box belonging to Dulcie Adams. *Dulcie Adams* – the name of that woman made him cringe. Was she set to haunt him for evermore?

Yes, he'd tried his very best to talk himself out of a connection, but it hadn't worked. No matter how many different slants he put on it, he kept coming back in a circle, the nigging suspicion of a link morphing into a clanging alarm.

The fundamental problem was, amongst everything else he'd done that he wasn't particularly comfortable with and although Teagan was a pain in the arse and a month ago he'd have been pleased if she'd disappeared off the face of the planet, since Alan's death and since, well... *everything*, he didn't want anything to happen to her. But whichever way he looked at it, he couldn't shift the horrible thought that something *had* happened to her and that *he* was partly responsible for it.

And he didn't know what to do about that.

Joe scowled. There was only one thing *to* do about it, but it he didn't want to get involved. He wanted it all to be over, full stop. That was the plan in the first place, was it not? The whole point of ditching Teagan was to get his life back, but since he'd done that, his life had literally become hideous.

Sighing resignedly, he too got up, knowing what he was going to have to do. But he was having a couple of drinks first.

• • • •

ANOTHER NIGHT WITH LITTLE SLEEP left Robert both exhausted and irritable. He stood outside Footlights and stared up at the imposing property. *Did he really want to go in here again?*

No, he didn't, but he didn't want to stay in the flat either. Something was really not sitting well about all of this. His mother's revelation last night had done nothing to assuage his fears. As much as he struggled with the stark contrast of how much his opinion of her had changed in the last couple of days, nothing was much worse than realising every new thing coming to light only gave more reason to distrust every single thing that came out of her mouth.

No matter how many different ways he slotted the pieces together, stuff did not fit together at all.

Robert stared at the lit cigarette in his hand, his mind quickly returning to what his mother had in her possession. *Those diamonds.*

He frowned. She had not been overly forthcoming when it came to explaining why she had them, where they had come from and why his father had given them to her. Was it to do with any of those 'big jobs' she'd referred to in that notebook?

He felt quite sick. The diamonds were stolen, but from where?

Resentment grew. His mother was hiding something big. This theory would also explain why she didn't want the police involved. After keeping the identity of his real father a secret for so long, she still wasn't being straight. Pinning it on Teagan made things even less palatable.

Robert pulled Teagan's phone from his jacket and sighed. No missed calls. *Two days and still no word.*

Letting himself into Footlights, Robert walked into the sitting room and looked around, not wanting to remain in this house any longer than necessary.

Grabbing the wastepaper basket, Robert carried it towards the kitchen to empty it, when he stopped dead.

That night… that night he'd discovered about Michael Pointer, was the night Teagan had mentioned the box; he remembered now. But she'd said something else…

Dumping the bin in the corner, Robert ripped off his jacket and slung it on the kitchen table.

Thundering up the staircase, his mind raced. Teagan said his mother kept the box under the floorboards in the bedroom. Had she put anything else there? Something that might still be there?

• • • •

TEAGAN FELT DREADFUL. She retched violently into a bucket at the side of the bed, her head pounding. She desperately needed a drink, her mouth parched. Racked with pain, she was unable to stop her body from shaking, the continuous trembling making the bleeding sores on her chafed wrists weep.

Her mind rolled through a constant state of mist, blurred with red hot pain and confusion, her thoughts looping, unable to separate what was reality and what was not; shadows and shapes looming menacingly behind her closed eyelids.

Hearing what she thought could be movement, she stiffened, before realising she had probably imagined it. Was she imagining everything? Where had her life gone? What had it been like before? She had no recollection.

'You awake? It's the afternoon already.'

The deep growling voice made Teagan wince. She recognised that voice. She'd heard it several times. It might have been twice, three times, four, ten? She had no means of knowing how long she'd been lying here listening to that voice and her mind rolled again, the process of thinking causing physical pain.

Saul sat on the end of the bed, staring contemptuously at the half-full bucket, along with dried piles of vomit on the carpet which had clearly missed its intended target. He watched with satisfaction as the girl brought her knees up to her chest, her face contorting with pain. *She was progressing nicely.*

Keeping levels topped up for a couple of days, then cutting the supply off usually gave a good indication as to what extent the body had attached itself and how susceptible a person was. Something else he'd learnt spending time at Her Majesty's Pleasure. From what he was seeing, this one had already become nicely attached.

Waiting until the girl's cramps passed, Saul ran his thick fingers between her breasts and down along her stomach. Playing games were so much easier when he didn't have to mess about with clothes. She didn't need them and was so out of it she hadn't even noticed them being removed the other day.

Teagan's mind fluttered, the fingers tracing over her skin like hot needles. She was so thirsty, so, *so* thirsty, but her head hurt too much to speak. She couldn't remember how to speak.

She just needed... needed...

Feeling fingers push inside her, Teagan yelped, still unable to warrant the energy to open her eyes. *Who was she with? Where was she?*

Her temples pounded, her stomach crunching again as another cramp gained pace. Hearing the sound of a zip being undone, Teagan rolled into a lucid moment. *This was that man. The man who'd...*

Bucking away from the exploring hands, Teagan gasped for breath, panic forcing her one working eye open, the sudden blinding illumination of the overhead light scorching her retina. 'No please...' she croaked, fresh waves of pain crashing over her.

'Need some medicine, girl?' Saul growled, pumping his hand down his rock hard erection. Pulling Teagan's head back by her hair with his other hand, he smiled. 'You'll get some as soon as you've made me feel better. We do things for each other, sweetheart, remember? Now open wide.'

Teagan gagged as Saul shoved himself deep into her mouth, her nerve endings crying out in agony from the combined movement of her gag reflex.

'Now, no biting,' Saul warned. 'Or you'll get nothing!'

Tears rolled down Teagan's face but she wasn't sure why she was crying. She couldn't remember. *What was wrong with her?* Nothing made sense.

Suddenly feeling the cold rush as the medicine she so desperately craved flooded into her veins, she relaxed. She was no longer thirsty and even whatever was pushing against the back of her throat didn't bother her anymore.

Twenty Nine

WALKING INTO HIS MOTHER'S BEDROOM, Robert realised it appeared like nothing had been touched. The matching silver comb, hairbrush and hand-held mirror were placed neatly on the dressing table, along with elegant bottles of perfume and a few bits of makeup; a can of hairspray and a large fluffy powder puff sitting on the top of a glass jar. His mother's dressing gown hung on the back of the wardrobe door and all the things that had been here since he could remember were still in place. It was like the room that time forgot.

Although she'd brought a good amount of things with her to his flat, it was difficult to see what, looking at the contents left in this room.

He stared at the thickly carpeted floor and confusion spread. Teagan said the box was hidden underneath the floorboards. How could something be kept under the floorboards if the room was carpeted?

Wait! The *pink* bedroom. Even his mother had mentioned that was where she'd seen Teagan snooping around.

Rushing from the room, Robert made his way along the landing and stood outside the room where Helen was shot; the room which had been thoroughly turned over and the truth rapidly dawned.

The people that had shot Helen hadn't been something to do with her – they'd been looking for the diamonds! Someone had come to Footlights that night to retrieve those jewels?

Even if he hadn't been so completely lost in his thoughts, there were too many thick walls between the pink bedroom and the kitchen to hear Teagan's phone ringing in the pocket of his jacket on the kitchen table and the back of Robert's neck became clammy with sweat as he pushed open the bedroom door. His mother had said Helen had found out about Michael Pointer, so was it possible that she also knew about the diamonds? Had it been *her* who had turned over the room in search of them?

But if it was Helen who had been after them, then who was the man? Someone Helen had told about the diamonds killed her when he couldn't find them? *Which?*

Sweat now beaded over Robert's forehead as 1001 possible scenarios ran through his brain. His eyes skirted around the floor. It was floorboarded. He peered at the varnished Victorian boards, unable to see an area which looked like it might lift up.

His mind tracked back to when he'd cleaned the bedroom after the police had finished their investigations. After scrubbing the bloodstains away and removing the splatters off the walls, it had taken *hours* putting the clothes and scattered items back in the wardrobe and drawers. Placing the rug back along the side of the bed…

The rug...

Darting around to the far side of the bed, Robert got down on his hands and knees and rolled the rug up to one end. He stared at the floorboards, feverishly looking for any trace that one of them may lift.

There it was. A slight indentation along the edge of a board. Twisting around, he glanced at the dressing table for something to prise at the floorboard. Remembering the Swiss Army knife he always kept in his pocket, Robert pulled out the largest blade and slotted it into the crack with the slightly bigger gap than the others. Heart racing, he applied pressure.

It was only then he noticed the nails in this particular board were missing. Using the blade as leverage, he pressed on the back of the floorboard and it raised up with surprisingly minimal effort.

Remaining motionless with the floorboard hinged like the lid of a tin, Robert questioned what he was expecting to find? In his mother's eyes, the most important things to keep safe all of these years were in that little wooden box, which was in his flat. There was no logical reason why he was hell bent on looking in here. All he knew was that he was drawn to it. A really strong hunch.

Fully bracing himself to find an empty space, Robert lifted the board out of position and peered into the hole. It was a lot deeper than he'd expected and looked pretty much as he'd expected. *Empty.*

Or was that something at the bottom?

Reaching across for the bedside lamp, he turned it on its side and aimed the dim illumination down into the hole.

It was another box...

Reaching in, Robert pulled out the box. Whatever was in it was fairly heavy.

Gingerly opening the box, he frowned at the contents wrapped in a towel. Lying the towel on the floor, he unwrapped it, blinking several times before hesitatingly picking up the gun. By the looks of it, it was old. Not that he was by any means an expert.

Checking the safety catch, he flipped open the barrel and checked the chamber. *Shit. It was loaded.* But there was one bullet missing.

Feeling fear ripple, Robert stared at the gun more closely. As said, he was no expert, but by the traces of residue on the barrel, he'd warrant this gun had been fired. And *recently.*

Gingerly, he lifted the gun to his nose and smelt the very faint scent of sulphur and oil. Yes, the gun had been fired relatively recently.

Carefully putting it back on the towel, he leant back against the side of the bed and closed his eyes, his breath ragged. He didn't have a clue who the man present that night Helen died, but he was fairly certain it wasn't the person who had fired the gun.

Sweat poured off Robert's brow. *That man hadn't killed Helen, his mother had.*

THIRTY

KEITH LET HIMSELF INTO THE FLAT with the key Saul had given him. He wandered into the kitchen and plonked himself down at the small table, eagerly pulling the packet of sandwiches from his pocket.

It was almost 3pm and he hadn't even had any lunch. *No wonder he was fucking starving.*

He picked at the heat-sealed cellophane, the fact that sandwich packets always required a degree to get inside them never failing to irritate him. Why did they feel the need to seal them so a blow torch was required to get in the bloody things?

Scowling, he slammed the packet down and stretched his bulky frame over to the tiny work surface, just able to reach one of the knives from the small knife block. Impatiently puncturing the cellophane with a satisfying 'pop', Keith dug his finger into the newly made slit and ripped the top off the packet, gratefully pulling out one of the sandwiches.

Taking a large bite, his face screwed up at the half-stale bread, wondering how something more preserved than Michael Jackson could possibly be so rank.

His mouth worked at the chewy bread and whatever it was allegedly supposed to contain, coming to the conclusion that seed bread with its revolting doughy consistency, along with bits of gravel should be banned. Couldn't places use normal fucking bread, rather than weird shit?

What was it even supposed to be? He glanced at the packet. Turkey salad? *Yeah, right.*

Pulling apart the sandwich in his large hand, he scowled at the single anorexic strip of turkey, three limp shreds of lettuce and a slice of tomato that not only looked like it had been cut by one of those machines used for making wafer-thin cross-sections for microscope slides, it also had a distinctly green tinge to it. Or was it cucumber?

Shrugging, Keith shoved the remains into his mouth. However pointless and revolting it was, he was so famished, his stomach was convinced his throat had been cut so he had no choice but to eat it.

He looked at the clock on the wall. Still another half an hour before Saul was due. He could have waited in the car, but what was the point of that when there was a perfectly good flat to sit in? Well, it would be perfectly good if it wasn't for the chick locked in the bedroom.

Personally, he couldn't see the point of hanging on to her. If she hadn't got the gear, then at least put her to good use by taking her back to that Footlights place. The haul must still be within those four walls and being as she'd lived there, she more than anyone should have a good idea of where to look.

Jonah would be the first to admit he'd barely had chance to look anywhere before having to scarper. The police were no longer digging around and the old bag wasn't there, so it was the perfect opportunity, but Saul was adamant that wasn't happening.

Keith's forehead furrowed. Doubts as to the validity of Saul's handling of this crept up on him and he couldn't say he liked himself very much for that. Above all others, he was loyal to Saul, but to question why the man was doing the things he was doing didn't make him feel loyal.

He also felt bad for not including Jonah. After Saul had got banged up Jonah had taken him on, no questions asked. He could have easily been passed over, but that hadn't happened. He'd even been given a shed load more responsibility, but now Saul was back on the scene, he'd all but jumped ship. And in all fairness, that wasn't making him feel great, especially since Saul had now gone down this road.

Finishing the second sandwich, Keith wiped his mouth with the back of his sleeve and stood up. He'd just have a quick piss and check on the girl before Saul arrived.

That was another thing. Saul expected him to do all the shit like emptying slop buckets and that didn't make him happy. He was an enforcer not a carer in some old folks' place. He didn't agree with the girl being held anyway, but maybe that was why Saul had asked him here? Perhaps he'd taken what had been said on board and was letting the girl go?

Hearing noise within the locked bedroom, Keith paused. What was the stupid woman up to? She had no chance of escaping. Even Houdini would struggle to get out of those manacles. Besides, the way Saul had been lacing her up with the brown, he was amazed the poor girl hadn't OD'd, let alone had the energy to move.

He didn't agree with that either, but who was he to argue? Keith's brows knotted. Saul had made it very clear with non-too subtle reminders that *he* was in charge and no one else had the right to an opinion.

Trying the handle on the off chance, Keith was surprised when the door opened, but nowhere near as surprised as to what he saw in front of him.

• • • •

NERO HAD TAKEN A CHANCE parking where he did. Keith could have gone to any of the flats in this block, being as the Powells owned all of them, including the ones not visible from the road, but he'd got lucky. He'd seen exactly which one on the third floor Keith entered.

Admittedly, he hadn't relished the prospect of waiting

whilst Keith got his end away with whichever tom he'd chosen, but at least he could report back to Jonah that Keith wasn't up to anything, apart from being somewhere he should have been on his *own* time, rather than the firm's.

Nero couldn't say the same for Saul though. He had no idea where he was.

He opened the can of Fanta wedged in his drinks holder, wishing it were something stronger and toyed with trying Saul's mobile on the off chance or perhaps even swinging the car around and heading back to the club. There was little point sitting outside whilst Keith poked some hooker, although in retrospect it was best to hang around in case he went on somewhere else afterwards.

He was about to flick through the paper when movement above caught his eye. Looking up, he squinted, seeing Keith leaving the flat, closely followed by Saul. *Saul was in there too?*

Nero watched the two men stride along the walkway towards the stairwell. Although he was a fair distance away, he could still recognise the thunderous look on Keith's face and the equally rabid look on Saul's.

Losing sight of them as they entered the stairwell, Nero shuffled down in the driver's seat even though he'd taken great pains to park nowhere near Keith's car. But where was Saul's? He was pretty certain he'd have spotted a shiny new beamer gleaming like a star amongst the motley collection of motors in this estate. That he *did* know.

Nero clocked Saul and Keith appear from the stairwell, Saul's arms waving around wildly. They were clearly having words. Whatever was going on had undeniably caused friction between the two of them.

As to what that was, he had no idea, but had the sneaking suspicion he would need to find out.

Thirty One

HEATH SAUNTERED UP to the Feathers entrance in his tuxedo, knowing he looked the bee's knees. Although outwardly exuding confidence, inside he was jittering like a bag of leaves.

He was finally going inside the infamous Feathers club. Well-known in its own right for being one of the oldest, most esteemed clubs in Soho, there was also the personal connection from his side. This was the very club his grandfather had worked at and the very same club which was still owned by the family who, according to his sour-faced grandmother, had killed her husband.

Furthermore, if his speculations were correct, somewhere inside here were the jewels that, by rights belonged to his father and so, by proxy, *him*. This was the closest he'd come to getting his hands on them since everything had gone Pete Tong with the Helen Shepherd plan.

Heath took a deep breath as he loped up the gold steps. Flashing his email membership confirmation to the intimidating bouncer, he made his way inside, hoping he hadn't trodden in dog shit, picturing clumps sticking the deep pile burgundy carpet in a trail after him, leaving no question who the culprit was.

He'd have been less self-conscious with a woman accompanying him, but who could he have asked? He'd have asked Teagan if she'd bothered answering his messages, but she was probably getting far too much grief off that miserable bastard, Robert Adams. Still, he was here and the whole point was to get a decent inside look at the place in the hope that it might offer answers or at least hints as to which way to go next.

Heath glanced around the large reception, inwardly applauding the sumptuous décor; massive gold chandeliers oozing class as well as illuminating the lavish gold and burgundy colour scheme and the impressive feathers emblem, resplendent and gleaming on the wall behind the front desk.

He nodded at a couple milling around, glad to see that they too were dressed to the nines; the man in a well-tailored tuxedo and his attractive companion, splendid in a red evening dress.

'Good evening, Sir.'

Following the voice, Heath moved to the reception desk and smiled confidently at the doll-like woman standing motionlessly behind it. He blinked, unsure whether the woman's mouth had actually moved, fleetingly wondering whether she was a mannequin.

Throwing caution to the wind, he kept his smile fixed. 'I'm a new member – Platinum VIP.' He fished in his pocket. 'I have the confirmation here somewhere and…'

'If you take the first staircase on the left Sir, the VIP area is up there,' the woman said, proving that she was a real person after all. 'They'll have your new membership card and be able to show you what's what.'

'Thank you,' Heath nodded, moving in the direction the girl indicated.

Pushing through the double doors, he made his way up a darkened flight of steps, each stair illuminated by neon strip lights; the mirrored walls creating a strange sense of surrealism. The top of the staircase opened into another square lobby, complete with black chaise loungues and a gold and black reception desk - the edges lit with tiny lights.

This really was the business, Heath thought, heading towards a desk manned by a woman with perfectly styled long blonde hair.

Lena eyed the handsome young man, unable to stop herself from drinking in the cut of his tuxedo jacket that emphasised his wide shoulders and narrow waist. She hadn't seen him before, but he looked like he had a few quid to spare. 'Good evening, Sir,' she smiled, exposing her perfect white veneers.

Heath smiled at the overly made-up woman and tried to work out whether her long, thick eyelashes were real or whether they were the stick-on variety. 'Hello there,' he said. 'You'll have to excuse me, I don't know what I'm doing.'

Lena raised an eyebrow. 'That I *very* much doubt.'

Heath's face cracked into his award-winning smile. 'I meant, I'm a new member. Platinum VIP?'

'Ooh!' Lena squealed excitedly, holding out her hand for Heath to shake. 'I'm Lena Taylor, Head of Events and the Manager of the VIP suite. Did you receive an email with your membership details?' She batted her eyelashes, then leant forward, making sure the man got a decent glimpse of her more than ample cleavage.

Feeling unable to draw his eyes away from the stunning blonde's voluptuous bust, Heath reached into his inside pocket for his membership confirmation and handed it over.

Lena kept her long-nailed fingers in contact with the man's just that little bit too long as she took the paperwork, then pulled a small box from under the desk. Flicking through, she retrieved his plastic card. 'Here you are, Mr...' She double-checked the card. '...Pointer. This is your membership card. Go through those double doors on your right and make sure to help yourself to canapes and a complimentary glass of champagne.' She pulled her bright red lips into a smile. 'We have a wonderful show on tonight.'

Heath grinned. 'I'm very much looking forward to it. I think this will be the ideal place to hold future events. I'm a music producer.'

'A music producer? How exciting,' Lena gushed. *Definitely lots of money and influence here.*

'I take it I won't be lucky enough to see you as part of the show?'

Lena laughed, a high pitched tinkly sound, her long talons twiddling one of her long blonde extensions. 'Not these days, although I used to be one of the star acts,' she boasted. 'But there's many beautiful dancers here and I'm sure you won't be disappointed.'

Heath slipped the membership card into his pocket. 'I'm sure I won't be. Not if they look half as good as you.'

Smiling ingratiatingly, Lena glanced around. 'No guest accompanying you tonight, Sir?'

'Please call me Heath,' he said. 'No, unfortunately my date couldn't make it.'

'Oh, what a shame. Well, have a good evening and I'll pop over later to see how you're settling in.'

'Please do,' Heath grinned. 'I'm not a big fan of drinking champagne alone.'

Lena watched Heath strut through the double doors into the VIP suite. If all the new customers the Platinum membership scheme brought in were of *that* vein, she'd be more than happy. She'd make sure she dropped by his table later - she could do with a glass or three of champagne. Everyone knew it paid to mingle with the customers. This one was clearly of good stock, so once she let it be known that she was intricately connected with the club's *owner*, she had the feeling he would be happy to recommend the club to his associates. Being in the music industry, he'd know plenty of famous pop stars and if she could entice him to make a booking *tonight* then that would be something else to rub in Gwen's face.

• • • •

BY THE TIME ROBERT HAD LEFT Footlights he'd been so shell-shocked by his discovery he'd barely been able to remember where he'd parked, let alone anything else.

There was absolutely zilch point approaching his mother about the gun. She hadn't levelled with him about anything and certainly hadn't mentioned she'd shot and killed her own daughter! Neither was she likely to.

He'd been so side-tracked, he almost hasn't bothered checking Teagan's phone, but now he was very glad that he had made the effort to look.

Well, *sort* of. Since returning the missed call and hearing this Joe character say that he thought Teagan may have been taken against her will and that he knew who it might be had caused jangling at the base of his spine.

Robert's teeth clenched. The man's words were bothering him more with every minute that passed. Why the fuck hadn't the man just told him the rest? Why had he insisted on meeting up?

Pulling up outside the Plough and Harrow, Robert yanked on the handbrake and glanced around for anyone who might resemble how this person had described himself. He hoped he wasn't walking into a set-up by some monged-out timewaster.

The bloke on the phone had sounded drunk and he could ill afford having time wasted by a pisshead. His only concern was finding Teagan and that was the singular reason he was giving this Joe person the time of day, but if the man spouted crap, then he'd be sorry.

One thing was for sure and that was his mother was definitely linked to something bad and he had the very real fear that Teagan had been dragged into it.

Robert clenched his fists and rolled his neck in a bid to release the heavily building tension. He'd slam this Joe whateverhisname's teeth down his throat if it turned out he was pissing about, but through the drunkenness, the jittery and worried undertones were obvious during the short, garbed conversation they'd had.

Robert sparked up yet another cigarette and raked his fingers through his hair. Was this something to do with that smarmy bastard, Darren Harding? If it was anything to do with that shit-for-brains, then he'd…

A knocking on his window made Robert swing around in the driver's seat and glare at the dishevelled creature peering through the glass. If this was one of those bloody junkies asking for money… He stabbed his finger on the electric window button, opening it a crack. 'What?'

'R-Robert?' Joe stuttered. 'I'm Joe.'

Robert stared for a moment longer, trying to deduce whether the man was telling the truth. He wasn't anything like he'd expected, but then again, he didn't know *what* he'd expected. Just not *this*. He jerked his head to the passenger side. 'Get in.'

Joe hesitated before moving around the other side of the car. He glanced around several more times before finally getting in. 'Can we drive?'

'Drive?' Robert glanced at Joe. 'Drive where? I just want to know what's going on.'

Joe swallowed nervously. 'I'll tell you everything, I promise, but I can't stay around here. In case… in case they see me.'

Robert fired the engine and slammed the car into gear. 'In case *who* sees you?'

Joe looked out of the window, hunching down to make himself as small as possible. 'Please… just drive…'

Slamming his foot on the accelerator, Robert screeched off. He hadn't got a clue where he was going, but it would be somewhere close by and then this prick could tell him what the hell was happening.

THIRTY TWO

'I'M FINE,' KEITH GROWLED. 'Why wouldn't I be?' He busied himself turning towards the bar, nodding to the barman to pour his usual. He made a point of not looking back at Nero, knowing the man was directly behind him, studying him suspiciously.

Keith had made the conscious decision to go into the main club area of the Feathers rather than an office or the VIP suite like he would normally, purely to avoid being around anyone. He didn't want a conversation - mainly because he was terrified of what he might say. And now Nero had showed up? Nero *never* came into the main club. It was just so typical. Why couldn't he be left alone?

Taking his fresh drink, Keith returned to his table, the one he'd purposefully picked well away from everyone, right at the back and knew Nero would shortly follow him. He didn't want to be followed. He just wanted to be left the hell alone. He *needed* to be left alone because for once in as long as he could remember, if not *ever*, he didn't have a clue what to do about what he'd witnessed. What he'd seen put him in a position he didn't want to be in at all.

Sitting down, Keith took a long slug of his pint and fished

his cigarettes from his pocket, wasting no time in shoving one into his mouth. Realising his fingers were unconsciously rubbing the angry red mark around his neck where Saul had grabbed him, he jerked his hand away. The last thing he wanted was to draw attention to that.

Short of the handful of injuries he'd received on the few occasions where he'd been jumped by a multitude of men, no one ever got the chance to lay a finger on him.

Like most of the Powell firm, Keith was notorious for his speed and viciousness, but this had been Saul and Saul was one step beyond when it came to speed, stealth and mode of attack. Keith had never dreamt that Saul Powell would lay a hand on him, but then neither had he dreamt he'd be faced with what he'd seen tonight. It had thrown everything out of the water, but the question was, what was he going to do about it?

Keith turned his pint around on the table and reflected sadly. Out of all the years he'd known Saul; the situations they'd found themselves in, the beatings they'd doled out, the shit they'd done and the schemes they'd engineered – they'd done it all together.

Like two peas in a pod, everyone always said that they were more like brothers and Keith had always taken that as a compliment – a *massive* compliment. To be classed on the same parallel as the infamous Saul Powell was akin to the highest accolade men like him could have. It was something he'd always been proud of. *Until now.*

Keith might have the same way of thinking where violence and enforcement were concerned and might also like his women on tap, but he was no fucking rapist pervert.

He dragged deeply on his cigarette, blanking one of the dancer's enticing come hither looks. Normally, he'd be on that like a shot, but tonight that prospect was the furthest thing from his mind.

His weather-worn face crumpled into a scowl. Grabbing his drink, he tipped it down his throat. That was the crux of it, wasn't it? Opening that bedroom door he'd seen what Saul was doing. He'd seen it with his own eyes.

Drugging someone up and manacling to them a bed to get them to talk was one thing, but fucking them to ribbons when they were out of it and helpless was not. In the space of a few seconds, everything Keith felt for Saul – the brotherhood, respect and loyalty had been razed to a pile of wood shavings. Regardless of what he wanted or didn't want, he couldn't do anything to backtrack that. And he wanted to backtrack it. In fact, he wanted to delete this evening from his mind like a crap program by taping over it with something else, but he couldn't. He couldn't unsee it.

And all Saul had been bothered about was being interrupted and questioned over his decisions. Exactly what did that say about the man he'd spent so very long idolising.

'Are you going to tell me what's wrong or not?'

Keith's head snapped up, focusing on Nero's all-seeing eyes studying him intently over the table. He hadn't even noticed him sit down. 'There's nothing to say.'

Except there was. There was *plenty* to say, but if he told Nero, then Nero would tell Jonah. Jonah would kill both him and Saul for a) doing stuff behind his back over the Dulcie Adams' business and b) what had been done to the girl. Everyone knew Jonah's values when it came to women and to be fair, Jonah or not, the vast majority of people would also have an issue with what Saul had done.

Keith admitted he hadn't been comfortable with Saul's insistence on getting the girl as hooked on brown as possible, but at a push could see the reasoning behind that, but as for the rest… *No fucking way…*

'I don't know what's happened, but I don't fucking like it!' Nero said, shaking his head in frustration.

Keith watched Nero stalk off and stared at his now empty pint glass. Nero wasn't the only one who didn't like it and he didn't even know what *it* was.

He knew what he *should* do, but could he really betray his most long-standing friend and throw him to the wolves? Could he throw *himself* to the wolves at the same time? Because that's what would happen.

Keith dragged himself back to the bar. He didn't know what he was going to do, but he would have to do something one way or the other.

• • • •

WATCHING THE SHOW, Heath found it refreshing from the previous strip shows he'd seen - and there had been quite a few – mainly in low-end Soho clubs, strippers on stag nights and the slightly different range available in the strip and live sex shows he'd frequented during lads' weekends in Amsterdam.

The show – or cabaret, as they called it at the Feathers, was an altogether different type of performance – a burlesque show; more tantalising than straightforward strip or pole dancing offerings.

Aside from the gorgeous, scantily clad women moving fluidly like mercury on the stage, the whole atmosphere was enjoyable. The immaculately turned-out staff, impeccable table service, luxurious and opulent surroundings and the well-dressed clientele – encompassing an even number of both men and women, made the Feathers more akin to the Moulin Rouge. Not that he'd ever been to the Moulin Rouge, but he'd *heard* about it and seen plenty of photographs. Either way, he was impressed.

But now it was the intermission, he'd check his messages to make sure he hadn't received any frantic texts or voicemails from his father.

Heath frowned. Leaving work tonight, he'd had to make up some cock and bull about being invited to a mate's posh work do, hence the request for the tuxedo, but he couldn't help but feel paranoid that his father had found out what his *real* plans were. His father had almost had a coronary at the concept of going anywhere near the Feathers when he'd broached the idea as a possibility *weeks* ago.

Glancing at his mobile, he was relieved to see no

notifications and quickly shoved the phone back in his pocket, then looked around, not forgetting the whole point of coming here wasn't to ogle the gorgeous birds. The point was to gain insight into the nerve centre of the Powell firm where the latest boss spent most of his time - the member of the Powell family who was the most likely to have stolen the jewels from Dulcie Adams. The jewels that should be *his*.

By anyone else's logic, a car salesman taking it upon himself to steam in to pilfer jewels from under the nose of one of London's gangland firms might seem both insane and impossible, but Heath didn't care. Ability was only ever hindered by believing there were limits. And yes, he may be a car salesman, but his grandfather was involved in this game, so it must run in his blood too.

Suddenly feeling fingers tracing lightly along his collar, Heath turned to find the woman from the reception leaning over his shoulder. As she moved her manicured talons to rest on the edge of the table, his gaze moved to the cleavage now directly in line with his eyes. *Holy shit – this bird was as hot as shit off a shovel!*

'Hello,' Lena purred. 'I thought I'd see if you were enjoying the cabaret?'

'Take a seat,' Heath indicated to a spare velvet upholstered chair around his glass table and crossed his ankle over his knee, giving the impression of being laid back, when really he was desperately hiding his rapidly growing arousal.

He indicated to an ice cooler in the centre of the table. 'Champagne?'

Mimicking Heath's body language, Lena crossed one of her long legs over the other, the movement showcasing the length and shapeliness of her thighs. 'That would be lovely.' She allowed her full lips to part sensuously. 'So, what do you think? Of the show…?'

Heath could barely bring himself to take his eyes off this ravishing stunner long enough to even think about pouring the woman a glass of bubbly. He *must* concentrate, but by God, this chick was so fucking sexy it hurt. 'The show's fantastic!' he said, pouring Lena's champagne. 'Really good.'

'Glad to hear it,' Lena said, her eyes purposefully moving to Heath's mouth. Men loved it when a woman stared longingly at their lips. It gave their egos more of a hard-on than their cocks and she needed to get his cock hard as well as his wallet to make sure the Feathers benefitted from his business.

'Tell me more about your work, Heath. The music industry, you said? Do you know any famous artists?'

Heath grinned cockily. *Now this he could do.* He'd spun this old chestnut so many times recently he'd almost convinced himself he was a music producer for real. 'I've signed many well-known names,' he boasted, the practised lies tripping off his tongue like honey. He leant forward conspiringly, wishing only that he could bury his face in the heaven between this woman's massive knockers. 'But I'm sure you appreciate I can't give away names. Especially the artist I'm signing tomorrow.'

Lena feigned a look of impressed surprise and put her hand to her mouth to accentuate her alleged amazement of this egotistical prick's abilities. 'Wow! How exciting!' she gushed. 'Do you have parties to celebrate new signings?'

Heath leant back in his chair, like signing celebrities was an everyday occurrence. 'Oh yeah, all the time and…'

'Have you thought of hosting them here?' Lena asked. *No opportunity like the present.* 'Your Platinum membership gives you a substantial discount on catering or bar bill packages and I presume you're aware that you're guaranteed a booking for the VIP suite!'

Heath blinked. *You thick shit*, he thought. *Why did you not think of this?* 'What a great idea. I'd need some more information though.'

Lena smiled gracefully. 'Of course. Do you have a date in mind?'

Heath made a big show of thinking. 'Well, if the artist in question signs tomorrow – of which I'm fairly certain he will, then I'd be looking for a function around a week today?'

Lena could barely contain her enthusiasm. *Got him hook, line and sinker.* 'For roughly how many people?'

'Oh, erm…' Heath fidgeted. How many people would be invited to a pop-star's signing? As the intro music blasted out signifying the second half of the show, he had a brainwave – one that would get him behind the scenes – and, as an extra bonus if he played his cards right, between the legs of this hot chick. She was as much up for it as he was, so why not take a few perks as part of his detective work? *All work and no play and all that…?*

'I don't suppose you have an office? Now the show's started I can't hear myself think. It won't take long to see if you have the dates I need available and then I can get it booked in.'

Lena stood up. 'Please follow me.' *That hadn't taken long.* She'd only gone and bagged another massively influential event. Jonah would be pleased, but Gwen would be spitting chips which made it even more enjoyable.

Following the corridor to Lena Taylor's office, Heath surreptitiously glanced through the other doors. Although each one had a glass panel, there wasn't anyone about. 'It's like the Marie Celeste in here,' he joked.

Ignoring the comment, Lena motioned to the door in front of her. 'Please come into my office.'

Heath glanced down the end of the corridor at a room that didn't have a glass panel. 'What's that mystery room?'

Lena laughed. 'Nothing mysterious about that, it's the main office.'

Heath gave a dramatized cloak and dagger look. 'You mean the big bad boss?'

'Something like that,' Lena giggled, shutting the office door behind them. 'Take a seat and I'll find the diary.'

Heath's eyes remained firmly fixed on Lena's backside as she sashayed across the office, bending over in front of him to retrieve a book from her desk. Fidgeting uncomfortably, he dragged his eyes away from the far too tempting sight and instead tried to remember what he was doing.

With her back turned, Lena smiled, knowing damn well this guy's full concentration was on her. She suppressed a giggle. His tongue was almost hanging out – just the way she liked men to act. It was empowering having that effect and the day that stopped was the day she knew her power had diminished and it was time to get down to Harley Street for a top up of whatever new surgery was required.

She quickly double checked the button on her white jacket was done up. She didn't want him spotting the kitchen roll baby. That would break the illusion. It was vital to ooze as much charm as possible and dangle the carrot in front of his nose to get him to sign up for the most expensive event package possible. That would go some way towards placating Jonah.

Since some prat had ballsed things up by planting a seed of doubt in his mind about her allegations about Saul, Jonah had treated her differently and things had edged back to being less balanced. The situation was playing heavily on her mind and she needed to restore the faith.

Smiling widely, Lena turned and leant against the edge of her desk, glancing in the events book. 'We can cater for you next Friday or Saturday, but the only available room is our biggest function suite – the one that holds 600 people.'

Blatantly undressing Lena with his eyes, Heath stood up. 'It goes without saying that I'd want the best selection of wines and champagnes and of course a full buffet, as well as entrance drinks and canapes.'

The pound signs rolled behind Lena's eyes, but refrained from squealing out loud. She'd make a mint out of this. Doing some rough calculations in her head, tripling it and adding on another 40% for good measure, she placed her hand on Heath's jacket sleeve. 'Let's see… With the 25% reduction for being a Platinum member and the buffet for 600 covers… decorations… guest DJ etc… then I'd say you're looking at around £75,000. If you want a free bar then that would be extra, of course.'

Heath astounded himself by not twitching at the ludicrous figure. *75k for a party? Did people really do shit like that? Jesus!* 'That sounds fine,' he said casually.

Sidling closer, he figured he may as well push his charms. He grinned lazily at Lena, a little disappointed to see close up she had on at least fifteen layers of foundation on and wondered how deep the groove would be if he ran his nail down her cheek. 'How well do you know the boss? Maybe I could have a word and see if I can get a better discount? I'm thinking I'd like all of our events to be held at the Feathers. Especially if we can reach a mutual agreement.'

And if he could get some time with Jonah Powell, then he might be able to get a *proper* heads up as to where his inheritance had been squirrelled. Worth a try, surely?

Lena raised her painted eyebrows. 'You want to speak to Mr Powell about this, rather than me?'

Heath faltered. *Fuck. Now he'd offended her.* He just needed to see this man and weigh him up. There was also a certain amount of morbid curiosity in laying his eyes on the man related to his grandfather's murderer. 'I'd much prefer to deal with you,' he said hastily. 'I just thought th…'

'Jonah doesn't deal with this side of the business. This,' she said proudly, 'is all at *my* discretion.'

Heath forced himself to smile. *Bollocks.* 'Then I'll leave it down to you. I'm sure Mr Powell will be happy to hear you have convinced me to book all of my company's events here from now on.'

'Yes, I'm sure he will.' Lena returned the smile, but inside she was irritated. This bloke really thought he was something, but he was right on one thing – Jonah would be impressed with what she'd pulled off here tonight. Unable to resist, she couldn't help from grabbing back a bit of power. 'Although I assume Jonah's happy with me considering we're getting married in a couple of weeks.'

Blood draining from his face, Heath then noticed Lena's hand resting on a small, but distinctive bump that he'd previously failed to notice under her jacket. *Fuck*.

Controlling the combination of disappointment and nerves, Heath was just grateful for his acting ability. 'Then he's a very lucky man. Now, where do I sign? I'll book next Saturday, please.'

THIRTY THREE

'T-THAT WILL MAKE things difficult,' Joe blathered. *This was going from bad to worse.*

Robert glared at Joe as they sped towards the address he'd forced from the man. 'I don't give a shit it if makes things difficult.

Sweat dripped freely down Joe's back. So much for trying to do a good turn... Look where it had got him. 'But my housemate might insist I call the police and you as well as I know that will make everything worse.'

Robert scowled. That was probably the only thing he would agree with this waster on. He still could not quite believe what this man sitting in his passenger seat had told him. 'Then you'll make sure he understands *not* to involve them, won't you?'

Joe closed his eyes in despair. 'You don't understand what you're asking by wanting me to get back in contact with those men.' His eyes felt like they were sticking out on stalks and could soon pop out and roll around in the dusty footwell of Robert Adams' car. This was a nightmare – a total and utter nightmare. 'Christ, I've only just got rid of them and just because I decided I should do the right thing and tell y...'

'You what?' Robert abruptly swerved to the side of the road

and yanked on the handbrake. Lurching out of the driver's seat, he grabbed Joe around the neck and squashed him non-too gently into the seat. '*You* decided to do the right thing?' he roared. 'Giving these nutters a key to my mother's house; involving Teagan in whatever shit my mother has caused, then phoning up these bastards to tell them *she's* is in possession of their diamonds is the right thing? It didn't cross your mind that something untoward might come off the back of this sequence of events?'

Robert was incensed enough to spontaneously combust. This stupid bastard; this useless streak of piss was the problem all along. *After his mother, that was...*

'Wait. I-I didn't know this was about diamonds. Your mother gave Teagan a shed load of diamonds?' Joe gasped. He scrabbled at Robert's fingers around his throat. This one was almost as deranged as the fucking nutters. Why did this shit keep happening?

'What the hell does it matter?' Robert screeched.

Glad Robert had released his grip, Joe rubbed at his neck. How was he supposed to know things would turn out like this? 'We don't know for sure they've got Teagan.'

Robert clenched his jaw. 'No, but it stands to reason they have and that's why you're going to phone up and find out.'

'W-What?'

'You're going to ask this person, whoever he is, if they have Teagan and tell him that she doesn't have the diamonds, but *you* do.'

Joe swallowed hard, feeling that all too familiar thrumming of fear tingling in his feet and in the end of his fingers. 'You want me to put myself up to those nutters by pretending I've got their diamonds?' He thought he might gag. Gag so hard that his mouth turned inside out. 'You can't be serious?'

This time Robert grasped the shoulders of Joe's checked shirt and slammed him against the inside of the door. 'Do I look like I'm not serious? That's exactly what I want you to do. I should add, in case you don't quite get it, that you won't *really* have them. You'll merely be the decoy.'

'B-But...'

'Listen, you snide bastard, if you don't do this, then I'll kill you myself and these other people will be the least of your problems.' Robert hissed through gritted teeth, his anger raw. 'Now, let's go in your house, get the phone you've told me about and I'll wait while you call this wanker.'

....

'LENA? OH...!' Barging into the office, Jonah eyed the dark-haired man pointedly. 'Am I interrupting something?'

Heath's nerves pinged as the man's ice-blue stare penetrated every layer of his being. *This* was Jonah Powell?

He'd expected to feel antagonism towards the person whose family had killed his grandfather, but surprisingly he didn't. In fact, he was unsure *what* he felt, apart from the nervousness being in the presence of this man engendered within him. This larger than life man exuded authority and a steely kind of magnetism which radiated from every pore of his being.

Heath's usually overtly forward personality cringed into submission and for the second time he silently thanked his good fortune that he had escaped by a hair's breadth of making a play for this brute of a man's pregnant fiancée.

Lena glided towards Jonah, her arms slipping around his waist, underlining her position. 'Hello, darling. I was just sorting out the formalities for multiple bookings for the VIP suites.'

Heath was about to introduce himself when the immensity of the danger he had mistakenly dropped himself in whacked him somewhat dead in the centre of his brain.

Oh, you stupid, stupid fuck, he thought, his mind looping around the enormity of what he'd done. Giving his name when signing up for Platinum membership? His *real* name? What the fuck had happened to his brain? How could it have bypassed logical thought to such an extent not to take into consideration that using a name the Powells associated with the disappearance of millions of pounds worth of goods wasn't a great idea? The name 'Pointer' would undoubtedly be fixed in their mind for eternity.

Fuck, fuck, fuck it.

Refusing to start hysterically laughing at his own stupidness, Heath stood up and extended his hand. 'Pleased to meet you, Sir. I'm Heath. I run Assure Productions, a record company. We're looking for suitable venues to host our elite signing parties and,' he glanced towards Lena, 'your lovely wife-to-be has been confirming some dates for me.'

Quickly shaking Heath's hand, Jonah nodded abruptly. 'I'm glad you find my club to your satisfaction. Now, if you'll excuse me.' Giving Heath a cool glance, Jonah moved to the door. 'A word please, Lena?'

THIRTY FOUR

JONAH SCOWLED AT SAUL. That his brother had the audacity to sit there with a smug condescending look on his face wasn't doing anything to help his mood. 'Finally decided to show your face?'

'You think the reason I haven't been around is purely because someone's trying to stir shit between us?' Saul snapped. 'I've heard what's been said.' He'd see if Jonah owned up to what his tramp of a girlfriend had trapped off about before he decided how to retaliate.

Jonah folded his arms. 'And what shit might that be? Would you care to enlighten me?' *Who had run to Saul and told him?* It could only be Gwen or Nero. Or Lena herself... That was unlikely, but then he'd have hardly thought Gwen and Nero would have said anything either. He frowned, fast running out of knowing who to trust.

Saul leant back, bending the backrest of the leather desk chair at a worrying angle. Staring Jonah in the eye with a look that matched the viciousness of the one he was receiving, he sneered openly at the irritation on his brother's face. 'Yeah, I've heard all about what the daft tart you think you're marrying has been spouting. And do you know what? I won't lower myself to even bother denying the ridiculous allegations.'

Jonah was ready for this. He wouldn't give Saul the satisfaction of letting him know that Lena *had* stirred shit – not that she'd admitted it. 'Exactly what am I accusing you of by asking you where you've been these past few days?'

But he knew what he'd have said if he'd run into his brother before Nero had the sense to put things into context. At least that was a small mercy. 'I'd also appreciate it if you didn't talk disrespectfully about Lena. As I've said, what I choose to do is not your business.'

Saul's eyes narrowed. That's what Jonah thought, but he'd keep schtum for now. He had a plan where that tramp was concerned and if she didn't make the correct decision, then she'd be joining the stupid bitch at the flat. The trouble was, Lena would probably enjoy it, which would defeat the fucking object.

His eyes glinted with malice. Lena would be exposed soon enough if she didn't fuck off from his hard earned business. 'And how's the wonderful 'pregnant' fiancée? Still glowing?'

Ignoring the blatant attempt to rile him, Jonah instead changed tack. 'Contrary to your opinion of what goes round my head, I've been expecting an update from you about the police investigation, but I've heard nothing. What's going on, Saul? We had an agreement.'

Saul lurched forward, the back of the spring-loaded chair rebounding noisily. 'What the fuck is that supposed to mean?'

Jonah sighed. 'It's not difficult to understand. You were supposed to be digging with your contacts, but since then,' he clapped his hands together sharply, 'there's been sod all – *nothing*! And furthermore, both you and Keith are rarely around.'

Thinking quickly, Saul rose to his feet. 'I take it Keith didn't pass on the information I instructed him to give to you?'

Jonah frowned. 'I haven't heard anything?' Nero had brought him up to speed that he'd tailed Keith to one of those flats, but he wouldn't mention that. He'd wait and see if Saul mentioned anything... 'Forget Keith. Why haven't *you* told me? Why have you been thin on the ground lately?'

Saul paced around in agitation. He'd best make this sound good. It would give him a bit of cover at least, especially since Keith had made it clear he wasn't happy with his way of doing things. *Well, fuck you Keith! It's none of your damn business.* 'If you must know, the reason I haven't been around is because I've been sorting out turf war shite that's recently cropped up at the flats.'

Saying nothing, Jonah folded his arms and waited to hear what bull would come out of his brother's mouth.

'You know our flats the other side of town?' Saul continued, 'There's been some shit with cheap arse ponces moving in to pimp on some of the girls there.' His mouth formed a menacing scowl. 'The fuckers started putting the heavy hand on some of the tarts, so I've been, shall we say... addressing the situation.' *There, that was reasonable enough.*

Keith would tell Jonah fuck all. Last night he'd put across quite bluntly that if the man didn't like the way he did things, then he could get the fuck out of his firm for good. He knew the man well enough to know that he lived and breathed the firm and wouldn't throw away his life's work over some over-zealous morals he'd suddenly conjured up from God knows where after all this time, the stupid bastard. But if Keith *did* let him down, then he'd make sure the man didn't get a decent night's sleep again in his pointless fucking life.

Saul stared at Jonah, his expression unwavering. 'And before you ask me why I didn't tell you, let me remind you that it has fuck all to do with Dulcie Adams. This is *my* side of the business.' He sighed dramatically. 'Don't think I don't know that you've been presuming I'm up to things behind your back. I agreed we'd work together on this and I *meant* it, so I'd appreciate it if you didn't disrespect me by thinking otherwise.'

Acting suitably offended was usually enough to get the point across. Jonah didn't have a leg to stand on. Anything to do with hookers and enforcement was *his* bag, not Jonah's, so as long as Jonah believed this to be the case, then he was home and dry. 'As I said, I told Keith to pass on the info I got from my cop contact the other night, but from what you said, he hasn't. That isn't my issue. I presumed he had done what was asked,' Saul lied.

Let Keith take the rap, the useless bastard. Having the damn cheek to kick off at him about the girl? Silly cunt. Who the fuck did he think he was? Who the fuck did *any* of them think they were? He was sick of the lot of them.

Jonah pursed his lips. 'Ok, so what was said? From your contact? What do you know?'

Saul frowned. 'My contact has a mate in the CID from the nick investigating the Dulcie Adams case who says you're not in the frame. None of us are.'

Jonah breathed an inward sigh of relief. 'We can move on with the next phase then?'

Too late, shit for brains. I'm well ahead with that already, Saul thought acidly, yet smiled reassuringly. 'Yes, but he did say they're digging around for a few more days to tie all the loose ends for the paperwork up, so by my estimation, just to be on the safe side, we give it a wide berth for another week.' That would allow enough time to get the rest in place and whatever happened after that, Jonah would be too late. And there was fuck all he would be able to do about it.

Jonah nodded. 'Ok. Frustrating, but we'll just have to sit tight a bit longer then.' He'd been barking up the wrong tree with Saul. He should have given him more credit, both about Lena and about steaming ahead with the Dulcie Adams business. 'Do you need any help with this trouble at the flats?' he asked, deciding to extend an olive branch.

Saul shook his head, pleased that as usual, Jonah had taken his word. 'Nah, it'll all be sorted within a couple of days.' *And it would. More than sorted.*

'Just one more thing.' Jonah eyed Saul carefully. 'Give the shit about Lena a break. Whether you like it or not I'm marrying her, ok?'

Saul sighed. 'Point taken. I'll keep my comments to myself.' *But you're not marrying her, Jonah. You don't yet realise it, but you soon will.*

Nodding at his brother, Jonah stood up. 'Right, I'd best get on. Thanks for bringing me up to speed.'

Saul grinned. 'No problem. That's what brothers are for.' Meanwhile, Lena was his next port of call.

• • • •

WALKING DOWN TO THE CORNER SHOP, hands wedged deep in his jeans pockets, Joe resented that his fingers were touching the phone. *That* phone.

Waiting on tenterhooks for it to ring was not his idea of a good time. And furthermore, he didn't *want* it to ring, precisely because he knew who would be on the other end of the line.

End. Of. Story.

But what choice did he have with Robert Adams manhandling him into his own bloody house last night, standing over him as he called the only number on that burner phone? It was hardly likely he could do anything else.

Oh sure, he could have *pretended* to leave a message, but he got the distinct impression that Robert Adams wasn't the sort to glibly accept anything without proof. And he'd been right.

It had been Robert who'd snatched the phone off him, wanting to hear for himself that the call had gone to voicemail and Joe had been relieved for all of a nanosecond, thinking this meant he could do nothing further, but his hopes were dashed when Robert instructed him to leave a message.

It had only been when he'd been slammed up against the bedroom wall, his five-year-old cactus jumping off the bedside table with the reverberation that had again convinced him that doing what was asked was the best solution. So he'd done it; he'd left the exact message Robert wanted. He'd even managed not to sound like he was shitting a brick with a 6' 3" bloke pinning him up against the wall at the time either. He'd done well.

Robert Adams had finally left after telling him to phone as soon as a response was received and not to even think about doing a runner, because he'd find him. Worryingly, Joe knew that this was possible because, short of drowning himself or emigrating to Libya, it appeared *everyone* had the ability to find him, so there really was no point in trying to pretend otherwise, but now he was waiting. Waiting for that call.

Walking into the corner shop, half tripping over the step, Joe stood behind an old man at the counter, his gnarled fingers moving teeth-grindingly slowly as he meticulously counted out a pile of copper coins. Joe would happily pay for the old boy's five TV guide listings himself if it meant it would speed up the process, but then he wouldn't have enough for fags and if he didn't get a smoke soon he'd scream.

Tapping his foot impatiently, he stared at the back of the man's balding head in the vague hope of speeding him up.

'Twenty Lambert and Butlers,' Joe muttered the second the old man had finished, pushing against the counter in his haste. He dragged his change from his pocket and put it on the counter, hoping he hadn't mislaid any of it since he'd counted it earlier.

Suddenly the burner phone rang. *Oh, not now, not here. Come on!* Fumbling to get the phone out of his pocket, Joe glanced at the newsagent who was staring disparagingly as he counted the money. He also ignored the disapproving tuts from the woman behind him.

His shaking fingers stabbed at the answer call button. He could hardly talk about this in here, but at the same time he didn't want the call to drop out. 'Hello?' he gasped.

THIRTY FIVE

'WHAT THE FUCK are you talking about, prick?' Keith growled.

He hadn't expected any calls on this phone and although he made a habit of regularly checking all the burners as a matter of course, last night he hadn't bothered. His mind was overloaded with what he'd seen yesterday and after sinking far too many beers he hadn't got around to it. There was far too much to think about.

And now *this*.

Keith gnashed his teeth waiting for the stoner to speak. He could barely believe it when he was asked to hang on. He hadn't got all bloody day and neither was he in the frame of mind to wait for anything this moron had to say.

'I've got something I think you'll want,' Joe said, as he dashed around the back of the newsagents, amazed his voice held no trace of wavering.

Keith frowned. 'Yeah, you said that on the message. What could you possibly have that I would want?'

Joe took a deep breath and glanced around to check no one was in earshot. He pressed the mobile tighter against his ear, like it would make a difference... 'Before I tell you, I need to know - have you got Teagan?'

Keith almost laughed. He moved the phone away from his half-chewed ear and stared at it. 'Are you having me on? Why would I tell you that? More to the point, what the fuck has it got to do with you?'

Despite everything, a small knot of unease rolled around Keith's insides. The girl's disappearance had been noted, as expected, but did that mean the police were involved? He liked what was happening to that woman little enough, but the prospect of the cops, he liked even less. There was no way he was being implicated for what Saul done on this one. Robbery was one thing, but *that…*

'It's got nothing to do with me,' Joe stammered, fast losing his nerve. 'But Teagan hasn't got what you're after. That I *do* know.'

Keith sighed. 'Fuck off stoner. I haven't got time for this.'

'No,' Joe spluttered. 'I'm serious. The old bag Teagan looks after – the one… you know…? Well, she called me when Teagan didn't come back after the funeral.' *Think, think! What was the story again?* Sweat poured down his temples. 'I went round to see if I could help. She knew me and Teagan used to be…'

'Get on with it,' Keith growled, his ears pricking up the minute Dulcie Adams was mentioned.

'The old cow went to make me a cup of tea and it was then that I saw the box.' Joe laughed nervously, desperate to make things sound plausible. 'I remembered what Teagan said about… you know… about being given a box. The one she hadn't looked in? Well, I'm a nosy bastard, so I looked.'

Keith's heart hammered painfully. *Was it possible…?*

'I've got them! I took them. I left the box where it was, but I've got the stuff,' Joe continued. *Christ, this was like signing his own death warrant. Was the nutter buying this? Come on, speak!*

'Got what?' Keith growled. He'd soon know if this piece of shit was trying it on.

'The diamonds,' Joe whispered, the words burning his throat. 'There's loads of them... *pink* diamonds.'

Keith said nothing. Was the stoner winding him up? How would he know about the diamonds if he hadn't got them? Had anyone mentioned them before? No they hadn't – no one had ever spoken of them. A lucky guess, perhaps? No. It couldn't be. *Shit the fucking bed!*

'Are you still there?' Joe's confidence grew, realising the nutter was digesting the information. *Just the next bit now.*

'I'm still here,' Keith said, his mind racing.

'Give me Teagan and I'll get the diamonds to you,' Joe blurted.

Keith laughed. Who in their right mind would give up millions of pounds worth of jewels in exchange for some bird? Though remembering how dappy the stoner was, he was the sort of person to think it logical. Vegetable rights and peace and all that clobber, right? 'And why would you do that?'

'Because I love her,' Joe lied. 'Look, the diamonds are what you've been after all along, aren't they? Holding Teagan to ransom won't get you anywhere because she doesn't know anything, I've told you before she thinks you lot were looking for drugs. She never knew anything about me being in contact with you.'

Keith chewed his lip. Had the stoner splurged to the cops and now they'd pieced everything together and told him to call? No, they'd have descended on the club in their droves if there was any inkling the Powells were linked to that old robbery, not to mention kidnapping on top.

Joe closed his eyes in despair. 'Look, give me Teagan and take the diamonds. Job done.'

Keith faltered. If the stoner was telling the truth then *he'd* get the diamonds back for the Powells. Him and him *alone.* The vision of being handed one of those multi-million pound jewels for his services, glowed in his mind like a magic charm. But if this wasn't kosher and was a set up, then he'd be screwing the entire firm, himself and the Powells...

But what choice did he have? He had to do something about Saul's behaviour. His old friend's actions were haunting him something chronic. Although he hadn't found a way of getting around the problem which didn't involve him either being killed in retaliation or leaving the firm to spend the rest of his life in exile, he did know it was one of those things that he couldn't turn a blind eye to or brush under the carpet. This wasn't like the other things he'd ever been involved in.

If he could sort this, then not only would Jonah be forever indebted to him, but it would also mean Saul's behaviour wouldn't have to be exposed, so he wouldn't be betraying his buddy, plus the girl would get away, so it made sense.

Hearing nothing but traffic noise from the other end of the line, Joe began to panic. 'Hello?'

'I'm thinking,' Keith muttered.

'Whatever you're thinking, this isn't a set up,' Joe blathered, immediately wishing he hadn't. Didn't that make it sound that it was?

'I don't think even *you* would be that stupid.'

'Exactly.' Joe blathered. Although Robert hadn't outlined exactly what it was he intended to do, Joe was sure it wouldn't be straightforward and the persistent knocking inside the back of his brain made that glaring fact difficult to ignore. Whatever else he might be, he did owe it to Teagan to get her away from these people – not withstanding that Robert Adams hadn't given him any choice in the matter…

'I'll meet you tonight. 10pm,' Keith grunted. He'd have to take the chance. He just had to.

'Where?' *Shit, shit, SHIT.*

'The warehouses out the back of Dock Road. But just you – no one else. There will be no girl until I've seen the goods.'

Joe swallowed. *That wasn't part of the plan.* 'But how do I know you've got her?'

Keith laughed. 'You don't, but trust me, you'll get her back once Jonah confirms the stuff is his.'

'But that's n…'

'Take it or leave it.' Keith played his hand. '10pm at the warehouse.'

Hearing the call click off, Joe stared at the mobile, his hands shaking. *Fuck. Now what?*

• • • •

'HOW AM I NOT SUPPOSED to worry when you disappear all day and don't say a word?' Dulcie moaned. 'Anything could have happened!' Her bird-like fingers drummed on the table. 'It really isn't good enough. Teagan having no manners is one thing, but *you*?'

She stared at Robert as he tapped away at his computer. 'What with everything that's already happened, first with Helen and now Teagan, I'm on edge. Do you not think I've been through enough?' Not content that Robert hadn't acknowledged her words, she raised her voice. 'I'm a right state. A bag of nerves!'

Robert stopped typing and looked at his mother. It was taking all of his power not to blurt out that he knew – knew *everything*. That she was a liar, a fake, a phony and a murderer. But he wouldn't. He also had to act that Teagan's whereabouts did not bother him, when in reality it was driving him to distraction. Even more since Joe had called, recounting the conversation he'd had with that psycho. That had made everything 1000 times worse.

Adrenaline fizzed in his veins. He'd only got until 10pm to think of a feasible plan, but he was good at methods and plans – like programming.

Robert's blue eyes met with the equally blue ones of his mother. How had he never noticed how cold her eyes were? How had he missed the lack of empathy behind those cornflower-coloured eyes of hers?

Because she was his mother, that's why. He'd never had any reason to think she was anything else, but now she'd been exposed as being a lot of things and they read a lot differently.

'I'm sorry, I didn't mean to worry you.' Robert smiled. 'I

was at Footlights the entire day yesterday and you'll be glad to know it's now all spick and span and ready when you are.'

Dulcie's face lit up before her eyes narrowed suspiciously. 'You haven't thrown any of my things away, have you? Cleaned all my stuff out like you always wanted?'

Robert laughed – the sound unnatural. He wanted to walk away. Walk away as far as possible. *This woman was poison.* 'No, I've thrown nothing away. I think you've already lost too much to warrant me adding to it.' God, the words coming out of his mouth were sickening. He'd prefer to launch everything which had any connection to her, that place and her life out of the window, especially her gun which was now safely concealed in his wardrobe. 'I got rid of anything broken, but nothing else. Why? Was there something in particular…?'

Dulcie studied Robert suspiciously. 'Like what? I just don't want to lose anything else.' *Why was he acting odd? Had she not been convincing enough?* She changed her expression to a sad one. 'I think we have to presume that Teagan isn't coming back.'

Robert bit back his anger. 'I thought you said she'd return for those diamonds?'

Dulcie shrugged, her shoulders slumping. 'Oh, I don't know… I don't know anything anymore. Teagan must realise we're on to her and has decided not to risk it.'

Robert snarled inwardly. He knew exactly where Teagan was now and why - held to ransom at that fucking club - that bloody godforsaken Feathers club for the diamonds. Joe had confirmed the psychos had got her, so where else would she be? He knew what he had to do. They said they wanted to see the jewels? Well, that's exactly what he'd be doing.

He would see this Jonah Powell character and he could have his fucking diamonds back. It wasn't like *he* wanted them. In fact, he wanted *nothing* from the father he'd never met. Money and possessions meant little, but he wanted the person back who was awakening him. He wanted the person back who made him believe he could be normal.

Getting into the Feathers to see the big honcho wouldn't be easy, but if half of his henchmen were being led in the opposite direction by Joe, then that would at least help.

He stared at Dulcie, now rubbing lavender oil on the pulse points of her wrists. As for her, she wasn't keeping those diamonds. If *anyone* deserved them, it wasn't *her*.

Thirty Six

GWEN KNEW LENA wouldn't be in until later because Jonah had said so when she'd seen him briefly. He hadn't said why in so many words, but telling her to remind all staff that under *no* circumstances were any members of the public to be admitted into the staff areas, spoke volumes.

Since when did members of the public ever get admittance to the back offices? In all the time she'd worked here she'd never seen this happen. It was certainly nothing she'd ever entertained. For a start, she wouldn't be that stupid and couldn't think of one reason when it could be relevant.

From Lena's absence and the presence of the events diary and a completed booking form on her desk, Gwen came to the conclusion that it was something to do with her. Another example of the woman putting the firm in jeopardy. That girl would always be a liability. Despite the unexpected flair she showed for organising events and attracting customers, she had to learn and learn fast that in this line of business, or rather the *other* facets of the firm in addition to the club's front end, everything that was anything was held somewhere behind the scenes. There would always be people waiting in the wings for a chink in the armour – an opportunity to slip under the radar to get their hands on confidential information and if that happened, before anyone knew it, the police would be on their back or another firm would have the knowhow to muscle in. It was a hell of a risk doing something like that and one of the most important things in this game was not presuming people were who they *said* they were.

Moving to Lena's desk, Gwen glanced at the partly filled out events booking form and quotation for next Saturday. Her eyes widened. *£75,000?* Bloody hell, Lena had triumphed again by the looks of it. But not entirely if she'd allowed an unvetted person behind the scenes.

Gwen squinted at the scrawled signature, too untidy to properly read. Lena hadn't filled out the name and contact details either – just the membership ID. She'd cross reference it later. With a pending invoice of that amount there couldn't be any mess ups due to slack admin and paperwork.

However, if Lena wasn't due in until later, then wasn't now the prime time to get in that desk drawer of hers?

Gwen's mood brightened. Glancing over her shoulder, she first moved to her own desk and retrieved a small metal cash tin. Unlocking it, she pulled out a heavy bunch of keys. There were at least thirty on there, yet she knew what each and every one of them was for.

Rapidly locating the master key for the office furniture, Gwen moved back to Lena's desk when the door suddenly opened. Her head snapped up at the unexpected intrusion, heart sinking at the prospect of Lena, but to her surprise, found Saul.

'Morning,' Saul glanced around the office. 'Where is she?'

Gwen frowned. 'Lena? Jonah said she won't be in until later.'

'Right, ok.' Saul quickly retraced his steps.

'Wait a minute,' Gwen called. 'I need to speak to you ab…'

'Yeah, sorry I didn't return your call the other day. I'm up to my fucking neck, but I'll catch you later and you can fill me in then.'

'But I wanted to talk to you about Lena an…

'Don't worry about that. I've spoken to Jonah and we've sorted it out. Crossed wires, as you might expect…' He raised his eyebrows. 'It's all good.'

'But I…'

'Seriously, Gwen – no time. We'll speak later.'

Shutting the door behind him, Saul disappeared as quickly as he'd arrived and Gwen sighed despondently. She still hadn't told him that Lena really *was* pregnant, but if he'd sorted it out with Jonah, then she guessed everything was ok.

Her face creased into a frown, hoping he hadn't mentioned their previous conversation. No, he couldn't have because Jonah would have pulled her up about it long before now if that were the case and he'd seemed fine when she'd seen him. She'd still have to make sure she told Saul though. She had to put that right, just in case. But it would have to wait - at least until later on.

Gwen picked the keys back off the desk, determined to at least sort out *one* thing out whilst she had the chance. Unlocking Lena's bottom drawer, she pulled it open as far as possible on its big metal runners, immediately spotting the bottle of vodka at the back.

Just as she'd expected. Still drinking on the sly.

She contemplated putting a dot on the bottle with a permanent marker to show how full the bottle was, then check it again in a day or so and see how much had gone. Would that be enough to make Jonah see sense?

Carefully rummaging around, she stared in disappointment at the remaining contents. Apart from the vodka, there wasn't anything of great importance; a load of makeup, a hairbrush and a set of hair straighteners.

Gwen sighed. All of that for nothing. She hadn't known what she'd expected to find, but hoped more than *anything* there would be something incriminating – something that would be enough.

About to shut the drawer, Gwen faltered spotting a brown envelope blending into the wood right at the bottom underneath the makeup.

She tentatively pulled it out, recognising Lena's writing on the back:

20th July 1pm

That was the new date for the wedding - it wasn't like it was a secret because the change of date had already been announced.

Gingerly opening the envelope, she pulled out the registry office booking confirmation. *That was it?* About to slide the letter back into the envelope, Gwen froze. *Wait a minute...* There were additional things...

Pulling out the rest of the contents of the envelope, she held in her hands a passport and birth certificate.

Scrambling to open the passport, her eyes drew immediately to the professional-looking photograph of Lena. Looking a few years younger, her hair shorter and a brassier, blonde, it was still Lena through and through.

Gwen's eyes scanned the text, freezing at the details staring at her in black and white:

Surname/Nom (1)
O'HARA

Given Names/Prenoms (2)
Lena Margaret

Nationality (3)
BRITISH CITIZEN

Date of Birth/Date de Naissance (4)
11 AUG / AOU 78

Sex / Sexe (5)
F

Place of Birth / Lieu de naissance (6)
OMAGH

Date of Issue / Date de Délivrance (7)
17 SEP / SEPT 00

Gwen blinked several times, blood rushing from her head down into the soles of her feet. *Jesus Christ...* Lena Taylor was not Lena Taylor... Lena Taylor was Lena *O'Hara*. It said it there in black and white.

Suddenly everything fell into place. The name she'd heard

Lena say on that telephone call. The same name she'd seen on that mystery text message: *Noeleen.* She'd been referring to Noeleen O'Hara. Lena had said *Auntie* Noeleen…

Gwen felt vomit rise and she clutched her hand over her mouth, swallowing repeatedly to quell the bile from coming any further and stared at the passport again. The name resounding like a clanging bell whacking against the inside of her temples.

Noeleen O'Hara was Ron O'Hara's wife – she remembered her from years back when Ron had worked at the firm. Oh Christ… 'UR' – the contact on her phone. Ron O'Hara? UR – Uncle Ron?

It must have been Ron who had told Lena about her involvement with Jacky Powell. Gwen had no idea how he had known, but he'd been around at that time. It had to be him.

Perspiration beaded on Gwen's forehead. So Lena was Ron O'Hara's niece? But which of the O'Hara brothers was her father?

She frantically unfolded the other document: Lena's birth certificate, and her eyes scanned over the handwritten entries:

Sean Keith O'Hara **Father:**

Margaret Rose O'Hara **Mother:**

Shit, shit, SHIT.

The daughter of Sean O'Hara – the man who had been party to the Michael Pointer heist and the man who Saul had served seventeen years inside for? Lena was Sean's daughter? And Ron was attending the wedding?

Gwen put her head in her hands. Oh Christ, this was bad. *Really* bad… She had to stop this. She had to stop this now.

Jonah having a child with an O'Hara? This would kill him.

Quickly shoving the paperwork back in the envelope, Gwen placed it back in the drawer as carefully as she could with her shaking hands.

She'd go to Jonah's house. She'd go now. Jonah was here, so Lena would be on her own. She had to confront her and tell her that her plans were foiled. As much as she despised Lena and thought she should pay for what she'd done, she didn't want her to be *killed.* And that's what could well happen if word of this got out.

If the woman admitted to Jonah what she'd done before he found out from anyone else, there was a small chance, being pregnant with his child, that she might get away with her life. But if she refused, then Gwen had no choice but to tell Jonah herself.

Gwen knew her own secret would be exposed, but she couldn't allow this. Lena was shafting the family and it couldn't happen. She'd known there was something, but in her wildest dreams hadn't expected it to be *this*…

Grabbing her bag, she rushed from the room.

THIRTY SEVEN

'IT'S SOMETHING TO DO with the toms he rents the flats to,' Jonah said.

Nero frowned. 'Keith said that?'

'No, Saul did. He told me when I asked where he kept disappearing to. It looks like I've been worrying about nothing.'

Nero pursed his lips. He wasn't so sure. Keith was acting strange. Something was off with the man. He'd worked with Keith on and off for the best part of two decades and although he would hardly class them as best buddies, he knew him well enough to know when something was far from alright. He was keeping schtum about something and whatever it was, he sensed it was worse than toms having an issue with an uninvited pimp.

'I guess I'm expecting Saul to fuck up, but maybe I'm looking for problems when there aren't any?' Jonah continued. 'I also had to have words with Lena for inviting people back to the office and now Gwen's disappeared too. I could do without all this shite.'

Nero raised his eyebrows. 'What? Lena brought someone back here?' This was all they needed. 'Who the fuck was it?'

'No idea.' Jonah shrugged. 'Some jumped up record

producer prick. I came into the office and there they were.'

Nero really hoped Jonah would cap these mishaps Lena kept having. He knew more than anyone that there were eyes everywhere. But that still didn't solve the problem as to what was wrong with Keith and that was needling him a lot more than anything Lena had done.

'I'm not sure if Lena grasped the extent of the possible lapse in security with what she did,' Jonah muttered.

'She'd catch on if you got banged up and left her a single mother!' Nero griped.

Jonah nodded. 'I'm trying not to be too hard on her. She's fragile at the moment but doing really well with booking good events. She was quite upset when I balled her out about this earlier. That bloke is paying 75k for a function here on Saturday.'

Nero blew threw his teeth. 'And he's kosher, this guy?'

'I was hoping Gwen had checked him out, but I don't know where she's got to.' Jonah frowned, beginning to feel like he didn't know much of what was going on at all anymore. This was his firm, yet he felt side-lined – something he was not used to.

'Could you grab the form off Lena's desk and her membership file?' Jonah asked. 'The process is automated but she's got a printout of the details of all the new Platinum members.'

Nodding, Nero moved into the corridor, spotting Keith heading the other way. 'Where you off to?' he called.

Turning around, Keith scowled. 'Do I need to check in and out with you now? Got someone to meet. You know, the stuff I've been doing for God knows how many years?'

Refraining from catching up with Keith and knocking some manners into his head, Nero continued down the corridor, shaking his head in frustration. Was everyone hell bent on taking the piss around here? Things were going to shit quicker that he could keep up with.

Everything had been running nicely to clockwork before all

of this shit with Dulcie Adams started. Although he knew once it was sorted it would close an overdue chapter in the Powell's life, he couldn't help but feel it had upset the equilibrium with just about everything and everyone. And from his side, he was beginning to suspect the very people he'd always trusted implicitly.

• • • •

WALKING ALONG THE OPEN WALKWAY leading to the flat, Keith ignored the looks he received from an old woman peering through her net curtains. She was certainly no tom; at least ninety and looked like an extra from the *Tales of Narnya* or *Lord of the Rings*.

He shuddered inwardly with the uncomfortable thought of booking a tart and finding *that*. Mismarketing if ever he'd seen it.

Continuing, he stepped carefully over a pile of dog shit and the broken remains of a kid's ride-on bike.

'Ere!' a tinny voice yelled.

Keith glanced over his shoulder, half-expecting the wizened troll to have spirited herself outside in the futile hope of enticing him inside, but this one was definitely a tom – a stereotypical one at that. Unfortunately, not much more attractive than the other thing either.

He ran his gaze over the woman's straggly hair, overtight short skirt and sky-high heels, choosing to concentrate on her well-stacked chest rather than her face, which wouldn't win any beauty contests or adverts for blemish-free skin any time soon.

He wasn't in the mood for her either. At a push on any other normal day and ten pints he might have been tempted, but this wasn't a normal day. This wasn't a normal week. In fact, it hadn't been a normal *month* and he was about in as much the mood for sex as he was for being dismembered. He'd had enough of all of this. Dealing with the type of shit Saul was dishing out was not in his job description.

He fixed his beady eyes on the scantily-clad woman.

'Yeah? What do you want?'

The woman stomped over, her platform heels echoing on the concrete floor. 'This your flat?'

'What if it is?' Keith answered gruffly. If this woman started pawing him in the hope of securing a quick tenner, then she'd find herself launched over the edge of this stinking hallway. The whole lot of them could fuck off.

'Whoever the bird is in there, you need to tell her to shut her fucking rattle! All night she's been bastard screaming and crying,' the woman ranted, folding her arms over her large bust, meaning that Keith no longer had anything slightly acceptable to focus on. 'I've been banging on the fucking wall and I've even banged on the door several times, but the silly bitch won't answer. You need to tell her to keep a lid on it or I'll...'

'Or you'll *what*?' Keith growled menacingly, moving into the woman's face however much it offended him seeing her close up.

Even Keith's intimidating stance failed to dissuade this woman from backing down. 'I'll complain. It's putting off my punters. No one wants to listen to that! It sounds like she's being tortured! What the fuck are you doing to her in there?'

Keith smiled even though it was the last thing he felt like doing. 'Give me your name. I'll pass your concerns on to my boss.'

The woman eyed him suspiciously. 'And who's your boss? I'll speak to him myself, so I will.'

'Powell. Saul Powell...' Keith said slowly, amused as the nature of the woman's mistake flooded across her face. He glanced at the neighbouring flats. 'I take it one of these is yours? I'll get Mr Powell to come and see you and then you can sort it out with him.'

The woman stumbled backwards, almost tripping over the huge platform soles of her shoes in her haste. 'Y-You don't need to do that. I just wondered if she's alright, that's all. Forget I said anything. There's no problem.'

Hiding his chuckle, Keith watched the woman stumble off

in the opposite direction, glancing over her shoulder several times before she disappeared into the stairwell. Then his face fell. This was no good. Not only was keeping the girl in the flat and dosing her up out of order, but it was drawing attention too. This was asking for trouble – trouble he in no way wished to be associated with.

Reluctantly jamming the key in the scuffed door, Keith pushed it open, then quickly shut it behind him. If people were getting wind that something out of the ordinary was going on in here and put *his* face to the person coming and going, then that didn't sit well.

That was it. His mind was made up. He would tell Jonah what was going on. After checking on the girl, he'd go and meet the stoner and if the knob was telling the truth about the diamonds, which for all their sakes, he'd better be, then he'd take them straight to the Feathers. At the same time he'd tell Jonah about this girl and what Saul had been doing. Hopefully, the presence of the diamonds would offset from the unfortunate part he himself had played.

And if the stoner was lying… Well, Keith hadn't got a Plan B, so he'd just have to hope it didn't come to that…

Steeling himself to face the girl who he felt unusually bad for, Keith tentatively pushed open the bedroom door, immediately struck by the overpowering stench of urine, faeces and vomit that pervaded the stale air of the small room and quelled the urge to throw up all over himself.

His eyes adjusted to the gloom, dark in comparison to the outside, thanks to the drawn curtains. He looked at the girl writhing on the bed, awake but not anywhere near coherent. Her naked body was covered in a mixture of her own filth and blood from the red raw wounds where the manacles had gradually eaten away at her wrists.

He eyed the countless needle marks on the inside of her arms and shook his head in a mixture of anger and frustration. How many times had Saul jacked up this poor cow in the last few days? Countless times by the looks of it.

Teagan's eyes suddenly fluttered open, her eyes struggling to focus, her head thrashing from side to side.

Keith grimaced. Fuck's sake – this shit was cruel. The sooner he got the diamonds off the stoner the sooner this was over and the sooner this girl could get out of here.

His stomach lurched as the girl let out an eerie high-pitched moan, her legs pulling up towards her chest and he felt himself panic a little. 'Do you want some water?' He eyed the plastic bottle on the side which had been barely touched. How was she supposed to drink when she couldn't move her hands? *This was bad shit. Bad shit...*

'No water,' Teagan croaked. 'I need... I need... My head... Please...'

Keith frowned. He knew what she wanted, but he wasn't doing it. 'There's no more. You'll have to wait.' *Shit. What a fucking mess this was.*

'I can't!' Teagan wailed, her voice nearing fever-pitch. 'Please! I can't stand it! It's there. Look! There!' Her frantic gaze fell to the syringe on the side along with a small bag of brown and the rest of the kit.

'I'm not here for that. I...'

'You've *got* to. Please!' Teagan screamed. 'I can't stand it. I don't know what's happened, but I hurt and I can't cope. It hurts...'

Keith felt torn. He wanted to turn on his heels and get out of here. He didn't want to be responsible for putting a needle into this girl's vein. Saul had made that decision and it was fucking wrong. This was his fault. It he hadn't grabbed her – if he'd refused, then she wouldn't be here. She wouldn't be in this position and neither would he. If he'd have known this was what Saul had on the cards, he wouldn't have done it.

Keith suddenly felt even worse. Deep down he knew that even if he had been aware what Saul was planning to do, he'd have gone along with it because he *always* did what Saul wanted, but not anymore. Not after this. This was one step too far.

Teagan's groans got louder. They sounded almost unholy. Creepy. *Possessed.* '*Please…*' she wailed.

Keith snatched up the syringe and shuddered. He'd go to hell for his, but it was like watching a lamb in a mantrap. He'd give her a small hit and then get the hell out of here to meet the stoner. This would have to be over tonight one way or the other.

THIRTY EIGHT

GWEN DROVE ALONG THE ROAD, for once not caring if she was going over the 30mph speed limit. It was more important dealing with Lena than getting points on her licence.

Tutting impatiently as the set of traffic lights ahead turned to red, she drummed her fingers on the steering wheel, then used the opportunity to dial Jonah on her mobile. She would tell Jonah to come home as a matter of urgency. Whatever happened, Jonah would hear the truth either from her or Lena today.

There was no point in pretending to think there was anything Lena could say which would suffice as a valid reason why she hadn't disclosed her real name. And there was no point, even for a second, contemplating whether Jonah was *aware*. None whatsoever. The concept of him willingly becoming involved with one of the O'Hara's was not something that he would ever consider – baby or not.

He would be furious, but also devastated. Although it had never been his plan or wish to marry Lena, Gwen knew Jonah had come round to the prospect of being a father. That was the only thing driving the marriage, but now there was no escaping the sinister and disturbing undercurrent of Lena's intentions.

Gwen clenched her teeth at the audacity of the woman. Lena must be planning to publicly unveil who she really was *during* the marriage to cause the utmost uproar, embarrassment and humiliation. Lena, along with the rest of the O'Hara's would be forever attached to the Powells, both in name, blood *and* money and she was relying on Jonah honouring the wedding to save face and uphold his morals.

Lena was certainly a lot cleverer that anyone had given her credit for and she despised the woman four-fold. She'd planned this all along. Planned to combine the two families through marriage and joining with a family part of that godforsaken heist was the ultimate insult.

Frowning as Jonah's phone rang out, Gwen ended the call, not waiting to leave a message.

The light changing to amber, she wasted no time putting her foot down and chewed her lip as she continued along the road. Her heart pounded in her chest.

What a mess.

Perspiration built under Gwen's clothes and she stabbed at the electric window for fresh air, unable to see any acceptable way out of this. If Jonah let Lena live, the woman would make it her life's work using that poor child as leverage. She'd bleed every single penny, as was her intention from the off, but now, Jonah would also be cut out of his child's life.

Another issue hung heavily in the air in Gwen's car. Her past with Jacky Powell would undoubtedly be exposed, but so be it.

Dialling Jonah's number again, hearing it ring out and then click to voicemail, Gwen felt like throwing the phone into the footwell with frustration. *Come on, Jonah! Where are you?* He very rarely didn't answer his phone. She'd try him again once she'd parked up.

Rounding the corner into Jonah's road, nerves mounted. She turned into the long drive to the house seeing another car parked up by the property.

Parking next to the black BMW, she frowned. *This was*

Saul's car... What was he doing here?

Hurrying from the car, Gwen rushed towards the house.

• • • •

'YOU'VE DONE *WHAT*?' Mike gasped, staring at the proud expression on his son's face.

Heath's smile slid. 'I thought you'd be pleased?'

'Pleased?' Mike cried. 'How can I be pleased? Telling me you've gone into that club? Mixed with those filth who killed my father, potentially exposing yourself to them as to who you are? Who *we* are and I'm supposed to be *pleased*?'

'They won't know!' Heath said defensively. 'As far as they're concerned, I'm just another punter who's got more money than sense.' He folded his arms and leant back in the chair, gaining back some of his confidence. 'They think I'm a record producer.'

Mike scowled. 'Who's *they*?'

Heath grinned widely. 'The woman who organises the events, who... wait for it... is only engaged to Jonah Powell.'

Mike flinched. 'Don't mention the fucking Powells!'

Heath shrugged. 'Ok, well... she's with him and I have to say, she's as hot as hell. I got the impression she wouldn't have said no...' He wouldn't mention just yet that he'd all but been about to make a move on Lena Taylor until Jonah had walked in. He'd keep that bit to himself.

Mike rolled his eyes. 'Oh yes, wouldn't that be a good idea? Trying it on with a psycho's tart!'

'He didn't look that psychotic to me,' Heath countered. Not exactly true, but his father was jumpy and he didn't want to unnerve him.

'You *met* him?' Mike gasped. *Had his son lost his mind?* 'And this is why you wanted my tux? Work function eh? What else are you lying about?'

'Nothing! I didn't tell you beforehand because I knew you'd freak out and try to stop me, but everything's fine.' Irritation bubbled. 'In case you hadn't noticed, I'm trying to make things right. I know they've got those diamonds – *your* diamonds. Who else would have got them from Dulcie Adams home and killed the daughter without getting nicked?' Heath nodded in agreement with his own theory. 'No one else would have the knowhow to pull off something like that, leaving no trace, unless it was a professional outfit.'

Mike was unsure whether Heath was insane or simply pure dense. 'Ok, so let's say you're right. How then do you propose to go any further with this? You've spoken to the wife, girlfriend – whoever she is, deduced she ranks a 10 and you've met the man whose father killed mine. Oh, and you reckon he's got the diamonds, which I might add your grandfather nicked from *them* in the first place, so what now? What does any of this achieve?' Hadn't he got enough problems with debts slowly drowning him and his business, without Heath wandering around like a Ronnie Kray impersonator? 'Come on! What are you really thinking any of this will *achieve*? Powell jovially slapping you on the back, saying *'I didn't realise it was you... My mistake... Please have the diamonds with my compliments'* Is that it?'

Heath pursed his lips. His father didn't have to be sarcastic. He was doing this for him, wasn't he? Would anything he did ever be acceptable? 'I've arranged an event. Or at least, *they* think I have. Not that I would pay 75k for a function!'

Mike spat his coffee over his desk. '75k? Are you crazy?'

Heath laughed. 'As I said, I'm not really, but they don't know that. My plan is to keep going there to arrange things. I'll act super interested and say I want to be hands on with the planning of the event.'

'I already know where the main office is. The events woman – Lena Taylor, seems fairly pliable.' He grinned widely. 'Personally, I think she's the key to getting exactly where I need to be.' That Jonah was a snotty fucker, so she'd be putty in his hands if he played his cards right.

Mike sighed. 'You're being oversimplistic about this. Christ knows what your mother would do if she knew...'

'She's not going to though, is she?' Heath snapped. 'A bit like that she's unaware that you're a gnat's knacker away from losing the business and your home.'

Mike shuffled uncomfortably. *Yes, he was well aware of that.* 'What's he like?'

'Who?'

'Powell.' The name scorched Mike's tongue. 'What's he like?'

Heath shrugged. 'Standoffish? Cold? Tries to come over as intimidating.' He wasn't about to admit that Jonah Powell *was* intimidating. 'Not a lot else to say.'

Mike frowned. 'And he didn't look at you funny?'

'Why would he look at me funny? It's you that looks like your father, not me.'

'You've got certain traits…'

'He didn't look at me funny, ok?' Heath repeated. Well, he hadn't. Jonah had barely looked at him at all and for the short time he had, the look had been nothing other than indifference.

'And you used that name - Darren Harding again, I presume?'

'Well, no but…'

'What? You gave your *real* name?' Mike spluttered. 'You used the name 'Pointer'? For fuck's sake. You're dead. We're all fucking dead!'

'Their system is automated. I had to sign up with my real name for verification purposes,' Heath blurted. 'It's all done via a central server, not real people. That lot are far too busy to physically look at member's names.'

He couldn't mention that only half of that was true. He could have used a fake name but he'd been so rushed to sign up before the Platinum member slots ran out, he hadn't been thinking. It had been idiotic, but he just had to hope he hadn't flagged himself up. That Lena woman had said *'Mr Pointer'*, so if the name was such a red rag, then surely the wife-to-be of the club's owner would not be unaware of a long-standing feud.

His father was paranoid. The Powells had more important

things to do than worry whether a relation of someone from thirty years ago might wander into the club. It was more likely they couldn't even remember his grandfather's name by now.

Thirty Nine

JOE TOYED WITH THE ALTERNATIVES. He could continue making his way to Dock Road to meet a psychopath who had not only attempted to drown him, but had killed his housemate and more than certainly murdered Helen Shepherd. The same nutter who now had possession of his ex-girlfriend and who had arranged to swap her for a pile of stolen diamonds that, oh yes… he didn't have… *Or* he could lie in the road and wait to be run over – preferably by something large and heavy, leaving no room for error.

Although the second option seemed by far the most preferable of the two, Joe also knew it wasn't feasible because whether or not it pained him to admit it, he lacked the courage to top himself. Unfortunately, he also lacked the courage to meet the nutter, but at least there was slight hope that he could walk away unharmed, providing he kept himself calm and his head straight.

If he could only force himself to revert to the jovial, chilled-out and confident guy he'd been just a month ago, then he'd have a lot more faith in his ability when it got to the part where he was supposed to hand the diamonds over.

It was strange - before any of this he was a dab hand at

blagging his way into or out of most situations, but now – now he needed that ability more than ever, it had deserted him. Along with the rest of his life.

Joe scowled as he made headway towards Dock Road. Sweat pooling in the small of his back, unsure whether it stemmed from the exertion of his brisk walk or pure unadulterated fear. Why was it when he *really* didn't want to do something, time speeded up. If only there was an earthquake or a massive sink hole should conveniently appear just at the junction of Dock Road, then everything would be a lot easier.

Feeling his mobile buzzing from inside his pocket, Joe's heart leapt. Seeing a text from Robert, Joe could barely open it fast enough. Was the whole thing off? *Please let it be that…*

`On way now. Do exactly as we agreed.`

With shaking fingers and a crushing sense of disappointment, Joe stuffed the phone back in his pocket and instead sparked up a cigarette. How he wished he'd had a joint or two before doing this. He stood more chance of being coherent if he was stoned. It disturbed him even more that he didn't know what Robert was planning. All he knew was that the man was going to see Jonah Powell. If Robert got killed, which based on the facts seemed likely, then where did that leave *him*?

Joe shuddered. Neither did he know what he was supposed to say to the nutter who, in a few seconds time, was expecting him to round the corner with a shed load of jewels. Robert's instructions of *'do whatever you need to buy me time'*, weren't particularly helpful.

He tried his best to continue putting one foot in front of the other, the dark silhouettes of the warehouses on Dock Road looming into view like a line of Grim Reapers doing nothing to help his overall mental state.

Chucking his fag end into the gutter, Joe reached for another, feeling familiar waves of panic rumble over him. He didn't even know which warehouse he was supposed to be going to.

The sudden and unexpected clanging of something smashing into tall railings, accompanied by a hideous growling noise made Joe jump out of his skin. His eyes darted to the side, immediately spotting a slathering German Shepherd rabidly trying to get to him. The iron bars impeded the animal, but did nothing to slow the further shredding of his nerves. He was so on edge he felt like he might shatter into a thousand pieces.

Upping his pace past the snarling dog, Joe's mind dared to wander to Teagan. The nutter said *after* the diamonds had been inspected, Teagan would be released. He'd offered no guarantee, but Robert was adamant it would work. Whatever Robert had planned must be more in depth and thought out than he'd been made party to, but he could do nothing but trust the man's word, despite the man being stranger than a van load of badgers.

Passing the high-gated entrance to the second warehouse, Joe didn't expect the voice which came from nowhere. His head snapped to the side, seeing the dark, yet distinct silhouette of the nutter behind the iron railings. Frozen to the spot, he waited while a small passenger gateway creaked noisily into life.

'Get in then!' Keith hissed, still partly concealed by the gatehouse box.

Hesitating, Joe glanced around, knowing once he'd stepped into the fenced off area there was no turning back.

'Hurry up!' the voice growled and Joe jumped through the opening, the gate clanging shut loudly behind him.

Saying nothing further, but jerking his head slightly in Joe's direction, Keith walked towards the warehouse, and Joe found himself obediently following. *Remember the brief*, he chanted silently. *Buy some time. Drag it out.*

Taking a deep breath, he made the concerted effort to convince his brain that this was an entirely different situation – one where he didn't have so much to lose and one where he wasn't scared shitless.

• • • •

ROBERT HAD WATCHED the club for over an hour. Parking his car two roads away, he was now safely concealed in a back doorway of a building opposite the side door of the Feathers. He glanced at his watch. Just gone 10. His heart rate increased. Joe should now be with the henchmen. He'd better be anyway.

He'd spent time around the front checking the lie of the land and the rest of the time he'd used searching for other entrances around the side and the back. There were several comings and goings, but aside from the massive bouncer on the front door, the large showy entrance was now closed since the show had started. The side entrance was the only real option. And if offered a plausible way in too.

Three times now Robert had seen it open by a man bringing out empties to put in the trade bins. The door was left ajar - the clink of light visible in the otherwise pitch black alleyway. On each of these occasions it was the same man – a young, slim guy in a white shirt and black waistcoat, most probably a barman and each time he'd come out he'd slipped around the side of the bins to have a sneaky fag.

He had no idea where this door would bring him out inside the building or where Jonah Powell was in relation to it. All it would take was one person to spot him and he'd be done for, but it was the only option he had.

Robert watched the barman smoking and his fingers twitched against his jacket pocket, the urge to light one up himself, intense. But he couldn't. Not now. This was the only chance he'd get.

Dashing across the alley, Robert slipped inside the door of the Feathers and made the decision to head straight up the dimly lit stairwell in front of him, rather than chance going through the door to the left.

Based on guessing the layout of the club from the outside he presumed there would most likely only be stock at this level – drink, food, chairs – that sort of thing, but he also knew from the research he'd done on the web, the VIP suites were at the top of the building with the main club below. But that was all it was – a *presumption*. He had no way of actually knowing. The offices could be anywhere, but more likely situated somewhere along with the upper echelons.

As he moved up the back stairs as quietly as possible, all Robert could hear was the thundering of his heart and his breathing, convinced it was so loud it would make him easily detectable.

He'd gone to the trouble of wearing his little-used dress suit so he would blend in with the customers and just had to enter somewhere that would bring him into a main area, rather than the parts with reception desks or added security.

Nearing the top of the stairs, Robert heard the muffled sound of the cabaret, but as to where it was coming from exactly, he couldn't gauge. He stared the metal door in front of him. *Fuck*. It might be a fire door and if he opened it, it could trigger an alarm. But apart from going back down the stairs he didn't have any other options. He'd been undetected so far and he wanted it to stay that way.

Throwing caution to the wind, Robert gave the door a hefty shove and it opened out onto a square lobby. Glancing to his left, he saw the back of the bruiser doorman and quickly ducked back behind the door into the stairwell. This was the main lobby, but the reception desk wasn't manned.

Peering back out, he spied the double doors opposite and another set to the left, as well as a single door off to the right. Which ones led upstairs and which opened onto the main club?

Robert's breath hitched. He couldn't afford to be spotted by the doorman, who luckily for him was busy on his phone. He had to make a decision and fast.

• • • •

LENA SCRUTINISED HERSELF in the trifold vanity mirror of her dressing table. Her lashes were looking a bit ropey and spidery around the edges. She'd have to order a few more pairs and get what was left of her real ones dyed again before the wedding.

She smiled, checking her lips were symmetrically plump. They wouldn't need topping up for a few months yet either. She had toyed with the idea of getting them done again, but it was too much of a risk. One of the times she'd had fillers her lips had taken a few days before they settled down and she didn't want to risk anything like that happening so close to the big day.

No, she'd do just perfectly, thank you. It was all good. And next Friday she'd be meeting Uncle Ron. It was disappointing that Auntie Noeleen couldn't make the new date, but at least Uncle Ron was coming.

Lena placed her mascara back on the dressing table. Despite all of the bad feeling resulting from her decision to leave in the first place, she missed her family greatly, but this marriage to Jonah would show her sentiments were for valid reasons. If it didn't, then at least *she'd* be nicely well off.

It was also possible things could go the other way when the truth came out. She patted her kitchen roll bump. But whilst *this* was in situ she couldn't see it going in any other way but hers. It would be ok. It *would.* And there wasn't long to wait now.

Glancing up at the sound of the doorbell, Lena huffed. *Who the bloody hell was that?*

Getting up, she moved to the bedroom window and craned her neck, but couldn't see past the porch overhang. She'd told Jonah they needed cameras installed that could be seen from any room, but he'd always been reluctant; coming out with crap that the day he lived like someone from *Star Trek* was the day his reputation no longer proceeded him, signifying he was finished.

Lena couldn't envisage Jonah ever being finished and wanted the cameras regardless.

Begrudgingly making her way down the galleried landing, the doorbell rang again, this time more urgently. She tutted in irritation. Why did the postman insist on ringing the bell over and over? Why couldn't they leave the bloody parcels on the doorstep? It wasn't like anyone would pinch something from *this* house.

Lena's eyes brightened. Maybe it was her dress? She'd received an email from the bridal company saying it had been despatched via courier so it could be that. Oh, she hoped so. She couldn't wait to see it. The dress she'd commissioned may have cost an arm and a leg, but it was worth every penny. Jonah wanted her to look the business on their wedding day, didn't he?

Reaching the bottom of the stairs, Lena's heels clacked across the wooden floor of the large reception hallway whilst the ringing of the doorbell was replaced with banging. 'Alright, alright! I'm coming!' she shouted. *Christ, a courier with a wedding dress or not, there was no need for this.*

Lena yanked open the door, her eyes accusing. 'You don't have to knock the bloody door down y… Oh!'

Saul barged past Lena into the hall. 'Mind if I come in?'

Lena's mouth flapped up and down as she froze against the door.

'Shut the door,' Saul instructed, his voice neutral, but his eyes conveying an entirely different story.

'What's wrong?' Lena spluttered, nerves jangling as she hastily closed the door, well aware of Saul's intimidating presence dwarfing everything around him. 'Has something happened to Jonah?' *If something had happened to Jonah when she was this close to the wedding it would ruin everything.*

A strange half smile slid across Saul's face. 'Nothing's happened to Jonah, he's fine. Or at least he will be until he discovers about *you*?'

Ice flooded Lena's veins. 'M-Me?'

FORTY

NERO'S JAW CLENCHED as he walked back into Jonah's office. Jonah wouldn't like this. *He* didn't like it either.

This was the guy that Lena had invited behind the scenes? The stupid, stupid bitch. There was no way this was a coincidence.

Jonah glanced up from his phone. 'I've missed two calls from Gwen. I'd better call her back.'

Nero placed the Platinum members folder in front of Jonah. 'Before you do that, you need to take a look at this...'

Seeing the expression on Nero's face, Jonah placed his phone back in his pocket and looked down at the paperwork.

'I cross-referenced the details on that booking form with the memberships that came through Lena's automated system,' Nero explained.

Reading the details in front of him, Jonah visibly blanched, then his face twisted with a combination of sheer disbelief and rage. *Pointer? Heath Pointer?* The guy in Lena's office last night was a Pointer?

Nero stared at Jonah deep in thought. 'Surely the man wouldn't be so stupid as to come here? To come here into your club if he w…'

'The stupid, stupid bitch…' Jonah hissed, his eyes bright. 'She let a fucking Pointer into *my* club? She brought him back here into *my* space, falling for his bullshit about an extortionately overpriced event he wants to book?' He got to his feet and slammed his fist on the desk. 'I'll kill him!'

'It does seem the man has a death wish. That's if it is one of *those* Pointers?' Nero muttered.

'It's got to be!' Jonah raged. 'I'll wring Lena's fucking neck for this. Does she not have any sense?'

'I presume she knows about the link with the Pointers?'

'How could she not?' Jonah spat. 'She's taking the piss, she has to be!' He grabbed the whisky from the side and poured himself a large shot, his fingers shaking with rage.

'I'm presuming you're thinking this guy is aware of the connection then?'

'Why else would he be here and squirrelling his way in via Lena?' Jonah's eyes narrowed. 'He's pulling a stunt. I'm not sure what as yet, but I intend to find out.'

Nero frowned. 'Do you think it could have been him that was at the Adams' house? You said someone had got there first.'

Jonah dug his teeth into his bottom lip thoughtfully, his anger although raw, not clouding his logic. 'The Pointers would think they had a claim on the diamonds, but if it was him – or them, whoever the rest of them are and they *did* manage to lift the diamonds from the house, then why come here? Unless…' Jonah sat down heavily. 'Unless they think *we've* got them?'

Nero whistled through teeth. 'This is fucked up!'

Jonah's face broke into a snarl. 'Well, whatever this Heath Pointer's game is or what he has or hasn't got, I'll be paying him a visit. A *personal* visit.'

Nero flinched. 'Is that wise? If y…'

'The address is here.' Jonah stabbed his finger on the membership details form. 'I wonder if it's his real address or a fake one, like the rest of his fucking family.'

'If he's stupid enough to give his real name to the Powells

for a membership card, then I suspect it's the real address,' Nero said, unable to help but smile. He watched Jonah get up and unlock the large cupboard at the back of his office – the one with the secret compartment which concealed a healthy assortment of spare guns. 'You're going there now?'

Jonah smiled. 'No time like the present!'

• • • •

BEFORE LENA COULD SAY ANYTHING ELSE or deduce what Saul meant by his comment, her power of logic was cut off when a hand shot out and grabbed her around the throat.

Eyes wide with shock, Lena's fingers grappled against the hand wrapped tightly around her neck, a weird strangulated sound coming from her mouth.

Pushing himself into Lena's face, Saul snarled, 'You're not marrying my brother, you money-grabbing tart. I'll give you one last chance to do the right thing and call it off. Do you understand?' *There would be no more chances, but he'd see what she'd got to say before continuing with what he'd come to do.* Slightly relaxing his grip so Lena could speak, he waited.

Indignation overtook Lena's fear and her eyes narrowed. Saul couldn't come in here demanding stuff. Was he insane? She wouldn't call anything off, regardless of what he said.

Oh, she'd heard all about him. Everyone knew he was tapped with a twisted head. She contemplated whether it was worth turning on the charm. She'd always got what she wanted by using her God's given guiles, but maybe not this time. She needed to know what the issue was before she decided which way to play it. *Sex or tears?* Whichever one worked would suffice.

'I don't know what's been said, but I won't call off the wedding. If this is about money, I've already told Jonah I'll sign a pre-nup.' *Not that she had any intention of doing that either.*

'You've told Jonah a lot of things….' Saul spat. 'Like me trying to get in your knickers. In your dreams, you whore.'

'He told you that?' Lena cried, wide-eyed. *Shit.* 'I've never suggested that.' She'd begged Jonah not to say anything to Saul, but he'd gone and done it anyway, the stupid bastard.

Saul laughed. 'Jonah didn't.'

'Well if it wasn't him, who was it? Who would sa.... Ah, of course... Gwen!' Lena sneered. 'And Jonah believes her? As do you! What a surprise!' She laughed sarcastically. 'And to think I had you down as not being gullible.'

Despite her head being forced at a painful angle, Lena pushed her large breasts against Saul. He could take her against this wall right now if he liked. Running her tongue over her bottom lip, Lena's eyes twinkled. 'It wasn't like you didn't make it obvious that you'd like to get me into bed. I suspect that's also evident now...'

Her hand traced over Saul's crotch, fully expecting to find him hard and ready, but disappointedly found no trace of excitement.

Saul grinned, his exposed teeth making him look crazy. 'Although I'm well known for screwing anything that moves, *you* do nothing for me at all. I'd rather stick my cock in a dead badger that put it anywhere your plastic gold-digging cunt.'

Colouring furiously, Lena masked her shock with a sneer. 'You sure know how to make a girl feel good with your remarks... Anyway, you don't have to come near me – Jonah does and has done so on countless occasions!'

Irritation festered. It was this pretend baby that put him off, wasn't it? That was probably why the rich music producer hadn't jumped on her too. Anyway, it didn't matter because Saul could fuck off. She was marrying Jonah and there was nothing he could do about it.

'Does Jonah know you're here? I wonder how he'd feel if he knew you were threatening me,' Lena spat. 'He'd run you out of the very firm you're so desperate to have for yourself - you know, the one that ran perfectly well without you whilst you were busy getting fisted by some big black man in the nick!'

Red mist descended on Saul and he raised his fist. 'You

little fucking tramp!'

A flash of fear ran through Lena. *He'd ruin her face! She couldn't have that!* 'No! Don't. What about the baby?'

'What baby? You're not even pregnant!' Saul spat, his eyes flashing. 'You think I don't know? My brother's so fucking thick he believes your lies, but I don't!'

FORTY ONE

CREEPING ALONG THE deserted corridor, Robert held his breath, every nerve ending alert for movement or noise. He could hardly believe his good fortune in finding the staff area of the club so empty.

He'd been beginning to think no one was around at all, including the man he so desperately needed to see, meaning all of this had been a waste of time, but then he heard voices from a room at the bottom of the corridor. Edging closer to the wall, hoping no one was monitoring the CCTV, Robert hastened towards the door. This was the only one without a glass panel and he had a hunch this was the place he was looking for.

His adrenalin pounded. Fear was absent; rage and desperation overshadowing any nerves and fuelling the driving force behind every action.

Slamming his shoulder against the heavy door, Robert's large frame burst into the room, immediately spotting two equally large men and knew straight away he'd picked the correct place.

Wasting no time, he stormed towards the man he knew to be Jonah Powell. He'd seen photos on the web whilst he'd been researching his plan and *this* was him. 'You bastard!' he roared.

'What the fuck?' Spinning around, Nero watched Jonah effortlessly swing the gun towards the stranger.

Robert stared at the gun unperturbed. This man could shoot him if he wanted, but not before he released Teagan. That was all that mattered. 'Jonah Powell, I demand you release the girl,' he roared. 'Release her and you can have what you want.'

Jonah stared at the man in front of him, his finger steady on the trigger of his revolver, unable to believe what his eyes were seeing. This man – whoever he was, was a spit of Michael bastard Pointer. The face of that snake in his father's old photographs was indelibly ingrained in his brain and now it was standing in front of him. *The dead had come back to life.*

This must be Robert Adams - the son Nero and Keith had told him about. One thing was for sure and that was he was undoubtedly a Pointer. Why were the Pointers coming out of the woodwork all of a sudden? He knew there had to be a reason that music producer prick was here last night. They were in it together. This was all part of the same thing. This was Lena's fault, but he'd be stopping this. Stopping it *now*. 'I've waited a long time to personally make you pay for your family, Pointer.'

'I'm no Pointer. I'm Robert Adams and I don't care about that. I'm here for one thing only and that is Teagan. Tell me where she is,' Robert snarled.

Jonah almost laughed. It was surprising the Pointer bloodline wasn't extinct! The guy had a loaded pistol pointing into his face and all he cared about was some girl? Glancing at Nero, he frowned, then his eyes darted back to Robert Adams, whose hand moved to his pocket. 'Oh, you're a Pointer alright and I wouldn't make any rash movements if I were you.'

Ignoring the warning, Robert continued blindly. 'This is what you want isn't it? Courtesy of my mother!' Pulling the wooden box open, he threw it on the desk in front of him. 'These are yours, I presume? I don't want them – never have. Now let the girl go.'

Jonah's eyes fixated on the collection of pink diamonds rolling loosely around on his desk. *What the fuck?* For the first time in a very long time Jonah was rendered speechless. The man didn't even have a gun – he had nothing. Just *these.* And he'd thrown them on the desk, just like that?

A grudging and unexpected sense of admiration Robert Adams washed over Jonah.

Robert twitched with frustration. 'We're wasting time. You've got what you wanted, now release Teagan.'

Jonah lowered his gun. 'Teagan? Who the fuck is Teagan and where did you get these from?' He nodded at the jewels.

'Like I said – my mother. Dulcie Adams. I'm sure you're aware of her? You or one of you broke into her home to retrieve them.' Robert jerked his head at the diamonds. 'I thought it was you who killed my sister, but now I know it was *her.* I have found out a lot of things recently - the diamonds being one of them. You've got them back, so give me Teagan.'

He dragged his hands through his hair in agitation. 'Look, I have no argument with you. I didn't know anything about these until two days ago. A bit like I didn't know anything about my father being Michael Pointer either. I believe he stole these from your family and I presume that's why you were at the house?' His eyes narrowed. 'But I *will* have a problem if you don't give me Teagan. I know that's why you snatched her and why you're holding her, but she's got nothing to do with this. She doesn't even know about them, so be a man and let her go.'

Jonah's face was outwardly neutral, but inside his blood was boiling - his mind a seething mass of conflicting emotions and confusion. This was one hell of a mind fuck and he was wary of how much he was prepared to believe. It could be an elaborate plan? 'And what do *you* know about Heath Pointer?'

'Who?' Robert roared. 'Stop pissing about. I know you've got Teagan because I have someone with one of your henchmen at this very moment. They think *they're* getting the diamonds, but I diverted them as I wanted to speak to *you.* I want this done and I want Teagan back. As much as I don't like the prick who's dealing with your men, they'll probably rip him to pieces when they find out he hasn't got the jewels and I don't think that's very fair, do you?'

Jonah's eyes flashed menacingly. 'I haven't got your girl, whoever she is. I don't know what you're talking about with henchmen either. All my men are all accounted for. Now get the fuck out of my face.'

'One of you has her!' Robert raged, his fist slamming down on Jonah's desk.

Jonah moved forward at the speed of light, grabbing Robert, the two men equally matched in size.

Suddenly a horrible thought flashed into Nero's mind. 'Saul?'

Jonah froze, his head swinging around to Nero. 'What?'

'Saul and Keith…' Nero continued, his voice clipped. 'They could have her…'

A wave of cold washed over Jonah. Could Saul have lifted the girl to use as collateral to get the diamonds behind his back? His head flicked back to Robert. 'This man you say has been in contact with one of ours. Who is he?'

'Some idiot that used to go out with Teagan. Joe. Joe Singleton – that's his name. He gave you keys to my mother's house, apparently,' Robert snarled.

Jonah's eyes narrowed. That was the stoner – the one he'd given instructions not to bother with anymore. *The bastards.* He'd been right all along. Saul and Keith had been working behind his back… His teeth clenched. He would have Saul for this, the lying cunt. And to snatch a woman? *For fuck's sake.*

'The flat,' Nero muttered. 'They must be holding her at the flat.'

Robert shrugged Jonah's hand off the shoulder of his tuxedo. 'Tell me where the fucking flat is!'

Jonah had to give this guy credit – he had balls, that much was certain. And Nero could be well on to something there. 'Have you seen either of them?'

'Not for a while, no,' Nero answered.

'We need to get there now!' Robert cried, moving towards the office door. 'We need to get to her before they do. Once your men realise Joe hasn't got the diamonds, they'll take it out on Teagan, I'm sure they will.'

Nero thought this Joe person would be the first casualty, but didn't bother voicing it. It was pretty bloody obvious. It was also feasible that Saul and Keith had this girl – more than feasible. And if they had, then they would be keeping her at that flat he'd seen them coming out of. His nerves fizzed. Unease stirred and gained pace.

Jonah shoved his pistol in his waistband. 'We'll check it out.'

'I'm coming with you,' Robert barked, his eyes showing that he was deadly serious. 'Once I've got Teagan, then I'll tell you everything I know.'

• • • •

'STOP!' GWEN YELLED, pushing through the front door of Jonah's house, glad she remembered that unless it was deadlocked it opened from the handle like a standard internal door. 'Stop Saul! Lena's pregnant.'

Eyes locking onto Gwen, Saul's fist remained poised in mid-air, his other hand still holding Lena tightly by the jaw.

Gwen looked from Lena to Saul. She had to bring this down. She would blow the rest as to who Lena really was in a moment, but she couldn't stand by whilst Saul punched a pregnant woman in the face. Even if that face was Lena's.

Lena blinked rapidly. Through her fear, the ever present certainty of winning overriding logic. Even knowing Saul could smash her face beyond recognition was not enough to dampen her drive to get the last word in. She wanted to have the last laugh and get one over on this prick. This prick who deemed himself above her charms. And as for Gwen, why the bloody hell did she feel the need to come steaming in here like Maid Marion. The old bitch had told Saul she wasn't pregnant and now here she was saying the opposite?

Oh well... if she thought that this meant she would be grateful, then Gwen would get a very rude awakening. This was the perfect opportunity. Gwen was backing up her pregnancy and so she now had nothing to hold her over a barrel. *Absolutely nothing at all.*

'Saul?' Gwen moved forward, placing her hand on his arm. 'Did you hear me? I said, Lena is pregnant.' She glanced at Lena, sure she saw a flash of triumph in her eyes. 'I-I was mistaken. She *is* having Jonah's baby.'

Beads of sweat ran down Saul's rugged face, the veins in his temples bulging. He glared at Gwen, his eyes raging with unbridled fury. 'Keep out of this,' he hissed. 'She's an usurper bitch. She shouldn't even be here. She should *never* have been here. She's trying to break the firm up and she won't be marrying my brother.'

'I *will* marry him, whether you like it or not,' Lena cried, quickly adopting a scared doe-eyed look as Saul swung his hate-ridden glare back on her. Gwen may have seen her turn it on, but that hardly mattered. Gwen would be finished any second now.

She'd ride the pleasure derived from this fascinating stand-off watching Gwen beg Saul not to lay a finger on her a bit longer. Christ, it must be Gwen's worst nightmare and all to save the blue-eyed boy she thinks so highly of. The blue-eyed boy that would want nothing more to do with the old cow once *she'd* finished.

The hypocritical sly old hag had it coming. Lena smiled inwardly, the urge to laugh out loud with unbridled glee was almost unstoppable, but luckily she held a look of gratefulness when Saul lowered his fist, his cold stare still firmly embedded onto her. *A stare she could deal with.*

Turning on the waterworks, Lena slumped back against the wall, making sure her shoulders heaved in unison with her sobs, her broken nailed hands covering her face to hide her bone-dry eyes. Feeling felt Gwen's arms fall protectively around her, she resisted the urge to throw the older woman across the other side of the room as if she were poison ivy.

'Christ,' Gwen gasped, staring at Saul, his chest heaving as he fought to remain in control of his breathing. 'What are you thinking? She's pregnant, for God's sake.'

Saul took a deep breath. He was going through with his plan come what may. If what Gwen said was true, then it was more important now that ever. 'Sorry Gwen, you shouldn't have to witness this…'

'You won't be sorry once you know what she's done,' Lena cried.

Gwen froze. Lena wasn't stupid enough to say anything now, was she? She wouldn't rile the situation up any further?

'You think this is all about me?' Lena rubbed the kitchen roll bump. 'Like Gwen said, I'm having Jonah's baby but she's the one who hasn't been honest. She's n…'

'Shut it!' Saul roared. Grabbing Gwen's jacket, he pulled her none too gently out of the way, causing her to stumble onto the wooden hallway floor.

Gwen could do nothing as Saul moved like a panther, smashing Lena full bore in the stomach with his fist. For a split second she was rendered motionless with horror, as letting out a blood-curdling scream, Lena crumpled to the floor, her face twisted in agony. She watched, transfixed as Saul kicked at Lena so violently, her whole body shunted several feet along the polished floor.

'Saul! NO!' Gwen screamed. Scrambling to her bruised knees, her feet slipping on the shiny surface, she rushed to stand up.

'There will be no fucking baby!' Saul barked, driving another horrific kick to Lena's stomach.

Bile rising, Gwen rushed forward, blind that Saul's fury could easily be turned on to her in the blink of an eye. *He couldn't do this. Oh, Jesus – that baby!* 'SAUL! STOP!'

Grabbing his arm, she pulled and pulled, Saul still kicking out wildly. Animal-like howling came from Lena's mouth, her eyes wide and panicked like a barbie doll in a horror film.

'SAUL!' Gwen screamed so loudly her throat felt like it was being slashed with razors. *Oh, dear Jesus*. Jonah would kill

Saul for this; kill him stone dead. This was *her* fault. She shouldn't have told Saul of her suspicions. He was crazy; unhinged. 'SAUL!' She pulled as hard as she could, kicking at the back of his legs, *anything* to break his frenzy. 'You'll kill her! Stop it!'

All of a sudden, Saul stopped and stood panting heavily. His eyes glazed, he hawked up a ball of phlegm, spitting it in Lena's face.

Gwen dropped back to her knees at the side of Lena and feeling for a pulse, she was relieved to find one. 'Lena?' She patted her face. 'Lena, sweetheart – can you hear me?'

Whatever her issue with the girl; whatever she'd been about to say that would drop her right in it and ruin her life, she didn't warrant this. *No one* deserved this. Saul must have killed that baby – nothing could withstand a kicking like that. She looked up at Saul, tears streaming down her face. 'How could you?'

Saul nodded at the pool of blood steadily forming underneath Lena and smiled thinly. 'Job done, I'd say?'

Following Saul's emotionless gaze, Gwen gasped, her heart thudding painfully. 'Call an ambulance. *Now*!'

Saul shrugged. 'Why the fuck would I do that?' Internally, he was dancing with joy. *Baby no more*. 'Now there no need for my brother to marry the whore.'

Gwen stared at Saul in disbelief. 'I cannot believe you've done this. What sort of animal are you?' This would destroy Jonah. He wanted this baby and was proud to be becoming a father and to know that Saul had deliberately kicked it out of Lena... well, she dreaded to think what the result would be. 'Call the ambulance...' she repeated, gently stroking Lena's face. 'Come on, sweetheart. Can you hear me?'

Coming to, Lena immediately howled in pain, her face screwed up, she began retching.

'It's ok,' Gwen muttered. 'Help is coming.' She glared at Saul and jerked her head towards the phone. Unbuttoning the last part of Lena's dress, she frowned seeing a swimming costume. She audibly gasped at the visible dent in Lena's bump, her own stomach rolling with the thought of that poor baby.

'Shut her up?' Saul barked. 'Or I will.'

Ignoring Saul, Gwen slipped the swimming costume off Lena's shoulders and eased it down over the pink lacy bra underneath, wincing at the purple bruising already vivid over the woman's ribs. Pulling it lower, she froze as a pile of kitchen roll fell out of the swimming costume onto the floor, revealing a blackened and purple, but perfectly flat stomach.

She paused, trying to make sense of it. Only Saul's sarcastic laughter broke Gwen from her confusion.

'Seems you were right all along, so you can get off your high horse about me being this, that or whatever now.'

Gwen stared at the wad of kitchen roll. *The sly bitch.* Lena wasn't pregnant and never had been, but she was bleeding from somewhere and needed urgent treatment.

'Get her cleaned up. Do you want to tell Jonah about her lies, or can I have that pleasure?'

'Something's ruptured. We have to get her to hospital.'

Saul laughed nastily as he pulled his phone from his pocket. 'Nah, fuck it. Leave her as she is. Jonah will kill her anyway, so there's no point.'

Lena glared at Gwen. Even through the agony of broken ribs and whatever had ruptured inside of her, she still found enough energy to spit out her venom through gritted teeth. 'Talk about me all you like,' she hissed. 'I don't care. I may not be having a baby but at least I didn't fuck Jacky Powell, like you...'

Saul looked between Gwen and Lena, before fixing his glare on Gwen. 'What the fuck did she just say?'

FORTY TWO

ROBERT'S HEART THUNDERED as he sat in the back of Jonah Powell's Range Rover. He was more than aware of being scrutinised in the rear view mirror by the piercing eyes of the man himself whilst the car moved at a breakneck speed along the inner city roads.

Robert hadn't even thought it was possible to get through London this fast, but it was being achieved somehow. This was the least of his concerns, but at least it gave his rolling brain a few seconds' respite from what was *really* on his mind.

From the reaction of these two men about Teagan's possible whereabouts and the fact they had moved so quickly on it, he knew that wasn't a good sign.

Dread pooled as Robert's mind scrolled through a selection of various scenarios. He was scared. Scared of what they might find. Looping thoughts of Teagan pushed back into the forefront and he clenched his sweaty fists. *What if after all of this, he felt nothing?*

Fumbling to work his lighter with shaking fingers, Robert lit a cigarette and stared out of the window at the none-too pleasant surroundings. He eyed the never-ending blocks of flats rising from a maze of littered streets as they navigated the warren of roads into an estate and wrinkled his nose in distaste at the general mess and groups of unsavoury people loitering around. 'You own all these flats?' he muttered.

'Not all of them. Just that block over there.' Jonah heard the accusation in Robert Adams' tone and couldn't say he blamed him. It had been a long time since he'd clapped eyes on this hell-hole and it was a lot worse than he remembered. And that was saying something!

From what he could see, Saul's continuance of running the enterprise from prison, he'd concentrated only on getting as many undesirables into the properties as possible. The sort who either wouldn't care or *dare* question the state of the accommodation they were renting for extortionate prices.

Jonah pursed his lips, wishing he'd taken more of an active interest in how Saul was managing this project, but he'd never given it much thought. Not until now.

And this Robert Adams was a strange one. Jonah had always presumed he'd have immediately gone berserk being faced with the offspring of Michael Pointer, but Robert's demeanour had impressed him – as had his lack of fear and intent come what may to achieve what he came for. That, and of course, the non-irrelevant factor of returning the diamonds…

He hadn't even got his head around that yet, nor had he even savoured their long-awaited return. He'd slung the diamonds into his office safe before running to the car. If what Robert said was true and Keith and Saul were keeping a woman hostage in one of these dismal flats, then he needed to deal with that first and foremost. His jaw clenched. Women were not used as pawns in his firm. They haver had been and for Saul to pull a stunt like that, although unsurprising, was inexcusable.

Again, the glaring truth that his brother had schemed behind his back, blatantly breaking their agreement, throbbed in his temples, but he didn't have time to mull that over. It was his duty to release the girl and hope she wasn't harmed. Saul's well-known lack of respect for women was legendary. As for Keith's part in this betrayal...

Parking up against the kerb, Jonah yanked on the handbrake and glanced at Nero. 'Let's go!'

Robert followed Jonah and Nero up the stinking stairwells and along mazes of walkways, his heart thundering painfully.

Pulling out a large ring of keys, Nero flicked through them as they hurried along the third floor walkway. 'It's number 235.'

Robert waited impatiently for Nero to put the key in the lock, everything taking an extraordinary length of time, when in real life it was only seconds. 'Come on,' he hissed through gritted teeth. He'd kick the door down if he had to.

As the chipped, cracked front door was stiffly pushed open, Robert barged his way inside behind Jonah, the stench immediately assaulting his nostrils.

'Holy fuck!' Nero gasped, putting his hand over his mouth and nose. This smell alone signified things were far from alright.

Trying not to gag, Robert rushed into the nearest room, finding a tiny kitchen, the table strewn with empty sandwich packets, an overflowing ashtray and a collection of empty beer cans.

Jonah craned his neck through to the lounge, seeing it empty, his unease increasing. 'She must be in the bedroom,' he said, hastily turning on his heels to the short hallway and the door opposite. Trying the handle, he couldn't altogether say he was surprised to find it locked. *Saul, you utter bastard,* he thought, his anger intensifying.

'Fucking open the door!' Robert yelled, banging his fist impotently against the hallway wall.

Raising his foot, Jonah gave the door one almighty boot, the wood splintering as the door gave way. Enveloped by a blast of stronger stench, the men rushed into the dark room, Jonah's fingers fumbling along the wall to find a light switch.

As the room suddenly illuminated, for one moment in time all three man stared in silence at the scene.

• • • •

DULCIE STARED AT HER REFLECTION resenting how old she looked. She'd been stunning back in her day, yet with each hour, further despised how the years had gradually chipped away at her perfect looks, leaving her… *old.*

Her face screwed into a scowl. How had it come to this? It was bad enough dealing with the unanswered questions surrounding Michael's abandonment, but she'd lived for the day when it was safe to share the insurance the love of her life had left her with her most priceless possession of all – Robert.

But Robert had changed. He'd always been steadfast in his unwavering devotion, but now it had crumbled. She'd felt it disintegrating bit by bit. He hadn't said or done anything in particular, but he didn't have to. She could *tell.* The looks he'd started giving her – the suspicion she'd witnessed lurking behind his eyes… The comments he'd made and the questions he'd asked, underlined it all.

Her son no longer believed or trusted her.

Dulcie's bottom lip trembled. Anyone else was fine, but with Robert, it wasn't. She had to have Robert's full trust, attention and love. That was the only thing to hold any importance since Michael had left. It was all Teagan's fault. If the stupid girl had minded her own business, then everything would be alright.

Even the knowledge that the Powells and possibly the other Pointers were on her trail after all of these years wasn't something that unduly fazed her. She'd always half-expected them to show up at some point and was only surprised it had taken them so long, but even that wasn't a problem. She could deal with *anything* whilst Robert was in her corner, but he shouldn't have found out about his father the way he had.

Dulcie scowled into the mirror once more. She'd been so close. So, *so* close. With Helen removed it left the way clear to move forward unhindered with no awkward questions from her unwanted daughter. Bloody silly bitch that Helen was. Selfish to the core like her bastard of a father.

She turned her head from left to right, hating the saggy jowls now dominating her once pristine face. They spoilt her side profile. They spoilt *everything.*

After Helen's funeral the time had been right to tell Robert. They'd go abroad, cash in the diamonds and start again. It would have been perfect…

How she rued the day when she'd made the decision to employ the stupid slut. With her self-effacing simpering personality, she'd thought Teagan perfect, but she couldn't have been more wrong. It must have been the girl's aim from the start to fleece everything she possibly could.

She may have now disappeared off the face of the earth, but it was too late. The damage was done and her beloved son had lost faith.

Biting back the sting of tears, Dulcie stomped determinedly down the hallway to her bedroom. She hadn't seen hide nor hair of Robert since last night either. He'd do anything to be away from her now, that was clear. She'd really thought she could turn his sudden change of attitude around with the latest stories she'd worked so hard to concoct, but she'd lost her power.

It was over.

Well, if Robert hated her then there was nothing left around here. Being as he thought so little of her, she'd leave him alone. *For good.*

Dulcie plastered a smile across her face. She would do what she'd planned all along, just with the exception of doing it alone, rather than with her son at her side. Then Robert would wish he'd remained loyal. Tough luck – it was too late.

Right. That was settled. She'd take the diamonds and go.

Pushing open the door to her bedroom, Dulcie reached around the back of the chest of drawers to remove the box. Sighing when she couldn't quite reach it, she got down further on her knees and extended her hand further.

With a blinding jolt of panic, Dulcie flopped back against the wall. They were gone. Her diamonds had gone.

FORTY THREE

IT DIDN'T MATTER ANYMORE. None of it did. Keith scowled. He'd had enough.

He hadn't expected to get a call. Saul sounded high as a kite and Keith had immediately thought his plans to meet the stoner and get the diamonds had been uncovered, but nothing was mentioned. All Saul said was that he needed a hand. Keith hadn't bothered asking what for because he didn't care. He didn't care about any of it.

After he'd done what was needed, he'd tell Jonah what Saul had done. He'd explain everything and if Jonah asked why this muppet was with him, he'd say it was because he was trying to get that girl away from his psycho fucking brother.

He knew he was finished. Jonah would never stand for him going behind his back, but even on the off chance that Jonah *did* forgive him, Saul would not.

Keith glared at Joe, his broken nose and smashed mouth bleeding profusely as he lay bound in the boot of his car. *Wanker*, he thought as he slammed the lid shut and clambered into the drivers' seat. Now this stoner prick had double-crossed him like everyone else did, he had no diamonds to placate the situation or guarantee release of the girl.

Keith knew he'd done some shit things in his life, but he wasn't being party to this cruel bollocks any longer. Enough was enough. He'd dump this prat at the house and do whatever it was that Saul wanted him to do. That would be the last thing he'd ever do before he served Saul up to Jonah, then he'd go round and release the girl. Once he'd released her then he'd take on the chin whatever Saul or Saul *and* Jonah would have in store for his betrayal. But he wouldn't take it until the girl had been set free. He hadn't got anything left to lose – not now… But he did have a small shred of self-respect left that he was determined to cling on to before he was killed.

Nerves pricked at the thought of being ripped apart by the Powell brothers like a pack of hyenas. But he would not be leaving this world until he had exposed what Saul had done. That would be his parting gift.

Driving rapidly through the streets to Jonah's large house, Keith sighed. After everything, his life had amounted to sod all. He'd got jack shit for his life's work for the Powells and now he would die in shame as a traitor.

Lighting up a cigarette, Keith turned into Jonah's road. Turning up the drive, he frowned at Gwen's car parked next to Saul's BMW.

Absentmindedly shrugging, Keith turned the engine off and got out of the car, flicking the boot open. He unceremoniously hauled Joe out of the boot, not taking a blind bit of notice when the man's head thwacked against the bumper.

• • • •

THE SILENCE WAS DEAFENING. Gwen knew Saul had said something in response to the words Lena had uttered about Jacky, but all she could hear was high-pitched ringing deep inside her ears.

How long had she sat motionless for? How long had everything carried on with and without her? She tried to look at Saul, at Lena, but found herself paralysed in a state of suspended animation.

She could hear a muffled voice, like she was deep underwater. Her head swam, unable to believe that her worst nightmare had finally come true. *Saul knew about her and Jacky*. Saul knew and Jonah would soon know. Everyone would know…

Somehow forcing herself back to the present, Gwen realised that only seconds had passed.

'I asked you what the fuck Lena was talking about, Gwen,' he spat, his voice rising. Reaching down, he grabbed Gwen by her suit jacket and pulled her to her feet, his eyes searching hers. 'Tell me it isn't true. Tell me you weren't sleeping with my father…'

Gwen swallowed, her eyes locked on to Saul's – his vicious expression also holding a hint of desperation. She opened her mouth to speak, but the words became jammed in her throat.

'Gwen!' Saul cried, his eyes mere slits, knowing her lack of response confirmed everything. Adrenalin pumped wildly in his veins and his body tremored. He'd always liked Gwen, but all along… White fury descended. 'You disgusting bitch!' he snarled, grabbing her around the throat.

'L-Let me explain… I…' Gwen spluttered, Saul's fingertips crushed against her neck. Oh dear God, he was going to kill her. He would kill her and she'd never get to explain to Jonah how it really was.

Saul pushed himself closer to Gwen's face. 'Because of you, my father wasn't there when my mother died. I remember no one could find him that night and it was because he was between *your* legs, you dirty whore!'

Tears poured down Gwen's face at Saul's venomous diatribe, his words slicing like knives. 'It wasn't like that! Please! We…'

'Get away from me, you despicable witch!' Saul roared, backhanding Gwen.

Flying across the room, Gwen landed heavily against the wall, pain shooting through her shoulder. 'I understand you're angry, but if I can just explain. It…'

Eyes flashing with menace, Saul strode over to where Gwen lay, smirking as she cowered from his reaching grasp. 'Shut it! There's fuck all you can say!' Grabbing her by the lapel of her jacket, he lifted her off the floor like a limp doll. 'I've had enough of all of you pointless bastards!'

Dragging Gwen with one hand, the other grabbing a dining chair, he plonked her onto it, wasting no time in binding her to the slatted wooden back. His mind seethed. He'd had enough of people taking the piss. And to think he'd been happy to have solved the grating problem of Lena thinking she could lie her way into the family, when all along – all these years, there had been another lying whore in his midst.

Oh, he'd had enough alright. Even his right hand man didn't like how he did things anymore, the stupid bastard having developed a conscience for the slag in the flat. Well, fuck him and fuck all of them. Keith would be here any minute like he'd instructed and he could deal with getting rid of these two. Once he'd done that, he'd be joining them.

Saul's brow furrowed. He was Saul Powell. No one, but *no one* took the piss. Things had slipped too far in his absence. People had forgotten and he wasn't having it. Those diamonds were his and if Jonah failed to step up after all of this… If he still insisted pussy-footing around whilst everyone around him was taking him for a mug, then brother or not, he was done too.

'Saul,' Gwen squeaked. 'Please stop this and untie me. We can talk about this an…'

'I'm done with talking!' Spinning around, Saul paced up and down the hallway, his mind racing. Yanking one of the hall curtains clean off its pole, he tore at it, fashioning a strip of fabric. Storming over to Gwen, he ignored her pleading eyes and pulled her head back by the hair.

'I need to tell you about Lena. I…'

'What is this shit? School?' Saul roared. 'Lena's told on you and now… What? You're going tell on her? If you had something else on her then you should have spoken up in the first place!'

Gwen was about to say that she was coming over to do just that, but her chance disappeared when Saul expertly gagged her with the strip of curtain fabric. Fresh tears sprang from her eyes as the thick material cut into the sides of her mouth.

'It's a bit unfair, don't you think?' Saul sneered, tying a tight knot that painfully pulled strands of Gwen's hair, a sinister cackle escaping his mouth. 'It's not like the other party can defend themselves from your accusations.' His bright manic eyes fixed on Lena's crumpled body.

Gwen's eyes followed Saul's, panic spreading as she stared at Lena's inert body, the pool of blood underneath her having considerably grown in size. 'NNNN!' she squawked through the gag in the hope that Saul would do something. He couldn't let Lena die like this.

Her heart lurched when, almost in answer to her prayers, Saul moved towards Lena, then recoiled in repulsion when he dragged her up from the floor by an arm, her head lolling against her chest.

Haphazardly tying Lena to a second chair next to Gwen, Saul chuckled – a guttural noise deep in his throat. 'Don't know why I'm bothering,' he said, almost to himself. 'It's not like she'll be saying anything, but it is kind of artistic.'

Stepping back, he thoughtfully appraised the scene, putting his finger to his mouth. 'Hmm, yes... Artistic. My version of the three monkeys. One dead, one soon to be dead and the third monkey isn't here yet, but soon will be.'

Gwen blinked in horror, realising Lena had died. *Oh Jesus Christ. Saul was completely mental and there was no way out.*

With the sound of the doorbell, her heart palpitated and her already dry mouth became drier as a flash of hope flooded through her.

FORTY FOUR

HEATH FROWNED, MOST PUT OUT. He was a Platinum VIP member and this bozo wouldn't allow him through the door? 'What do you mean, 'not available'?'

The doorman studied Heath, his face expressionless. 'Like I said Sir, Miss Taylor is not available at the moment.'

Heath pursed his lips. 'Then when *will* she be available? I want to discuss my event next weekend.' He folded his arms. 'I'm paying a lot of money to host it here, yet you're telling me that I can't see h…'

'Miss Taylor isn't here, Sir,' the doorman repeated patiently. 'The club isn't open yet, but I'll make sure she knows that y…'

'But I'm…'

'Perhaps booking an appointment might be a good idea, Sir? At least then you wouldn't have a wasted journey.'

Heath stared at the doorman. *The patronising bastard.* Book an appointment? Did they think they were royalty or something? Pushing himself up on tip toe to look around the man's bulky frame, he peered into the Feather's lobby. 'What about Jonah Powell? Is he around?'

A slight twitch passed across the doorman's face. 'Mr

Powell is not here either, Sir. Even so, you would still need to…'

'To book an appointment, yes – I heard you the first time. No need to repeat yourself. I think you've spelt everything out quite clearly.'

Turning on his heels, Heath stomped back down the entrance steps before he did something stupid – like lose his temper.

Well, this ruined his plans. How was he supposed to get acquainted with the place and find his bloody stuff if he couldn't even get in the goddamn building? Picking up the pace, Heath hurried along the road towards the overpriced car park where he'd left the Lexus, deciding he'd use the time to visit Teagan instead. Thanks to that discarded invite he'd grabbed from the wake, he knew where Robert Adams' place was, so he'd take the chance of going there. With any luck, he wouldn't be present and would have gone into work like a normal person.

Ok, so it meant having to trek to Maidenhead again, as well as putting up with seeing that creepy old girl, Dulcie, but he may as well try his luck, if only for further info. Teagan should know a lot more about what was going on by now. Besides, it was better than returning to the car showroom to get more disparaging grief off his bloody father.

If his father no longer wanted the benefit of his plans, then that was his prerogative, but *he* did. He very much still wanted that benefit.

• • • •

JOE'S EYES WIDENED IN TERROR as he was dumped unceremoniously on the tiled hallway of the large house. Blinking, he squinted up at the overly bright lights, willing his vision to adjust after the blackness of the car boot.

No longer being confined in the oily-smelling space and being thrown around during the short journey was good. Even having his head whacked on the way out had seemed like a bonus.

'What the fuck is that?' A voice roared.

Joe froze, his confused senses rapidly realising that the initial elation of being released from Keith's car boot was premature. His ordeal was far from over - it appeared to have got worse. He had no idea where he was, but judging that he was lying on the floor of the large hallway of a rather swish house and someone who didn't sound too friendly was roaring at the psycho who had dragged him here in the first place, did nothing to convince him that his situation had improved.

'This is the stoner,' Keith muttered, eyeing Saul blocking him from fully passing into the hall.

'Why is he here?' Saul barked, detecting a hint of nervousness behind Keith's usual staid, expressionless exterior. 'I thought we were done with him, or was that something else you didn't agree with my judgement on?' Spinning on his heels, he turned. 'I was expecting it to be just you, Keith, but I guess the stoner can be added to my artwork.'

As the sight of Gwen and Lena was exposed behind Saul's retreating back, Keith paled. *Holy shit.* 'What the f…'

Saul grinned – a manic wide garish smile. 'My version of the three monkeys… What do you think? Impressive or what?' *Keith had been the third, but now he'd use this guy instead. Maybe he could do the four monkeys?*

Keith had vaguely heard Saul's words, but his concentration was solely fixed on Lena; the pool of blood; her glassy eyes staring sightlessly in front of her like a ghastly doll. 'Jesus Christ, is she… is she..?'

'Dead?' Saul shrugged. 'Yeah, sad huh? And Gwen here, well, unfortunately for her she's been exposed for the lying whore she is too.'

Gwen stared pleadingly at Keith, her frightened eyes speaking volumes behind her forced silence.

'The girl in the flat – you've got to let her go, Saul,' Keith muttered lamely. This was a lot worse than he'd expected. A *lot* worse. He wouldn't bother asking what had happened to Lena or why. Frankly, he didn't care, but Gwen? What had Gwen done? Everybody loved her – especially Jonah, but there was no point in trying to rationalise with Saul, he'd clearly flipped. The best he could achieve now was securing that young bird's release. The rest of them, including himself were fucked.

'Since when did you tell me what to do?' Saul roared. 'You work for *me*, remember? Not the other way around! The girl stays where she is until I get my diamonds.'

'The diamonds, they…' Joe began. He hadn't meant to speak, it just kind of slipped out. He blinked, wishing with all his heart he hadn't been such a brainless fool. If he'd remained silent he might have melted into the background. These nutters were so busy scoring points, they might have forgotten about him. Unlikely, but sometimes convincing himself of unplausible outcomes was better than facing up to reality. Most of the time this attitude was helpful, yet now – when it *really* mattered, he'd failed to use his brain in a logical fashion. *Stupid, stupid…*

When the larger of the two psychos bent over him, two crazy flashing eyes staring down at him with an amused glint, he realised he'd made a cardinal mistake. It was only when he spotted a dead girl strapped to a chair and an older woman next to her gagged and bruised, did he realise exactly how much of an error he'd made.

Oh fuck. *Fuck*! He'd right ballsed this up. This must be one of the Powells. It had to be. Christ! He was finished.

• • • •

ROBERT STARED AT TEAGAN, no longer smelling the stench.

He looked down upon her face twisted with pain, her skin a ghastly grey pallor and his anger increased tenfold. He didn't think it was possible to get angrier that he had on seeing Teagan manacled to this stinking bed, her thin wrists cut to ribbons from the cuffs. They'd even stripped her of her clothes, taking away her dignity.

His fury built even thinking about it; the image forever

ingrained. His fears had been realised. *He felt nothing, apart from revulsion.*

Teagan cried out in fear and agony. 'No! Leave me alone. Leave me alone!' she screamed.

Robert's face creased into a worried frown, not having a clue how he should react. He glanced at Jonah watching from the other side of the room, his face thunderous. It stood to reason Teagan wouldn't know Jonah or the other man, Nero, which at least proved they weren't lying about their involvement, but she didn't seem to recognise *him* either. And that further backed up his theory. It had all been a one-off. Nothing had really changed. But he had to say *something…* 'Teagan, it's me. Robert.'

Teagan's wide eyes darted around wildly. 'When…? When am I…? She lashed out at Robert. 'Don't touch me! DON'T!' Tears flowed as she curled into a foetal position.

Robert turned to Jonah, irritation mounting. He didn't want to be here anymore. He'd had his questions answered, so he didn't need to stay. 'What's wrong with her?'

Nero glanced at Jonah knowingly, his brows knitting deeply. 'As I suspected, the kit's over here.'

Stomping across the littered bedroom, Jonah eyed the assortment of items on the chest of drawers with utter contempt. 'The bastard!' he spat, a vein in his neck pulsing. 'He's done her up like a kipper. I'll kill him for this. He *knows* I hate this shit.' Slamming his fist into the wall, he punched a hole straight through the stud partition.

'We need to get her away from here first,' Nero said.

'Will someone tell me what the hell is going on?' Robert barked.

Jonah stepped forward. 'My bastard of a brother had been injecting her with drugs. He *knows* I will not stand for something like this. *Ever*!'

'Drugs?' Robert spluttered, only now noticing countless puncture marks scattered over the insides of Teagan's arms. *Those bastards had been injecting her with drugs?* His head span. 'What sort of drugs?' Swallowing dryly, he glanced back down at Teagan and forced his hand to move and brush a tendril of her usual luscious, glossy dark hair, now greasy and limp off her forehead. *They'd ruined everything!*

Nero glanced at both Jonah and Robert. 'Heroin. He's been injecting her with heroin…'

'*Heroin*?' Robert screeched. 'What kind of people *are* you? Is this a normal kind of day for your sort?'

'I am *nothing* like my brother!' Jonah spat, moving towards Robert. 'Whether you believe it or not, I'm angrier than you are.'

'That I doubt…' As much as he was reluctant to touch Teagan, Robert scooped her into his arms. 'I'm getting her to hospital.'

Jonah regained his equilibrium. Now was not the time to concentrate on Saul. Getting this girl sorted had to be priority and *then* he would deal with his brother. 'That's not a good idea.'

Robert's head flicked up, his anger evident. 'Why not? Because the police will get involved and you lot don't want *them* sniffing around your fucking firm or finding those diamonds.'

'It's got nothing to do with the police or diamonds. It's about *her*. You think the hospital won't inevitably involve several drug agencies and the social? Do you think having 'heroin addict' on her records will help? Do you really believe being labelled with that will do her any favours? If so, then crack on!'

'Addict? What do you mean 'addict'?' Robert cried, the words sticking in his throat. He looked down at Teagan. 'How much has she been given?'

'By her behaviour and the state of her, I'd say a lot for several days. Saul has been trying to make her dependant and by the looks of it, has succeeded,' Nero added, his voice flat. 'It's evil shit. Some people become reliant from the first hit, others take weeks or months. I'd say she was pretty much reliant.'

'I agree,' Jonah said sadly. 'She'll be ok, but she needs to go cold turkey behind closed doors and get that shit out of her system.' He moved towards the bedroom door. 'We need to get her out of here. She can stay at my home to recuperate.'

'*Yours*?' Robert cried. 'Are you insane?'

Jonah's eyes flashed with irritation. 'My brother's already ballsed her life up, so it's the least I can do. I have a big house not far from here. You can stay with her or I'll arrange for a private nurse to see her through this. I will ensure she gets clean without disruption and no stains on her record. Alternatively, you can take her to hospital. Your call.'

Robert blinked rapidly, unsure which way to turn. Was what Jonah suggested the best thing to do? How could he stand being around Teagan now?

'She will be ok,' Nero added. 'But Jonah is right. We need to leave.'

Robert looked down at Teagan once again, realising he had little choice. 'Ok, I'll do as you suggest.'

FORTY FIVE

'FORGOT YOUT KEY in your desperation to be away from me?' Dulcie snapped, opening the door. 'The first thing you can do is tell me wh... OH!' She stared at the figure in the doorway, momentarily thrown off guard.

'Hello Mrs Adams. I'm Darren Harding, do you remember? I saw you last at the fu...'

'I'm not an imbecile, young man! Of course I remember you. I thought you were Robert for a minute, that's all. Teagan's not here, so you've had a wasted journey.'

Heath wondered what could have happened to Dulcie Adams to make her look so frazzled and stressed. And Teagan wasn't here? Recalling the telephone conversation he'd had with Robert, he inwardly frowned. Robert had been looking for Teagan, but then made out Dulcie must have got her wires crossed. Was that not the case? 'Do you know when she will be back?'

'No and quite frankly, I don't care!' Dulcie placed her hand defensively on the door frame. 'Now, if you'll excuse me?'

Health faltered. Teagan's absence affected his plans somewhat. *However...* 'Are you alright, Mrs Adams? You look... look rather flustered.'

Dulcie's mind worked overtime, her bitter and crushing disappointment over Robert's betrayal threatening to overwhelm her. 'I thought you might be part of this, but you're not are you?' she muttered, beckoning Heath inside the flat.

Heath hesitated, then followed Dulcie inside. 'Part of what? What do you mean? I don't underst…'

'Oh, I thought the stupid girl had run off with you and that you'd both schemed to take my things.' Dulcie stopped suddenly and turned to look accusingly at Heath.

Heath successfully managed to contain the shudder the look in Dulcie Adams' beady eyes caused inside of him. 'What are you talking about? I don't k…'

'That's it then. It must be Robert. That whore has turned my own son against me. Can you believe it? Was it not bad enough to develop feelings for the little tart, but then to do a runner with her and take the very things I've kept safe all these years...'

Waving her hands around, she strode down the hall into the lounge. 'Come in here, Darren. I only told Robert the other day and now he's done this to me!' Her eyes narrowed to small slits. 'That girl has ruined everything. *Everything*, I tell you!'

Heath glanced around Robert's lounge. This woman really was barking mad. She was talking as if he'd been party to her and Robert's conversation, but he hadn't a clue what she was referring to. And Robert had a thing for Teagan? That couldn't be right! Teagan couldn't stand him from what he remembered. He was a right odd-ball, so surely she'd never…

Hang on... Heath's brain whirred at record speed as the penny dropped. This hideous old bag was actually telling him that Teagan and Robert had disappeared with the diamonds? *His* diamonds? Was that what she was saying? He could barely breathe. The jewels had been at Footlights all along and then moved here to Robert Adams' flat?

A sickening feeling crawled over him and he forced himself not to scream out loud. Jonah Powell wasn't in possession of the diamonds at all, so he'd wasted all that bloody money on a stupid VIP membership for nothing? Not to mention the disaster of using his real name, which had he not been so lucky and the Powells so stupid, could have got him into serious shit. All this time, all he'd had to do was to ramp up wooing Teagan and it would have been plain sailing. He'd have got his hands on those diamonds by now.

'They concocted this together. I gave the box containing them to Teagan to look after and she must have told Robert, even though he pretended otherwise.' Dulcie scowled. 'He fooled me! My own flesh and blood has fooled me. It's *her* who has made him behave like this. I should have got rid of her when I had the chance!'

Heath stared at Dulcie, her nostrils flaring as she continued raving. His eyebrows pulled into a deep frown. What should he do? If this was true, then Teagan and Robert had played a blinder. An absolute *corker*. But where the hell did that leave him?

'Haven't you anything to say? You were sweet on her too.' Dulcie spat the words through her gritted teeth.

'I'm really disappointed,' Heath lied. 'Robert called only last week asking if I'd seen her.'

'Oh he did, did he?' Dulcie sneered. 'All part of the plan to make out that he didn't know what was going on and together they were fleecing me!'

Heath weighed up the situation fast. At the moment Dulcie's mouth was loose enough for his idea to work. He made a big point of shrugging sadly. 'I called and messaged her several times and wondered why she didn't call me back. I presumed her phone must be broken, hence why I came round.'

'Too busy planning how to steal my things.' Dulcie griped.

'I don't know what's been taken, so I can't comment. All I know is that I'm devastated. I thought she liked me… I really thought we might have a future. That we…'

'My diamonds, that's what they've taken!' Dulcie spat, her eyes glazed. 'Rare diamonds, worth millions! First Helen tried to get them, then the Powells and I even thought *you* had come for them at one point…' She laughed shrilly and gazed at the ceiling. 'I sometimes wonder whether I really am mad! I was genuinely convinced at one point that you looked a bit like…'

As Dulcie's voice tailed off, Heath could barely breathe. 'Looked like who?' he pushed tentatively.

'Oh, it doesn't matter.' Dulcie pointed towards the sideboard. 'Be a good lad and pour me a gin will you?'

Heath got up from the chair and walked obediently to the sideboard, turning his back so he could afford to crack a smile. So, she *had* suspected he was related? There might be something he could salvage from this situation after all. But how should he play it? There was one or two ways and either could backfire, but it was worth a try, surely?

Heath poured a larger than average gin into a tall glass, despite his shaking hands. Fixing a sympathetic smile, he handed Dulcie the glass. 'Well, I think it's dreadful how your son has treated you. I also had no idea Teagan was capable of something so underhand. She… she seemed so lovely…'

'Didn't she just?' Dulcie scoffed, snatching the glass. 'Lots of people aren't what they seem. Everyone has an agenda.'

'Well, *I* don't!' Heath exclaimed – the first of many lies to come. He grabbed Dulcie's bony hand. 'I'm all too aware of how awful people can be. Is there anything I can do to help you get your diamonds back? Why don't we call the police? They've stolen from you, after all.'

Dulcie paled. 'I can't call the police!' she snapped. Quickly remembering herself, she looked down at her hands, ensuring her bottom lip trembled. 'Not after Helen… It would remind me too much of… of…'

Sniffing loudly, she pulled a handkerchief from the sleeve of her cardigan and dabbed at her face. 'It probably sounds bizarre to a young man like you, but although I know the diamonds are worth a fortune, when you get to my age it's betrayal that's more important.'

No it wasn't – well, a *little*. Robert's betrayal stung, but those diamonds were her insurance. The one she'd been waiting to cash in for decades, but she had to make Darren Harding believe otherwise. The last thing she wanted was him thinking he was doing her a bloody favour by involving the police!

Heath nodded. *A likely story.* Dulcie wanted those diamonds as much as he did, but he didn't want the police round either. If he played his cards right, then he'd talk her into believing he was the key back to happiness. He'd step into her beloved son's shoes.

Here was an opportunity – a good one and he was going to take it. 'I do understand – at least to a certain extent. My own grandfather was murdered because of underhand people.' He sighed dramatically. 'It was a scandal because he was having an affair with a dancer at the club he worked at and he was murdered by the dancer's husband or someone connected to him. I don't know, but it's something that's haunted my father all his life. You'd think he'd be cross that his father was playing away, but he felt awful for the other woman too. I mean, two women left devastated by my grandfather's death.'

Heath shrugged sadly, hoping his acting skills weren't letting him down. *Would Dulcie fall for it?* 'After I was finally told why I didn't have a grandfather, I became convinced these people would come after me.' He laughed sadly. 'I felt the name I inherited was cursed, so the moment I turned eighteen, I changed my name. I haven't told anyone about this - not even tell Teagan, so I don't know why I'm telling you!'

Dulcie's beady eyes scrutinised Heath. 'Your grandmother must have hated this other woman.'

Heath shrugged. 'I think she did initially, but the few times she ever spoke of it she always worried something had befallen her too. She tried to find this other lady but never managed to track her down.' He smiled sadly. 'She never will now, because she died recently.'

Nerves fluttering, Dulcie weighed up the conversation and hid her inner glee to hear that Sophie Pointer, the sour bitch, was no more. 'I'm sorry to hear that,' she gushed. 'Can you remember the dancer's name?'

Heath wrinkled his face in mock concentration. 'I can't think now… Was it Faith? No, Faye. That's it - her name was Faye.'

Dulcie swallowed the newly formed lump in her throat and quelled the urge to reach out and touch the young man's face. *Another piece of Michael.* She'd been right all along. Right, in as much that this boy was a relation of Michael's but not right about him being after the diamonds. He'd clearly known nothing about them. Regret pooled, only to be replaced with a spark of hope. She may have lost Robert, but she could still have a piece of Michael through this boy here and his father.

Should she tell him? What did she have to lose? 'Out of interest, does your father use the name Pointer or has he changed his too?' Dulcie forced herself to ask, her voice dry. She hated to think that the legacy of Michael's name was forever obliterated from the record books.

Heath feigned surprise. *Gotcha*! 'How did you know his surname? I don't think I mentio…'

'Because *I'm* Faye…' Dulcie smiled, reaching out to stroke Heath's face. 'And Robert is your uncle…'

• • • •

'YOU'RE TAKING THE PISS, COCK-SUCKER!' Saul raged, pulling Joe up by the scruff of his checked shirt. 'Get us another chair Keith – that's if you can cope with that one small task without melting down?'

Mechanically, Keith lumbered into the dining room and pulled another chair into the hall, placing it next to Gwen. He couldn't look at her. He didn't want to see the expression on her face again. What he really wanted to do was knock Saul Powell clean out and stop this madness, but he couldn't. Saul still wielded a strange invisible control, like he always had. It was like being hypnotised and turned into a programmable robot.

As expected, Keith stepped back, not even bothering to look at Lena. He stood by, awaiting his next instruction, like he would until the end - until he silently allowed Saul to take his life, which would be soon.

Saul dragged Joe, his arms and legs flailing wildly, over to the chair. 'There's no point trying to pretend you know where my diamonds are, you pointless streak of piss,' Contempt dripped from his voice. 'Keith might be stupid enough to fall for your bullshit, but I am not.'

He secured Joe's wrists to the back of the chair with cable ties, closing them so tightly the skin bunched up and split. 'How much were you planning on demanding for your bullshit information?'

'N-Nothing! I didn't ask for anything, apart from the girl and it's not bullshit.' *He had to get this lunatic to see sense.* 'I know where your stuff is. I know who's got th…'

'Oh, shut up! Saul backhanded Joe, reopening his already split lip. 'I'm bored, do you hear me? Fucking *bored*!'

Spitting blood, Joe pulled against the immovable restraints, the thin plastic cutting deeper into his wrists. 'You have to listen!

'I have to do fuck all!' Saul roared. 'You've wasted enough of my time and *he's* allowed it!' He glared at Keith. 'And it's the last time!' He bent down, pulled his trouser leg up and removed a large knife secured to a strap on his ankle. 'Now, if none of you mind, I'll get on with editing my masterpiece.'

Joe's eyes widened as he stared at the glinting blade in this madman's hand. Was he going to cut him? If he'd just listen, then he'd know where his precious diamonds were. Opening his mouth to speak again, Joe found his voice box rendered useless. Any chance of uttering the words that could grant his freedom disappeared as Saul's nicotine-stained fingers were shoved into his mouth.

'Urrgh!' Joe gagged from the thick fingers pressing down on his tongue along with the overpowering smell of stale fags.

Saul glanced at Gwen, becoming more animated at the raw terror on her face. 'Back to my version of the three monkeys. Firstly, we have a slight differentiation from the classic line-up.' He nodded towards Lena's limp body. 'On the end we have

Ms Think-No-Evil.' He laughed shrilly, his eyes manic as he turned to Keith. 'Do you get that one? 'Think-No-Evil'? Yep, she can't think fuck all. Not much of a change, but I like it. Like it a lot.'

Keith stared at Saul, finding it impossible to move his face into any form of expression. There was nothing to say. Nothing at all. Lena was dead – yeah, he got it. *Very clever...*

Saul gestured to Gwen, his fingers still embedded firmly in Joe's mouth. 'Next we have our lovely *trusted* colleague and long-standing family 'friend', Gwen Vella. Gwen will be Ms See-No-Evil.'

He laughed loudly once again, heartily enjoying the panic behind Gwen's eyes - the eyes that would shortly see nothing. 'Gwen has seen and more importantly *done* a lot of things... You'll go last though, Gwen. Purely because I want you to see everything else I do first.' He looked thoughtful. 'Although, if I was delivering like for like, I'd make you wait another twenty years. Imagine twenty years of being lied to…? Alas, I haven't got that sort of time to waste.'

He bowed theatrically. 'Moving swiftly on to our new friend here.' Saul pulled Joe's tongue forward, making Joe squawk in pain. 'Our stoner friend here likes talking shit. Unfortunately for him, he's wasted too much of my time because *some* people are stupid enough to believe his crap. Predictably, there can only be one choice for this muppet.'

'NNNGH!' Joe screeched as the knife lowered, his body stiffening as it pushed inside his mouth.

Pulling Joe's tongue forward further, smiling as the man's eyes bulged almost out of their sockets, Saul grinned with deep satisfaction. 'Introducing Mr Speak-No-Evil.' The knife sliced through Joe's tongue, only requiring a small amount of sawing at the end to detach the last bit. *This knife was good. He was most impressed.*

With thick blood mixed with saliva flowing over his hands, right up to halfway up his forearm, Saul proudly held up the detached tongue. 'Ta-da!'

Joe sat bewildered as thick blood dripped onto his jeans, presumably from his chin. Whatever had been done hadn't hurt. His mind was unable to rationalise what had happened. He tried to ask, but nothing came out apart from an intelligible sound.

As the truth sank into his addled brain, the pain started. Heaving with agony and shock, Joe vomited a mixture of stomach contents and thick blood over himself, howling in loud guttural bursts.

'Why do people always puke?' Saul muttered uninterestedly. 'It pisses me off.'

Moving to Gwen, he smiled at her petrified face. 'And now onto my favourite. Save the best until last, don't they always say?' His smile was replaced with a snarl. 'Like my father did.'

He rubbed the remains of Joe's tongue along Gwen's cheek, leaving a thick smudge of blood. 'Did he lick your face while he screwed you? Or was his tongue too far down your throat? LIKE THIS?' Saul rammed the tongue into Gwen's mouth, shrieking gleefully when she spat it onto the floor.

Saul span towards Keith standing like a statue, his expression void. 'Get me a spoon – a teaspoon. There will be one in the dresser in there.' He nodded towards the dining room.

'I think you've done enough now. This is out of order, Saul. Just like you forcing yourself on that girl in the flat. It ain't right!'

'What the fuck do you know about being right?' Saul roared. 'I don't give a flying shit about your opinions. Now, get me the fucking spoon!'

Robotically, Keith moved into the dining room, hating himself even more for his weakness and retrieved a silver teaspoon from the drawer of the Welsh dresser. He knew what Saul was planning to do. He'd seen it done before. It had been quite funny the last time, but only because the bloke on the receiving end was a Grade A tosser. This wasn't funny though. And all done in Jonah's house too? This was one hell of a fucking mess.

Finding a resolve he didn't think he had, Keith replaced the spoon back in the drawer. He wasn't being party to this. He turned around to return to the hall empty-handed only to walk straight into Saul.

'You ended up a pointless bastard, Keith. Such a waste. Hey ho, not a problem, I'll get it myself.' Saul said slowly. Retrieving the spoon, he pushed past Keith and moved back to the square hall, knowing the man was following him like the puppy he was. He grinned. 'Time for Ms See-No-Evil.'

Pointlessly struggling from within her bindings, Gwen whimpered through the gag.

FORTY SIX

JONAH KNEW SOMETHING was very wrong the second he turned into his driveway and clocked the cars. 'What are they doing here?' he muttered.

His heart pounded. Had something happened to Lena or the baby? His clammy hands slipped on the handle as he scrambled to get out of the Range Rover, unwelcome thoughts of what had befallen his mother during pregnancy crowding his mind. Life wouldn't be so cruel as to replay a similar situation with his own child, would it?

He turned to Robert lifting Teagan out of the back seat and looked at the poor girl; her head lolling against Robert's chest. He felt sick to the stomach that Saul had done this. Knowing that, judging by the black beamer, his brother was inside his house at this very moment, wasn't doing anything to calm his rage.

But as much as he wanted to go for Saul, his priorities had to firstly be whether Lena and the baby were ok and then getting this girl settled and on the way to recovery.

'Take her straight upstairs. Put her in the third room on the right,' Jonah said to Robert as they moved towards the front door. Lena would undoubtedly have an issue with the sudden presence of a strange woman up to the hilt on heroin, but it was *his* responsibility to take ownership and put it right. If that was possible?

Frowning at the ajar front door, Jonah's unease increased. Pushing it open, he moved quickly in the large square hallway, the sight all but knocking him for six. He'd seen and done many things over the years, but this…

'What the fuck is this?' Jonah screamed. Rushing forward, he yanked at Saul's arm, the spoon clattering to the floor out of Saul's hand.

Saul's face twisted, his manic expression worsening seeing Robert and Teagan. 'That's the Adams bloke! What the fuck are you bringing a Pointer cunt in here for? You've brought one of those bastards into your own house?' His eyes narrowed further. 'And the girl. That girl is mine!'

Nero stood in the doorway looking at the stranger tied to a chair and covered in blood. The man, panting heavily paid no attention to their entrance. He looked barely alive. He'd also seen what Saul had been about to do to Gwen. His stomach rolled. And then he saw Lena. *Oh shit.*

Flicking his head around, he looked at Robert, standing transfixed, his mouth agape in horror. 'Get her upstairs. Now!' he hissed, jerking his head in the direction of the staircase. 'And stay up there.'

'Did you not hear me, Jonah?' Saul raged. 'That's a fucking Pointer. And the girl? Why have you got the girl?' His eyes traced to Keith. 'Is this you? Is this something to do with you, you two-faced bastard?'

It was only as Saul moved that Jonah saw Lena – or what *had* been Lena. His eyes scanned the massive amount of congealed blood, her sightless eyes staring through him, her face twisted into a grotesque mask. A muffled howling escaped from his throat. Lena was dead. *His baby?*

'NOOOO!' Jonah roared, cold dread replaced by white hot fury. He lurched towards Saul. 'What have you done?' he screeched, pure hatred enveloping him.

Saul took the brunt of Jonah's tackle head on and using his shoulder, sent his brother sprawling to the floor.

Relieved that Robert had now got the girl upstairs whilst Saul was distracted, Nero's urge to go to Jonah's aid was unbearably strong, but also knew at this stage, it had to remain between the two brothers. He glanced at Keith the other side of the room. He'd been party to all this? He'd been working behind everyone's back with Saul? That would not be forgotten.

Moving to Gwen, Nero's fingers fumbled to untie the tight knot of the gag, trying his best to keep his eyes averted from Lena, whilst attempting to convey reassurance to Gwen. Why would Saul turn on Gwen of all people? Christ, he'd burnt his bridges this time – there was no doubt about that. 'We'll sort this. You're ok, I promise,' he whispered.

'What's the problem, Jonah?' Saul raged. 'I've saved you the problem of marrying the whore, haven't I? I told you she wouldn't get her hands on the firm, or on you, but you wouldn't listen.' His mouth cracked into the widest smile. 'I really enjoyed kicking that baby from her too… That was until I discovered it was a bunch of kitchen roll which spoilt the satisfaction!'

He paced around like a prowling tiger. 'It was all bullshit, do you hear? *Bullshit*! But she's gone now. You're my brother and this is *our* firm.'

Jonah scrambled back to his feet and launched himself at Saul, too irate to feel upset. *Lena was pregnant – he'd seen it with his own eyes. This was all lies. It had to be.* 'You piece of shit,' he hissed, his hands closing around Saul's throat.

Still fumbling with the knot, Nero's eyes darted to Jonah not knowing which was worse. That Jonah's own brother had kicked his child out of his fiancée or that Lena had set Jonah up?

A high-pitched strangulated laugh escaped from Saul's mouth. 'Yeah, go on – kill me if you like… You can't face the truth. Our father must have been gutted leaving you in charge. You with your bunch of henchmen who are more use in a knitting circle! Even Keith's turned out a useless shit. You're all bunch of fucking slaves, yet none of you can see it!'

'Shut the fuck up!' Jonah yelled, spittle flying from the corners of his mouth. He pressed down harder on his brother's neck, his rage incessant. 'You're mental. Unhinged!'

'If you say so…' Saul counteracted the pressure of Jonah's hands with his own force, the glint in his eyes, goading. 'But then again, our father wasn't particularly choosy. I mean, ask Gwen… She'd know, considering she was shagging him the night Mum died! Wasn't that right, Gwen?' He laughed at Jonah's expression. 'Go on, ask her! She won't deny it.'

Without wanting to, Jonah felt his eyes move to Gwen and saw by the look on her face that what Saul said was true. His mind reeled. Was that why she'd wanted to leave the Feathers? Was that what Lena wanted to tell him about Gwen? Unable to help it, his grip on Saul's throat slackened as his head reeled.

Immediately homing in on the lapse in Jonah's concentration, Saul seized the opportunity, twisting his brother's fingers away from his throat and throwing him on to his back. Springing up like a cat, he delivered a boot to Jonah's stomach, leaving him winded. Surveying the scene, Saul's mouth split into a crazed grin. Throwing his head back, he made a whooping noise. He'd done it. He was taking charge. He'd re-established his authority and removing every single person who had hindered, doubted or didn't trust him.

He'd given years for his family and he would have that respect. He *deserved* that respect. All those taking the piss or slowing him up were going. *Every. Single. One.*

Pulling the knife back out from the holder on his ankle, Saul lurched towards Keith. This one was a shame. He'd always felt a kindred spirit in Keith, but that had gone. Keith had severed the connection and disconnected their pairing. He thought about voicing something along these lines, but decided it wasn't the best use of his time and instead, without a second thought, cleanly sliced through Keith's windpipe.

A moment of utter shock passed across Keith's face before

his massive frame slid to the floor, the wide gash in his throat emitting a strange hissing, gurgling sound as bubbly purple blood frothed in torrents from the wound.

'Holy shit!' Nero muttered as Saul stepped over Keith's body. His eyes then darted to Jonah, still gasping for breath on the floor. There was little point in going to Keith's aid. Whether he liked it or not, the man would be dead within minutes.

Dropping his hand from the knot of Gwen's gag, Nero moved towards Saul, his eyes fixed on the position of the knife. His heart raced as he steeled himself. Saul would go for Jonah next and he couldn't let that happen. 'Saul, you n...'

'Get out of my way, Nero. I have no argument with you, but I'll remove you if I have to,' Saul spat.

Saul barged past Nero, his immense frame more than capable of displacing a giant. Nero grabbed at Saul's arm and twisted it with all his might. He couldn't let Saul destroy Jonah, Gwen or the girl upstairs.

Howling with pain and rage, Saul span around, the blade slashing out wildly. The knife cut across Nero's cheekbone, forcing him to drop his grip, leaving Saul free to move in on Gwen.

Gwen's eyes bulged as Saul neared, his movements happening in slow-motion. Her eyes darted around the room. The man next to her couldn't help. She'd heard his laboured breathing slow and then stop not a few minutes past. Lena was long dead and Nero was now hindered enough not to be able to reach her in time. She couldn't even see Jonah, but he was on the floor somewhere...

Saul had won. It was over. And now she wouldn't even get chance to tell Jonah what had happened with his father or who Lena was. It was too late.

Knowing what was imminent, she clenched her jaw and looked up at Saul with resolve, no longer frightened.

Seeing a flurry of movement from behind Saul, Gwen watched his mouth form an 'O' and his eyes widen with a jolt of unexpected shock. Stumbling forwards, Saul attempted to turn around, but the Swiss Army knife stuck in his back was quickly pulled out and plunged into his chest.

She watched with a weird sense of detachment as Saul's hand opened like a starfish, his knife tumbling to the floor with a clatter before he too sank to the ground like a punctured inflatable toy.

Gwen blinked several times in succession as the space opened up behind Saul, revealing a man who, following Saul to the floor, sat astride him and continued driving his small knife into his chest over and over. After what seemed like hours, although possibly only seconds, the man stopped his frenzied attack, threw his knife down, then scraped his sweaty hair from his face with blood-soaked fingers.

Panting heavily, his empty eyes locked onto Gwen's but remained silent.

Forty Seven

THE NIGHT HAD BEEN THE LONGEST OF JONAH'S LIFE. He stared out of the window, past the large patio area, complete with a brick built BBQ and bar. His eyes moved past the canopied hot tub and out towards the first of three good-sized ponds, which for reasons unknown to him, he'd forked out a small fortune stocking with top grade Koi Carp last year. He didn't know why he'd bothered. What did any of his material possessions matter now everything he'd deemed important had been deleted? He also didn't know why he was expending any brain power thinking about it. Nothing could be done to change what had happened. But it was better than thinking about everything else.

Inhaling deeply, he focused on the cup of tea someone had brought in for him some time ago. He couldn't remember who, but it must have been Nero because there was no one else left.

Closing his eyes, Jonah concentrated on breathing. Everyone and everything was gone, leaving his life and everything it stood for as a pile of rubble. He hadn't left this room, the one he used as his home office, since he'd been shepherded along the back hallway and steered into here by Nero last night.

He didn't know how long Nero had stayed with him. He didn't know what had been said. In fact, he could remember very little of what had happened following the nightmare which had unfolded last night. He remembered every single last vivid detail of *that*.

He vaguely remembered hearing things further back in the house as he'd sat unmoving and mute in the leather desk chair. Motors coming and going. Doors slamming. Muffled voices…

He didn't know what had been going on and didn't care because it seemed he hadn't known what had been going on in any facet of his life for a very long time.

Jonah picked up his mug of tea and raised it to his lips. It was stone cold. *Like him*.

He wanted a drink. A *proper* drink. Not tea. If only he could summon the energy he'd fetch the bottle of whisky from the cabinet, but he didn't think he'd ever be able to summon any energy ever again.

Pulling his eyes away from the tempting bottles of alcohol, they instead fell on a framed photograph on his desk. He didn't mean to look at it – didn't *want* to look at it, but his eyes focused on it regardless. A lone tear rolled down his unshaven cheek at the image of his father in the filigreed silver frame. He wasn't going to be a father anymore.

He'd almost choked on the spot seeing Lena posed in the grotesque position Saul had meticulously arranged, blood pooling underneath. He'd fallen down a bottomless lift shaft with the unavoidable knowledge that his child, along with Lena, was dead. But he'd been mourning the loss of a child that had never existed. Lena had played him all along and he'd fallen for it. *Stupid, stupid bastard that he was*.

How he hated her. He hated her more that he'd ever hated anyone.

Angrily wiping his face with his sleeve, Jonah focused instead on the dried stains over his once pristine white shirt.

Saul's blood. His brother's blood. The blood of the brother Robert Adams had killed.

• • • •

NERO WAS EXHAUSTED, but there was still a lot more to do. This next part would be by far the hardest and a whole different kettle of fish compared to arranging for bodies to be removed and disposed of. His body ached for sleep but that was a long way off.

Nero glanced around the large square entrance hall of Jonah's house once again, doing a final double check. Even the damaged curtain had been replaced. He nodded to himself in approval. The boys had done a good job. Everything was looking back to normal now. On the outside, at least.

Once the last of the men had left just under half an hour ago, he'd initially been relieved to have a break from the noise and bustle the clean-up operation had caused, but now the silence weighed heavily. The stillness only accentuating what had to happen now.

Taking a deep breath, Nero moved down into the narrower part of the hallway that spanned the length of the big house, keeping an ear open for any noise or movement from upstairs. It was still quiet.

He glanced at his watch. *Coming up to 7.30am.*

Moving into the back hallway, Nero tapped on the office door, waiting a couple of seconds before entering.

Walking into the room, Nero frowned when Jonah didn't turn around or acknowledge his presence. Jonah was in exactly the same position as he'd been the last time he'd seen him. He'd half hoped the man may have got some sleep, even if for only half an hour, but he should have known better. He knew Jonah too well and it was unlikely that he'd sleep for a very long time, if ever.

Moving straight to the cabinet, he poured two large whiskies. He needed one and guessed it wouldn't hurt Jonah either.

Pulling up a chair opposite, Nero sat down, placing the whiskies on the desk and looked at his boss, his usually sharp blue eyes dull and bloodshot. 'Everything's done.' His voice was unnaturally loud in the silence. He wouldn't elaborate further. There was no need. Jonah was well aware what clean-up operations consisted of. They'd both had their fair share of being part of the clean-ups during their early days in the firm. They'd got their hands dirty along with everyone else and the contacts they'd used back then were the same ones they used to this day.

Getting no response, not even a flicker, Nero pushed the glass of whisky nearer. 'Drink that,' he said. 'I know I need one!'

Jonah surprised Nero by unexpectedly looking up. 'Gwen? And the girl?'

Nero lowered the glass from his mouth. 'They're upstairs. It's all quiet.' He watched Jonah nod imperceptibly, his face immediately closing. 'You know he did the right thing, don't you?'

Jonah slowly raised his eyes and fixed them on Nero. 'Yes, I know.' It didn't make him feel any better though. Saul had to die. His own life, Nero's and Gwen's sight had been saved by Robert Adams' actions. There had been no choice, but it went against the grain. Saul was his brother. *Was…*

They were family. Now Saul was dead.

His head was mashed. Was he grateful to Robert Adams or resentful? Jonah didn't know and that was the crux of it.

He should have dealt with it. He should not have allowed Saul to incapacitate him. What did *that* say? Saul had floored him and he'd been able to do nothing apart from impotently watch the proceedings unfold. He should have been stronger than that.

But if he hadn't been incapacitated, what would *he* have done? Stand by whilst his unhinged brother pulled out Gwen's eyes, killed Nero, most likely him too and then disappeared off upstairs to Robert and the girl? Or would he have done exactly what Robert Adams did? It was a bitter realisation and one he couldn't ignore.

And what about Gwen? Jonah swallowed dryly. He hadn't properly processed that yet. He wanted Saul's words to be lies, but knew in his heart they weren't. He clenched his jaw. *She'd slept with his father?*

He wanted to hear her side of things. He wanted to know what had possessed her? But he couldn't do that now. He couldn't face hearing her voice. Hearing the words. Wondering what was truth and what was lies.

Raking his fingers through his unkempt hair, Jonah jumped up from his chair.

'Where are you going?' Nero asked, concern written over his face. Jonah was in no fit state to go wandering around. He looked almost as manic as Saul.

'I need a shower,' Jonah muttered as he walked stiffly to the door. Opening it, he turned back to Nero. 'Thanks for sorting out the mess. I appreciate it.'

Nero nodded and watched with much trepidation as Jonah disappeared along the hallway.

• • • •

HEARING HIS MOBILE BUZZING, Heath irritably glanced at the screen:

```
Incoming call:
Dad
```

Gritting his teeth, he stabbed on the reject call button. His father had called twice yesterday – no doubt wanting to know why he'd failed to show up at work. He'd have to call him at some point, but not now. *This* was far more important.

'I still can't believe it!' Heath said, shaking his head in pretend fascination over the 'remarkable' coincidences.

Dulcie smiled to herself despite her deep-seated sadness. At the crack of dawn this morning she'd found herself unable to contain the urge to rush down the hall and stick her head around Robert's bedroom door, only to be crushed once again with the sight of his empty bed, dashing the small sliver of hope that she'd been wrong in her conclusion. But she wasn't - Robert had gone. He'd taken the diamonds and gone. *With Teagan.*

But every cloud had a silver lining and life worked in mysterious ways. It had brought her a replacement. Not quite the same, but whichever way she looked at it, she'd still got a piece of Michael. Even a small diluted piece, such as Heath – or Darren Harding as she now knew he preferred to be called, was better than nothing.

'Are you alright?' Heath watched the emotions pass over Dulcie's face, hoping she hadn't changed her opinion about him since last night.

Dulcie looked up and smiled. 'Yes, dear. I'm fine.' There was no point crying over spilt milk. Robert had made his choice and so she'd made hers. 'What were you saying?'

Heath smiled. It would be hard work being ultra-nice to this creepy old cow, but he had a good feeling that his altruism would be handsomely repaid. 'I was just saying that fate must have drawn me to you via Teagan. Your strong connection to my grandfather must have made things move in certain directions without either of us being aware.' *There, that sounded deep and meaningful.*

He poured Dulcie a cup of tea, having already made sure he noted exactly how she liked it. 'You had more of an instinct for it than I did. You saw the resemblance, whereas I'd never have guessed!' he lied.

Dulcie nodded appreciatively, seeing the amount of milk in her tea was perfect.

'By the way, thank you for letting me stay last night,' Heath continued.

'I should be thanking *you*. After everything that happened yesterday, I didn't want to be on my own.' Dulcie looked at Heath fondly.

Heath fiddled with his cup. He hated tea and would much prefer a tot of that nice-looking whisky on the sideboard, but if this charade got him in the old girl's good books and enabled him to turn this around, then it was worth it. But this next bit was a long shot. He had to make his intentions look genuine. 'I've been thinking about that and I've come up with a solution I'd like you to consider.'

Dulcie frowned. 'What are you talking about? A solution? To what?'

Heath reached for Dulcie's hand. He'd grabbed it so much over the last twenty-four hours the feeling of the skeleton-like object wasn't half as off-putting as it had been. 'I don't want you being here on your own now Robert had abandoned you... especially with the Powells hanging around. How do you feel about me moving in with you here for a while? I know you don't know me all that well and there's not much room, but I'm sure we'd manage.'

Dulcie's heart melted. 'That is so sweet of you, but I couldn't possibly expect that.'

Heath's face fell. The only way he'd could do this was if he was around her all the time. *Try a different approach...* 'Then at least promise I can come and check on you as often as possible. I probably won't be able to get up from London every day, but...'

'You can't move in here, but you *could* move to Footlights?' Dulcie interrupted, her eyes sparkling.

'M-Move to Footlights? *Great. Move in somewhere where someone had just got murdered.? What a fantastic idea... Not...* But then again, it wouldn't be for long...

'It's ready and there's plenty of room. I'd move back too. I've been stuck in this poky flat for far too long.' Dulcie looked at Heath expectantly.

Heath maintained a surprised expression, but inside his mind was spinning.

'Oh, I'm being silly. You've got your job and life in London. You can't just up and leave,' Dulcie said, sensing Heath's hesitation.

Heath grinned. 'No, but I can take some time off. So, yes - let's move to Footlights. I'll feel so much better knowing I'll be there to look after you. I would never be able to concentrate back in London knowing you were up here on your own.'

Dulcie clapped her hands together excitedly. 'That's all settled then!' If Robert ever came back then he'd know he'd been replaced. That was what happened to people who treated their own mothers with contempt. *Teagan was welcome to him.*

FORTY EIGHT

ALTHOUGH ROBERT HAD BARELY SLEPT for two nights, short of accidentally occasionally dropping off in the chair, each renewed cry from Teagan had immediately woken him. He had no idea how long he'd been in this room watching Teagan like she was made of brittle china. It could have been one day or ten. All the hours merged together and felt like a lifetime, yet minutes at the same time.

He'd expected to experience the same amazing rush of *something* the minute he set eyes on her, but there had been nothing. Absolutely *nothing…*

Yesterday was the worst. As her body ramped up expelling the poison that had been injected into her, he'd lost count of how many times he'd held her head over the side of the bed while she vomited green bile. He'd also lost count of the number of times he'd dragged her into the en-suite bathroom and supported her on the toilet as her body had purged itself. The whole thing had made him feel sick.

His throat constricted. And there was worse… No one had yet broached it. Not yet. No one actually needed to mention what Teagan's clothes being removed and the line of bruises visible on the insides of her thighs meant.

He'd always been funny about second-hand goods and this was no different. Everything was ruined and damaged beyond repair.

Despite Nero bringing him countless plates of food. Nothing fancy: sandwiches, bowls of soup – that sort of thing. Robert wasn't hungry. He knew he should eat something, but he couldn't. Not eating wouldn't kill him. The only indication of lack of food was the constant dull throbbing in his temples and behind his eyes. Headache or not, he couldn't face the prospect of putting anything in his mouth.

Nero had even attempted to make conversation in his gruff way, saying something along the lines of *'It was over'*, but this had only made Robert angrier. It certainly wasn't over for Teagan and it would *never* be over for him either. What he'd seen and what he'd done, courtesy of these people, would forever be stuck in his mind. Each tiny piece of killing Saul and seeing Teagan had contributed to closing his brain and stealing his chance of a life.

He was well aware that if he'd just stayed where he was, like Nero instructed, then he wouldn't have this on his back in addition to everything else. If he'd just ignored the growing yelling and screaming downstairs, instead of creeping back down there. If he hadn't had that Swiss Army knife in his pocket…

Sweat trickled under Robert's collar and down his neck. But he *had* gone down there and he *had* the knife in his pocket, so he'd used it. He'd used it well. He hadn't hesitated plunging that blade into Saul Powell's back.

In his mind he could see the scene as clearly as if it were a cinema screen. He'd seen the devastation that filthy bastard had caused. That bastard who had snatched Teagan and injected her with shit. That bastard who had killed Joe.

A small twinge of guilt fluttered before remembering that Joe had been instrumental in involving Teagan with this in the first place, though Robert hadn't wanted him to lose his life.

He shook his head in bewilderment. Saul Powell had also

butchered that woman, floored Jonah and cut up that other bloke too, as well as offing one of his own henchmen. It had been impossible to avoid missing the mountain of a man crumpled on the floor with a gaping slash across his windpipe. And what he'd been about to do to that older woman…

It wasn't rocket science to guess where that psycho would have headed afterwards...

Robert swallowed the fast-rising bile. He'd had no choice but to finish it. Besides, he'd wanted to. The curse of his father's blood ran through his veins and had drawn him into this world with these people, but he didn't belong here. He didn't belong *anywhere*. Less so now than ever before…

Robert's eyes moved back to Teagan sleeping fitfully, her face drawn but not quite as grey as it had been. Today her delirium and general malaise had improved, but having no experience in this kind of thing, he had no clue how long the process of cold turkey or whatever they called it, lasted. That was the only thing he'd asked Nero, but the man offered little in the way of advice, just that it was different for everyone.

But now he was trapped. Trapped here with these people and having to sit here with this… this *thing*…

He glanced at Teagan and quickly looked away again, his stomach rolling. She was now surplus to requirements, yet he was still having to pander to it. Like an automaton, he'd do it because he had little choice unless he wanted to draw unwanted attention.

A sudden tapping at the door made Robert look up.

Nero's head appeared. 'Jonah wants to speak with you.'

Robert scowled. He didn't want to talk to Jonah Powell. He didn't want to talk to *any* of them. He resented being here. In this house. With *them*. Breathing the same air as these bastards. It was *their* fault this had happened. 'I'm not leaving Teagan,' he muttered, hoping that sounded a feasible reason for his reticence, when realistically it was difficult to decide which option was the most unpalatable.

Nero entered further into the room. 'Jonah needs to speak

to you now. I'll get Gwen to sit with Teagan in your absence.'

Robert glanced towards the wall of the adjoining room. *Gwen*? He presumed that was the woman on the chair? The one that had watched him drive that knife into Saul over and over? The one who he'd since heard sobbing from the next bedroom the whole time he'd been here.

'You're not convinced Gwen will be ok sitting with Teagan? Trust me, she'll be fine. Gwen could do with something to concentrate on, so it will do her a favour too,' Nero said, beckoning to Robert.

Sighing, Robert stood up, his legs stiff from lack of use. He might as well get the conversation over with. It was only a matter of time being as he'd promised he'd tell Jonah Powell everything, but he needed to concentrate now. Needed to concentrate on who was going to pay for stealing his soul and exactly how they would pay for it.

He glanced at Teagan, still asleep. 'I'll wait for this Gwen woman and then I'll come,' Robert promised.

• • • •

IT TOOK ALL OF GWEN'S COURAGE to walk across the landing and down the stairs to *that* area.

Unsure whether the tears she'd cried over the last couple of days had been for Jonah, that poor girl Saul had held hostage, Keith, the young man next to her on the chair – the list was endless… Or Saul?

Or had her tears been solely for herself?

All Gwen knew was that she'd cried enough tears for everybody, but she couldn't hide away for ever.

Sitting with that poor girl whilst Robert Adams went to speak with Jonah was what had finally given her the push she'd needed to venture further. Admittedly, she'd been terrified how she'd feel setting eyes on the man she'd watched launch the frenzied attack on Saul.

Terror? Gratefulness? A combination of both?

If it hadn't been for him, none of them would be here now,

but Robert Adams had barely acknowledged her as she'd entered the neighbouring bedroom.

Gwen had stayed for as long as Robert had been away – a good few hours and in that time the girl hadn't stirred, save for a handful of anguished cries within her sleep. It had been difficult to stomach, knowing what that evil son of a bitch had done.

The girl would need a lot of support to get through this and Gwen swore to do everything possible to help erase Saul's despicable acts. But first she had to take the plunge venturing down into the house.

Taking a deep breath, Gwen hurried through the reception hallway, not wishing to see the surroundings she wanted to permanently blank from her mind, but her eyes looked anyway. It was like nothing untoward had ever occurred and easy to believe she'd been dreaming if she unfortunately didn't know otherwise.

Hurrying, Gwen made her way down the corridor with a back door to the garden. There was no way she wanted to risk going through the lounge in case Jonah was in there. She knew she would have to face him soon, but she couldn't bear the look of contempt on his face again like she had as he'd learnt of her past with Jacky. Neither could she stand hearing the words that would inevitably come out of his mouth…

Maybe he would kill her? She wouldn't say she blamed him, but the crushing guilt of losing his love and respect would hurt more than what Saul very nearly achieved with his plans. It would hurt a *lot* more.

Gwen's face creased as tears threatened, her breathing laboured. All but breaking into a run to be out in the fresh air, she centred on the door.

Pushing it open, she rushed outside. Leaning against the brick wall of the house, Gwen closed her eyes and tilted her face up towards the welcoming rays of the approaching midday sun.

Inhaling deeply, she felt her panic begin to wane. That was until she opened her eyes to find Jonah standing a couple of metres away studying her intently.

• • • •

EVEN THOUGH THE SUN WAS BRIGHT AND STRONG, Gwen was chilled and shivery. Seated at the patio table opposite Jonah, a jug of iced water and a plate of sandwiches in the centre, it would look to anyone watching like a relaxing early afternoon break.

It was anything but.

The sandwiches, untouched and exposed to the warm air had already hardened and the edges were beginning to curl. Gwen stared at them, almost longing to pick one up, but knew without even attempting it that her mouth was way too dry. Thanks to her trembling fingers, she'd almost spilt her glass of water countless times whilst she'd explained everything to Jonah.

The night she'd truly believed Saul would put an end to her life – all she'd wanted was the chance to tell Jonah the truth about his father. To tell him how it *really* was and what had really happened. And why. That she'd never meant to hurt him. Or to lie to him, for that matter.

And she'd done it. She'd now told Jonah everything: that the affair with his father was not a cheap and random thing. They really had loved each other.

She'd cried. She'd cried a lot. She'd cried more when Jonah said nothing. He'd listened, but offered nothing in response. Asked nothing. Questioned nothing. And Gwen wanted him to. She *needed* him to. She needed him to react – shout, scream – say he hated her if that's how he felt. She just wanted him to say or do *something*.

Was she being selfish? Probably, but she needed to know he was taking in everything she said. There was also a part that wanted his acknowledgement, forgiveness, anger – *whatever*, for means of allaying her own guilt, but it wasn't just that... There was the part that she hadn't yet told him. The part that she'd found out the day all of this happened. But how could she dump that on him on top of everything else?

Always able to read Jonah well, it was now like looking at a blank slate. Had he closed himself off completely or was he just empty?

Had what Saul, Lena and she herself, had done, removed his soul? Was *she* partly responsible for inadvertently ruining the most important person in her life? Against her every intention not to break down yet again, Gwen felt the tears building. *Stop it, Gwen. You knew one day it might come to this...*

Raising her eyes, she looked at Jonah, finding his cold blue eyes staring straight at her. Almost *through* her. She cleared her throat. 'Jonah, I…'

'Why didn't you tell me…?' Jonah cut in, his voice hollow.

Gwen blinked. 'I-I've tried to explain. I didn't want you to hate me. I know it doesn't make it any more excusable, but I didn't want you think that I'd…'

'To think that you'd lied? Lied to me for years?' Jonah snarled.

'I-I've never lied! Just no one asked… It…it all stopped after your mother died,' Gwen pleaded, her face pained. *Please understand, Jonah. Please!* 'I never purposefully hid anything from you.'

'But why stop then?' Jonah pressed, his eyes burning. 'Why not carry on? After all, there was nothing to stand in your way...'

A tear slid down Gwen's cheek. 'It wasn't a conscious decision by either of us. It was never even discussed. We both knew… My and, I'm sure, your father's only concern after that was you. You and Saul.' She stared at her trembling hands. 'You were my priority and were lost enough as it was, without us making things more confusing. You were only a young boy.'

Jonah remained silent, his eyes far away. Gwen sat for a few minutes, before tentatively reaching across the table. 'I'm sorry, I really am. I wish now I'd told you a long time ago. I wish both me *and* your father had told you once you were older.

At least then you would know that what we said was the truth and you wouldn't doubt about how your father felt about your mother. He loved her more than anything.'

'But he also loved *you*!' Jonah spat. 'If he'd really loved her then he couldn't have loved you too.' His voice trailed off as he pulled his hand from Gwen's grasp.

Gwen stared at Jonah's retreating hand. 'It is possible to love more than one person.' He hated her now. This could never be undone.

Jonah's eyes focused on Gwen. 'You should have done it.'

Gwen frowned. 'Done what?'

'Married him. You should have married my father.'

'I don't think either of us could have after what happened.'

'Guilt, you mean?' Jonah said, his eyes accusing.

Gwen flushed red. 'Yes, guilt. We spoke about our guilt frequently before, but never afterwards.'

'But you never married anyone else?' Jonah said – a statement, rather than a question.

Gwen smiled sadly. 'There was and never will be anyone else.'

'Do you know, when I was young after mum died, I used to dream that my father would marry you. Don't get me wrong, I didn't want to replace my mother, but you were always… always there for me. I felt comfortable with you.'

Gwen sat back in shock. 'That's because I've always loved you. you were the son I never had. Whatever you may or may not think of me now, I will always see you as my son.'

Trembling, Gwen watched Jonah rise from his seat. Moving around the table, he enveloped her in his big arms. Breaking down in surprise and relief, she sobbed into his chest, her fingers clinging to the back of his shirt. 'Do you forgive me?'

Pulling away and holding Gwen at arms' length, Jonah stared down at her. 'Forgive you for what happened between you and my father? Things happen, Gwen, I'm not stupid, but I'm glad it wasn't an affair for the hell of it.'

'Your father never looked at anyone. He could have had the

choice of anyone, but he never even…'

'Until you…? And that's the point. You're a special woman, Gwen. But will I forgive you for not telling me? That's harder. Although I understand why you didn't, I wish you had and that will take longer.'

'I, understand… I…'

'She knew, didn't she?' Jonah hissed, immediately deleting Gwen's relief. 'Lena knew about your affair, that's why you wanted to leave?'

Gwen nodded sadly. 'She did, but I didn't know how. No one knew…'

Jonah sat back down and indicated that Gwen should do likewise. 'You said you *didn't* know how? But now you do?'

Gwen took a deep breath. *It was now or never*. 'I found out the night she… the night Saul… I came over here to tell her that she had to tell you what I'd discovered or I would. I tried to call you…'

Jonah folded his arms. 'And?'

'I was going through her drawer in our office and I heard her on the phone to her Uncle Ron. I didn't believe she was pregnant at first and then I did, but now I know I was right.'

Gwen knew she was gabbling but couldn't stop. There was too much to say and she had been holding back for so long. 'I knew she was hiding something. I snooped around and found some papers: her passport; birth certificate. It's all on there. Lena is… *was* an O'Hara,' Gwen said quietly, the words sticking in her throat like broken glass.

'An *O'Hara*?' Jonah cried incredulously.

'The very same…'

Jonah raked his fingers through his hair. 'Then… then she must have been… Oh, Jesus, then she's one of the O'Hara brother's children. Mark? Or, fucking hell – Sean? Is she Sean O'Hara's?'

Gwen looked at Jonah, saw the desperation in his face, the realisation. 'Yes, she's Sean O'Hara's daughter.'

Jonah's face morphed into a scowl. 'And Ron? Ron fucking

O'Hara? The one in the loony bin?'

Gwen nodded. 'From what I gathered, Ron and Noeleen were coming over for the wedding.'

'Christ!' Jonah processed the implications. This was getting worse by the minute. 'I'd have been tied to the O'Hara's... Jesus Christ...'

Getting up, he paced around the table, his face awash with fury. The O'Hara's would be over for the wedding - the wedding, that as far as they were concerned was still on. He had to find a way to deal with this.

Gwen watched Jonah closely. 'What are you thinking?'

Jonah's mouth creased into a twisted smile as he turned to walk into the house. 'I'm thinking how I'm going to use what I now know.'

'Where are you g...'

'I need to make sure no one gets wind that anything's amiss,' Jonah said, his face resolute stating loud and clear there was no room for manoeuvre. 'And I'll need your help with that. We need to get back to the club.'

Gwen frowned. Get back to the club? How would they explain not only Lena's absence, but Keith's and furthermore, Saul's? It was already unheard of that they should all have been off the radar for two days as it was. 'But how wi...'

'I'll think of something, trust me.' Jonah interjected.

Forty Nine

IT HAD BEEN EASY moving Dulcie back to Footlights. There were only a couple of bags worth of stuff. It also meant Heath could breathe a sigh of relief. Every extra minute they remained at Robert's flat was an additional minute that made it more likely the man himself would return and put a stop to his plans. Of course there was also the chance Robert could show up at Footlights and he certainly didn't want that happening.

He didn't want anything to balls this up. *Couldn't* have anything balls this up, but he would have to make a trip back to his own flat at some point. It might have only been two days, but there was only so long he could exist without a proper change of clothes. Borrowing the ones of Robert's Dulcie had insisted on was unpalatable enough. The man was a lot bigger than him, making him resemble a dodgy geezer who'd nicked a shed load of ill-fitting stuff from the local charity shop.

At least he'd been able to shower and brush his teeth. Without Dulcie having a spare toothbrush he'd have been buggered. Having a mouth like a dog's arse was not something Heath would entertain.

He'd also borrowed one of Robert's phone chargers, but he'd still need his proper stuff – including his laptop.

Furthermore, he had to explain his absence to this father. There wasn't a right time for any of these things but they would all have to be done if he were to get anywhere.

Heath pulled his attention back to Dulcie. 'Did you remember everything? There's nothing you may have accidentally left at Robert's?'

'No, there's nothing missing apart from the diamonds, but as you well know they aren't available!' Dulcie remarked caustically.

Heath laughed weakly. Dulcie had been excited on the way over, but the minute they'd stepped across Footlights' threshold, she'd changed. Gone was the excitability, replaced by a sullen, antagonistic attitude and he wasn't sure why. All he could do was play things by ear and hope for the best. 'I'm presuming you still haven't heard from Robert?'

Dulcie scowled. 'No and I'm not likely to. He's got what he wanted.'

Heath smiled kindly, unsure whether it was too soon, but he had to put out the feelers. He needed to get things moving in his favour. 'I still think we should try and locate him. I can certainly try if you'd like me to?'

Dulcie flapped her hand. 'I'm not sure. I'm still too hurt to think.' Regardless of the diamonds, she'd discovered something else. Whilst Heath was settling into a bedroom, she'd felt compelled to check. Prising up the floorboard in the pink bedroom, she'd seen straight away the gun was missing. Only Robert could have taken it. And if he'd taken it, then he'd worked out what had really happened to Helen. *And if he knew that, what did it mean?*

• • • •

'SHE WON'T BE IN until after our wedding.' Jonah smiled at the club staff he'd amassed in the VIP function room. 'Any issues with the rotas or general club stuff, your port of call as usual, is Gwen. Due to Lena's absence, event booking and anything VIP related will also be handled by Gwen for the time being.'

Noticing one of the dancers looking at him, concern on her face, Jonah gestured. 'Terri? You have a question?'

Terri shuffled nervously. 'Mr Powell, I-I don't want to speak out of turn, but we'd heard... I mean, there's rumours that Lena's pregnant and... well... I just hope everything's ok with the baby...?'

Biting his cheek, Jonah stopped the immediate flicker of rage. 'For once, I'm pleased to say the rumours are correct.' Hearing several gasps of pleasure, he looked around the sea of faces once again. 'And yes, everything is fine,' he lied. 'The doctors have advised Lena take a few weeks' off for some relaxation, but she'll be back soon.'

Watching his staff nod happily, Jonah clasped his hands. 'That's about it. Please carry on preparing for tonight's show. Well done and thank you for all your hard work in helping make the Feathers such a success.'

Without waiting for anything further, Jonah left the function room, hastily making his way to his own office. His clammy hands slipping on the door handle, he stumbled into the office, dropped into his desk chair and put his head in his hands.

Following, Nero closed the door quietly behind him. 'That went ok.'

Jonah looked up, no longer needing to maintain the mask he'd perfected for public use. 'Why would they suspect anything else?'

Gwen's idea of saying Lena was taking a medically-suggested break was good, even though the irony of using the pregnancy stung. It didn't alter how they'd explain her permanent absence, but it did allow a couple of weeks' grace which was the most important thing. *Nobody* could get wind that she would not be coming back.

Sitting down, Nero stretched his long legs out across the room. 'As far as everyone is concerned, the wedding's still going ahead. I think the only issue might be the hair and makeup people. Won't they think it strange if Lena doesn't attend a million and one dress rehearsals over the next week or two?'

Jonah's lips formed a thin line. 'Gwen can call them and come up with some bullshit about Lena deciding to use someone else.'

Nero raised his eyebrows. 'That will go down well…'

'They'll get over it,' Jonah scowled. 'I just want to concentrate on O'Hara.'

Nero frowned. Hearing the news of Lena's true identity was still sinking in. 'But surely they will have arranged to meet Lena beforehand? Won't they smell a rat if she doesn't show up?'

'That's why Gwen's monitoring Lena's phone. I'm planning on finding out what arrangements have been made – or make new ones myself,' Jonah answered. 'If possible I'll intercept them before the wedding day itself.'

Nero had a bad feeling about the O'Hara's and still couldn't fathom how meticulously Lena had planned this: from getting a job at the Feathers, wheedling her way into Jonah's home and life; trapping him into marrying him… She was certainly nowhere near as thick as he, or any of them had assumed. 'Which of them are coming?'

Jonah shrugged, his eyes drawn once again to the paperwork Gwen found. 'I know that cunt Ron O'Hara will be there. As to any others, I don't know.'

Nero studied Jonah. He'd pulled himself out of the shocked trance he'd been in, but inside his mind must be total mush. 'How are things with Gwen? You've taken all that stuff better than I think I would have.'

Jonah sighed. Yes, he probably had, but as much as he hated the situation, he wasn't losing Gwen too.

Getting no response from his last comment, Nero knew better than to push it. The unexpected issue between Gwen and Jacky Powell was an awkward one. There was also another issue… 'The show staff might have swallowed the shit about Lena, but we've still got the enforcers to deal with.'

Jonah nodded, his mouth curling contemptuously. 'I'll tell them Saul and Keith are undertaking surveillance for a new contract. Saul's been absent a lot so it won't be unusual for him not to be about.'

Jonah stared at Lena's passport once again, before locking it back in the bottom drawer of his desk. 'Have you heard how the girl is today?'

Nero shook his head. 'No, but I'll find out. What are you going to do about her? And the Adams bloke?'

Jonah walked across to the safe. He retrieved the small wooden box and opened it. Unfolding the fabric inside, he picked up one of the exquisite pink diamonds. *These are finally back in their rightful place, Dad – just like I promised you.* He held the jewel up the light and admired the flawless quality. 'I've decided to bring Robert Adams into the firm.'

'But he's a Pointer!' Nero spluttered.

'His lineage isn't important. What matters is his capacity. Now we're two down from the inner circle, we need someone who knows the score and I want to use his computer knowledge,' Jonah said.

'But there's something odd about the guy,' Nero frowned. 'I don't trust him…'

'Adams has already proved his worth by returning my goods and saving all of our lives.'

Nero considered Jonah's words. 'I suppose so. If you think he'll do the job.'

Jonah smiled thinly. He was quietly confident Robert Adams was up to the job. Yesterday, the man had filled him in with a shed load of information about what had gone on behind the scenes – more than he'd expected and most of which he'd had no idea about and with his IT skills, he'd be perfect for what he had in mind.

'The main thing to concentrate on now is the O'Hara's. That must take priority above all else. They need to be reminded there is no place for them here and that their plan to infiltrate my family and firm is over,' he continued. 'Once they've been deal with, then we'll look at Heath Pointer. Don't think I've forgotten where we were going with him before all of this took precedence. And finally, Dulcie Adams. Regardless that she no longer has my diamonds, I still want to see her. I want to hear from her own mouth her reasoning for turning my family over. And then…' he smiled. 'We can finally put this to bed.'

FIFTY

TEAGAN SIPPED FROM HER WATER, making sure that she didn't meet Robert's eyes. Even during the last five days of floating in and out of consciousness feeling the worst she ever had in her entire life, she'd been aware of his presence.

She wanted to feel something other than disgust, but it wasn't possible. It wasn't disgust for him, it was with *herself.* Although mercifully, thanks to her consciousness sliding and looping down endless tunnels, she couldn't remember every single thing, but *did* have vague glimmers… Being covered in her own filth, the horror on everyone's faces… Robert holding her up on the toilet… What *all* of these people had seen…

All she'd been able to focus on at the time was getting more of whatever she'd been given that robbed her from thinking and stopped her from feeling. *Blissful oblivion.* But now it was different. The short but vivid recollections flashed back through her mind, taunting her in a cruel, endless nightmare.

Her cheeks burned. That man - the monster... She hadn't stopped him, had she? In fact, she didn't think she'd even *tried.* Had she even cared?

With mounting sadness, she realised she couldn't remember. The only way anyone could look at her now was with shame, disgust or pity. She was dirty. A drug addict. *Soiled.*

Teagan glanced at her bandaged wrists. They were healing, but their presence underlined that she hadn't imagined any of it. It was *real*… She wanted to scream. She wanted to scream and scream and *scream*. How had any of this happened?

Dulcie… It was coming back. It was the people who had killed Helen and who had come for the diamonds. They'd been asking her about diamonds… What about Dulcie? Had they hurt Dulcie? Oh no… no… NO!

Teagan tensed as Robert perched on the edge of the bed. 'How are you feeling? Are you up to getting some fresh air in the garden today?' His deep voice vibrated through her body. Her skin felt so thin, so sensitive that she feared her bones may crumble.

She stared at the thick cream curtains framing the large bedroom window. The sky outside looked blue and inviting, but nothing held any enjoyment any more. How could it? 'Dulcie? Is she ok? Is she…'

'Don't worry about that, just concentrate on getting back to normal.'

Teagan flinched. *Back to normal?* There was no chance of ever being back to normal. *And what was this about Dulcie? Was she dead?* Turning her back, she curled into a foetal position, the tears now flowing freely.

Robert edged away. Wasn't this what he was expected to do? Offer words of support and reassuring gestures? He didn't want to be here. He didn't want to be in this room dealing with this. 'We'll make this better,' he said flatly.

Teagan stared at the wall, anger replacing the tears. She dug her nails into her palms. The drugs might be out of her system, but the rest wasn't. None of it. 'Please leave me alone,' she whispered. Nothing would ever be alright again. *Nothing.*

A tap at the door made Teagan's blood freeze. *Who was that? Who was it?* Colours flashed behind her eyes.

'Sorry to intrude,' Jonah said, entering the bedroom. He

glanced at Teagan and then fixed on Robert. 'When it's convenient could I have a word?'

Teagan scrabbled up the bed, her nails scraping against the crisp cotton duvet. 'CAN EVERYONE LEAVE ME ALONE!'

• • • •

'SHE'LL BE FINE WITH GWEN,' Jonah poured Robert a large whisky. Gulping at his own drink, he gestured for Robert to take a seat.

Robert took the offered drink and sipped at it gratefully. Teagan's reaction was worrying and it made the situation he wanted nothing to do with, harder. 'I don't know why she's being like this.'

Jonah rubbed his hand over his chin and knocked back the rest of his whisky. That was a strange thing for Robert to say? Both he and Robert Adams knew Saul had done more to Teagan than the drugs. It had been impossible to miss that tell-tale bruising. How he wished he'd killed his brother the moment he was released from prison. He never thought Saul would sink to such depths.

'Try not to worry too much. Gwen will be good for Teagan. She's great with stuff like this. She understands people,' Jonah said, his voice tailing off as he skirted around the uncomfortable elephant in the room. 'Christ, I don't know what to say? What the fuck *can* I say, apart from that my brother was a cunt and I'm sorry?'

Robert's eyes glazed over. Finishing Saul had been far too quick and in retrospect, he should have tortured the bastard for weeks. *Months*. He clenched his fists, his nails digging into the palms of his hand. Between Saul Powell and his own mother, they had ruined everything.

Jonah cleared his throat. 'It might help if you tell Teagan that Saul's dead?'

'What, so you want me to tell her that as well as failing to protect her from your bastard brother, I'm also a fucking murderer too?' Robert hissed. That was the upshot, wasn't it?

Saying it out loud made it real. Now on top of that, he was back to square one. And he couldn't deal with it.

'Listen, Saul was my brother, but if you hadn't done it, I would have.' Jonah said. 'I'll help put this right for the girl in whatever way I can. Tell me what you need.'

'What *I* need?' Robert stared at Jonah incredulously. How could anyone give him what *he* needed? No one could.

'What either of you need,' Jonah corrected. 'Say the word and it will be done.'

Robert shook his head and helped himself to another whisky. He felt like necking the whole bottle. 'Not to be involved in any of this would be good.' He'd almost had a life for a while back then. *Almost…*

Jonah shrugged. 'I'm afraid you have your mother and father to thank for that. If it will help, you and Teagan can move to another one of my properties. You can have some time together there. It might make things easier?'

Robert swallowed his scowl. Going somewhere with Teagan was the *last* thing he wanted. Even being surrounded with of this lot was preferable than being left to deal with her.

Jonah folded his arms and looked directly at Robert. 'Whatever you want to do is fine, but as I said to you yesterday, I want you to help me with things. You may be a Pointer, but not the one I want.'

'I am NOT a Pointer,' Robert snarled. 'I'm a computer programmer, not someone like… someone like *you*!'

'I think that's where you're wrong.' Jonah raised an eyebrow. He was playing a wild card here, but he had nothing else to lose. 'Helping me to finish this will ensure it will be over quicker for you and that girl of yours.'

'She isn't my girl,' Robert said hollowly.

Jonah smiled weakly. 'It's just a term of phrase.' He frowned inwardly. Robert Adams was indeed an odd one, but he had the knowledge for what was required.

Robert nodded numbly. Now Saul had touched Teagan, it had changed everything. That was the wrong thing to think, wasn't it? But it was the truth. Despite this, he felt that he had to at least listen to what Jonah had to say. It was unlikely that he could return to his job – however much he dressed it up, he was no longer the same person that he had been. He couldn't return to his flat either.

'Ok, I'm listening, but I think we'd be better remaining here for the time being. If Gwen is as good as you say, then Teagan will benefit more from being around her, rather than me.' Robert said, silently hating himself further knowing that he didn't want to go *anywhere* with Teagan.

Jonah nodded. 'As you wish. From your side though, I need focus and a straight head. Using your IT skills, the first thing I want you to do is look into how we can locate and intercept the O'Hara's.

FIFTY ONE

RUBBING CREAM ON HER WRISTS, Teagan stared at the angry red scars, then pulled the long sleeves of her top down to cover the constant reminder.

Today was the first time she'd looked at herself in the mirror. Gwen's words had made a difference and she felt stronger. Gwen was right. She could and *would* not let what Saul had done colour her life.

She would not let him win. Neither would she let what Robert had said about Dulcie destroy her. The woman she'd cared so much for – that she'd risked her life for. It had been unthinkable that Dulcie had killed Helen, but it was true. The woman had manipulated everyone, yet despite this, Teagan still found herself worrying about the old lady.

She looked at Robert, his face drawn and lined. There was something behind his eyes that wasn't there before and much to her horror it had crossed her mind whether he'd been in on this business all along? That *all* of them were behind Saul's abuse?

Luckily Gwen had put that into perspective too. Learning Robert had risked his own life by approaching Jonah in the first place and bartering the multi-million pound diamonds in exchange for her had made the world of difference. He'd risked himself and given it all up for *her*. It has also been Jonah Powell who had guessed where she was being held and between them, they'd saved her. But Joe… Joe had paid the ultimate price and to discover that he'd been involved with feeding information to that monster Saul, hurt beyond comprehension. It was a blessing that she had no recollection of the scene when they'd first entered the house because regardless of everything, seeing Joe like… like *that* would have crucified her.

At least all of this violence and grief was now over, but listening to what Robert was saying now was something she hadn't expected and couldn't say she was comfortable with. 'Staying *here*? Staying here for longer with these people? What about your job?'

'I'll be doing some work with Jonah for a while. Contractors don't get leeway for time off like employees, so I won't be welcome at my job by now.'

Teagan's eyes widened. 'You're working for Jonah? Aren't they…? What about Dulcie? Your mother?'

Robert's eyes narrowed. 'There is no longer any need for you to be involved with looking after or worrying about my mother. You're free to do what you like.'

Teagan felt winded. She really had become too attached to the family, but she was purely an employee. She didn't even warrant as a friend - Robert's cold attitude bluntly reminded her of that.

Standing up, Robert forced himself to look at Teagan, seeing her eyes filled with unshed tears. 'Of course, you don't have to go anywhere until you're ready. I'll stay around until you are,' he muttered. He was trapped and getting angrier about that by the minute.

He knew he should place his hands reassuringly on Teagan's shoulders or something like that to make her feel protected, but he couldn't… He just *couldn't…*

'Just so you know, Saul Powell is dead,' Robert said bluntly.

Bittersweet relief coursed through Teagan. 'Dead? Did

Jonah…? Did he…?'

'It doesn't matter how,' Robert said hastily. 'He's dead and it's over.'

Without thinking too deeply about what she was about to do, she threw herself against Robert's chest, burying her nose into the cotton of his shirt.

Stiffly, Robert put his arms around Teagan's body. He lasted all of ten seconds before the urge to break the physical contact became overwhelming. Gently pushing her away, he straightened his shirt and moved towards the door. 'I really must go. I have to meet with Jonah.'

Stepping from the room, unable to look at Teagan again, Robert hurried along the landing, ignoring the quiet sobbing he could hear from the girl he could no longer bear to be around.

• • • •

'YOU CAN PUT A TRACE ON O'HARA THEN?' Jonah asked, tapping on his keyboard. 'Judging by the calls and texts Gwen is receiving we need to move on this quickly.'

Robert nodded. 'I'll do it via his phone.' He frowned. 'I'll need a laptop though and a good one. Mine is back at my flat.'

'No problem. I'll sort one out for you straight away,' Jonah said. Scribbling down Ron O'Hara's mobile number on a scrap of paper, he handed it to Robert. 'While you're here, I want you to have a look at the bloke I told you about. The one that came into this office with Lena.'

Just uttering Lena's name make Jonah feel like he was choking. *The lying bitch.*

Throwing his concentration back to his screen, Jonah scrolled through the dates of the previously stored CCTV footage to locate the evening in question. 'This isn't priority, you understand? The O'Hara's are, but you might as well take a look.'

'This is the bloke you reckon is a relation of the Pointers?' Robert frowned, glancing at the membership details of a print-out on Jonah's desk:

Name: Heath Pointer
Membership No: 57862
Address:14 Panama Street, Shepherd's Bush, London

'One of *your* relations, yes,' Nero said pointedly, eyeing Robert suspiciously. He didn't like Jonah's decision to bring a Pointer into the fold. In fact, he *hated* it. Although he could understand Jonah's reasoning, he still didn't like it. It seemed a recipe for disaster. A Pointer involved in the Powell firm? And an odd one at that.

Jonah shot Nero a warning look. Out of courtesy he'd already explained his logic behind his decision, but wasn't having the equilibrium upset with snide comments. He needed all hands on deck. 'Here it is - the recording from the evening of 5th July.'

Opening up the playback screen, he moved the timer along the playline. 'From what I remember, the footage is at about 10 o'clock.' Jonah glanced at Robert. 'If I'm correct, this guy is the grandson of *the* Michael Pointer – your father. Making him your nephew.'

'*Half* nephew,' Robert muttered, not liking the reference. 'And you want to confirm this man at this address?' He tapped on the printout.

Jonah nodded. 'At some point. With your computer skills I'm thinking you can find links to him – social media profiles etc. confirming an address – even if it's not available to the public.'

Robert nodded. Getting around system security was what the corporates had paid him handsomely for nigh on twenty years.

'Wouldn't it be easier to just watch the address?' Nero cried. 'I could have had that done by now.'

'We want to avoid any of us being around the address if we want this to work,' Jonah explained. 'We can't afford being flagged up on any level after that debacle with Dulcie Adams.'

Nero stood back and silently watched Jonah play the footage of Heath Pointer and Lena in her office. 'I still can't believe the cheeky twat had the audacity to come in this club and…'

'Wait a minute!' Robert leant closer to the screen. 'This is him?' He snatched the mouse from Jonah's hand and backed the footage up several seconds. Hitting a combination of keys on the keyboard, he zoomed in on Heath Pointer's face, then paused the footage. He turned to face Jonah and Nero. 'This guy - I know him. He goes by the name of Darren Harding…'

Jonah frowned. 'What?'

'Darren Harding - he took Teagan out a few times. He even viewed some of my sisters' houses and came to her funeral. He made out he was an old school friend of Teagan's, but when I checked him out, I found he never went to Teagan's school. He's an imposter.'

Jonah's mouth flapped open. 'You're telling me that he's not anything to do with the Pointers? He just picked an unfortunately connected name?'

Robert shook his head animatedly. 'No, not at all. It makes perfect sense he's a Pointer. I knew something wasn't right about him and now it adds up.'

Nero raised an eyebrow. 'Does it?'

Robert paced around the desk. 'Don't you see? Harding or Pointer, whatever you call him, was getting in with Teagan for the diamonds. He must have worked out – like *you*, that my mother was in possession of them.' His face formed into a snarl. 'My mother thinks the sun shines out of his arse.'

Nero blew threw his teeth. 'Fuck me, so this guy who is now trying to muscle in here, was also previously trying to get his feet under the table with Dulcie and Teagan?'

Robert nodded. 'Yep and when that didn't work, he made here his next port of call.'

Jonah grinned. 'So we know he's definitely a Pointer and why he's here. Just the address then, but like I said, I need the

O'Hara's first. And, Robert, it goes without saying there must be no contact with your mother.'

Robert nodded and took the laptop Nero handed to him. He had an idea, but he'd keep that to himself.

FIFTY TWO

'HI, MR ADAMS, it's Darren Harding. I was hoping it would be Teagan who answered, rather than you,' Heath said, determined to sound upbeat. He had to be careful how he did this, not wanting Robert Adams to get a whiff of any suspicion.

Robert thought rapidly. Darren Harding, or should he say, *Heath Pointer* calling him today couldn't be better timed. 'Yes, it's me,' he replied gruffly.

'Sorry to call out of the blue, but I've been worried. I still haven't heard from Teagan and now…' Heath forced a worried tone into his voice. 'Since you've answered her phone, am I correct in thinking she's still missing and not with you?'

'With me? Why would she be with me?'

'Oh, I… erm… I presumed she'd have returned to your flat,' Heath blustered. *Christ, he was ballsing this up.* He shouldn't have bowed down to Dulcie's nagging and should have thought how to handle Robert's responses before calling.

Seeing Dulcie waving her arms and mouthing something he couldn't decipher, he faced away. She was putting him off. 'What did the police say?'

Heath waved at Dulcie to stop signalling. He couldn't think with her flapping. Yes, he knew she wanted to know whether

Robert had involved the police and to find out if he was with Teagan. That's what he was asking, wasn't it?

'The police? I haven't called them. Teagan called me a week ago. She's made the decision not to return. Disappointing, but there you go.'

'But I dialled her phone and *you* answered,' Heath pressed, moving quickly to one side as Dulcie's Grandfather clock boomed out its hourly chimes.

Robert's hackles rose. He'd recognise that sound anywhere. Thanks to a stretched cord on one of the pendulums, the second half of the chime was distinct. He'd listened to that grandfather clock for half his life and could pick it blindfolded from a shop full of them.

Heath Pointer was at Footlights with his mother. His eyes narrowed. 'Teagan didn't want the phone. She was quite rude. I don't think any of us will be seeing her again.'

'Oh, that's such a shame!' Heath blathered. 'How's Dulcie?'

Robert inwardly snarled. The man knew *exactly* how she was because by the sound of it, he was standing right next to her... 'I haven't seen her for a few days.'

'Where are you then? Are you working? I mean, are y...'

'You have a lot of questions, Mr Harding?' Robert snapped. 'If you must know, I'm working away and before you ask, my mother insisted she would be fine on her own. Now if you don't mind...?'

'I...' Heath began, but the call had already disconnected.

'That was pathetic!' Dulcie barked. 'We know Robert's not at work because you've already called there. He's with her, I tell you. *Her*!'

Heath nodded. Pretending to be one of Robert's clients, he had indeed called up the office. The woman he'd spoken to had apologised for Robert's absence and confirmed he hadn't been contactable for over a week. 'It could be feasible Teagan *has* called him and said she isn't coming back. He didn't sound happy.'

Dulcie's face screwed up as her bony legs carried her around the sitting room. 'Don't be so ridiculous. Robert's *never* happy! She's with him and they've got my diamonds!' Her sharp eyes homed in on Heath. 'You said you wanted to help? So do it! I want my diamonds back!'

Heath stared at the phone's screen, seeing another text notification from his father. He wanted the diamonds back too, but before he did anything else he would have to make a trip to his own flat to pick up his stuff and also go and see his father.

• • • •

BOOTING UP THE LAPTOP Jonah had given him, Robert perched on a chair in the corner of Teagan's bedroom. Now he knew where Heath was, he could put the trace in on him at the same time as O'Hara.

Robert watched Teagan mirrored in the screen of his laptop reading a book that Gwen had thoughtfully brought to try and get her mind off things. She seemed a lot better physically but mentally - still paper thin.

His anger of being tasked with Teagan's fragility, the burden of Saul Powell and the hatred for his mother grew. On top of that, Darren Harding – now known to be Heath Pointer, infiltrating his mother's life was the last straw. At least he no longer had to spend the nights perched on a chair in Teagan's bedroom and instead sleep unhindered in a separate room - one far away from *her* and the reminders. But he was still lumbered with keeping an eye on her half of the time and that had to stop.

This was all his mother's fault. She was personally responsible for bringing all of these people out of the woodwork. Well, she was too late. The diamonds were gone, but Robert knew without a doubt that by now she'd have worked out that he'd taken them and would be arranging to get them back by whatever means necessary. His mother and Heath Pointer were either working together to track him down or working each other without the other one knowing.

He snarled silently. It didn't matter either way because they were both going to pay and he knew exactly how that would happen now.

'What are you doing?' Teagan asked, placing her book in her lap.

Quickly putting his screen to sleep, Robert turned and forced a smile. 'Just a bit of scripting.'

'Oh, you mean for your job?'

'No, a little freelance project,' Robert said. If Teagan knew what he was really doing there would be endless questions. Ones he didn't want or couldn't answer. 'How's your book?'

'It's good, but...' Teagan frowned. 'Do you not think we should check on Dulcie? I mean, I know what she did to Helen but she's still your mother and we don't know all the details – she may have had no choice. You said yourself th...'

'You need to stop worrying about my mother. She's got someone looking after her – I arranged it,' Robert snapped. *Yeah, Heath Pointer and that he hadn't arranged.* If only Teagan knew what was in that notebook and about Heath – or should he say, *Darren Harding*... 'If it will make you feel better I'll go and see her at some point this week.'

'Yes it would,' Teagan said. Smiling, she picked her book back up and continued to read.

Robert glanced back at Teagan in the laptop's reflection and satisfied she was now concentrating on something other than him, he brought his screen back to life. Tapping in the credentials for his proxy server, he waited until the screen scrolled with events and watching closely, a smile crossed his face.

Entering the necessary details, Robert hit the enter key with a flourish. All he had to do now was hope his plan worked. It would be the only sure fire way he would know when the coast was clear, but suspected it wouldn't be too long.

FIFTY THREE

HEATH SCOWLED AT HIS PHONE. Another configuration setting update? Bloody thing! Why did mobile networks keep insisting on this? Update this, update that, security patch this… all the bleeding time! Sometimes it would be easier not to bother with a smart phone and have one of those antiquated ones that just sent texts and made calls.

Stabbing the OWA CP configuration notification, Heath selected *Install* and rolled his eyes when the phone pinged gleefully stating the install was successful.

'Shall we go for a drive somewhere?' Dulcie asked, breezing into the sitting room. 'I quite fancy a pub lunch – maybe out by the river?'

Heath looked up. 'Not today, I'm afraid. I really must go to my flat and pick some of my things up.'

Dulcie's eyes narrowed. 'You're going back to London? Today? What about me? You said you wouldn't leave me.'

'I won't be long.' He might have known she'd play up over this.

Dulcie pouted. 'But you've got all those clothes of Robert's! Do you think it's wise swanning about fetching clothes when you're supposed to be locating where Robert is hiding with that little tart and my diamonds? Don't tell me you fell for his lies when you spoke to him on the phone?'

Heath refrained from smashing Dulcie in the face with the large teapot sitting on the coffee table and instead smiled graciously. 'No, I certainly didn't fall for that! Robert's clothes are fine, but I'd like my own, plus I need my laptop. Without that I can't do any digging on their whereabouts.' *Plus Robert's clothes were crap...*

'Oh, I see...' Dulcie said, contrite. 'I never thought about that. Will you be long?'

Heath got up and walked over to Dulcie, putting his hand on her arm reassuringly. 'Just have a relax while I'm gone. I might pop in to see my father whilst I'm over that neck of the woods too. I need to tell him I'm going to be away for a while and I don't want him to worry.' His eyes brightened. 'Or you could come too? Once I explain who you are, I'm sure he'd love to meet you!' *Please say no...* His father would not want to meet Dulcie Adams under any circumstances. It would be bad enough explaining everything as it was. 'What do you think?'

Dulcie frowned. 'I-I don't think that would be a good idea. I'm not up to seeing another double of Michael, especially after all of this with Robert. I will meet your father once all of this business is over.' She patted Heath's hand. 'Besides, you have a resemblance to Michael and that's enough to get me through the day.'

Heath grinned. 'Ok, well, I've got no intention of hanging about. I'll text my father now and tell him I'll be down later this afternoon.'

Pulling his phone from his pocket, he tapped out the message. His father had made it clear that he didn't approve of his plans and he couldn't see the latest one of moving into Footlights with Dulcie Adams in an attempt to catch up with her missing son and the diamonds going down too well either. But surely his father could manage for a few weeks without him? He could even place the car adverts remotely from Footlights if needs be. Not that either of them would need to bother with a poxy dealership if his plans pulled off.

Heath smiled to himself smugly. Even if finding Robert, Teagan and the diamonds didn't work out, there was a back up…

Now Dulcie had washed her hands of Robert and Helen wasn't in the picture any longer, who else did she have to leave her worldly possessions to? After all, as she kept saying, he did remind her of the beloved Michael Pointer.

Ok, so the diamonds not being included was more than disappointing, but then a massive house and tons of antiques which would sell for a tidy amount was better than nothing.

• • • •

TEAGAN SMILED WARMLY AT GWEN, feeling for the first time in weeks there might be light at the end of the tunnel.

Sitting in Jonah Powell's beautiful garden that gave Kew Gardens a run for its money with its amazing landscaping and huge variety of stunning plants and flowers, she couldn't have wished for nicer surroundings.

She took another of the sandwiches from the plate in the middle of the patio table and smiled cheekily. 'I probably shouldn't have another one. I've already had four!'

Gwen grinned. 'Getting your appetite back is a very good sign.'

Teagan smiled shyly. It was true. Despite the lingering trauma of the last however long, she was feeling, dare she say it, a little better.

Gwen was easy to be around. She had one of those faces that calmed and reassured everyone and Teagan was sure that if Gwen had not been here, she wouldn't be coping half as well. Robert, however, was a different story. She knew his intentions must be good, but they were having the opposite effect and only accentuated what had happened. Ignoring the issues made everything still very much alive, but however much she needed him to, he wouldn't discuss anything. Worse, he recoiled even if his hand as much as brushed hers.

'I'm glad you've decided to stay.' Gwen said. 'It's nice to have another woman around here.' She too hadn't been home and had snapped Jonah's hand off when he'd offered for her to stay for a while, both to get over her ordeal and also to help with Teagan. Helping this girl had been just the tonic she'd needed, giving her something to focus on other than dwelling on herself.

'Robert didn't want to return to his flat, but I have to admit I don't want to stay here after… after everything,' Teagan said. 'Also, I keep telling Robert he should check on his mother. He says he will, but I don't know… He seems different…'

'A lot has happened, love, but I'm sure Robert knows what he's doing,' Gwen said. She didn't know much about the state of play with Dulcie Adams – but by the sounds of it, even that was more than Teagan did.

She didn't want to stop the girl discussing anything, but she was stuck between a rock and a hard place. She'd been briefed that Teagan was to be told as little as possible – especially over the night in question. Robert particularly, was adamant Teagan was to learn nothing about his involvement in Saul's demise.

Gwen frowned. She understood, but enough lies had been told already and her personal feeling was that the girl shouldn't be kept in the dark. 'I don't want to pry, but are you and Robert… together?'

Teagan fiddled with the paper napkin in her hand, twiddling the end into a point. 'No, it's nothing like that. I thought we were becoming friends, but now he can't even bear to look at me…'

'And you thought there could be something more?' Gwen asked. That Robert Adams was a strange one. *Far* too detached to suit Teagan, who was open and warm – the complete opposite. And there was something about him. Nero felt it too, she knew he did.

Teagan's eyes widened. 'God, no! Definitely not.' She looked down sadly. 'We were arguing the day… the day that man took me…'

'Men aren't great at dealing with certain things, sweetheart.

It's early days.' Gwen focused on Teagan. 'Apart from that, how are you feeling now? I mean, *really* feeling?'

'Sometimes I'm ok, other times I'm wracked with disgust.' Teagan inspected her wrists. All that was now left were smooth red scars and even those would probably fade further with time. 'Physically I'm much better, but not quite so in here.' She tapped her head. 'In here, I'm a mess.' She twisted the napkin further. 'Everyone has betrayed me. Joe, Dulcie, even myself...'

'You've done nothing wrong,' Gwen reminded Teagan. 'You must keep sight of that..'

'But people are dead because of my stupidity.' Teagan felt the tell-tale sting of tears. 'My actions caused people's deaths.'

'*Their* actions caused their deaths, not yours,' Gwen said sternly.

'And I'm not comfortable being around these people.' Teagan looked up at Gwen hastily. 'Sorry, I didn't mean you. I sound dreadfully ungrateful, don't I? Jonah has allowed us to stay here and it I know it was down to him that I was found, but... this violence... It terrifies me...'

She looked back at the house. 'I'm staying somewhere that several people were killed, but I can't remember anything about it. I don't even know if I was there when any of it happened. I don't even *know* what happened. Robert won't go into detail...'

Gwen pursed her lips. *So Teagan presumed it was Jonah who had killed Saul?* 'I've worked for Jonah for years and his father before him. I can tell you straight up that Jonah is one of the most decent people out there. Despite what you may think, he has good values.'

Teagan looked down at her hands. 'I didn't mean to insult anyone, I...'

Gwen squeezed Teagan's hand again. 'I know what you're saying, but Jonah really is a good man. I won't deny that the firm he runs includes things many people would shrink away from, but he's not a lunatic. He's fair and extremely loyal - not like his brother. Now *that* one was despicable.'

Watching Teagan pale, Gwen smiled. 'I won't pussy-foot around. Men deal with problems by either ignoring them or removing them, but I don't!' She laughed to herself, then her face grew serious. 'Saul was a certifiable nut-job. Aside from a list of things too long to mention, the guy was dangerous. A psychopath. I know what he did to you... He deserved everything that happened to him. It's good riddance too.'

Teagan was almost relieved someone had spoken of what had occurred out loud and in a strange way, it helped. 'Robert's gone to Jonah's club today. He said he's doing some work there?'

'From what I gather, he's helping with the IT side.' *That was sort of true*. 'Jonah needs someone he can trust, like we all do and Robert might be a moody one, but he's got balls, I'll give him that!'

Teagan frowned. 'Robert's changed. I can see something behind his eyes.' She twisted her hands in her lap. 'He looks at me strangely. What Saul did...'

Gwen smiled and patted Teagan's hand. 'Robert's a bit cold, I agree, but what man is going to think any less of someone because of an attack?'

Teagan looked at Gwen hopefully. 'I hope you're right.'

Gwen pursed her lips. She had to change the subject otherwise she might let slip that she wasn't at all sure about Robert. She topped up Teagan's water. She wanted to personally extract Saul Powell from whichever block of metal at the car crushers he was embedded in and kill him again for what he'd done. 'Now have a drink of that. It's getting hot out here. Oh...!'

Hearing a phone buzzing, Gwen reached into her bag, her heart plummeting realising it was Lena's.

With fumbling hands, she retrieved the mobile and stared at the screen. *UR*. The second time he'd called today. He'd called yesterday too and like she'd promised Jonah, she'd texted back adopting the same language Lena would use in her replies. She'd said she'd call him back when she could, but *she* couldn't. And Lena certainly couldn't…

'Is everything alright?' Teagan frowned.

'Yes.' Gwen smiled. 'Just one of those annoying withheld numbers. I'm getting besieged with them. It must be the time of year for double glazing quotes and phone upgrades.' She laughed loudly, until the phone buzzed with a text notification:

From: UR

You said you'd call? Are you ok? We are arrivg Fri and need to know where we are stayg? Everything still on? Call me. Ron x

Gwen shoved the phone back in her bag. *O'Hara was definitely suspicious.* 'That was Jonah,' she lied. 'I need to pop over to the club. Will you be ok on your own for an hour?'

Teagan looked around, flustered. 'Oh, erm… I…'

'There's a problem with the rota. They'll never sort it out without me.'

Teagan smiled. 'I'll be fine.' It was about time she got herself back to normal. She couldn't have babysitters for ever. 'And Gwen, thank you.'

'What for?'

'For being so nice. You've made such a difference to everything and I really appreciate it.'

Standing up, Gwen pulled Teagan into a hug. 'You don't need to thank me, sweetheart. Now go and have a chill out inside away from this midday sun. I'll be back as soon as I can.'

Fifty Four

TEAGAN HAD TRIED RELAXING in the bedroom, but she couldn't stop her mind flinching from all the noises: the crack of expanding floorboards; the water immersion coming on. The large house was quiet with no one in it and being alone was unnerving her more than she liked.

Venturing down the stairs, she wandered into a large sitting room and marvelled at the beautiful upmarket and expensive furniture and accessories. Although she'd been in this house for over a week, she hadn't ventured outside the bedroom in all of that time, apart from into the garden with Gwen earlier.

She hadn't even seen Jonah Powell – apart from that once when he'd come into the bedroom to speak to Robert. Even then it was only a vague recollection. And of course the night they'd found her, but she could remember nothing of that.

Teagan found herself wandering across to a polished glass shelf and picking up an ornament – one of those crystal figurines that the light refracted off in a thousand different directions. It looked the sort of thing a woman would buy – as did the cushions and matching curtains, but Jonah wasn't married as far as she could gather. Hadn't Gwen said it was nice not to be the only woman here?

But then, who was that on this picture? Teagan picked up the gold-framed photograph and looked at a devilishly handsome man, who she presumed was Jonah Powell, standing with a stunning blonde.

Her hands suddenly became clammy. *It was him!* That man she'd seen rushing from Footlights the night of Helen's death. Although she'd only got a fleeting glimpse, she was sure it was him. *Those eyes…*

Hearing a noise, Teagan stiffened and quickly placed the photograph back down. *What was that? Was Gwen back?*

Unnaturally scared, Teagan made her way out of the sitting room and cautiously peered into another reception room, stopping in surprise to see Robert bent over his laptop. 'Oh, you're back!' she exclaimed.

Robert swung around startled, wearing an expression of deep irritation, making Teagan shrink from the look on his face. She watched with growing sadness as he clumsily tried to hide his reaction, but no matter how much he tried to conceal it, he didn't want to be around her.

'I didn't want to disturb you,' Robert muttered, his attention already back to his screen.

From her position, Teagan could only see a screen full of green scrolling text. 'I'm going stir crazy sitting upstairs, so I thought I'd have a wander,' she babbled for want of something to say. 'Are you still working on that project?'

'Project?' Robert frowned. 'Oh yes, yes, I'm still doing that.' He paused the scrolling text and turned back to face Teagan. 'Do you need something?'

'No, I'll erm… I'll leave you to it.'

Robert shut the lid of his laptop and stood up. 'Stay here if you wish.' He picked up the laptop. 'I'll be back some time later.'

'Please stay!' Teagan begged. 'I don't like it here.' She glanced over her shoulder. 'I saw a photograph… This Jonah… it was *him* at Footlights that night Helen died. I know you said it was Dulcie who shot her, but can you really be sure?'

Teagan wanted to reach out and touch Robert as he neared her. She needed some kind of contact - for him to touch her hand, her arm – *something*, just so that it might make her believe she wasn't poisonous. But she couldn't in case he refused. Being refused was worse than being ignored.

Robert's jaw clenched. 'Oh, for God's sake, Teagan! There's so much you don't understand!'

'They why won't you tell me?' Teagan cried. 'You won't tell me anything, yet you say I don't understand.' She moved closer when Robert got up. 'Where are you going?'

'I've got things I need to do.' Robert sighed, waiting until Teagan moved to one side so that he could pass through the doorway without brushing against her.

Teagan stared at Robert sadly. His actions spoke volumes. '*Please* don't leave me here!' She lowered her voice to a whisper. 'I know what you said, but look what happened here. That man killed his own brother!'

Robert swung around, his eyes flashing. 'Would you have preferred to have stayed at the flat with Saul Powell then? Is that what you're saying?' He shook his head in contempt before storming from the room, leaving Teagan to stand frozen from his words.

• • • •

WILLING HIS CAR TO GO FASTER, Robert raced up the M40 towards Maidenhead, his breathing increasing with his heartrate. He felt like he was drowning – running out of oxygen and sinking fast. A myriad of unwanted thoughts revolved endlessly in his mind in a faster ever-increasing loop. He was suffocating, truly suffocating and everyone around him was part of that.

Throwing his cigarette end out of the window, he struggled to see through the film of tears. If he blinked, they would roll down his cheeks and he refused to allow one single tear to escape. Not now. Not *ever*.

He clenched his jaw and gripped onto the steering wheel

harder, squinting through his reduced vision as the speedo hovered on 90 mph.

It was all about timing. Timing was of the essence now more than ever.

Spotting the sign for the one mile warning to the Maidenhead junction, Robert mentally checked his calculation. Working backwards from the mirrored texts he'd received from Heath's phone, the man should be arriving to see his father or be there already.

His focus shifted to the dashboard clock and his thundering pulse slowed. Providing nothing had changed, he was within time. *Good, because he had to be.*

Hearing a notification, Robert snatched his mobile from the passenger seat and stabbed in his PIN number. Balancing the handset on his knee, he changed down gear and exited onto the slip road. Coming to a halt in the queue, he opened the server message.

An alert from the other trace. The O'Hara number. There had already been one this afternoon, but this was a new one. He'd check it out as soon as he'd finished here.

Come on, come on!, he thought, inching his way to the head of the roundabout. Everything now hinged on what *she* was doing.

Effortlessly navigating through the backroads, utilising every single shortcut he could think of, Robert's adrenalin pumped wildly. He had to get this done today and it had to be done without anyone being any the wiser.

Pulling up outside Footlights, he yanked on the handbrake and waited. He glanced in his rear view mirror. No one was about, but that didn't necessarily mean no one was watching.

Picking his phone back up, he clicked on his satellite app and entered in the details, waiting as the phone picked up the signal. Pointer was at White City. Something else Jonah would want to know, but not today. Today was *his*.

Robert pulled his key from his pocket and got out of the car, overriding the shiver as he looked up at the house. The house that had always been associated in his mind with protection and routine until recently. It wasn't now. Now he knew it was a viper pit of lies.

Clambering up the overgrown steps to the front door, Robert glanced at his watch. 3.10. His mother liked her routines as much as he did, so there was every possible chance today would be no different.

Every chance indeed...

Slipping the key into the lock, Robert turned it carefully, entering Footlights as silently as physically possible.

FIFTY FIVE

DECIDEDLY SWEATY, thanks to an uncomfortable journey home in his Range Rover with an air conditioning system fault, Jonah was glad to be out of the car.

Seeing those latest texts O'Hara had sent, Gwen was right to bring them to his attention and he'd rushed straight back to see what Robert made of them. He knew he could have called, but now knowing how simple it was to infiltrate other's texts, calls and location with a bit of know-how, he was more reticent than usual to do anything over a mobile.

Once O'Hara reached the place he'd instructed Gwen to suggest they stay, then surely Robert could confirm it, meaning O'Hara would be intercepted before the alleged wedding. The man was getting twitchy and if he suspected anything had befallen Lena, it would cause problems - even a total disaster.

Although Jonah felt it unlikely that Ron O'Hara would involve the police if he suspected Lena had gone off the radar, he couldn't risk it. Who could be certain how someone's mind worked where logic was concerned with a history of residing in loony bins? He couldn't leave anything to chance. He wanted to get his hands on O'Hara and wanted that as soon as possible.

Walking towards one of the sitting rooms, Jonah stopped in

the doorway. *That wasn't Robert!*

Feeling uncharacteristically uncomfortable like he was trespassing in his own home, Jonah faltered, unwilling to disturb Teagan as she stared transfixed out of the window into the garden. She looked a damn sight different to the other times he'd seen her – stunning, in fact.

With hesitation, he cleared his throat, watching Teagan jump and swing around in his direction. 'Don't let me startle you,' he said, momentarily knocked off balance with the sadness visible in the woman's eyes. 'I'm looking for Robert.'

Teagan blinked, unable to say anything, her heart racing. *This was Jonah Powell? It had to be.*

Jonah walked into the room and outstretched his hand, trying his best not to appear intimidating. He could almost smell Teagan's fear. 'I don't think we've properly met? I'm Jonah Powell. Teagan, isn't it?'

Swallowing her nerves, Teagan took Jonah's hand, surprised by the warmth. What had she expected? A cold reptilian grasp? *He wasn't his brother, remember.*

Clasping her hand, Jonah smiled. 'Glad to see you up and about. Can I get you a drink?' He didn't really have time for this, but he should make the effort to allay the woman's nerves. She was clearly terrified and there had been enough misery.

Teagan flushed, knowing the last time this man saw her she was in a state she would have preferred *no one* to have seen, but the feel of someone else's hand was like soothing balm. Despite yearning to cling on to Jonah's hand for longer, she pulled it away. 'Robert's gone out,' she spluttered. 'I-I'm not sure where.'

'Whisky ok?' Jonah asked, glancing over his shoulder as he poured two large measures. *Why had Adams gone out suddenly?*

Teagan faltered, then nodded. She shouldn't really have a drink, but she was suddenly desperate for Jonah's company. *Anyone's* company. If she had a drink with him he'd stay, wouldn't he? Was that so wrong of her? Or was it just plain pathetic?

Jonah placed both crystal tumblers on the coffee table and shrugging his suit jacket off, flopped into a chair, gesturing for Teagan to do likewise. 'Apologies if I honk. The air con has packed up in my motor.'

Aware he was spouting nonsense rather than acknowledging his brother's misdeeds, Jonah knew he should at least say *something*. Wasn't skirting around it insulting to this woman? His brows furrowed. Although conversely, Robert had made it clear she was struggling and he didn't want her kicking off.

Despite this, he couldn't help but study Teagan perched uncomfortably on the edge of the opposite armchair, clearly nervous in his presence, but beautiful. *Breathtakingly* beautiful.

He waited until Teagan finally raised her eyes. 'I want to say I'm sorry for what my brother did to you. I can offer no excuses, and nor would I, because there aren't any. Neither can I change it, otherwise I would. I know you're uncomfortable being here, but we aren't all like him.'

Teagan swallowed and nodded, finding herself unable to drag her eyes away from the penetrating ice-blue of Jonah Powell's gaze. She hadn't expected him to broach that subject and now he had, she didn't quite know what to say.

'Is there anything you need? Anything at all?'

Jonah's gravelly voice vibrated over Teagan and she shook her head. 'You don't need to apologise for your brother's actions,' she croaked, her throat dry. But it was nice that he had. Robert's insinuations that her nightmare had been something that she'd enjoyed, still burnt painfully.

The silence weighed heavily and she gulped at her whisky for want of something to do. Like a trapped bird, she felt unable to leave the room with this man with the overwhelming presence, but equally felt unable to stay. Neither could she bring herself to refuse the top-up of whisky he offered her.

Teagan's heart banged relentlessly, dreading further questions, along with the persistent nagging urge to ask this man how he'd killed his brother.

She knew Jonah was scrutinising her – she could feel it. He was most likely comparing her to how she'd looked when he'd first seen her. Did he think the same as Robert? That she'd *enjoyed* what Saul had done? Shame threatened to push her under, so she instead stared at Jonah's hand on the bottle as he tipped more whisky into her glass. She concentrated on every single hair on the back of his hand and on the pronounced muscles of his forearm.

Did those hands strangle his own brother? Or drive a knife into him? Which?

She dare not raise her eyes because she sensed the moment she connected with Jonah's gaze, he'd ask her something she didn't want to answer. His eyes were… were too deep…

Finishing pouring her drink, Jonah topped up his own and moved to sit back down in his chair. Teagan fought within her mind for something to say. Her eyes tracked over to the framed photograph – the one of Jonah standing with the beautiful blonde, his hand resting around her tiny waist.

'That's a lovely picture. I take it that it was a professional photographer?' Teagan inwardly cringed. What sort of rubbish was she saying? 'I mean, it's obviously a proper photographer.' She laughed nervously. 'Sorry…' *Oh God, shut up, Teagan!* 'Is that your wife?'

Jonah's eyes moved to the photograph, his eyes narrowing menacingly. He'd asked Nero to get rid of anything of Lena's, so how had *that* been missed? 'That's not my wife,' he spat, venom sliding into his words.

Teagan's mounting unease grew as Jonah tipped the entire glass of whisky into his mouth. Striding over to the photograph, he snatched it up and slung it viciously into the fireplace where the glass shattered into several pieces.

Teagan began to tremble. 'Sorry… I…' Why had she asked him that? She'd deduced earlier that he couldn't be married after the comment Gwen made.

Immediately regretting unnerving the woman who had

already been through far too much, Jonah smiled. 'Forget it,' he muttered. 'It shouldn't have still been in here.' Snatching up the bottle, he refilled his glass once more.

• • • •

MIKE LEANT BACK IN HIS SEAT, acting more laid back than he actually was. *Days* he'd been trying to get in touch with Heath and today he'd finally deemed it acceptable to bother making an appearance, yet only to say he was leaving the business in the lurch?

He wouldn't give his son the satisfaction of knowing know how much his behaviour riled him, but he was disappointed. *Really* disappointed. *Heath was losing the plot.*

Heath glanced at his phone to make sure Dulcie hadn't called. He wasn't comfortable leaving her alone in case she wandered off or did something to mess up his plans, but she hadn't called, which was good. As long as he made sure this was a fleeting visit and didn't allow himself to be dragged into family arguments, then it would be fine. Correction – he *wouldn't* be dragged into any arguments, nor would he get berated by his father. If he was quick, he'd escape the London traffic before it started stacking up and could be back in Maidenhead within the hour.

'Exactly how long do you intend to continue this ridiculous charade before you accept it won't work?' Mike asked. *Moving in with Dulcie Adams? Was the boy mad?*

Heath grinned. 'No longer than I have to, believe me!' It was clear his father had no belief in his plan, but that was ok. If he didn't want the gains at the end of it, that was fine. 'How's mum?'

'She's fine,' Mike mumbled. 'I won't be telling her about your latest brainwave though!'

'Being as you haven't told her about anything else, that will hardly be anything new,' Heath chided.

Mike sat forward, his calm act deteriorating. 'You've got a nerve!' he spat. 'Deciding to bugger off from the family firm and then making comments?'

Heath laughed out loud. 'The family firm?' He made a big show of looking through the wide expanse of glass into the showroom. 'Oh, you mean the one you've made such an effort to fill with customers? It was hard enough getting them in here in the first place, but the minute I'm not driving that, you've done nothing! There's not a soul here.'

He picked up the sales receipt pad, flicked through it, then chucked it back on the desk. 'Not *one* sale since I've been gone. What does that tell you? Have you even opened or did you just do so today being as you knew I was coming?'

Mike reddened, his anger rising. 'You think you're so bloody clever, don't you?'

Heath raised an eyebrow. 'Let's put it this way, I have no intention of walking away from this empty handed.'

'You're a stupid fool!' Mike spat.

Heath shrugged. 'That's your opinion. No doubt you'll change your mind once everything comes to fruition.'

Mike snatched up the desk phone, glad for its interruption. 'City Car Sales, Mike Pointer speaking…'

Heath rolled his eyes listening to his father putting on his telephone voice. He scraped his phone off the desk and shoved it back in his pocket. He needed to make tracks. There was no point hanging around – everything needing to be said, had been. At least he'd picked up his clothes and laptop from the flat on route, so he could head straight back up to Dulcie's.

Seeing Heath get up from the chair, Mike indicated that he should wait. '2 o'clock on Friday? Yes, that's fine. I'll look forward to seeing you then.' Replacing the phone on the cradle, he folded his arms. 'See? Ye of little faith! That was a new customer – he's coming on Friday. Very interested in the gold Audi over there.'

Heath sighed. 'Oh good, that will sort everything out!'

'You can scoff, but someone doesn't come all the way from Ireland to look at a car if they're not serious!'

Heath smiled patronisingly and stuck out his hand. 'I'm off

now.'

Mike reluctantly shook hands with his son. 'Whatever you're doing, promise me you'll be careful, ok?'

Flashing his father a self-assured grin, Heath sauntered through the showroom. By the time all of this had come off he'd never have to bother setting foot in a car sales showroom again, unless he was buying a flash motor for himself, of course.

FIFTY SIX

AFTER LOSING HIS TEMPER and throwing the photograph into the fireplace, Jonah hadn't planned on telling this stranger about Lena, but there was something about Teagan Fraser which had unexpectedly opened the gates. He had just about blanked what Lena had done from his conscious mind enough to function, but his reaction proved her betrayal was still eating away at him every single minute of every single day and that chafed hard.

'I really didn't mean to pry,' Teagan said quietly, the pain on Jonah's face raw. To make the man believe he was going to be a father was low. *Really* low. What sort of woman would lie about something so important?

'Don't worry about it.' Jonah stared at his fourth glass of whisky. He hadn't intended drinking so much and was beginning to feel the effects. His eyes rested back on Teagan and suddenly he laughed loudly. 'It's ridiculous! I didn't trust anyone to start with and I certainly won't now!'

Teagan forced a smile. She felt very similar.

'At least you've got Robert,' Jonah said gruffly. 'When he shows up again, that is.' *Where the hell was the man?*

Against her will, Teagan's bottom lip quivered. She

wouldn't cry. She *wouldn't*. This drink – it made her guard slip. *Stupid, stupid.* 'I don't know why everyone thinks we are together?'

'I suppose they just presumed… I know I did. People presume a lot of things…' Jonah frowned, suddenly noticing the bereft expression on Teagan's face. 'Has something happened?'

Teagan flushed. 'Just something Robert said,' she muttered, looking at her feet with embarrassment.

Jonah walked over, his dark eyebrows knitting together. 'Is he not behaving decently?'

Teagan raised her head, surprised to find Jonah had moved so close without her sensing it and found her gaze travelling over the strong sculptured lines of his jaw and the shadow of dark stubble under his skin. She had a strong urge to reach out and touch his face to see if she could feel it. The man exuded raw power and it was hypnotising. 'Robert has no obligation to treat me in any specific way.'

'Yes he does,' Jonah said. 'You're a woman and women should always be treated decently and with respect.' He watched Teagan's eyes moving over his face, trying to read him and found himself drawn to her mouth, wondering what she'd do if he traced his thumb over across her lip, wondering what she tasted like…

His groin aching with the beginnings of arousal, Jonah shook his head angrily. He clearly needed to get a grip. It had obviously been too long, but his thoughts and reaction were unforgivable, considering this woman had recently been attacked. For fuck's sake, what the hell was wrong with him? Perhaps Gwen was right after all – maybe he should cut down on the drink.

Jonah purposefully moved his vision over to the mangled photograph of Lena – that would quell his urges straight away. *Christ, was he some kind of wanker, like Saul?*

Teagan watched Jonah scowling at the image of the woman in the smashed frame. 'I know she hurt you, but do you think you could forgive her? You must have felt something if you were getting married?'

Jonah's eyes flashed. 'Married? The only reason I was marrying the stupid bitch was because of the baby – you know, the one that didn't exist!'

Teagan blanched with the raw vitriol in Jonah's voice, his sporadic temper scaring her. They were all the same, these people. *She'd lost sight of that for a split second.*

'And no I wouldn't forgive her even if she wasn't dead!'

'D-Dead?' Teagan spluttered. No one had mentioned anything about a woman having died? *What else did she not know?*

'Yeah, dead,' Jonah spat. 'They're all fucking dead.'

Teagan felt like she might pass out. Had Jonah killed them all? Saul, his fiancée, Joe and that other man? 'So it was you? You that…?'

Jonah swung around. 'It was me, what?' he barked. 'Go on… say it! Accuse me!' He smiled viciously. 'I *dare* you…' *He was so sick of everything being so bloody wrong.*

'Is everything alright?' Gwen entered the room, eyeing Jonah first, then Teagan and finally the shards of glass and pieces of picture frame around the hearth. Her eyes narrowed accusingly at Jonah seeing the glass in his hand and then looked at Teagan. 'Teagan, could you give us a moment?'

Not needing any excuse to get away from this man and his loose temper, Teagan scrambled towards the door a little unsteadily. 'I'll be upstairs.' She nodded at Jonah and then quickly left the room, heart pounding.

In the hallway, she leant against the wall and inhaled deeply, hearing the raised voices of Gwen and Jonah muffled behind the closed door. She couldn't be around men like this – especially when her body wasn't responding to logic.

• • • •

STANDING IN THE HALLWAY AT FOOTLIGHTS, Robert listened carefully – every fibre of his body alert.

A strange tingling, vibrating sensation thrummed in an incessant hum along his veins. The anticipation, the nerves, the anger; expectation and apprehension all rolled into one. He was doing this come hell or high water.

He could have had something. For the first time in his life, he could have achieved what he'd always presumed unobtainable. The piece of him that was missing had been *so* close, but now it had slipped through his fingers like fine white sand.

Making his way slowly up the stairs, Robert took extra care to avoid the ones that always groaned loudly even with the lightest weight. He had to be silent. *Always silent…*

Biting down hard to keep his concentration in focus, his jaw ached, but concentration was something he was good at. Probably the only thing, apart from computers. He could excel at those without attracting strange or confused looks, but what did he have now?

Now he was a murderer, he'd lost his job, couldn't return home, had a father who hadn't been his father and to top it all, had resumed feeling nothing about anything – including the one thing that had made him feel something – *Teagan*. And there was only one person responsible for every single one of those facets of his ruined life.

Reaching the doorway of his mother's bedroom, Robert's eyes narrowed. As predicted, she was having her afternoon nap. His skin crawled with the list of things and people she'd manipulated. The people she'd ruined. The people she had killed. And all because of something she believed, or rather *said*, was down to love. Love? There was no such thing. More like greed. Greed and personal gain.

Well, he didn't believe in greed or personal gain, he wanted payback for what he could have had.

Robert glanced at his watch. Would the window of time be enough? Were his calculations accurate? Things had to be perfect. Nothing else would suffice.

But before he could do what he'd come to do, there was one

other thing he needed and, if he wasn't mistaken, it shouldn't be too far away.

Treading lightly along the corridor, Robert poked his head around two of the neighbouring bedrooms. One of these rooms would be where the usurper was staying… Knowing his mother, she'd want her latest pet project close. Seeing a bag that was neither his, nor Dulcie's on the floor in the corner of the next but one room, he knew he was right.

Robert moved straight to the chest of drawers and opened the top one. His face morphed into a scowl. Heath hadn't wasted any time putting his things away, had he? And they were *his* things, Robert noticed, eyeing a folded pale blue shirt that he knew straightaway was one of his own.

His anger increased. His mother had not only moved this lying scrote in as a replacement for him, but also dressed the imposter in *his* clothes? She should have picked more wisely. Heath Pointer had abused her hospitality and generosity in the very worst way. *At least, that's what it would look like.*

Pulling a pair of latex gloves from his pocket, Robert forced them over his large hands, scowling at the shiny plastic feel against his skin. He grabbed a brush from the top of the chest of drawers and teased a couple of strands of hair caught between the prongs. He didn't need much – even one would do.

Pulling the bedroom door to behind him, he strode back along the landing to the room where his mother slept, holding the strands of hair in front of him at arms' length, like a diseased animal.

He paused outside the door, listening for the sounds of Dulcie's breathing. It was slow, steady. *Still asleep.*

Robert slowly pushed the door open and focused his eyes on his mother lying on the embroidered bedspread, her tiny frame dwarfed by the wooden headboard of the antique queen-sized bed. *Like 'The Princess and the Pea'…*

He swallowed a chuckle. None of this was funny, but it would be. When it was over, it would be *more* than funny as well as being a relief.

Stealthily edging into the room, Robert kept an eye on Dulcie, soft snores coming from her open mouth, her bony chest rising and falling rhythmically.

Brushing the strands of hair onto the bedspread, he methodically inspected his gloved hands, then smiled slowly as he pulled open the top drawer of her chest of drawers. It was encouraging to see nothing had been rearranged since he'd placed everything back where it belonged.

Grabbing a pale silk stocking from the back of the drawer, he scrunched it in his hand. These stockings – another memento from her vile days at the Feathers. The perfect accessory for the job in hand.

Making sure the sheer stocking was rolled tightly, Robert moved to the head of the bed and without further hesitation, shoved it into Dulcie's open mouth, pushing it to the back of her throat with a thick finger.

Dulcie's eyes immediately shot open, her expression firstly shock, then relief to see her son, before fast changing to fear when she realised she was choking.

'Don't struggle,' Robert hissed, holding a spare pillow against Dulcie's torso. He could not leave marks on her body, but she must remain still. Making sure he didn't break eye contact, he waited. He wanted, no, *needed* her to know it was him who was finishing this. After all the lies and betrayal, it was his turn…

A ghost of a smile broke across Robert's face. She hadn't thought he'd do this. Never in all of her schemes would she think of this being on the cards.

Well, mother, there was only so much one could take…

The muffled squawks coming from Dulcie's mouth caused nothing but irritation and Robert scowled inwardly. He might have known she'd drag things out. Nothing was ever easy, but he wouldn't waver. Not after what she'd done. 'I might have considered forgiving you if you'd apologised,' he said wistfully, glancing at his watch again. 'But you didn't…'

With a remote expression, Robert watched the life force

drain from the woman who had ruined everything. 'Goodbye, mother,' he muttered coldly.

Satisfied it was done, Robert replaced the pillow and wandered to the window to gaze out over the garden – the one where he'd found solace before realising normal life was unreachable for people like him.

A Goldfinch landed on one of the bird feeders and a smile spread across his face. Finishing things had been easier than expected, both physically and mentally. Although there had been a lot of things he'd wanted to say before she'd taken her final breath, when it came to it, he couldn't be bothered. It changed nothing. She'd never have accepted responsibility. She'd have continued making excuses. There was no point.

Robert took a deep breath, then turned around to face his mother's lifeless body, her unseeing eyes staring silently at the ceiling with a look of panicked terror. He'd have to sort that out, but didn't want to touch her in case she transferred more of her curse to him than she had already.

Sighing, he dragged his finger over both his mother's eyelids, suppressing the urge to poke her eyes out as a parting shot.

Heart thudding, even though he had nothing to fear, short of Heath Pointer returning thirty minutes too soon, Robert pulled the kitchen tongs from his inside pocket, gently feeding them into his mother's mouth. He hadn't pushed the stocking too far down – just enough to block the airways, so… ah! *Got it!*

Grasping the tong handles, he pulled the stocking slowly from Dulcie's throat and closed her gape with his gloved fingers. Now it looked like she was sleeping peacefully. But that wouldn't fool the police. And he'd be making sure they weren't fooled.

As the Grandfather clock struck the hour, Robert knew it was time to leave. He positioned the kitchen tongs, still clasping the saliva-soaked stocking, on the floor and carefully rearranged it at an angle to make it look like they had been tossed down.

Backing out of the room, Robert made his way down the stairs. He didn't look back as he left Footlights for the final time.

• • • •

WATCHING HIS TRACKER like a prize possession, each ten-second refresh feeling like ten years, Robert, wiped his hand across his sweaty brow.

Come on, come on – the window of opportunity was narrowing.

A-ha…!

The dot appeared in the radial distance he'd set for Footlights. *There he was.*

Getting out of the car, Robert hastily walked to the phone box and put in the call. It had to be done around the time Heath stepped across the threshold.

'Hello?' he said, as the line connected. 'Police, please.'

Robert waited, tapping his fingers together on the metal case of the public phone. 'There's been a disturbance… No, I'm not there. I've just walked past and I could hear shouting and a woman screaming.'

A smile broke across his face. 'I called as soon as I could. An old woman lives there, but there's been a young man hanging around the last couple of days – a stranger… Yes, I walk past every day to go to work… It's Frogmore Road… No… All I know is that it's a big house with a red front door. The place looks a bit dilapidated. No… No, I don't.'

Replacing the handset before any more questions could be asked, Robert returned to his car and fired the engine.

His job was done and now nature could take its course.

FIFTY SEVEN

HUMMING ALONG TO RADIO ONE, Heath grinned. Now his father couldn't say he hadn't been brought up to speed or accuse him of disappearing off the face of the earth without a word. Yeah, he may think this was a pointless exercise and that it might well be too late to save the business from the quagmire of debt, but that was neither here nor there anymore.

Heath stabbed at the radio volume button, increasing the noise. If his father had been honest about the trouble the business was in from the start, then perhaps there may have been more that could have been done. The same could be said if the original plan with Helen hadn't gone pear-shaped, but that was life, wasn't it?

His dad's general consensus of accepting defeat far from impressed him, it only made Heath more determined. Except *this* time around, he was doing it for himself – not anyone or anything else. He'd never aspired to be in car sales in the first place. He felt bad for his mother, but he couldn't spend the rest of his life wiping his parents' backsides – especially when they, or at least his father, had little faith in his ability.

No, he'd pull this off and then he'd be nicely fixed for the future.

Flicking his indicator on, Heath weaved through Maidenhead. Again, he'd made good time. Lady Luck was on his side again and he took that as a general sign of the good fortune ahead.

He glanced at the bag on the back seat of the Lexus. *Laptop. Chargers. Clothes. Yep – all sorted.*

And that was the next thing. He'd go back to the Feathers tomorrow and see if he could catch that Lena Taylor to cancel that event he'd booked when it had seemed like a good idea – that was if the meathead bouncer let him through the door this time.

From this point all he'd be concentrating on was Dulcie Adams. Oh sure, he'd be making a special effort to locate Robert, but only to make sure he stayed the hell away. He wasn't letting Robert wheedle his way back into Dulcie's good books once he realised that ship had sailed.

Turning into Frogmore Road, Heath smiled. The food he'd picked up from M&S would go down a treat in impressing the old goat. Duck Parfait was one of her favourites and these pre-prepared things with all the sides were perfect. Even *he* could manage to lob this lot in a bloody oven!

Yeah, Dulcie would be well impressed and when he'd told her he'd take her out somewhere for lunch tomorrow to make up for not doing so today she'd be even happier. As much as it grated on his tits, it was vital to show his supposed loyalty, family values and willingness to put her first. Until he'd talked her into amending her will it was all system go.

Parking up, Heath hopped out of the car with enthusiasm. He hadn't been too long, so if he acted suitably excited to be back and glad to see her, that would also earn further brownie points.

Slotting the key in the lock, he opened the heavy front door. He'd even got his own key now. Things were going very nicely indeed.

'Dulcie? I'm back!' he called, putting his holdall on the floor in the hall. *It was very quiet? Where was she?*

Frowning at the lack of response, he moved to the kitchen, finding that empty too. Quickly shoving the carrier bag of food in the fridge, he loped up the stairs. 'Dulcie?' She was probably asleep, the lazy cow. It wasn't like she'd had anything else to do.

Knocking on the ajar door of Dulcie's bedroom, Heath walked in. 'Wake up, sleepy head! Wait until you see what I've got! I've got your favourite for dinner tonight and...'

He broke off mid-sentence as he approached the figure in the bed. 'Dulcie...?' *Something wasn't right.* He touched her grey-tinged cheek, finding it cool. *Oh shit, she wasn't dead, was she?* She couldn't be fucking dead! She hadn't changed the will yet... *No!*

Unable to locate a pulse, perspiration beaded. *For fuck's sake. The old bitch had karked it. How bloody typical was that?*

So now what?

Heath feverishly paced around the room, frowning at something on the floor. *What the hell was that?* It was one of those things from the kitchen used for fishing bacon out of a frying pan! What on earth was that doing in here? And what was that at the end of it?

For a split second, he thought about taking a closer look, but realised he shouldn't mess about until he'd first dealt with this situation.

Heath ran his fingers through his hair, scarcely able to believe this had happened. He was sick of this. Was his life that doomed for every single set of well-laid plans to be ripped from under him just as he reached the finish line?

He glared at Dulcie, wanting to whack her. The fucking old bitch! She'd probably done this to spite him! Decided to die just because he'd dared to go elsewhere for the afternoon?

Heath sat on the edge of the bed. What was he supposed to do now? He rolled his eyes. Oh, this would give his father something else to bleat on about and could almost hear it already: *'I told you it was a waste of time...'*.

Glancing around, Heath sighed. Should he leave? No one

had seen him come back, so if he just went then he wouldn't be lumbered with dealing with any of it.

Oh Christ! Would he be expected to sort everything out? Things like the funeral and all that?

His eyes narrowed. Fuck that! It wasn't like he stood to gain anything. If only she could have dragged out dying for a few more weeks then he would have got everything sorted in time. *And* he'd wasted a tenner on that bloody Duck Parfait!

All but gnashing his teeth with frustration, Heath stood back up. Perhaps he should call an ambulance? Even though Dulcie was dead, wasn't that what had to be done? He didn't want to be accused by anyone of not reporting it…

Pulling his phone from his pocket, he fumbled to enter the unlock code when loud banging from downstairs startled him. *What the fuck was that?*

A wave of cold crashed over him as he heard shouting amidst the banging. *Burglars wouldn't shout, would they?*

Dashing to the window, Heath's mobile fell from his hand at the sight of several police cars.

Wide-eyed, he glanced back at Dulcie's body lying lifelessly on the bed, just as the front door splintered when the police entered by force.

FIFTY EIGHT

SINCE THE UNCOMFORTABLE and unnerving time spent with Jonah this afternoon, Teagan had remained in her bedroom to avoid running into him again, instead using the time to rid herself of the thick head the whisky had left behind. That and analysing the unanswerable questions of how she could leave this place – away from people who doled out violence in a way that was completely unfathomable.

She'd seen how quickly Jonah's personality had turned. For a moment, she'd almost been taken in by the strong magnetism emanating from every pore of his being and the unpalatable truth of his attractiveness – something which men like that invariably used to their advantage to wield power over stupid, gullible women, such as her.

It hadn't taken long before the mask had fallen though, had it?

Teagan fully admitted she liked Gwen – liked her a lot, but to say that Jonah was a decent man?

But if she left, where would she go? She was nowhere near ready to start again somewhere on her own. Her nerves were high and her diminished confidence at an all-time low, but how could she remain here?

Interrupted by hearing Robert return, she'd made her way downstairs and despite how much his earlier words still stung, she had to know if he'd seen Dulcie and also hoped he might feel it necessary to apologise and tell her he hadn't meant to say what he'd said earlier. In the sitting room, it was clear his mood had not improved and nothing was forthcoming.

Teagan waited patiently for Robert to answer her question.

'I called round this afternoon, but there was no answer,' Robert said finally, the resentment at Teagan's intrusion obvious.

Teagan knew she shouldn't press the issue, but this was too frustrating. Robert may no longer care for Dulcie, but *she* did. 'Did you not go in? Haven't you still got your keys?'

Robert slammed his pen down on the table and looked at Teagan, irritation leaking from him like a sieve. 'Why would I just walk in? I don't know whether you remember, but I don't live there and want nothing to do with the woman. I said I'd check because *you* asked me to, but no one answered, so that's all there is to say.'

His teeth grated. He needed quiet and concentration and to discover the upshot of whether his plan had worked. That was the only thing of any value. Until he got confirmation of that, he could not be disturbed.

'I'm just trying to help. I…'

'You're *not* helping. You never have!' Robert's temper ignited. 'Furthermore, I don't need your help. I've had nothing but problems since you arrived. If it wasn't for y…'

'If it wasn't for *me*?' Teagan interrupted, her voice small.

Robert banged his fist on the table. He couldn't think. He hadn't been able to think straight for what felt like *centuries* because of her. Because of *them*. Because of *everything*.

Teagan felt like she'd been punched in the stomach. *So he did blame her?* 'Why won't you just explain?'

Robert swung around, his eyes wild. 'Because I don't *want* to! I was quite happy with my life before. Then you and *her* are suddenly in my flat, giving me no space. Interfering…'

He had done alright most of his adult like by keeping himself to himself. Being alone meant no problems. It was easier that way. His mother had always said being alone helped his inability to fit in. *Yeah, his mother... and she was always right, wasn't she?*

Putting Robert's dismissal to one side, Teagan felt she had to keep trying. He was clearly upset. He'd always tried to do his best for her before, hadn't he? Biting back the tears, she moved closer. 'Please tell me what's bothering you. Is it Dulcie? I know you're worried regardless of what you say. And you're still here for me an...'

'You know *nothing*!' Robert snarled. 'I'm still here only because I have to be.' She needed to shut up. She should *always* have shut up. He couldn't listen. It only led to disappointment and distraction. And as far as his mother... He'd already ended that, but just because the bitch had given him life, that didn't mean she'd be taking his freedom as a parting shot from beyond the grave. No way! It wasn't difficult - all he wanted to know was if his plan for her and that Pointer twat had worked. *Why hadn't there been any news bulletins and why couldn't everyone leave him alone?*

Teagan placed her hand on Robert's shoulder, feeling him tense at her touch. 'I know this is difficult and I also know you didn't mean those dreadful things you said earlier.'

Robert threw Teagan's hand off, her touch making him cringe. 'Get the fuck off!' he screamed, his eyes narrowing. 'You see? You're doing it again – thinking you know what I'm thinking when you don't. And for the record, I meant *everything* I said! You disgust me!'

'What's happened to you?' Teagan cried, the malice in Robert's eyes making her step back. 'Why are you being like this?'

'I've always been like this!' he snarled. 'And you and my mother have made it worse, that's what.'

'Me? What have I done?' Teagan gabbled, her hands trembling.

Robert glared at Teagan, his eyes burning. 'What do you think? If you hadn't have done what you did with that freak, then… then… Oh, what does it matter? Everything is ruined and it's because of *you*.' Robert's hatred burnt into his laptop as he looked for a BBC bulletin notification. *Still nothing. Why was nothing being reported? Had his call been ignored?*

Tears poured down Teagan's cheeks. 'How can you say that? I-I didn't get a lot of choice. I can't believe that y…'

'*Everyone* has a choice, Teagan and you made yours.'

For a moment Teagan stood frozen with hurt before running from the room.

• • • •

JONAH STOOD TO THE LEFT of the doorway taken aback with everything he'd heard Robert Adams utter, any respect he'd initially had for the man diminishing rapidly. Was the man crazy? He knew what Saul had done, so how could he say all of those things?

As Teagan blindly stumbled through the door straight into him, Jonah had no choice but to grab her to prevent her from crashing headlong into his chest. His hands gripped her upper arms and he silently searched her eyes as she stared up at him, almost blind in her distress.

He was still simmering with anger over what had happened last time he'd seen her. Not anger for her, but anger for *himself*. Admitting to a total stranger that he'd fallen for Lena's lies couldn't have made it more obvious how bloody stupid he'd been and he resented that. Plus Teagan thought, or had been led to believe that *he'd* killed Lena. She believed he'd killed *all* of them. Jonah clenched his teeth. He'd seen her face – it had reeked of horror and disgust.

Normally, it wouldn't bother him, but this time it did. It *really* bothered him. Why had he not just told her the truth?

Jonah swallowed his growing anger. Why did he care what she thought or what anyone thought? Because what she believed made him seem incompetent, that's why… Or was it because he hadn't liked seeing the disgust for what she perceived he had done?

But now there was *this* problem and this made him even angrier. Seeing the raw pain in Teagan's eyes, fresh rage churned. 'He's wrong,' he growled.

Choking back a sob, Teagan pulled herself from Jonah's grip and without a word, rushed off in the opposite direction.

Jonah watched Teagan's retreating figure disappearing up the corridor and he turned back towards the room containing Robert Adams, his brows knitted with pent-up fury. How could Adams treat the woman like any of this was her fault? Like she was damaged goods no one would want? And on top of treating the woman like a piece of shit, Adams had been around to Dulcie's house even though he'd made it clear that everyone was to stay away?

Hearing the tapping of a keyboard, Jonah glanced back at the door. Adams would have to move to one of his satellite properties like he'd first suggested. He might need the man for locating O'Hara, but he wouldn't have him disobeying instructions, nor disrespecting women. He was fast beginning to wonder whether he'd got Robert Adams completely wrong.

FIFTY NINE

LOOKING AT HIS LAPTOP SCREEN, Robert scribbled down coordinates and times into his notepad before glancing over at Jonah. 'Your man is definitely making a move.'

Jonah frowned. 'Yes, but where to? That's the key.' It was difficult enough having to be civil to Robert Adams after what he'd witnessed yesterday, let alone put up with vagueness about O'Hara's whereabouts. He knew O'Hara was planning on turning up somewhere, but it was a question of *where*. He needed this to be over.

He turned his attention to Gwen. 'You're sure he wasn't more specific?'

Gwen pulled the phone from her bag and opened the text message Jonah was referring to. 'What I told you was exactly what he put. Look.' She thrust Lena's phone at Jonah:

> Something's not right and I don't like it. I'll stay with friends of the family until you call me. R x

Jonah arched an eyebrow. 'So, he's not going to that hotel I told you to suggest?'

Gwen reined in her irritation. 'Like I said before, he's suspicious. He wants to hear from Lena herself. I knew he would if all I ever did was text.'

Jonah chucked Lena's phone on the desk next to Gwen's mobile. 'Where's he going then if not the hotel? What family friend could he possibly have around here?' He glared at Robert still stuck to his laptop screen. 'How long will it be before we know?'

'He's on the way over to England now.' Peering closer at the slowly changing coordinates on the screen, Robert frowned. 'By the speed of this, I'd say via ferry rather than plane.'

'So how long?' Jonah pressed. *Could no one answer a simple question?*

'However long it takes him to get wherever he's going! I can't be any more exact than that!'

Jonah paced around his office in agitation. Adams' facetious comments were getting on his wick. The man wasn't levelling with him and he'd had plenty of opportunities to say he'd attempted to pay Dulcie a visit, but nothing had been said.

Nearing the drinks cabinet, his hand itched to pour himself a large one, but Gwen was watching with *that* look on her face. She'd already insinuated his increase in drinking was affecting his judgement.

Gwen jumped as her mobile rang. Snatching the phone from the desk, she glanced at the screen:

`Unknown number…`

With her eyes still firmly on Jonah, Gwen answered the call. 'Hello?' she snapped, rolling her eyes when the line disconnected. That probably served her right for giving Teagan an excuse about cold callers yesterday.

Suddenly, a wave of dread washed over her. *That was Lena's phone, not hers. And she answered it… Shit!* Thankfully, it wasn't O'Hara.

Relieved to see Jonah was still too busy pacing around the

office to take notice, Gwen quickly shoved Lena's phone in her bag, rather than putting it somewhere that it could get mixed up again.

Moving back to the drinks cabinet, Jonah grabbed the whisky bottle and poured himself a generous glass, ignoring Gwen's expression. *No one* was dictating when he had a drink or how many.

Also watching Jonah, Nero frowned. He was unsure what else had happened to rattle his cage, but something had. Robert going off radar yesterday hadn't helped either. 'Have you decided what you're doing about Lena yet?'

Jonah scowled. *Why did everyone have to mention Lena?* 'I've already said she's off under medical instruction. What else do you want me to say?'

'We can't use that indefinitely.' Nero pushed.

Jonah paced around some more. He knew that. Of course he did, but there was too much going on and he needed to think. He'd been rash bringing Adams into the picture. He'd needed his expertise, but now… well, he didn't know what to do and answers weren't forthcoming. 'I'll spell it out again, shall I? My priority is the O'Hara's. I don't know how many times I need to say that everything else can wait!'

Gwen watched Jonah top up his glass. 'I have an idea, but it would mean taking a dent to your ego that you might not like…'

Jonah span around, his eyes accusing. 'What's that then?' Wasn't not being able to sort Saul out himself; admitting to strangers that Lena had hurt him; having the son of his arch enemy come to the rescue on every level, but now doubting him as much as he'd doubted Saul. Another was being presumed to be the multiple murderer… Weren't all of these things enough to question whether there was anything left to be humiliated over?

Nero cleared his throat, seeing Gwen's reticence to continue. He'd broach the idea himself. 'Gwen mentioned her idea earlier and it's a good one. The best we've got, anyway.'

'Glad to see you've been busy discussing things in my absence,' Jonah spat.

'Tell everyone Lena's left you. Tell them she's walked out and you don't know where, therefore the wedding's off,' Nero said confidently.

Jonah stared between Nero and Gwen and clapped slowly. 'And that's it, is it? Announcing to all and sundry that my fiancée has decided to leave me? Oh yeah, that's great! The ultimate public humiliation!'

'If you want to see it that way, but it would work,' Nero added.

Jonah slammed his now empty glass on the desk. 'What does it even matter?' He yanked his suit jacket from the back of the seat. 'I tell you what, I'm going home! *You* decide - discuss it between yourselves and when you reach a decision, let me know and I'll simply announce it. How does that sound?'

Leaving Nero and Gwen in stunned silence, Jonah stopped on his way out to lean over Robert, still firmly entranced with his laptop. 'Let me know when you get the next lead, if that's not too much trouble? That's if you're not disappearing off for half the day again?'

Robert frowned, still fixated by his screen, Jonah's barbed dig going over his head. 'You'll be waiting a long time. Look.' He pointed to his screen, showing that no new coordinates of the trace had showed for twenty minutes and the blue dot on the corresponding map was static in the Irish Sea. 'Either the ferry has sunk or your man has offloaded his phone.'

'I don't believe this!' Jonah fumed, slamming the office door behind him as he stalked down the staff corridor.

Gwen stood motionless, wondering whether this meant she had inadvertently caused this problem by stupidly answering that call.

• • • •

BACK AT THE HOUSE, Jonah fumed silently and refilled his drink. His brain felt like it was melting.

Nero had already braved ringing since he'd walked out of the Feathers confirming the trace on O'Hara had still not moved. Two hours now and nothing. Oh, they were keeping watch on it, he'd promised. It could be that the phone's battery had died, he'd added. But they all knew that wasn't the case and what the significance of this lack of movement meant.

From Lena's lack of contact, Ron O'Hara had got wind that something had happened and had decided to leave nothing to chance. A pretty astute move for someone who belonged in a fucking straitjacket.

With mounting frustration, Jonah ripped off his tie and undid the top two buttons of his shirt. He was bloody hot and stressed. He was more than that. He was sick to the back teeth with everything! So now what? If the trace had disappeared on O'Hara, which it looked like it had, then where did he start looking for the bastard?

Jonah fished the wooden box from his suit jacket pocket. At least he'd brought *these* back with him.

Opening the box, Jonah unwrapped the collection of pink diamonds. Spreading them out over his desk, the afternoon sun through the large south-facing study window refracted a multitude of tiny rainbows across the room.

Moving the diamonds from the Feathers safe into his personal one achieved nothing, apart from giving him a modicum of control. It felt like he was doing something. Furthermore, he would tell *no one* that they were here. Not Nero, not Gwen and certainly not Robert Adams. He'd had enough.

'And those are what this whole thing has been about?'

Jonah's head shot up to find Teagan standing in his study doorway.

'I've been through all of *this* for those?' Teagan walked into the room uninvited, staring at the collection of sparkling jewels on the desk. 'Personally, they're weren't worth it!' Her voice was hollow. 'I don't expect you to understand that, of course. These sort of things are the only things important to people like you.'

Jonah wrapped the diamonds back up and placed them back in the box. Leaning his elbows on the desk, he knitted his fingers together and stared at Teagan. 'You might be surprised to learn that you're wrong because I agree with you.'

Getting up, he walked over to one of the many bookcases, opening a hidden safe very cleverly camouflaged as a shelf of books. He could feel Teagan staring into his back making the hairs on his neck stand up.

'These,' he said, placing the box in the safe and shutting the door securely, 'have been the bane of my life for as long as I can remember.' Turning around, he sighed. 'This problem arose decades ago and has followed this family ever since, now *I've* had to deal with it.'

He looked squarely at Teagan, noticing a slight twitch in her eye. 'You should never have been involved and I'm sorry that it ended up that way.'

Noticing Jonah looked tired and drawn, Teagan reprimanded herself for contemplating any slight sympathy towards this man. After what he'd done and what he'd sanctioned, he deserved problems. He'd murdered that woman... Ok, so she'd betrayed him, but *murdering* her?

Jonah moved to the drinks cabinet – a place he was visiting more and more frequently. 'Drink?'

Teagan shook her head. 'I don't think so.'

Jonah smiled, even though nothing was remotely amusing. 'I hope you don't mind if I do?'

'I doubt whether anyone would dare question you,' Teagan snapped.

Jonah's face darkened as he poured his drink. 'I may have spoken unnecessarily unfairly to you yesterday, but that doesn't give you the excuse to be rude.'

Teagan flinched, then regained her composure. Robert had already made it very clear what he thought and she wasn't having this man treat her like shit too. This man, whose greed had ruined countless lives and whose brother had personally completely ruined hers.

'No, you're right. This is your house and I'm a guest here – albeit an uninvited one. One here purely from misplaced responsibility to offset you and your family's wrongdoing.'

Jonah bristled. He'd had enough of women thinking they could say what they liked. 'I don't know what your problem is with me, lady, but I've been respectful to you, therefore I would appreciate the same courtesy. You may be pissed off because of Robert's attitude, but that is not my fault!'

Teagan flushed crimson. *He'd heard everything Robert had said?* 'I suppose you agree with Robert's opinion?' She wouldn't let him upset her. She wouldn't let these people get to her anymore. 'Are you going to kill me now as well? Add me to the list of women who have pissed you off?'

As soon as the words left her mouth, Teagan wished she could retract them. That wasn't fair of her. 'I shouldn't have said that… I…'

'No, you shouldn't,' Jonah spat, tipping the whisky liberally into his mouth. 'Shut the door on your way out.'

• • • •

MIKE IGNORED THE PHONE CALL. No doubt it would be Heath again, and he wasn't having his hot-headed sarcastic son taking up any more of his time bragging about his latest scheme or listening to digs over how much the business had failed.

As much as he hated admitting it, Mike had come to the conclusion that as much as he never thought he'd see the day, his son had turned into a self-obsessed, selfish shit and he wasn't putting up with it anymore. Neither would he put up with his constant jibes.

Mike knew he'd screwed up and hadn't dealt with things in the best way or the way he probably should have done, but he was trying to *protect* his family. That was all he'd ever tried to do.

So, he'd never been overly-enamoured with Heath's hair-brained idea of recouping his grandfather's stolen goods. He'd always endeavoured to stay the right side of the law and apart from a few suspect expenses he'd put through the books over the years, he had. And he was proud he'd done it that way. Mike had felt increasingly uncomfortable over Heath's penchant to chase after the other side of things – for one, he'd had first hand experience of what being involved in that sort of things led to. It had ruined his father's life, as well as his mother's and subsequently, caused him a great deal of heartache, so he wanted no part of it, but Heath was obsessed now and that could only be dangerous.

In a way, it was a relief that Heath was no longer involved in the business – at least for now.

Mike stabbed at the reject call button as it rang for the third time. He set his chin determinedly. He just wasn't doing it anymore. Once Heath had come to his senses – if he ever did, then maybe they could start again? Besides, he had to concentrate on this customer who was due in an hour or so. If he could sell that gold Audi, that would be a good start.

Yep, he'd just about had enough.

Seeing two men walk into the showroom, Mike sat up and grinned. This must be those Irish guys now. They were early but that didn't matter. In fact, it was good because it must mean they were really interested.

Standing up, he moved towards the office door, but the men beat him to it. 'Are you here about the Audi? We spoke on the phone?' Mike said, a wide smile on his face as he extended his hand.

The two men exchanged glances and the larger of the two smiled thinly. 'I'm afraid we're not here about a car, Sir. I am Detective Inspector Morgan and this is DC Blake. Are you Michael Pointer? Father to a Heath Pointer?'

Mike blinked, a rush of fear enveloping him. *Had Heath been in an accident?* 'Yes, I'm Mike Pointer. Heath's my son. What's happened? Is he alright?'

'Heath is unhurt, Mr Pointer. We'd just like to ask you a couple of questions, if that's ok with you?' DI Morgan gestured for Mike to step back into the office. Following inside, he waited while his colleague closed the door behind them.

'W-What's this about?' Mike spluttered. *If Heath wasn't hurt, then...?* He hadn't been back to that damn club and got himself killed, had he?

'Would you mind telling us if you saw your son yesterday?' DC Blake asked, fishing a notebook from his inside pocket.

Mike looked between the two detectives and fear glimmered. He'd thought Heath was in a rush to leave yesterday. He hadn't been going back to Maidenhead at all, had he? He'd gone back to that damned Feathers place in his mad bid for those blasted diamonds again, the stupid, *stupid* boy.

Whatever Heath had done to rile him and let him down lately, Mike wouldn't allow for this old business that had taken his father, to take his son too. *He'd fix this.* Moving his gaze to the larger man, hoping the sheen he felt on his forehead wasn't visible, he smiled. 'Yes, Heath was here yesterday and before you ask, I know that for a fact. I haven't seen him for a few days, so I know categorically that I saw him yesterday. Yesterday afternoon, to be precise.'

Mike watched the detectives exchange glances again. *They didn't believe him?* 'I can assure you he was here!'

'Yesterday afternoon, you say? Can you remember what time, Mr Pointer?' DI Morgan asked.

'It was around 3 o'clock. Yes, it was definitely 3. I know that because a customer with an appointment had just left. I was eager to see Heath because, like I said, I haven't seen him for a few days.'

'But Heath works with you, does he not? Why have you not seen him for a few days?'

'Erm, he's had a couple of days off. People do have days off, you know. Even in the car sales industry!' Mike laughed falsely.

'And what time did he leave, Sir?'

Mike thought for a moment. They were trying to place him at the club weren't they. He knew it! Well, he'd fix that! 'He didn't stay long. He left around 3.15. He wanted to miss the London traffic.'

'You're saying he left London around 3.15?' the detective continued. 'He couldn't have remained in London?'

Mike nodded. *He knew it. Well, ha ha.* They could try and catch him out all they liked, but it was true. Heath had left London – at least, that's what he'd *said.* Ok, so he must have lied and gone to the Feathers instead as part of his stupid mission, but Heath was his son, so he would do everything in his power to make out otherwise. 'I'm telling you, he wasn't in London. Whatever has happened, it wasn't anything to do with him! Heath was going to Maidenhead!'

DI Morgan frowned. 'Why would he be going to Maidenhead, Sir?'

'If you must know, he's been up there for a few days. He's, erm, he's staying with a friend.' Mike watched the detective scribble something into his notebook. 'Look, he wasn't in London.'

DI Morgan locked eyes with Mike. 'No one said your son was in London, Mr Pointer.' His eyes moved to the notebook his colleague handed to him. 'The times coincide and add up.'

Hearing this, Mike smiled inwardly. Heath owed him one for this, but he would certainly be expecting him to explain himself. After everything he'd said. He'd *told* him not to go to that bloody club! 'Is that all sorted then? You didn't even tell me what this was all about in the first place!'

'Your son was arrested yesterday on suspicion of murder, Mr Pointer. Now, thanks to what you have just confirmed, we will be able to charge him.'

'W-What?' Mike screeched. *Murder?* 'There must be some kind of mistake! Murder of who?'

The detectives stood up. 'I cannot say any more, but thank you for your time, Mr Pointer and of course for confirming your son's whereabouts and times. Someone will be in contact with you should we need any further assistance.'

Mike found himself unable to get up from the chair and his

mouth flapped open and shut. 'B-But…'

'We'll see ourselves out,' DI Morgan said, as they both left Mike's office.

Mike blankly watched the two men walk through his showroom, stopping momentarily to admire a Jaguar on the way, before putting his head in his hands. *What in hell's name had Heath done? Oh Jesus Christ!*

Nausea flooded over him and he was so distracted that he didn't even notice the man walk into his showroom and approach his office.

'Mike Pointer? The name's Ron O'Hara. We spoke the other day about the Audi?'

Mike slowly looked up, too tired to want to sell cars, but felt he might perhaps change his mind noticing the barrel of a gun pointing straight at him.

SIXTY

JONAH HATED ADMITTING he was wrong, especially when it concerned something he'd previously been warned of, but it had to be done. He also owed these people an apology.

Closing the folder on his desk, he looked at Nero and Gwen, both staring at him with uncertainty. 'First of all I need to apologise,' he said. 'I should not have taken things out on either of you yesterday.'

'It's not a problem,' Nero smiled. 'It's understandable what with everything that's happened. You've had a lot to deal with.'

'As has everyone,' Jonah remarked, his mouth twisting into a wry smile.

'But not in the same way as you,' Nero countered. 'Lena and then Saul… It's a lot to d…'

'Yes, well,' Jonah interrupted, not wishing Saul or Lena to be brought into the conversation. 'There was still no excuse to rally. You've both been invaluable, so I'm sorry.' He clasped his hands, pleased to see that at least one of the things he needed to say had been said.

'It was a double blow losing the trace on O'Hara,' Nero added. 'There's definitely been nothing since. Not one signal, so we have to accept that he got wind and ditched the phone.'

He sighed deeply. 'Back to square one…'

'I think that was down to me…' Gwen said, wringing her hands. 'It's *me* who should be apologising.'

She'd been dreading this, but after analysing it all night, there really was no other explanation. 'You may remember that call I got during our meeting yesterday? It was from an unknown number who hung up the minute I answered? I thought it was my phone… but it wasn't… It was Lena's…'

Jonah bristled. 'You answered Lena's phone?'

Gwen nodded sadly. 'Less than five minutes after that, the trace on O'Hara dropped. It must have been him calling from a different number in a bit to allay his suspicions. I'm so sorry. It was stupid. I should have checked. He'd have known immediately I wasn't Lena…'

Jonah raised his hand. 'What's done is done. We were cutting it fine to intercept him as it was. He knew something was up.'

'But we almost had him,' Gwen cried, angry for her stupidity. 'We have no idea where he is now.'

'I agree it's unfortunate, but we can't change that now,' Nero said. 'Talking of which, where is Robert? I asked him to put some checks out to make sure the trace hasn't been blocked. Although I doubt whether O'Hara has the nous to do that, I told him it was worth a try.'

Jonah frowned. 'That brings me to the next thing. I'm not happy about Robert. You were right to be concerned over him. I was rash to involve him.'

Nero sat forward. 'Has something happened? You think Robert's playing us? In it with O'Hara?'

Jonah shook his head. 'No, not like that, but I don't trust him. Something's not quite right with the man.' He tapped his temple. 'He's not quite the ticket.'

Gwen looked from Jonah to Nero. 'I'll admit he's a bit of an odd-ball, but that doesn't mean he's…'

'He went to see Dulcie,' Jonah cut in. 'He went there despite strict instructions of no contact.'

'What? What's he said to her?' Irritation seeped from Nero. He'd never liked Adams from the off. Knowing he had Pointer blood made it worse.

'He didn't see her. There was no answer,' Jonah explained. 'But the point is, he shouldn't have done it. Neither did he tell me. I overheard a conversation with Teagan. Robert lied about his whereabouts and then didn't level when he had the chance.'

'What's his excuse for this?' Nero spat.

Jonah shrugged. 'He doesn't know that I know. I figured it was better to keep schtum for now.'

'Maybe he was embarrassed?' Gwen suggested. 'Dulcie is his mother after all.'

'Instructions are instructions!' Jonah barked, his brows furrowing. 'But that's not all. You should have heard the shit he was coming out with to the girl. I wanted to give him a fucking kicking there and then!'

Gwen sat forward. 'He's a cold one, he is. If he's upset her…'

'Oh, he upset her alright,' Jonah spat. 'More than that – he upset *me*. Saying stuff like she wanted to be with Saul etc. etc. and that everything was her fault.'

'What sort of thing is that to say?' Nero choked.

'Like I said, I wanted to give him a slap, but I'm ashamed to say that we needed him for this O'Hara thing, so I didn't.' Jonah continued. 'But now that's gone pear-shaped, I'm going to suggest he takes one of the satellite houses and works from there.'

Nero clenched his fists. 'Why help him at all. If we've no need for him, tell him to sling his fucking hook!'

'He knows a lot about the firm and we can still use his expertise, but I won't have him in my house to lie to me and disrespect women.'

Nero nodded in agreement. 'Where is he now?'

'I left him working at the house.'

Gwen stood up, furious. 'Well, if no one minds, I'll go there now in case he's taken it upon himself to lay into Teagan again.

I won't have her spoken to like that, Jonah. She's lovely and for him to have said… Urgh, I can't bear it.'

Jonah also rose from his chair. 'No, I'll go. While I'm there, I'll tell him about his change of living arrangements that are to take immediate effect.' He shrugged on his jacket. 'Then I'll sit down and work out where we go next with O'Hara. Whatever happens we'll need to think about stepping up the security both here and at the house. He's bound to turn up at some point when Lena remains silent.'

• • • •

ENTERING HIS OFFICE after having firstly checked Robert was not causing any problems, finding him utterly entranced with lines of code on his laptop as usual, Jonah shook his head with a combination of bemusement and irritation and began sifting through the folder containing his properties.

There weren't too many empty at this present time, but there were a couple which would be both suitable, as well as being close enough to keep tabs on Robert.

Flicking through the paperwork, Jonah stopped at one of his smaller townhouses. The latest tenants had vacated this one almost a month ago and he'd kept meaning to phone the estate agents to get it back on the rental market, but what with everything, it had worked its way to the back of the priority queue.

Checking the reference number, Jonah retrieved the cashbox containing all the keys for his properties, when there was a tap on the door. He glanced up. Robert had clearly saved him the journey of going all the way down the other end of the house to tell him the 'good news' about his move. 'Come in,' he muttered.

Surprised to see Teagan standing in the doorway, he raised an eyebrow. 'Teagan! What can I do for you?'

'I don't want to disturb you,' Teagan said, warily glancing around the study.

Jonah pushed himself away from the desk and crossing his

ankles, beckoned Teagan into the room. 'You're not, providing you're not planning to launch more accusations!'

'That's why I'm here, 'Teagan said, making her way into the room. She perched uncomfortably on the chair the opposite side of Jonah's desk. 'I wanted to apologise. I lashed out at you yesterday and I shouldn't have… You've been very good to me and I had no right to say the things I said.'

Jonah studied Teagan. She really was a beautiful creature. 'I hope you know that Robert was wrong with what he said to you?'

Getting up from the chair, Teagan walked over to stare out of the study window, hurt washing over her. 'I don't know what's wrong with him,' she said quietly. 'He's changed.'

'You won't have to be around him anymore. I'm letting him know that he's moving to one of my other properties away from here.'

'Oh, you don't need to do that!' Teagan protested, swinging around.

'I do,' Jonah muttered. 'Weird shit does stuff to some people, but regardless of his reasons, they're not good enough. He's not staying here anymore.'

Teagan fidgeted nervously. 'I know it's none of my business, but you don't say the sort of things he did... And, well, with the stuff you've done…'

Getting up, Jonah placed the box of keys back in the filing cabinet, then turned to Teagan. 'Not all of us feel the need to throw shit because of situations, Teagan. And by the way, I didn't kill Lena. I *wanted* to, but I didn't. Saul did.'

Teagan blinked. 'B-But they said…'

Jonah moved towards Teagan. '*Who* said?'

Teagan faltered. *Who had told her?* No one had actually said… She'd just presumed…

'Come on. Who told you that I killed her? I didn't kill my brother either!' Jonah laughed, amused by the surprise on Teagan's face. 'Don't get me wrong, I'd have happily killed Saul, but someone beat me to it.'

His eyes dropped to Teagan's mouth. 'Amongst a whole host of other reasons, my main reason for wanting to slowly slit his throat was for what he did to you. You should never have got dragged into it. Listen, I may have killed a lot of people and hurt more, which I'm sure you already 'presumed', but my only regret is that I didn't get to Saul first.'

Just hearing Saul's name made Teagan blanch. *But if Jonah hadn't killed Saul, who had?*

Jonah was far too close for comfort. Flustered, Teagan stared at the smattering of dark hair underneath his open collar. Moving back to his eyes, she saw it. It was there, loud and clear. And she felt it too.

Desire.

Feeling the invisible pull from the man in front of her, Teagan felt faint. Regardless of what Jonah said about his brother and Lena, the man was still a murderer. A lunatic… He'd just admitted he'd killed others…

'I should have killed Saul a long ago because if I had, then he wouldn't have hurt you. I'm sorry I didn't.'

Suddenly a thought dropped into Teagan's head like a brick. *Christ, it all made sense now.* 'I-It was Robert, wasn't it?' she whimpered. Her eyes moved to Jonah's mouth, his full lips and her breathing quickened. 'Tell me, was it him?'

A ghost of a smile formed on Jonah's mouth. 'What does it matter?'

Without thinking too much about what he was doing, Jonah brushed a tendril of Teagan's dark hair away from her eye and then traced his thumb slowly along her bottom lip, just as he'd wanted to the other day. 'And nothing has ruined you. Nothing can, unless you allow it to. You're beautiful and let no one tell you otherwise.'

Putting one hand on the small of Teagan's back, Jonah pulled her towards him and she offered no resistance. Gently tilting her face up to his, slowly and very deliberately, he brought his mouth down on hers.

It flashed through Teagan's mind to question what on earth

she was doing, but Jonah's lips like soft velvet moving to her throat pushed all thoughts from her mind and the urge to feel his mouth all over her grew, wanting this man like no other. With one of his hands still at the base of her spine, the other now clutched in the back of her hair, her arms moved to wrap around Jonah's neck. Hearing herself whimper with longing when Jonah's mouth crashed back on hers, his kisses now deep and urgent, heat rose from her in blinding waves.

Effortlessly lifting her onto his desk, Jonah swiped the paperwork out of the way with one hand. As his fingers found their way under her skirt, Teagan pulled at his shirt, running her fingers over his heavily muscled torso and then fumbled with the zip of his trousers.

'Jonah? Are y… Oh!' Gwen froze in the study doorway.

Jonah pulled his mouth from Teagan's and glared at Gwen. 'Doesn't anyone knock around here?'

'Sorry, I'll wait out here,' Gwen spluttered, quickly closing the door behind her as she stepped out of the study, mortified.

'Oh my God!' Teagan cried, scrambling from the desk, hastily straightening her clothes.

Rearranging himself, Jonah stared intensely at Teagan, her mouth still swollen from his hard kisses. 'I guess I should see what the problem is.' He dropped heavily into his desk chair. 'GWEN!'

Re-entering the room, her face crimson, Gwen glanced first at Teagan, then at Jonah, who didn't look at all pleased. 'I-I'm sor…'

'Save it!' Jonah waved his hand at Gwen, indicating for her to take a seat. 'What is it?' He glanced at Teagan hovering uncomfortably near the bookshelves. *Christ, why had Gwen chosen that moment to need to speak to him?* He raked his fingers through his now tousled hair, glad the desk concealed his still raging arousal. 'What is so important to rush back from the Feathers for?'

Clearing her throat, Gwen placed the newspaper down in front of Jonah. 'I thought you should see this…'

Sixty One

ROBERT'S FACE SET LIKE THUNDER as he thraped his car along the road. The final insult – not only had Teagan ruined his life by sparking the capacity within him to feel something, but then allowing that bastard, Saul Powell, to manhandle her, now she was allowing *another* one of them to put their hands on her, the little tart.

And Jonah Powell of all people?

He'd have thought out of all of them, Jonah might have had enough self-respect to not want his brother's sloppy seconds, but apparently not.

Robert gritted his teeth. He might have bloody known. Crunching the gears loudly, he took the roundabout at ludicrous speed.

Now O'Hara had dropped the trace there was no need to hang around. In all honesty, he wasn't hanging around for that anyhow. O'Hara was sod all to do with him. All he'd been waiting for was confirmation his task was complete and courtesy of the breaking news on his laptop not half an hour past, he'd received it.

Robert's eyes narrowed. Why had be bothered though? When he'd heard noise from down the corridor he should have ignored it, but as usual, he'd felt he should investigate. Had he not done the man enough favours? And *this* was how he got repaid?

But now he'd seen it with his own eyes – Teagan kissing Jonah Powell, like the vile tramp she was.

Well, Jonah was taking the piss. Robert growled to himself. Teagan should have been *his* and would have been had everything not been ruined.

Grating his teeth harder, Robert stamped on the accelerator.

After that he wasn't hanging around for one second longer. He'd have just quietly walked away before, but now it was different. He wasn't staying in that nest of backstabbing freaks. Neither was he letting this latest attack go unpunished.

They'd planned it. *All* of it. They'd all manufactured this on purpose to rub it in. They'd engineered it so he would never have what he was owed.

But he could wait. He would wait thirty years if he had to.

• • • •

TEAGAN WAS TOO DISTRACTED with racing thoughts swirling through her mind with what would have happened had it not been for Gwen's interruption to take much notice of the expression on Jonah's face.

She forced herself to overcome her burning embarrassment to move her eyes in Gwen's direction, finding her studying her questioningly.

As their eyes met, she gave a weak smile. What would Gwen think of her now? Would she think she had thrown herself at Jonah – or the other way around? It wasn't like that – it had… just happened… And she had no explanation for it.

Suddenly, Teagan's attention was brought sharply into focus when Jonah jumped from his chair. 'I'll get Robert now. He'll want to know about this.'

Wide-eyed, Teagan looked from Jonah to Gwen as Jonah dashed from the study up the corridor. She edged towards Gwen, her hands trembling. 'Gwen, I…'

'Forget whatever you're thinking - you need to look at this.' She jerked her head towards the newspaper open on Jonah's desk.

Warily, Teagan moved around the other side of the desk, getting a heady waft of the lingering scent of Jonah's aftershave in the air. Shaking her head in a bid to concentrate, she peered at the article:

Murder Suspect Apprehended and Charged

Police were alerted by an anonymous caller to a possible attack in Maidenhead on 11th July. Although at first glance it seemed Dulcie Adams, 65, had died peacefully at her home in Frogmore Road, on closer inspection suspicious motives were uncovered, due to items found at the scene. The man present at Mrs Adams' property, claiming to be living there was arrested and after further investigation, has today been charged with murder.

Heath Pointer (26), of Shepherds Bush, will attend the preliminary court hearing on 15th July. This is the latest in a line of murders and attacks linked to this family. Anyone with any additional information to assist the police with their enquiries, are urged to call.

'Oh my God...' Teagan's hand flew to her mouth, her head spinning. *Dulcie was dead? Murdered?*

Her body trembled as sorrow engulfed her. Robert hadn't had the chance to make his peace with his mother. This would crush him.

Grateful for Gwen's arms around her, the tears escaped from Teagan's eyes. Regardless of anything else, she'd truly cared for Dulcie and always believed they could put things right. Now they couldn't.

'He's gone!' Jonah appeared back in the doorway of the study, breathless and agitated.

'Gone? Gwen parroted. 'What do you mean, gone?'

Storming straight over to the drinks cabinet, Jonah poured himself a large shot, downing it in one. 'Robert was in the sitting room. I saw him with my own eyes when I returned. I was about to go and speak to him.' His eyes narrowed. 'He's gone and so has all of his stuff.'

Snatching up the newspaper, he stared at it once more before given Gwen a pointed look.

Reading the meaning behind Jonah's eyes, Gwen gave an almost imperceptible nod, then steered Teagan towards a seat. 'Come on, love. Come and sit down.'

Bewildered, Teagan lowered herself into the chair. 'I-I don't understand how this could have happened. That must have been why there was no answer when Robert went round.'

Jonah placed a glass of whisky in Teagan's hand, watching Gwen slip out of the room. He wanted extra security at the Feathers with immediate effect and he also wanted men stationed here 24/7 and knew Gwen would call Nero and arrange it.

Teagan's mind raced and sweat soaked into the back of her cotton top. *Why would that man want to kill Dulcie? Unless...* 'This isn't because of those diamonds again is it? You've got them back, so I thought it was all over?'

Jonah dropped to his haunches in front of Teagan. He took the glass out of her hand and placed it on the desk before taking both of her hands in his. He would have to do this subtly. Teagan would be shielded from this – all of it. She'd already been through enough.

'It *is* over. What's happened has nothing to do with those diamonds. I don't understand it myself.' He looked deeply into Teagan's frightened eyes. 'You've seen them for yourself. They're here and the feud is over. I promise this is nothing to do with me. I would hardly have accepted Robert here otherwise, would I?'

Fear raged through Teagan and she clutched at Jonah's jacket sleeve. 'But who is this Heath Pointer person? That's the same surname as Robert's real father. Is there a link? Are we all in danger? I...'

'How could there be a link? It must just be a really weird coincidence,' Jonah lied, his reasoning sounding fake even as the words left his mouth. He could only hope Teagan was too distressed to pick up on it. 'Listen. Nothing bad will happen to you or any of us.

And it wouldn't. He wasn't going to let anyone else pay for the curse surrounding those bloody diamonds. He glared at the bookcase where they were safely stashed, wishing his father had never ever been involved in the heist all that time ago.

And he was certainly not going to let Teagan be hurt any further because of it.

But it was true that this wasn't about the diamonds. At least, not *this* part of it, but he had an inkling of what it *was* to do with. There were so many things Teagan didn't know about this whole situation and it had to remain that way.

Jonah stared deeply into Teagan's eyes. 'And I'm sorry about Dulcie. I know you cared for her deeply. This must be a dreadful shock.'

Teagan began sobbing again. 'I did. I loved her. I know what she did to Helen and that she'd lied to Robert about his father, but she was a good person. A *genuine* one. There must have been a reason for all of the decisions she made.'

Jonah nodded, pretending to believe he agreed. Despite the light of this next and unexpected situation with Robert and what it might mean, he couldn't help the overwhelming pull towards Teagan and that urgency of need unsettled him. Like it or not, it was there all the same.

He placed his hand on her shoulder, silently longing for it to be something more. 'Teagan, I...'

'Are you alright, love?' Returning to the study, Gwen looked to Jonah and then to Teagan.

Teagan sniffed loudly. 'I can't get my heard around any of this. I'm devastated!'

The proximity to Jonah was bothering her too. The distress of hearing about Dulcie was hard enough without having to allay the ravaging guilt, that as well as that, like a demonic alter-ego, the other half of her mind was centred on Jonah Powell. And that was wrong. *Plain wrong.* All she was thinking of was herself and what did make her in light of this present situation? She rose from her chair and stumbling forward, leant against the desk for support. 'I need some fresh air.'

Jonah glanced at Gwen as Teagan left the study. He waited until he spotted her figure through the window in the garden before sitting back down. Resting his chin in his hands, he exhaled loudly.

'Nero will be over as soon as he's put everything in place,' Gwen said.

Jonah nodded in acknowledgment, his eyes narrowing. 'Teagan is not to be made aware of the situation. She is to know nothing further than what she already knows. About *anything*.'

Gwen watched Jonah carefully. 'How much danger are we in? I mean, realistically?'

Jonah's lips set in a thin line. 'I don't know, but we have to err on the side of caution. I think you have already worked out that Heath Pointer didn't kill Dulcie Adams. It was Robert. He went round there that day but Teagan hasn't put two and two together yet and I'd like it to remain that way.'

Gwen nodded sadly. 'What I can't work out is *why*?'

Jonah shrugged. 'I have my theories, but that doesn't matter right now. What does matter is that I believe he is more of a threat to Teagan than us and of course O'Hara is here now too. *Somewhere*. And he'll be looking for Lena. That one's very much on *my* head.' He poured himself a small scotch.

And Heath Pointer was a problem – a big one. He was in police custody and knew things about the firm – he'd even been behind the scenes and God only know what Lena had told him. Regardless of what, if anything, she'd told him, his whole family – whoever they were, were deeply ensconced with the Powells. There were decades of bad blood and he could only guess at what the man might spill to the cops to get his own head out of the noose. Whatever he might say would be more than enough to put the whole Powell firm and everyone in jeopardy.

And then there was O'Hara…

Diamonds and payback aside, once O'Hara discovered Lena was no more – which he *would*, then he'd want retribution over that too. And he had no idea where they were and how many of them there was.

Jonah cracked his knuckles. 'Whatever happens it has to be business as usual, but I'll keep everyone safe.'

Gwen smiled. 'I know you will, love, but about earlier…'

Knowing straight away what Gwen was referring to, Jonah glanced up quickly. He could do without her casting aspersions. 'Whatever you saw earlier shouldn't be the most important thing on your mind right now Gwen.'

Gwen pursed her lips. 'That's as maybe, but I don't want Teagan getting hurt. And I don't mean by this latest threat either. I mean by *you*. All this bullshit with Lena will have left you presu…'

'As, I said. You need to not concentrate on that. It was just a case of heightened emotions from both sides, that's all. It shouldn't have happened,' Jonah muttered.

But it was more than that. A lot more and he couldn't explain it. Lena had indeed left a horrible legacy behind and as much as he swore he'd never get involved with another woman again after what she'd done, it was impossible to ignore that Teagan had sparked something. Something that he'd never felt and he wanted her to figure in his life. And he'd do whatever was needed to protect her from this invisible threat in whatever way was required.

Whether he was wanted to or not, he felt the distinct urge that Teagan was going to be instrumental. Not for the business, payback or for any other means, but for himself.

Epilogue

STANDING OUT OF EARSHOT of the strangers crammed around the dining table in her small kitchen, Tammy glared at Mike. 'Two days they've been here already! How much longer are they planning on staying?' she hissed.

Mike smiled amiably, even though he felt like he was internally melting. 'Not long. Their hotel was double booked so I said they could stay here. What's the big deal?'

'But who are they? You've never mentioned them before?' Tammy persisted, eyeing her husband suspiciously. 'We really haven't got the room.'

Mike sighed. 'If you'd ever listened to me then you'd know Ron's a friend of the family from years back.' *No he wasn't.* Well, his father might have classed him as such, but the man was certainly no friend of *his*. Not that he'd had a lot of choice about bringing them here anyway, but he could hardly tell Tammy that. 'Can't you just make them feel welcome? It won't hurt you.' *He hoped not, anyway.*

Tammy huffed loudly. 'I wish you'd consulted me before you descended here with them. Where are we going to put them for Christ's sake?'

'We'll make room.' Mike glanced through the ajar door,

spotting Ron O'Hara studying him malevolently through the crack.

'Heath's supposed to be coming around for dinner tomorrow and I was really looking forward to seeing him,' Tammy continued, blind to Mike's internal trauma. 'It's been *ages* since we've had a family dinner with our son, but now *they're* going to be here and it will be awkward.'

'No it won't!' Mike blustered. 'Because Heath can't make it tomorrow. I meant to tell you.' He wouldn't tell Tammy where Heath really was either. She'd have a coronary. He could barely believe it himself. It was bad enough having to hide the newspapers and keep her away from the television, but with any luck, Heath would be out tomorrow.

'He's not coming? Why ever not? You haven't been having a go at him again have you, Mike?' Tammy cried.

'No! He's, erm… he's been seeing a girl – you know, that first heady rush of love,' Mike croaked, willing a meteorite to land on his head.

'I can't remember that feeling it was so long ago,' Tammy snapped. 'So now I haven't even got *that* to look forward to.'

Mike sighed. He really thought his life was at the lowest ebb, but when Ron O'Hara had shoved that gun in his face and explained what was expected of him, he realised in comparison he'd been having a really good time before.

Underneath his jacket, Mike's shirt stuck to his skin as the weight of what he'd agreed to sank further into his veins. But what choice was he given?

The answer to that was *none*.

What else was he supposed to do with a gun in his face, apart from agree to O'Hara's demands? In all fairness, in comparison with what the man was asking in return was giving he, Heath and Tammy a lot more benefit, as far as he was concerned. Outwardly, at least.

But Mike didn't want to dwell on what else the agreement could drag him into.

He glanced around the utility room that he and Tammy

were crammed into, sure O'Hara must be able to hear every single word said. Sweat continued soaking the back of his shirt and he glared at his wife, wishing she'd just shut the fuck up.

Now he wouldn't have to break the news to Tammy that he'd fucked up and lost them their home and business. Neither, with any luck, would she ever have to know that Heath was at present banged up on a murder charge.

She may well have to find out about that in the end, but at the moment there was *hope*.

If this brief O'Hara had arranged was as good as promised, then it stood a chance Heath would walk permanently. And that was something Mike wholeheartedly agreed with O'Hara on. It *had* to have been a set-up by the Powells. The brief had already showed how canny he was by knowing his stuff enough to fudge things for the CPS to grant a bail hearing.

Yes, he'd been able to prove that Heath was no danger to the public; their evidence was either fake and planted, or at worst, circumstantial. Neither was there any previous, so the hearing to release him on bail was all but a formality. The full trial would be another matter, but at least they were heading in the right direction.

O'Hara had also offered to stump up the cost of the bail, as well as paying off the debts the business had run up.

Mike inwardly shrugged, blindly trying to override the constant rolling of his guts.

What person in their right mind would turn that down? And all O'Hara wanted in return was a place to build a life here and find his niece, along with as much dirt on the Powells as possible.

Well of course, Mike hadn't been able to refrain from telling the man that, as it happened, Heath knew *all* about his niece – that Lena Taylor from the Feathers he'd gushed over.

Whether there was any truth or not in O'Hara's paranoia that something had befallen the girl, courtesy of the Powells was something else, but surely Heath telling them what he knew was a small price for his freedom?

And as for Tammy, well, she wouldn't particularly be happy when he had to mention that the three strangers would be here for a lot longer that a couple of days. Aside from O'Hara, the young man was a bit of a weird and the girl wasn't quite the ticket either. He didn't have clue who they were, apart from related to O'Hara. That was obvious from the funny eyes the lot of them had. Far too close together.

But with any luck, they'd soon get fed up being crammed here with the lack of room and find their own place. As long as the cheque cleared they could do what they liked, but in the meantime, he'd just have to ensure Tammy remained patient.

Apart from that, there wasn't a lot else he could do, apart from hope.

THANK YOU!

Thank you for reading *Finders Keepers*. I hope you enjoyed reading it as much as I did writing it!

If so, would you please consider leaving a review on Amazon and/or Goodreads.

Reviews from readers are SOOOO helpful and especially important to us authors and without you we would have nobody to write for!

Thank you once again and hope you enjoy the rest of my books.

Edie xx

MORE FROM THIS SERIES

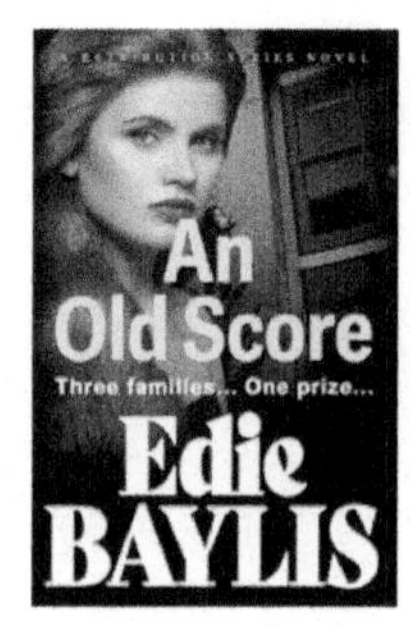

#1: AN OLD SCORE

Three families... One prize...

Teagan Fraser had no idea what she was getting herself into when she took on an assignment as a live-in carer for Dulcie Adams – a retired dancer from a Soho club. Dulcie has waited forty years for her lover, Michael Pointer, to return, but she's been living in hope for a time that never came and left looking after something important, which Jonah Powell and his firm want back.

In addition to the notorious Powell firm, there are others wanting to claim what they believe is rightfully theirs and they'll do anything to get it back. If only Dulcie wasn't around it would be a lot easier, but she's difficult to shift...

A lot can happen in the space of two weeks and Teagan might wish she'd never become involved.

#3: THE FINAL TAKE

THE TIME IS NOW...

Even knowing Ron O'Hara is somewhere in the vicinity, Jonah Powell feels it's time to finally get rid of the diamonds which have haunted his family for decades and caused so much trouble.

However, other problems start to arrive from unexpected and additional sources, some of which Jonah didn't expect.
Neither did he expect Teagan Fraser to be playing on his mind so heavily.

But what does it all mean? It may be apt to call time on the curse plaguing his family and of those around him, but how can this be achieved while so many other things are at stake?

More From this Author

ALLEGIANCE SERIES:

#1: TAKEOVER

Samantha Reynold hadn't bargained on unexpectedly needing to step into her father's shoes and take over the family casino business and known nothing about the rules of this glamorous but deadly new world. But she won't let her family down, especially when it looks like they could lose everything to their biggest rivals – the Stoker family.

Eldest son Sebastian hasn't got time to pander to pretty girl Samantha as she plays at being boss. Rumours are swirling around the streets of Birmingham that have the power to rip the Stoker family apart and destroy everything they've built.

#2: FALLOUT

With the odds stacked against her, Samantha Reynold is determined to prove she's tough enough to be the boss. But when a secret from the past threatens to ruin Sam's reputation, she suddenly feels very alone in this dark new world. There's only one man she can turn to – rival club owner, Sebastian Stoker.

Seb knows first-hand how secrets and lies can tear a family apart. He wants to protect Sam at all costs, but siding with her could threaten his own position as head of the Stoker family and risk accusations of betrayal.
With loyalties divided and two families at war – the fallout could be deadly.

#3: VENDETTA

Once bitter enemies, Samantha Reynold and Seb Stoker's powerful alliance enables their firms and casinos to go from strength to strength. With the families no longer in opposition, it seems that Sam and Seb are untouchable…

But not everyone is happy with the new power couple of the club world.

Unbeknownst to everyone, someone new wants to see Sam's perfect life ruined. And they will stop at nothing to seek their revenge – even if it means destroying everything - and everyone - in their path.

More From this Author

HUNTED SERIES:

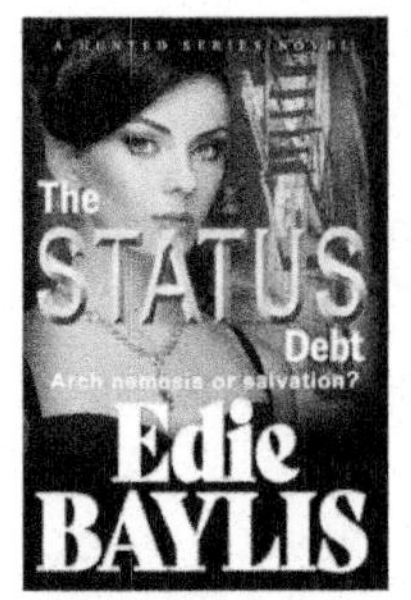

#1: THE STATUS DEBT

Lillian Morgan would do anything to regain the status she lost by marrying beneath her and to cover the sordid details of her husband's death. This includes blackmail and the hand of marriage of her own daughter.

Tori thought her life couldn't get much worse, but someone is not being honest and secrets have the power to rip everyone to shreds.

Especially when life is built on lies.

#2: THE FAMILY LEGACY

Unsure of whether Matt or Hunter has fathered the child growing inside her, Tori's unwanted wedding to Matt grows closer, but is there light at the end of the tunnel? Unfortunately, Tori hasn't counted on another man present in her life. One who is more instrumental in her misery than she realises.

Sometimes the truth is too late in coming and makes bad things happen and sometimes a hidden legacy can cause the most horrific thing of all…

#3: THE TARGET OF LIES

Neil Sparks has a score to settle. In fact, he has several… His first port of call when returning from France after a five year exile is to catch up with his estranged wife. Secondly, Neil wants to even a score with the people instrumental in his departure and thirdly, he wants an explanation from the man who promised his marriage would be free from hassle. The trouble is, he's not the only one with an agenda…

There are too many people about to become caught in the crossfire and everyone could become a target.

*** This series contains written depictions of graphic violence, sex and strong language. It also contains some themes that may be uncomfortable for certain readers. ***

MORE FROM THIS AUTHOR

DOWNFALL SERIES:

#1 - UNTIL THE END OF TIME

Dive into Seth and Jane's train wreck of a life, where drugs, alcohol and obsessional love means this downright dangerous pair will do *anything* to ensure nothing gets in their way.

They do bad things. *Very* bad things and their promise to love each until the end of time turns into a war against each other.

A war neither of them can win.

#2 - ESCAPING THE PAST

Things have changed and Jane has got on with her life.

Well, not *entirely*…

Embroiled in a bitter feud between two rival firms, it is clear that not everyone is who they proclaim to be.

The net is closing in and some things just can't be changed.

#3 - VENGEFUL PAYBACK

There is something missing. Something *very* important and no one is above suspicion.

Past vendettas are gaining pace and it is vital that whoever is behind this never-ending stream of cleverly engineered payback is discovered before it is too late and everything held dear is ripped apart.

*** This series contains written depictions of graphic violence, sex and strong language. It also contains some themes that may be uncomfortable for certain readers. ***

About The Author

Over the years Edie has worked all over the UK as well as in several other countries and has met a lot of interesting people - several of whom have supplied ideas for some of the characters in her books! She has now settled back in central England with her partner and children, where she is pursuing writing her gritty gangland and urban fiction novels.

Edie is currently signed to Boldwood Books for a 5-book gangland fiction series set in Birmingham. The first three in the *Allegiance* series, *Takeover*, *Fallout* and *Vendetta* have been released and the fourth in the series, *Payback*, is due to be released in January 2023. She is also concurrently writing the *Scarred* series - the first titled, *Mirrors Never Lie*.

Edie's other series are the *Retribution* series, the *Hunted* series and the *Downfall* series - all trilogies.

When she isn't writing, Edie enjoys reading and is a self-confessed book hoarder. She also enjoys crochet and music as well as loving anything quirky or unusual.

Visit www.ediebaylis.co.uk for the latest news, information about new releases, giveaways and to subscribe to her mailing list.

CWA MEMBER

CONNECT WITH EDIE

https://fb.me/downfallseries

https://www.goodreads.com/author/show/17153586.Edie_Baylis

https://twitter.com/ediebaylis

https://www.amazon.co.uk/Edie-Baylis/e/B075FQHWCZ/

https://www.bookbub.com/authors/edie-baylis

https://ediebaylis.co.uk/

info@ediebaylis.co.uk

https://www.fantasticfiction.com/b/edie-baylis/

https://www.instagram.com/ediebaylis/

https://www.tiktok.com/@edie747

https://www.pinterest.co.uk/ediebaylis/

JOIN EDIE'S MAILING LIST

Subscribe to Edie's mailing list for the latest news on her books, special offers, new releases and competitions.

https://ediebaylis.co.uk/signup.html

Edie Baylis

gangland | crime | urban

THRILLER AUTHOR

ACKNOWLEDGEMENTS

Thanks to the people that kindly read my drafts of *Finders Keepers* – you know who you are and I appreciate your time and feedback.

I would like to thank Sue John for her support, help and feedback. I would also like to give my thanks to Jess Richardson and Caz Finlay for all of their support and faith in me.
Thank you ladies! You are all very much appreciated.

Special thanks also goes to the people (you know who you are) – who were brave enough to allow their names to be adopted by some of the characters in this story (I must point out that these characters are in no way anything to do with, or connected to, their namesakes in real life!) 😊

Printed in Great Britain
by Amazon